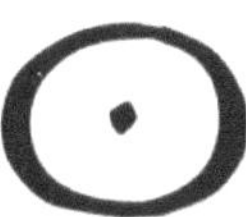

The Underland Tarot

XIII: Stories of Transformation
XVIII: Stories of Mischief & Mayhem

Underland Arcana Deck One
Underland Arcana Deck Two

UNDERLAND ARCANA
DECK THREE

edited by

Mark Teppo

Underland Press

Third, the Querent considers their question . . .

Edited by Mark Teppo
Book Design and Layout by Firebird Creative
Cover art by desertsands /stock.adobe.com

This Underland Press trade edition of the third year of *Underland Arcana* has been released in conjunction with the Autumnal solar eclipse.

Underland Press
www.underlandpress.com

DECK THREE

To E, once again.

B. waterways

~ Erik Kollmer

As my head prattles against Father's station wagon window to the cadence of the engine, I picture a massive green-scaled, three-headed snake sliding out of the wheatfields onto the single-lane road Father and I trace daily. Maybe it could grab the station wagon with its fangs and jostle it like a helpless cybernetic rabbit. Father would scream and I would laugh because that would be the most exciting thing that has ever happened to us.

The wheatfields have surrounded me my entire existence. The golden grain occupies every square meter that is not a building nor road in Damsel. A common point of conversation among families and neighborhoods is when children have their first inquisition as to what is deep within the wheatfields, colloquially called "W. moments". Ask any other nineteen-year-old what they remember about their W. moment, and they will respond with a scratch of the head and a shrug of indifference. It sears my heart.

"Lucina, you do understand how important today is for me, correct?" Father's apprehensive tone drags me back to the confines of the station wagon. He grips the steering wheel so firmly that his veins look ready to escape his skin. "Please be courteous and kind to everyone at the Community Center, especially Mr. Wingal. He has . . ."

"A silvery handlebar mustache and abnormally long eyelashes. His color is lime green, #3CFA3E. No child because he's on the Council. I remember him from the last Exhibition."

Father expels a soft sigh, then wipes his brow with the sleeve of the only tweed jacket he owns. It is a darker shade of burgundy, #6C011C, specifically matching my dress. Without it, there would be no other way to identify us as parent and child.

I turn my attention back to the wheat blurring together outside. A transmission tower looms over its agrarian subordinates, asserting its industrial dominance as electricity cackles through its wires.

The Community Center is a unique building. Many parents bring their children here after their W. moment to show them the parking circle, as it is the only piece of road in Damsel that defies the town's cartesian street grid. Once inside the Center, guests have the choice of entering either the theater or the ballroom. Of course, this is an Exhibition, so Father and I proceed into the theater and find our assigned seats. As I sit down, the rigid wooden slats rib my exposed back, but I've convinced myself that these seats are uncomfortable by design. As more people fill the theater, it becomes noticeably redolent of sun-kissed wheat.

As soon as the last seat in the theater is occupied, the audience's eyes snap towards the screen at the front of the room. It is a perfect square, 1300 pixels by 1300 pixels, mounted in front of a backdrop of gray curtains. In the center of the screen, the standard preliminary message is spelled out in blue pixels:

> *B. waterways. Iteration 4003029.*
> *Designed by Resident 6C011C-1.*

The audience blinks, and an image with a top-down aerial view of three parallel aqueducts appears on the screen, a thin coating of water flowing across the top of each. Underneath the three aqueducts is a riverbed, which disappears off the top and bottom edges of the image. Then, everyone in the theater begins to stand and clap with an unbridled passion. A spotlight showers down onto the seat next to mine. Whether Father was crying before they displayed his iteration on the screen, I am unsure. I stand up and perform the customary hug, then wipe Father's tears away with my thumbs for sentimental flair. I disgust myself.

At the previous Exhibition a month ago, a woman received a similar standing ovation for changing the pixel that is part of the central aqueduct's wall from a dry, dirty shade of brown (#bb5101) to a slightly darker, earthy brown (#934306). Father had essentially mirrored this color change at pixel (635, 799), which was part of the left-most aqueduct's wall.

"Brilliant choice, Maxwell! Brilliant!" a gaunt-looking woman in purple drab says behind me, still furiously clapping.

Another woman from a couple rows back joins in. "Such poise in selection, and such beauty in parallelism!"

"This is one of the most intelligent iterations I've seen in quite some time." Over Father's shoulder, I catch a glimpse of Mr. Wingal. My self-loathing only grows as I force a smile and extend my hand to the man outfitted with a pair of lime green circle-framed glasses. He shakes my hand with a mix of tenderness and assurance that, to my displeasure, puts me at ease. Father then turns and clasps Mr. Wingal's other hand in both of his. "Mr. Wingal, I hope this iteration is everything you've been hoping for."

Mr. Wingal grins. "Maxwell, your work is incredibly insightful. Many of the Council and I thought you would return to the contemporary trend of darkening the water pixels, but your adaptation of Gretchen's recent wall-focused idea underscores something . . . awe-inspiring I couldn't quite pinpoint before. Surely you will be remembered forever as one of the early adopters of dirt-brown wall pixelism. A renaissance is afoot!"

I watch as Mr. Wingal's words dismember Father. He staggers back from Mr. Wingal, and I notice a feral smile creep into the seams of Mr. Wingal's mouth. I pity them both.

Feigning affection has never been an issue for me, but I cannot bring myself to express appreciation for a process I find revolting. "Mr. Wingal, why do grafters only change *B. waterways* one pixel at a time? Is there some sort of rule around it?"

Mr. Wingal's eyelashes recoil as far away from his pupils as his eyelids permit. "Lucina . . . are you truly your father's daughter?"

My question also snaps Father out of his torpor. "Mr. Wingal! Please, for the love of Damsel, forgive my daughter. She doesn't quite understand the parameters of grafting yet."

"I see," Mr. Wingal says. He brings his thumb and forefinger up to the corner of his mustache, simultaneously pulling at and twirling the left end. "Let's do this. Lucina, for the Exhibition next month, you shall be in charge of grafting *B. waterways*."

Father and I slowly turn towards each other, our faces paralyzed with an unholy mélange of horror and shock. Father places his hand on my shoulder to steady himself, then turns to Mr. Wingal.

"With all due respect, Mr. Wingal, I do not believe she is ready for such an important task," he says, quivering.

"Maxwell, I appreciate your concern, but I have made my decision. I trust Lucina will surprise each and every one of us," Mr. Wingal declares, pursing his lips and narrowing his eyes in my direction. "With that, I must bid you both adieu. Maxwell, congratulations again on a job well done."

The silence hanging in the station wagon is finally pierced by the crackling of wheels on gravel. A soft *tunk* floats into the night air as the car's lights turn off. We sit in the darkness, staring straight ahead at our house, the wheatfields an omnipresent backdrop.

"Tell me why you don't think I'm ready," I finally say.

Father clears his throat with a practiced *ahem*. "I'm trying to protect you, Lucina. There are millions of pixels to choose from on top of millions of color palettes. The combinations scale exponentially. Six months passed until I realized how to best improve *B. waterways* for the future, inspiring others to find the beauty in the miniscule. For you to do the same in only one month, and at your age . . . I just don't want you to begin your life labeled a *derivative*." He whispers the final word with sacrilegious precision.

"It did *not* take you six months to decide on which pixel to change!" I exclaim. "You knew which one you were going to pick the instant you were appointed for this iteration seven months ago. The rest of the time you just spent second guessing yourself."

Father stares at me, mouth agape. "Lucina, I . . ."

"You're afraid to ask the bigger questions, Father. You always have been. How did *B. waterways* even come to be if no one in Damsel has ever seen water? Not a single person understands its physics. The concept of water is so abstract to us that we admire it initially, but have you ever wanted to actually *experience* water? How it might actually *degrade* the aqueducts over time, changing B. waterways as we know it?"

Father goes quiet, staring blankly at his palms in his lap. He begins to knead his thumbs together. "Lucina, you're really beginning to worry me. All I ask is for you to make me proud at the next Exhibition."

I kick open the passenger door and step out into the darkness. *It's only now he pays attention to what I have to say.* "Whether I make you proud is your choice," I mutter, shutting the station wagon door with more force than the old car would have liked. As I walk towards the front door, my fingers rub the middle of my bare back and make acquaintance with the impressions the theater seat left etched into my skin. They always linger longer than I expect.

It is only when I reach my bedroom that I allow myself to laugh uncontrollably. Defiant as I am, the opportunity to have an Exhibition all to myself is surreal. For as long as I can remember, I have partaken in the ritual of Exhibitions, but only out of reluctant compliance. Month after month, each iteration tampers with my soul, tempting me to bury my W. moment in a reality plagued with mundanity and the people who proliferate it.

I stare at my posterless bedroom wall, dilate my pupils, and allow Father's version of *B. waterways* to project itself through my eyes. I then tap my right temple to allow my eyes to move freely around the image. They instinctively dart to Father's most recent change at pixel (635, 799), where Mr. Wingal declared a "renaissance is afoot." I shudder. *Could changing one pixel in an image really be the genesis of an entire art movement?* I focus on the other wall pixels around Father's chosen one and use my pupils to draw a virtual perimeter. In my head, I calculate the hex code of the average color across the different shades of brown: #66484a. I search my memory for what I learned in my browns class in school, and recall that #66484a is a red-tinged brown. The color of Father's pixel, #634547, is only slightly darker. *Fitting for him to take as small a risk as possible. He didn't even try changing the color to something more interesting.*

Despite all my misgivings with Father's work, I thought I would have a better idea about what I wanted to add to *B. waterways*. My teachers in school had always dictated that Exhibitions are solely about improving the aesthetic appearance of the whole image. At my core, I always knew that my iteration would break that unspoken rule. But now that I finally had the chance to do so, I found myself struggling to come up with what exactly would establish me as a derivative.

What's beneath the wheatfields?

The thought felt internal, as if something dormant had just awakened within me. An incredible compulsion overcomes me. Whether this thought is going to drive me to madness or inspiration, I am unsure. But I soon find myself walking barefoot in the backyard towards the seemingly impenetrable wall of yellow grain. A friendly full moon assists my hands as they begin to dig at the base of one of the stalks.

About three hand-lengths deep, a cool liquid greets my fingers. I bring my hand back out of the hole and see that my fingers are covered in a viscous, dark liquid. I begin to tremble uncontrollably. *Is this . . . water?* Knowing that I can only verify the color under proper light, I dash back across the lawn and wrap my forearm around the backyard doorknob to open it without tainting the handle.

Under my bedroom light, the dark liquid becomes a deep shade of crimson. From a quick calculation, I can tell it is, on average, #a81117. This is not water. My senses continue to investigate: a soft, metallic scent. A thick texture that does not disappear as I trace my finger along my arm.

Shadowy notions of despair begin to crawl into the back of my consciousness. The Council could have invented this ink to brand those who had the derivative idea of digging through the wheatfields. While only a moment ago being a derivative seemed like liberation, feeling this viscous substance seep into the cracks of my skin makes me pause and consider a new potential reality: social exile.

I consider showing Father, but decide that confiding in him is the same as telling all of Damsel. Instead, I return to the backyard and try wiping my hands on the lawn. To my delight, the crimson liquid begins to adhere to the grass, and I direct my hands to make large sweeping motions, turning them over intermittently to eliminate the foreign substance. After verifying the cleanliness of my fingers and palms by moonlight, I return to my bedroom. *B. waterways* is still projected on the naked wall.

Fear not, Lucina.

An overwhelming sensation of warmth reverberates throughout my entire body. Once again, its source feels entirely internal. The very fiber of my being tells me the sensation can only be one thing: unconditional love. I try calling out to the source with my thoughts.

Are you my savior?

The only reply is the humming of the power lines that pass close to my bedroom window. I cast an unwavering gaze at *B. waterways*, allowing the image to etch itself into my eyeballs. I shut my eyes tight and allow the patterns of light to appear on the back of my eyelids.

Fear not, Lucina.

Mr. Wingal's condescending smile no longer feels as condemning. The opinions of the Exhibition audience no longer fetter me. I try to explain away every possibility that this overpowering sensation could be some type of ploy by the Council to let my guard down. And yet, it is as if this notion had always been present within me, simply waiting to be untapped.

Is that you, Mother?

Whoever is responsible for the sensation does not respond. A pang of loneliness shoots through me, but is quickly erased once I flutter open my eyes. *B. waterways* is not the same as when my eyes last left it on my bedroom wall. Every single pixel that used to be a watery blue had suddenly recolored itself to a deep crimson - the very same crimson I had just wiped my hands clean of in the backyard. My arm hairs defy gravity for the first time in their life. I blink, and *B. waterways* returns to Father's iteration. No matter. A glimpse is all I need.

The morning of my Exhibition arrives quickly. Father and I don the ceremonial burgundy, and he doesn't even seem to contemplate asking me if I want to drive before he sits behind the steering wheel of the station wagon. Once again, my head finds its familiar resting place between the roof and the passenger seat's headrest, while my eyes silently observe the wheatfields blur together into their trademark soft yellow, #F9EB27.

Father maneuvers the station wagon into our assigned spot in the parking circle. I step out onto the street and prepare to simulate my typical brooding demeanor, but am surprised at how difficult it is. Excitement is not something I have experience concealing.

"Lucina," Father calls from behind me. "I just want you to know . . ." he trails off, a sheepish expression overcoming his pale face. "I just want you to know that whatever your iteration might be today, I will be proud of you."

"You'll regret saying that," I say without hesitation. Out of the corner of my eye, I see the edges of Father's lips descend simultaneously. I turn and walk into the Community Center before my lips do the opposite.

As I sit down, I catch Mr. Wingal's gaze from far behind me. He and the other Council members are the only ones who are aware of my assignment, which explains the fourteen other eyes I feel relentlessly dissecting me. I quickly make note of where they are all seated so I can compare their reactions after I present my Exhibition.

Father is one of the final residents to find his seat. The curvature of his spine is more pronounced than usual, a sign of his utter exhaustion. He does not look at me as he sits down.

The lights dim, and the standard message shows itself once again.

B. waterways. Iteration 4003030.
Designed by Resident 6C011C-2.

A millisecond after the message disappears, I focus my eyes directly forward and use them to project my iteration onto the screen, hearing a soft whrr come from my temples. I gently tap my right temple, freezing my iteration on the screen for the entire theater to see.

At first, I am unsure if I projected my iteration correctly, as an anticipatory silence still hangs in the dusty theater air. But then an array of sounds begin to surround me: sardonic chortles, frightened cries, uncensored gasps. The spotlight finds my seat, and I slowly rise. I thought I would be able to withstand any sort of audience-led persecution, but tears begin to nestle themselves inside my eyelids. A few seats to my left, a girl my age rolls her eyes and slightly shakes her head. *You dumbass,* she mouths to me with lips painted blue.

Father does not stand to hug me as I did for him. He remains seated, his lips slightly parted while he gazes forward in a petrified state. Realizing now that he would be the only one to support me, I bite my lip and cast my eyes to the side. *Tch. Why am I expecting to be rewarded after all my unrelenting bitterness towards him?*

There is only one thing remaining in the room that can console me, and I am still projecting it on the 1300 by 1300 theater screen. I consider terminating the projection, but that would be admitting defeat. I admire the way the crimson liquid splashes across the aqueducts the way the water once did. It was difficult for me to illustrate the heaviness of the liquid in only two dimensions, but I tried to minimize the number of waves in the river that runs underneath the aqueducts . . .

Lucina, this is called blood. B-L-O-O-D.

"Mother!" I exclaim to no one.

I collapse into my seat. There is no way for me to verify Mother's claim, but there is something about it that feels inherently *irrefutable*. I cannot stop myself from laughing. Infantile as it may seem, Mother's acceptance is the only thing that matters to me now.

And then I realize that the auditory assault towards me has completely halted. I look around and see that all of the other Community members are seated, their heads compressed between their palms. Their shouts are no longer directed at me.

"Father, is that you?"

"Mother, is that you?"

"What exactly is *blood*? Why is it like that?"

Gradually, like how the wind chooses which wheat stalks to shake first, the heads around the theater turn towards me. Their faces all have the same expression: awe.

"Lucina, you're a prophet!"

"Such beauty in elegance, such composure in form!"

"How did you do that? How did you know that replacing water with blood was the key?" an authoritative voice asks from behind me, urgency at its heels. Mr. Wingal.

I turn around, placing my knees on the seat—a difficult accomplishment in this dress.

Feeling confident as ever, I answer Mr. Wingal's question with one of my own. "What do you mean, 'key'?"

Mr. Wingal clears his throat and centers his lime green glasses. "Lucina, surely you must have wondered at some point what the whole point of *B. waterways* was. Having pixel-by-pixel iterations of the same image without an end goal serves no purpose. We at the Council observed your frustration building at each Exhibition. Allow me to explain why Exhibitions even exist to begin with.

"The creators of Damsel founded the Council to determine what constitutes the most objective definition of art. We know this is accomplished when the internal parent microchips—what you know as 'Mother'—are activated. This only happens whenever there is sufficient electrical current directed towards them. We Damselians are designed to allocate electrical current to our parent microchips only when we are inspired. Clearly, your iteration of *B. waterways* elicited enough inspiration to awaken several of the audience members' parent microchips."

I look around at the theater crowd again, then cross my arms. "If you knew this much about how we operate, how are you not frustrated time and time again after each Exhibition like I am?"

"All Councilmembers undergo a certain training before they are appointed. We learn that when Damsel was created, everything was generated based on a template. Damsel as we know it is just one random variation of this template. Certain new features were added, like blood underneath the wheat stalks, and certain features were removed—water being the most notable. Everything about Damsel, from the parent microchips to *B. waterways* itself, is to accomplish one goal: to determine which environment is best suited for inspiration."

Mr. Wingal nods with a sort of acknowledgement towards me that I never thought he would be capable of. "No one knows who designed us, or how they were able to codify inspiration as electrical current," he says. "But do not dwell on that for now. Look around—you have enriched the Community's lives with a beauty they never even thought as possible."

He was right. The same Community members who had crucified me seconds ago were now glowing with an undeniable happiness. I allow myself a smile and look above the crowd at my iteration on the screen one final time. It does not fascinate me anymore. Interchanging water for blood is too simple of a transformation to be called "art." *My parent microchip must require a lower amount of electrical current to activate it. Inspiration comes easily to me, but leaves just as quick. Damn whoever programmed me into this vicious cycle.*

I turn to Father. He is sitting complacently in his seat, eyes still fixated on the screen.

"Father." He pivots his head slightly towards me. "Did you hear a voice inside you when you saw my iteration?" I ask.

"A voice . . ." Father goes quiet. I have never seen him this calm. There is no more urge to appease hiding beneath his beady eyes.

"Lucina . . ." he says slowly. "Today, you allowed me to fulfill my function as your Father. I serve no more purpose. You have made me undeniably proud."

A soft smile rests on Father's face, and his eyes go still. I watch as the soft light behind his pupils gradually dims. My eyes instinctively avert themselves, and they find my hands. I rub my fingertips together, still flecked with the dry blood from digging beneath the wheatfields.

You'll Never Believe What this Norse Monster Did to Keep His Mother Out of His Man Cave

~ Sarina Dorie

My nefarious cronies and I had been waiting for Ragnarok to come for ages and it still wasn't here, so we figured the best way to pass time was to enjoy ourselves at least. I sat down to play cards with Jarl the Ogre and Bjorne the Troll. Aarne the Fenrir Wolf couldn't join us for our monthly poker match because it was a full moon and he tended to go a little crazy, even for the likes of us monsters.

Jarl nodded to his cup of watered-down ale. "Hey, bro, you got anything stronger than this?" His leathery gray fingers held his hand of cards. His beady eyes darted about. I knew exactly what he was looking for.

I glanced over my shoulder at the torchlight casting flickering shadows over the walls of my underground lair. The coast was clear. I heaved the jug of mead out from where I'd hidden it under my chair and poured us drinks. Jarl took out the tub of special brownies, and by special, I mean the ones with the fermented shark in them. Yum!

"So, about those humans that keep attacking us," I said between bites. "Don't you think it's time we stand united and get rid of that ass-hat, Heorot?"

Jarl belched and patted his ashen belly. "My dad says we should ignore bullies and their childish attacks. Sticks and stones, you know, bro?"

Bjorne gulped down his mead and poured himself another. "The thing is, Gee, I don't care, so long as they don't kill anymore demon-li-cious monster babes. There's a scarce commodity of them as it is."

I shook my head. "You two have your priorities in the wrong places."

Bjorne barked out a laugh. "Whatever. Not everyone can satisfy their sexual appetites with a sock fetish."

"Shut up! You're high on hákarl again, aren't you?" I munched on another brownie. Pretty soon I would be high too if the night went according to plan. "You two really are bad influences."

"Complement accepted, bro!" Jarl poured another drink.

We were on our third round of mead and just starting to have fun when—wouldn't you know it?—my mom slithered in. Part she-giant and part sea monster, she loomed nearly as high as the stalactites on the ceiling. I took after her in size, though I didn't know where I got the horns, hairy posterior or bulging eyes. I was a big-boned, handsome devil—wherever those features came from—and the terror of all Denmark.

Bjorne's jaw dropped as he ogled my mother.

I elbowed him. "What's your problem?"

Jarl wisely tucked away the brownies.

Mom dusted one set of scaly hands across her polka-dot apron and carried the vacuum in the other set. She crouched to pick up a sock from the floor and held it away from herself, glaring at it with disdain. "Pumpkin, please don't leave your socks on the floor like that. I just found three of them in the adjoining cavern and one in here. I can't understand why you insist on—"

My face must have turned purple in humiliation. I nodded toward my friends, trying to make her understand she was interrupting.

She stopped, her vexed expression changing once she saw my friends. "Oh, gentle demons, I apologize, I didn't realize we had company. Just pretend I'm not here." My mother tucked the dirty sock into a pocket and vacuumed around us. I slipped the jug of mead back under my chair and arranged my abundance of leg hair to hide it from view. She was such a teetotaler. She'd probably dump it into the swamp if she caught a whiff.

"Sorry," I mumbled, some of my big, bad monster persona slipping. "She'll move on to a different chamber soon and then we can have some real fun."

"This is what you get for living in your mom's basement, bro," Jarl said.

I glanced at my mother. She hadn't seemed to hear over the roar of the vacuum.

Bjorne clapped me on the shoulder with a hulking, hairy hand. "What? That's your mom? Dude, introduce me! She's so hot!"

I stood so fast my chair toppled over. "If you ever say that again, I will uncoil my wrath and get all Ragnarok on your ass."

"No need to get your panties bunched up, man. I just think she looks kind of like, well, you know . . ." Bjorne winked at my mother, who was now dusting stalagmites.

My mother giggled. The sound grated on my ears. Didn't she realize how embarrassing it was when she flirted with my friends?

"No, I don't know," I said. "And I don't want to know."

Bjorne and Jarl exchanged glances. Bjorne whispered, a decibel that was only slightly under his shout. "You know, like that pin-up girl in the centerfold of my magazine."

"Well, she isn't!" I pounded on the table hard enough that some of the poker chips flew off. One of them rolled across the cavern floor, stopping when it smacked into my mother's webbed feet.

She stopped dusting. "Gee, are you playing what I think you're playing? After our last talk about gambling?"

"Mom, chill. It's just a game. It's not like we're playing for human heads or anything." We only did that at Aarne's house.

She pursed her lips. "By the way, I was cleaning your room and let the humans out from their cages. They were really making the place stink to Valhalla."

"Mom! How could you? They're just going to go back to Heorot and stage another attack on us. I needed those captives to take over Denmark."

"That's nice, dear." My mother shrugged her immense shoulders. "I guess you'll just have to capture some more tomorrow. After you muck out the swamp and mow the lake weed." Her gaze shifted from my horn-covered face to my shaggy leg hair draped over my chair. I followed her gaze. The jug of mead. I pushed it further into the shadows.

Mom pursed her lips. "Is that what I think it is? You know you're too young for that."

"Mom, I'm over a thousand years old."

"This is totally lame." Jarl threw down his cards and stood. "I'm going to Aarne's lair. I don't care if he tries to rip my face off because it's his time of the month."

My mom raised one of her many hands to wave goodbye. "Tell your mother I said hello, Jarly."

Jarl crossed his arms. "I don't have a mother."

"Oh, really? Then who did I run into at the monster suffrage meeting last week? Do demons just birth themselves? That is so like a male ego to think it can create the world all by itself."

By Thor's hammer! She was off on one of those tirades again. My day kept getting worse by the minute.

"Us, she-demons do have names, you know," she went on. "Just because humans aren't willing to write us down in their histories doesn't mean we are any less important than male monsters. I, for one, am sure I'll do something noteworthy to be recorded for all time."

This coming from the woman who fit the image of a Stepford wife.

Jarl edged closer to the exit. "Um, I'll tell my mom you said hi, Mrs. Borghild. Bye!"

Bjorne smiled, a lecherous gleam in his eyes I knew all too well from his exploits. He bellowed. "So where's your dad, bro?"

"By the powers of Asgard, she isn't a MILF," I growled under my breath. I prayed she hadn't heard.

As usual, Odin ignored my prayers.

"My husband? I ate him," Mom said with a shrug. "I guess I'm a real man-eater."

Of all the indignities, she had to bring that up again. When would it end? Couldn't she see she was ruining my life?

"You know, it really is empowering to be a liberated monster who permits herself the same appetites as male monsters. And by appetites, I'm not just talking about eating humans." She wagged a finger at Bjorne. Her smile was too cloying for my liking. Flirting with my friends was not allowed!

I cleared my throat. "Mother, could we get a little privacy? We're trying to have a guy's night."

"I'm sorry, dear. I didn't realize I was interrupting your big boy party. I should be getting back to the kitchen anyway. I tried to bake something from scratch and ended up summoning a demon instead. Now I've got a hot date cooking in the oven. A gingerbread golem." She feather-dusted her way out of the chamber.

I clenched and unclenched my fists, watching her go. I didn't think my day could get any worse. When I turned back to Bjorne, he was reading one of his dirty magazines. He opened the centerfold. A she-monster sprawled suggestively across the double page.

My jaw dropped.

There she was. My mom. Naked. Ick! I was going to be traumatized for the rest of eternity.

"I'm into golems. Do you think your mom would be into a three-some?" Bjorne asked.

Odin, have mercy! I thought I would die a thousand deaths right there. I was so grossed-out I puked up my mead and then passed out in a pile of my own vomit.

So there I was, alone in the underground lair, abandoned by my friends who had cooler places to be. I tried not to think about where Bjorne was. It made me nauseous when I thought about that son-of-a-troll and my mom.

I grabbed a club out of my trove of weaponry and headed to the kitchen, ready to pulverize my former friend. The only evidence they'd been there was a mess of gingerbread crumbs.

I couldn't even wallow in my misery in peace. The humans were at it again with their loud partying. The noise echoed from their stronghold above and into the swamp and our caverns. I usually didn't mind the ruckus, but today it reminded me of how alone I was—and how no one was around to party with.

Feeling grouchy and having nothing better to do, I decided to storm the humans' keep.

By the time I trudged through the swamp, passed a golf course, the row of fast food joints, and scaled the fortress walls, most of King Hrothgar's men were drunk and passed out in the great hall. They'd probably been celebrating the return of their escaped heroes after my mother let them out of their cages.

"Disgusting," I muttered, mostly because I could have been enjoying a similar state by now if my night had turned out differently. I considered stomping on the heads of the humans on the floor, killing them in their sleep. I was too depressed to bother.

A warrior stepped out of the shadows. He was tall, blond, and bearded like the rest of them. I couldn't tell if he was the king or someone else. These humans all looked the same to me.

"Ah, you must be Grendel. I've been searching for you," he said.

I crossed my arms. "You know, if you're going to throw a loud party, the unspoken rule is to invite the neighbors so they don't mind."

"I hear you have a problem with your mother. I might be able to assist."

Hope alighted in my heart. "By the power of Asgard, I'd give my right arm to be rid of her!"

A mischievous smile flashed across his face. He cracked his knuckles. "That can be arranged. Allow me to introduce myself. The name's Beowulf."

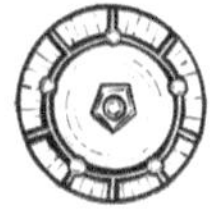

From a Serpent, Jade Bentasillus

~ Reggie Kwok

To Whom It May Concern,
I would like to express my interest in the Entry Game Designer Position at Slay Them All Games. I discovered this job through Monsterous.com. I am a serpent from Mammoth Cave in Kentucky.

I obtained my B.F.A in Animation from Scab University. My individualized internship at the indie company, Dontblink Entertainment, exposed me to several talented beings working in animation. In collaboration with others at this indie company, I demonstrated my creative and communication skills within the award-winning video game, *Life Is Scales.*

My portfolio is available at Fromagreenserpent.com. I am willing to relocate to California if accepted for this position.

From a Serpent,
Jade Bentasillus

☉

Dear William Banker and John Smith,
Thank you for the in-person interview on January 28. I enjoyed discussing the plans set for this company.

My portfolio contains several demo videos and images. In the attachment marked sample project, the characters delve into the meaning of the twenty-first century dragon. They encountered many situations in both urban and rural environments, and the list of assets from my portfolio can assist in creating an environment that anyone can enjoy regardless of species.

Every dragon has an element, and I am no different. My parents' breath magic related to health and medicine led to my own ability to produce cough drops on a whim. Co-workers will never go cough-drop-less ever again. I left a jar of mint and thyme cough drops with the secretary as a gift.

I am interested in this position. As requested, I have enclosed my references as an attachment. I am eager to work with you. I am available via DRAGON SHOUT, the translation slash email app, and email.

From a Serpent,
Jade Bentasillus

☉

Dear John Smith,
Why do humans respond to me via DRAGON SHOUT when I am able to type using several sticks strapped around my ten claws? I've increased in proficiency over the past few years, and I demonstrated my typing skills in front of the entire company. I don't understand why I am assigned to these typing tasks when other humans from this exact company cannot type with all ten fingers. Yes, I've seen at least one person using the two-finger strategy.

Every time that I listen to some fake dragon noise echoing from DRAGON SHOUT, my hearing orifices cannot take it anymore. I have been waiting to find a human who can actually speak in dragon tongue. No human from the company can solve this problem.

However, I need several solutions to move into place. First, the cubicles are too small for me. My co-worker has to work in the break room while I'm taking up the space of two cubicles. Everybody stares at me while I'm working.

Second, these human computers aren't working for me. I've been breaking these keyboards and computer screens left and right, and one time, I broke the ceiling from a surprise. You three expect me to pay for the six pieces of technology, which is unacceptable.

I'm not going into details until I receive a response. I don't understand why nobody responds to my emails.

From a Serpent,
Jade Bentasillus

☉

To: William Banker and John Smith
From a Serpent: Jade Bentasillus
Subject: A Report on the Outrageous Discrimination against
Dragons and Rectification Measures
Date: February 1

The purpose of this memo is to declare how outdated and dumb human memos are. Why haven't you responded to my emails? More importantly, why is there this requirement to submit complaints in this format? The true purpose of this memo is to offer strategies against interspecies discrimination.

Incident #1: The Typing Assessment

The madness all began on day one. For some reason, the company asked for a demonstration of my typing ability, and I was willing to demonstrate this through my lovely ten sticks designed to interact with technology without blowing it up all the time. However, co-workers planned for this event, for the whole office flocked to witness the typing dragon.

This simple exercise transformed into a game where co-workers demanded that I type until my fingers were ready to rip the keyboard in half. Co-workers were betting money on whether the dragon could type simple sentences humans could write.

After typing ten pages, I stopped.

According to the employee handbook given on the first day on my desk, the company prohibited gambling for all employees. I demand a very public announcement reminding others of company policy. I expect the supervisors to enforce this policy.

Incident #2: Modeling

At first, I thought that I was providing a decent service for my fellow workers by providing a proper image of a dragon. A co-worker asked me to enter her office one day and to strip down my clothes to the bare minimum for dragon anatomy practice. To protect the worker's identity, I chose a rather fitting name, Steak.

Steak went straight to work with her drawing and scribbled on her tablet at a very fast rate.

But then her tablet flashed once at my crotch.

She swore and thrust the tablet toward another direction.

I asked, "Since you have a picture of me, may I have my clothes back?"

She said, "Not until I shoot your face."

She proceeded to take more pictures. When I reached for my work clothes, she shoved them into the office drawer. I chopped the desk in half and then grabbed the clothes. I ran straight for the nearest bathroom. William Banker spotted me naked and gave a verbal reprimand when I was fully clothed. I was not even able to explain myself because the boss did all the talking and none of the listening, and I refuse to repeat the words that he said to me.

Incident #3: Interruptions for Cough Drops

I am unable to concentrate on work at the office. The cubicle doesn't cover half of my height. Every fifteen minutes, a co-worker taps my body and asks for a cough drop. I've placed visible signs all over my cubicle to drink water. My cough drops are not a cure all for colds.

Let me explain a little bit about dragon breath. Every time I breathe cough drops, I feel a little sick. With co-workers asking for cough drops every fifteen minutes, that's a total of thirty-two times a day when I feel like vomiting. For a whole three days, I had to call in sick due to my very own nausea, cold, and fever.

Then, the co-workers began slapping at my back the morning that I arrive on sight waiting for their free cough drops.

Incident #4: The Saddle

I received a gift with brown wrapping paper and a black bow on my desk. I unwrapped it with a neighboring co-worker and many more flashing their smartphones toward me. I even paused to ask them a question about the gift, but they didn't respond and continued to record.

They gave me a horse's saddle. They proceeded to pin me down and to attach the saddle against my will. I tried to resist, but I was outnumbered and outmatched. They also recorded themselves riding on top of me.

Incident #5: Paying for Office Equipment

I received a bill and a citation for the office equipment designed for humans. I am refusing to pay it.

Instead of buying the same thing for a dragon that he could crush every time, why not buy a decent sized computer with a dragon proof keyboard, so that every being can work without threatening one's wallet.

I am willing to provide resources on proper human-to-dragon interaction and etiquette. Please respond in a day's time.

☉

Dear Abby Tuffer,

Thank you for our lunch and meeting on February 10. Speaking to another serpent relieves me of every pound of headache from other co-workers. I've learned much from your portfolio. I'm interested in how the art and the game design combine together in the portfolio.

I cannot help but to point this out. During our lunch at the local coffee shop, a group of four teenagers pointed at a dragon.

One of them said, "Go back to China, where you belong!"

The poor dragon did not have features of an eastern dragon: no whiskers or slender body. In fact, the dragon looked like a western dragon with wings at the back and horns. Humans can be so offensive.

I said during our meeting that I would give the details to my meeting with the supervisors via this email, for, as I mentioned, that it did not go so well. In fact, everything went horribly wrong, to the point where if I ever were to mention specific names, I would wind up in another netherworld filled with trouble.

For starters, one of the supervisors decided to call me a snake for even requesting this meeting in the first place. From then on, I knew that they weren't going to do anything about my issues. The employee, Steak, denied all of the sexual assault accusations that I made against her. The supervisors placed my cough drop making as an additional duty, as if I was the official cough drop maker of the company. They regarded the horse saddle incident as absurd. They said that some insurance covered the damage done to the office equipment, but in the end, they still deducted extra money from my pay stub.

I have no faith in this company at all.
I want to eat my phone because nobody is responding to my emails.

From a Serpent,
Jade Bentasillus

☉

Dear Abby,
I got your package of six plastic bobble heads in the mail today. Did you really make these for my office? I'm not sure if the humans would approve of naked humans wearing underwear as hats and T-shirts as pants. Instead, I keep them in my apartment, where I flick my claw at them every time I feel like eating an office worker.

By the way, the whole I-ate-somebody-for-a-whole-two-minutes thing is a complete hoax and fiasco. The same bitch who took a picture of my crotch decided to Photoshop herself into my snout. The supervisors believed her, and now they are talking about dragon muzzles to protect human lives.

I'm on paid leave for a week.

Before I left, we were talking about the new dragon hire that was supposed to have a programming job but earned the design position since "he was a dragon." We spat out twenty different ideas during our last lunch before going on leave, and we agreed to keep the top four ideas in an email.

1. Check his portfolio. One or two of us should teach him the ropes to animation since they think that all dragons are artistic scholars for some reason.

2. Convince him to come to our two lunch spots at the pond and the coffee shop.

3. Support him during the typing assessment. Everybody is going to be there. With the power of two dragons, perhaps our growls and protests can end the taunting and the gambling.

4. I should remind him never to serve as a physical model. They have digital pictures on the Internet for a reason.

That could assist the new hire with blending into a toxic work environment.

From a Serpent,
Jade Bentasillus

☉

Dear Tobert Dell,
Welcome to Slay Them All Games! As a fellow coworker and dragon, I would like to offer a tour of the building to meet the other co-workers.

One of the supervisors may request a typing assessment as a part of company protocol. Given the programming background, I trust that this can go well. Abby, the other dragon co-worker, and I can check the surroundings of the testing area. This is a private affair after all.

I've set up a learning module on Fromagreenserpent.com. I would complete this module within the week. After the week, I must remove it. I don't want the supervisors and bosses to know what I'm up to.

If anybody asks you to serve as a model, I would say no and go elsewhere.

Could you accept Abby's invitation for lunch at the local coffee shop? We have a lot to discuss, including work culture, fellow employees, and much more.

From a Serpent,
Jade Bentasillus

☉

Dear Tobert Dell,
On behalf of the company, I would like to apologize for the incident on May 16. It was the last straw when they asked us to stop using the human bathrooms.

Abby and I didn't understand the cost to all of the electronic gifts. The entire electrical surge came from your ability to barf electronics.

Abby and I share the same weakness of becoming sick after using our breath magic, so we assumed the same for you. We would like to apologize for our mistake.

The electricity popped two light bulbs and almost set the lampshade on fire. Lucky for us, two other employees, a female and a male, assisted with putting out the fire, but the female employee complained about the dung-like odor.

She said, "One of the dragons pooped in the break room."

The female and male human left. Then, one of our bosses decided to escort all three of us to the lawn so that we could go to the bathroom.

This was so wrong. I felt like eating the boss and telling his family that I ate him, so that way, I could go to jail to protect myself from all of this hatred. It never made sense.

We don't have to deal with this. We have to talk.

From a Serpent,
Jade Bentasillus

☉

Dear Steaks,
As of June 1, Jade Bentasillus, Abby Tuffer, and Tobert Dell are resigning from our positions.

From the dragons,
Jade Bentasillus
Abby Tuffer
Tobert Dell

☉

About This Game:

> *Dear potential employee,*
> *Congratulations! Out of the fifty thousand jobs available on the Internet that are clearly advertisements, you stumbled upon the most important thing in the world: work. When drag-*

ons have taken over every possible job possible, learn about the meaning of this activity called work.

GET A JOB
Take a job as a button presser, a saliva spitter, a taste tester, a vomiter, or six other fabulous opportunities. Remember, the ability to eject bodily fluids is a requirement.

FLY TO WORK
Use your wings to fly to work. Cry when you realize that you don't have wings. Listen to authorities complaining about your lack of wings.

HAVE A LIFE
Stressed about work? Leave! Plenty of other opportunities provide real spambots bombarding the internet with advertisements for restaurants and retail stores. Search for a new job.

The first thousand customers who purchase this game will receive an exclusive puke bucket from Tufferware!

From Dragons United,
Jade Bentasillus
Abby Tuffer
Tobert Dell

☉

Tufferware Teams up with Dragons United to Promote VR Game

Dear fellow consumer,
Tufferware assists Dragons United, a new indie company, with promoting Dragon Job Simulator, a new virtual reality game on Volcano's PC gaming platform, Lava. Gamers can experience the true meaning of work in a dragon society.

Tufferware is teaming up with GamePit to display the power of virtual reality through several demos throughout the stores. Game-

Pit.com contains a map with all of the possible demo spots available.

Tobert Dell, founding chief architect and coder, describes the origins to the game: "It all started when we all agreed to quit our jobs. We started to spit out ideas, which turned into us spitting random objects out our mouths. After our brainstorm, Tuffer and Bentasillus were sick for a whole week, and I had to avoid technology for a whole day to remove the electricity out of my body. The next day, I received an email from Bentasillus containing a document with a novel's worth of ideas."

Dragons United began in response to policies from Slay Them All Games, a company preparing to declare bankruptcy from poor sales. The three founding dragons all worked in one apartment to create this game.

Abby Tuffer, founding creative game designer, states, "It was a dark time, having three dragons in a two-room apartment. One of us would often sleep on the floor or would continue working while the other two shared the same bed. While working on this game, I contacted an uncle who knew the CEO for Tufferware. I pitched the game to the CEO, who laughed so much that he needed several tissues to remove the tears from his face. Our lives changed so much after that point."

In *Dragon Work Simulator*, the gamer plays as a human who is searching for a job. Several occupations require the human to spit objects out the mouth and to carry a puke bucket, the same bucket that Dragons United designed and Tufferware manufactured. The puke bucket received many comical reviews on Forest.

"Depending on identity, the game can become really dark," states Jade Bentasillus, founding art director, "but any being, human or dragon, can enjoy this game. After all, the game came from personal experiences from our previous jobs. Once we received news about both GamePit and Tufferware supporting us, I promised my founding members that we would never have to worry about a second job ever again."

Dragons United reported that *Dragon Work Simulator* is updating until fan support dies down. With high demand for the puke buckets, Tufferware and Dragons United are working together to produce and to promote the famous bucket found in the game.

Voyeur; or, Helen of Troy, the Most Beautiful Woman in the World

~ Daniel David Froid

Ernestine told me she had just returned home from her travels. "*Just*," she said. "Got back this morning and I haven't even unpacked."

We sat inside her grubby kitchen, at a table piled high with junk. I glanced at my sister across the landscape formed by a few weeks' worth of mail, a pot full of soapy water, another, lidded pot, made of enameled cast iron in pink, several bottles of vitamins and pills, and a couple of boxes of food, with crackers in one and cookies in the other. The boxes were closed, and no food was on offer. A small patch of space had been cleared in one corner. I made a mental catalogue of all this accumulated junk while she moved around the kitchen, making coffee. Her house, in a state of unnerving disorder, could not be blamed on her extensive travels but on her regular habits, ever feeble, as a housekeeper.

She poured a cup of coffee for each of us and sat down. Cheryl, her dog, an elderly Vizsla, brushed past us before perching on a bed in the corner. She—Cheryl—had one in every room.

Ernestine was telling me she had once again gone to the Furono system. "At least that was the plan," she said. Lately, whenever she returned from one of her trips, she would call me and insist that I visit. Dutifully, I always did; I suppose some shred of sororal devotion lingered on in me. She never used to call me at all, until she had, in her retirement, taken up traveling. Or what she referred to as traveling. I'll admit that I could never quite say whether, or to what extent, I believed her. And yet, after so many years of silence, silence that at times felt vaguely menacing, I welcomed her gesture. I listened with tolerance to stories I scarcely believed. They seemed to me not far off from the stories she fabricated in our youth, stories in whose telling I once partook, full of magic and secrets, incantations we whispered in the dead of night in the forest just behind the house.

As she spoke, my mind flashed to the face of our brother, who did not like her stories, who did not like to play; quickly, I cut him out of my mind and turned to Ernestine.

"That far?" I asked. "I'm impressed."

Ernestine chuckled and lit a cigarette.

"Furono's not my favorite, but I got a good deal. And it's not so far, you know. Just one system over. But then I ended up going to Videro, and *that* is a place worth seeing."

While Ernestine spoke, Cheryl glanced at us with a look I can only describe as beatific: eyes narrowed, gazing toward the heavens and waiting to receive a sign from God. She often looked this way, and I wondered how often she received such signs in return. About as often, I thought, as her human companion traveled among the stars.

I smiled and sipped the coffee, which was rich and strong. In Videro, the coffee is expensive but very fine—or so Ernestine says. I had never been myself. I asked, "This is good. Is it Videran coffee?"

Ernestine smirked. "Yes indeed."

"But is it actually coffee?" I asked and looked down at the thick, dark liquid, which swirled thickly when I tilted the cup back and forth. "It just occurred to me to wonder. Are we actually talking about the same plant here? I mean, we can't be."

Ernestine tutted. "You have such a narrow mind. There are only so many elements in the universe, you know. Here we have a composition that is as close as anything you'd like. Closer than some swill I've had on Earth in my time." Her mug was already empty, and she rose to refill it. Mine remained nearly full.

"Well. Okay then. Tell me about the trip."

"The plan," she said. "was to stay in Furono. I had to leave because everything moves too slowly there. And I can't stand the people. Perhaps I shouldn't say that, but it's true. They all sit around and have these lengthy, abstract conversations about what it means to exist. I mean, this is dinner table conversation. This is what they discuss with their kids! There was this little girl in the hotel where I was staying. . . . My first morning, I sit there sipping my coffee and eating some very good pancakes—and yes, pancakes, even if they were not made of good old earth flour and eggs and whatnot." She raised a finger at me and jabbed it, once, decisively, before continuing: "And this girl comes up to me, and she asks me my name and I tell her, and I ask her hers. It seems like a perfectly pleasant interaction, and I tell her she seems like a very nice little girl, and then she says, in this lisping little-girl voice, 'Is my niceness your perception or is it a true quality of mine? Is it an essential quality of my being?' She went on like that, about the inherent nature of qualities, for a few minutes—minutes that felt, I am telling you, like hours. And at last I simply excused myself to use the bathroom and fled to my room. I could not bear it."

"She was trying to make conversation," I said, "in the only way she knew how." My coffee had lasted for this anecdote's duration, and, now my cup was empty, I wanted more. I stood up, prompting Cheryl to bark, weakly. She lifted her head from its pillowed recline, said her piece, and then let her head drop.

"Forgive her," Ernestine said. "She doesn't like sudden movements. Not at her age." She laughed and said, "I don't either." After a pause, she continued, "I personally cannot bear the tedious philosophical speculations of others; I do not care one whit!" Ernestine scrunched up her face in disgust.

"You know who questions like that remind me of," I said. My sister's face changed, from disgust to a darker emotion. Something flashed in her eyes. I was the one *who* said it, yet suddenly I did not want to grant that who a referent. "Our little brother," I whispered. Pursing her lips, looking away from me, Ernestine said nothing. My cup full once more, I returned to my seat.

"Anyway," Ernestine said, "when I was there, I heard all about this new interstellar liner that would be swinging by before moving on to Videro. *The Voyeur*. It was another guest at the hotel who told me, this very tall and very thin hairless man whose name I can't remember. But he was a human, and quite pleasant, and he said he knew the owner and could get me a discounted ticket. Now, I did not fall off the turnip truck yesterday, Cloris, and ordinarily a bland and pleasant man with such an offer would give me pause. To say the least."

"I would say so."

"Yes. Ordinarily the offer of a trip past the edge of the system, on a ship called *The Voyeur* no less, would be a sign that I should turn tail and run all the way home." Now she stood up, walked to the fridge, and paused to look back at me. "Are you hungry? I'm starved."

I demurred with a shake of the head. She busied herself, gathering things—eggs, a green pepper, an onion—to fix herself something to eat.

She said, "So I may have been tempted to see my way out. To flee. Whatever. And yet. What can I say? The devil of curiosity overtook me, and it prompted me to ask him to say a little more. And he did, he went on about how fabulous *The Voyeur* is. He said, 'Anything you'd like to take a peek at, you can, if you pay for the pleasure.' And, anyway, everyone says that Videro will dazzle you. The most spectacular sight in the galaxy." She paused mid-chop, one hand clutching a knife and hovering over an onion. "A spectacular sight: is that redundant, Cloris? I think it is. Spectacle is inherent to any sight. Or, better: to be worthy of being seen is inherent to a spectacle."

"Careful, Ernestine. You're beginning to sound like the little girl from Furono."

Her eyes glowed; she barked out one singular laugh. "The beaches— in colors you've never even dreamed. The cities—as tall as the sky. So he said, and I began to believe him, or perhaps it was only that my travels had left me dazed and debilitated. Interstellar journeys take a lot out of a woman, you know."

What was there to do but wait, patiently, for her to continue? That these tales seemed to me mendacious has already been noted. The extravagant telling of tales has long been a passion of Ernestine's— her whole life long. The first time she told me she had just returned from a journey beyond our solar system, I decided neither to argue nor to question her but to take her at her word, just to see what would happen, to see how she would proceed. With plentiful details and a coherent narrative thrust, her tale at least amused me if it did not altogether convince. As then, so now. If what she offered were lies, I accepted them anyway. Now, I waited. Cheryl rustled the blankets as she shifted her slumbrous body. Eggs sizzled in a pan that rested above flames of blue and white. My sister banged the pan against the stove and cursed. I pictured her, sitting glumly on a rocket that rattled through the cosmos, white fire trailing behind it. In my mind, Ernestine in her ratty housecoat, cigarette in one hand, straddled the rocket like a pinup girl riding a bomb as it shot across the sky, smirking and waggling her fingers at me in a patronizing wave.

"And so I went. I boarded *The Voyeur*." She sat down, soon, eggs fried hard and doused in hot sauce, the edges crisp if not burnt, and for a long moment she wielded the fork as though she were about to conduct an orchestra.

"That guy, I lost him. I didn't need him anymore. He seemed like a bit of a shady character, however useful I found his tips. The ship itself was grand. Not a rocket, sister, but a proper starship, enormous, equipped for deep-space flight, and painted the most beautiful shade of red."

"How did you know I imagined a rocket?"

"The wide and deep grooves of familiarity, worn into the paths that a mind daily treads, may occasionally be mistaken for telepathy."

"Ah," I said, and felt faintly embarrassed as the image of Ernestine straddling the rocket flickered in my mind once more. One might have thought, from the look on her face, that she had uttered God's own word. Even if she had, stubbornness would still forbid me from admitting it. I began to sort the mail on the table by category: bills, circulars that I would take home and recycle myself, and other. Ernestine's face spasmed for a moment: surprise, irritation, or gratitude? However she felt, I continued my sorting.

"And so I boarded the ship and went straight to my room. Rather small, yes, cramped and dark, but this was an adventure, and adventure often yields privation, which demands fortitude, which I have in abundance. The berth was truly no more than that, a small enclosed bed with scarcely enough room for my trunk. But it met my minimum needs, and what could I do but be grateful? Sleep beckoned, even in those unideal conditions, and I duly gave in. But the next day I awoke ready to take on my favorite role: voyeur!"

I snorted.

"Laugh all you want, Cloris. I have always been a great watcher of people, an outside observer, and relish what I learn from that purview. To board *The Voyeur* seemed almost too perfect, rather too suited to me, and the gentleman was right that what it offered was, simply, everything: everything you could ever want to see. Now, of course, much that comprises this 'everything' was simply shocking, disgusting, crude, and lewd. I did not wish to observe the act of copulation, nor did I wish to glimpse nude bodies writhing to the beat of an unfamiliar music."

"Ernestine, you boarded a cruise ship—pardon me, a starship—called *The Voyeur*. It sounds sleazy as hell to me. What would you expect but that sort of thing?" The mail before me lay in three piles. The vertiginous stack of circulars teetered on the verge of collapse. I divided that pile in two and folded my hands before me, awaiting a response.

She glared above her empty plate. I noticed that her housecoat had a yellow stain on its collar but did not dare point it out.

"Oh, Cloris," she began, settling into a familiar argumentative mode. "You're a real pill sometimes, you know that? Excuse me, but have you ever bothered exploring the galaxy around us? You'd find that lots of people elsewhere have minds quite a bit broader than yours—less inclined to sleaze. And you will have to take it on faith that there was much else there to draw the eye and mind for us voyeurs of nobler calling, a few of the carnal pleasures notwithstanding. If you don't want to listen, to give me your attention sans judgment— well, you can feel free to go home and return to your macramé. Or whatever it is you do to fill your time."

In silence we met each other's eyes. A long minute passed and then another. I stood up and walked to the sink, where water flowed weakly from a rust-stained faucet, and tried but failed to erase all trace of coffee from my mug. Back at the table, I sighed and waved my hand, prompting her to proceed.

"A zoo full of alien creatures—but you probably wouldn't care much about that. A library, granting access to the greatest volumes known to the galaxy. I couldn't help but slip a copy of my own book in there. Fortunately, I rarely leave home without a spare. I could go on, but there was one thing in particular that really drew me in—one thing I wanted to tell you about." Her voice quavered for a moment, and something in her manner shifted. It seemed that her muscles tensed; she grew defensive or wary. Then she cleared her throat and resumed.

"I spent all day wandering the ship, going in and out of the zoo and the library and the coffee shops and so on. And at the end of the day I wanted a meal, and maybe just a little drink to calm my nerves. So I asked around, and the word was that there was one bar you just couldn't miss. That's what they said. The name of this place was Sco-pophilia. It took me quite a while to find—way at the other end of the ship, the opposite end from the sleeping berths. It looked funny. The lighting was dark, but all the walls and the tables and chairs, every-thing, were in pastel colors. The pastel and dim lightning made it feel sort of eerie—haunted. It's been my experience that interior decoration on other planets is often disarming. Really, all judgments of taste—they differ so much from one species to another.

"Anyway, a young person led me to a high, round table near the back. I had to ask to be seated closer to the stage, and she complied but not without a look of disdain. Oh well. I had arrived just in time for the show, and I was not about to miss it because some gaggle of aliens in front of me were blocking my view. Onstage, a heavy black curtain made its squeaking way into a recess in the ceiling. No light shone; whoever stood there stood in shadow. But, soon, a thin trickling spotlight cast the performer's face in light, and I could see her pale and blue-toned skin, covered in garish makeup; her long flat limp blonde wig; her diaphanous garment, which might have been a sheet, cheaply sewn into a dress. If you could call it a dress. A voice resounded from somewhere behind me; the emcee said, 'And now, Helen of Troy, the Most Beautiful Woman in the World.'

"Now, that's a subjective judgment if ever I've heard one, not least because we spectators represented a good number of worlds, all of which, one might think, would have more to offer in the realm of beauty than this bedraggled performer. Nonetheless. We were there to enjoy the pleasure of looking, and I assumed that Helen of Troy, the Most Beautiful Woman in the World, not only offered a worthy prospect but enjoyed being looked at."

At this point, Ernestine's voice began to quaver. Her eyes roved around her kitchen and settled on her dog. Despite her apparent disapproval, despite her terse tone, it was clear that something that night had disturbed her.

"She sang. If you can call it singing. She sang a strange song that seemed a little familiar, though I could not recall having heard it. Something about how magic dances on a clock, how time is the magic length of God." I murmured "Buffy Sainte-Marie," but Ernestine ignored me, went on: "She didn't move at all, really, just barely swayed onstage in her terrible, booming voice. No: she *incanted*. She was reciting a spell on the unwilling masses. If you have not registered the fact, Cloris, she was a drag queen. And her voice pierced me like a needle, and it stung that badly. Oh my god. The thing is, Cloris, the thing is that I noticed, as she sang, that she looked remarkably like . . . She had blue skin—the slate-blue color of a corpse—and a terrible blond wig, but, when she moved in the spotlight, I saw it. She was the precise likeness, beneath false skin and hair, of him. Branson."

Ernestine, ever steely, looked suddenly so desperate. As though the cold night had come to claim her and found her bare—defenseless. As though the galactic paths she traveled had been totally evacuated. As though she had seen our brother.

My face must have been a mirror of hers. She said, "I had thought that he was . . ."

I nodded. My mouth felt dry. The room around us contracted, disappeared, and we floated alone with the remains of what we had thought to be unassailable truth.

My sister nodded. "And yet. There he was, I swear it. And doesn't that name just sound like him? 'Helen of Troy, the Most Beautiful Woman in the World.' The entire epithet, every time; no abbreviations. No compromises!

"Was beauty," Ernestine asked in a voice that was soft, shorn of its typical brash confidence, "our perception—we in the audience—or was it an essential quality of her being? She looked like a corpse; perhaps she was dead, and her body lived on in some other state we scarcely understand. She. Or he. Branson. I swear it was him. He was singing of the magic length of God and swaying, very gently, on his feet. And it was a very pretty thought to imagine that Helen of Troy, the Most Beautiful Woman in the World, was looking right at me as she swayed. But such a thought ended in conjunction with the song, and that is when she fled the stage; the lights went up; the show was declared, by that selfsame master of ceremonies, to be over. Helen of Troy, the Most Beautiful Woman in the World, had departed, and so had he."

Ernestine clasped her hands before her plate. She sat and said no more. Cheryl stirred behind us. And, after a very long spell of quiet, I said, "Ernestine."

"Yes, Cloris?"

"Is there more to the story?"

"There is not. The end has come. I retreated to my berth and slept all night. The next day, I found a trader whose little ship would depart that afternoon and bring me very close to Earth. I just got back this morning. Haven't even unpacked."

She stood and ambled to the sink, where she deposited plate and fork. From one pocket of her housecoat her hand drew out a purple leash, which she clipped to the collar around Cheryl's neck. After some exaggerated stretching, Cheryl followed her companion to the door. The thick sourness of dread suffused the air as I sat at the table, looking at the piles of my sister's mail. She and the dog left me alone with the faint sense that Branson could be here with us, except that I knew that to be impossible. An image surfaced that I would have preferred not to see: his face, his face, his face.

When at last Ernestine and Cheryl returned from their walk, neither of us spoke. Her face looked drawn, nearly corpselike. It seemed to me that her gaze was fixed on a point so distant it might have been that alien sun. For a moment the image occurred to me—a flaming star that sped our way and swallowed us whole, obliterating not just us and the house that held us but the entire wretched planet. And it occurred to me to speak it aloud and allow it to sit there between us, though I did not indulge the impulse.

Of course I did not believe her story. And after Ernestine gave Cheryl a treat and lumbered to her chair and sat down once more, I felt moved to say so. Perhaps the surge of perversity that then pulsed within me should have encouraged me to pursue a line of inquiry or to deny her stories outright, to insist that she was an inveterate liar and charlatan (which she was). But instead it drove me to take a different tack.

Hands clasped, eyes sure, I looked at my sister and said, "Ernestine, what really happened after you returned to your booth? Why don't you tell me the end of the story?"

She gave one miserable shriek of a laugh. "I gave it to you; you've got it!" Her face took on a bleak cast as she sighed and lit a cigarette.

"Couldn't you have smoked that outside?"

She shook her head, a firm no. "If you want the end of the story, dear sister, then why should I not oblige? Once the show ended, we began to stand up. Some of us, I presumed, would stay to chat and drink and do the other things that patrons do. But self-restraint is my watchword when I travel the galaxy, and no energy remained in me for such leisurely pursuits. My little sleeping chamber beckoned, and in that direction my feet swiftly took me. The halls of *The Voyeur* are narrow and, at that time, they were dimly lit—evoking the night that did not exist for us, then near no sun. Rather, nothing but night existed. Anyway, scarcely any others traveled those corridors; for a time I had the feeling, stoked by the show at Scopophilia, of having slid into an empty world.

"As I left, I happened to spy the master of ceremonies shuffling away, in the same direction that I was taking. The temptation to follow him rose within me, but a more direct approach seemed wise. I sped up and soon overtook him.

"'Sir,'" I called, combating distaste at his tiny form, which resembled that of a pill-bug, though he stood as upright as I did. And he evidently possessed vocal cords of some sort or another. Or made use of a technology I could scarcely imagine, which permitted communication, as well as the deception of my senses. Would he—I dared wonder—roll away if frightened? He stopped and waited for me to speak. And I did: 'Where did Helen of Troy, the Most Beautiful Woman in the World, scamper off to? I would like to offer her my deepest and most profound respects.'"

"The pill-bug continued to stare. And I heard a voice, which to my ear now sounded distinctly robotic. He said, 'Oh. That's a hologram. We just use her for the shows. There's no real person.'"

"I said, 'A hologram? But surely she must be based on a real person—a simulacrum of the real, composed of light and strings of code, no?'"

"The pill-bug replied disappointingly: 'I don't know, lady. We've used her for years.' And then he turned and began to walk away, ignoring me as I called after him: 'But how could I find out?'

"I made my way to the berths. I entered mine and slept. And now. The end. The real end."

"That's all, Ernestine?" I asked. I felt ready to stand up and leave.

"That's all, sister. The genuine end. I am afraid, Cloris, that what I have given you is no more than a shaggy dog story. A tale to entice you—but one that has neither moral nor point. One whose mystery is perhaps irresolvable."

"Well, that's true. There was no reason to tell me any of this. To bring up all of this about—about Branson. Completely unnecessary." I rose and moved to retrieve my coat.

Ernestine had begun to mutter. Perhaps she meant me to hear, but the feeling struck me that I was eavesdropping, intruding on an intense and sudden privacy. She said, "Is it only when we believe ourselves most in control that we are most caught within time's trap?

You see the shadow, the shadow, the beast within the shadow, the undying flame that burns at the heart of the darkest well in the world, and you think a way out is imminent, no? But delusion, utterly absolute, forms a hard and impenetrable shell around the sticky sorrow at the center of every single sorry life. I wonder whether she knew it, whether she understood the fundamental nature of our condition."

At that point she stopped, and she cleared her throat, and she lit another cigarette and looked my way.

"Do you understand it, Cloris?"

I sighed. "No," I said. My coat bedecked my shoulders. My bag was in my hand. The front door stood only a meter or so away, as the crow flies, though it suddenly seemed as distant as whatever desolate planet *The Voyeur* might now idly circle.

Ernestine cleared her throat and said, "I don't either. Not a whit. I'll call you after my next trip. I'm sure you'd be eager to hear all about it."

I smiled, made a gesture with my head that could have indicated yes or no or something altogether ambiguous—even I am not sure where my intentions lay and what it was I wanted her to see—and left her there alone at the table.

Many Deaths Before Dying

~ *Warren Benedetto*

The empty lot next to Eddie's house was the football field where Joe Montana threw the game-winning touchdown to Jerry Rice. It was the baseball diamond where Mark McGwire beat Jose Canseco in the most epic Wiffle ball home run derby in MLB history. It was where Rambo took down the Predator with a Nerf gun, and where Robo-Cop blew the Terminator's head off with a Super Soaker. It was my favorite place to hang out with my three best friends.

And it was the last place I saw them alive.

The four of us had known each other since we were toddlers. We lived in the same neighborhood, went to the same schools, and played on the same Little League teams. Eddie's house was our main hang-out spot, partially because of the empty lot next door, but also because his mom kept the best assortment of Tastykakes stocked in the pantry. Even better, his house had a big finished basement with a ping pong table and a Nintendo with its own dedicated TV. He had all the best games, too: *Mike Tyson's Punch-Out*, *Metroid*, *Double Dragon*, *Contra*. He even had *The Legend of Zelda*, the one with the shiny gold cartridge that I coveted so much.

The lot was nothing special, but that's also what made it so special. It could be anything we wanted—a sports field, a war zone, an alien planet, or whatever else our imaginations could conjure. Some of my earliest, fondest memories were of the four of us running around in that lot, having squirt gun battles in the summer and snowball fights in the winter, then retreating to Eddie's house for Elio's Pizza and Fanta Orange Soda.

The lot was mostly dirt, about the shape of a football field, with a row of dark green hedges separating it from the neighbor's yard. The ground turned into a mud pit when it rained, but it hadn't rained in weeks. That's why we were so confused about the enormous puddle that had appeared there overnight. There were no sprinklers, fire hydrants, or water mains nearby. The nearest hose was coiled up way over by Eddie's front porch—it was nowhere near long enough to create a puddle in that part of the lot. And yet, inexplicably, there it was: a perfectly round circle of water, maybe fifteen feet across, with a mirror-like sheen that reflected the cloudless sky overhead.

"You're telling me you have no idea where it came from?" Marco asked Eddie.

"Dude, I swear." Eddie held up his fingers in a *Scout's Honor* gesture. "Jack, tell him."

I nodded. "Yep. We were inside all night."

The previous evening, the four of us had been out in the lot until well after sunset, tossing a baseball around while listening to my Def Leppard cassettes on Eddie's boombox. We only stopped once it was too dark to see the ball anymore. Marco and Shah went home, but I spent the night at Eddie's, watching Indiana Jones movies on his VCR until 2:00 A.M. We were together the whole time.

"This sucks," Marco complained. "Now what do we do?"

The plan had been for us to play Wiffle ball all afternoon, but the puddle was directly in the middle of our infield, in the exact spot where the pitcher's mound was supposed to be. It was so big that it even encroached on the base lines we had scratched into the dirt with the heels of our sneakers the day before.

"We could run around it," Shah suggested.

"Or through it," Eddie added. "We'll just take our shoes off."

I peered at the puddle, trying to examine it from different angles. "I don't know, guys. Looks pretty deep."

There was something about the thing that just felt *off* to me. The puddles in the lot were usually muddy and brown; the water in this one was perfectly reflective and oddly still, with a surface unbroken by mosquitoes or water striders. That was unusual—any standing water in our area was usually a breeding ground for insects. But not this one. It was like someone had left a giant compact disc in the middle of the dirt, shiny side up.

"It can't be *that* deep," Marco said. "It's a puddle, not a lake."

"Why's it so shiny then?"

"Don't ask me. Ask Mr. Wizard." Marco pointed at Shah.

Shah Patel was the resident genius of our friend group. While Marco, Eddie, and I spent most of our free time playing video games, Shah preferred hacking into government computer systems using his dad's dial-up modem. He couldn't *actually* hack in—he had no idea what he was doing—but that didn't stop him from running up exorbitant long-distance phone bills while he tried. His favorite movies were *War Games* and *The Manhattan Project*: he was a real "let's steal plutonium and make a nuclear bomb for the Science Fair" kind of kid.

"Hold this." Shah handed me the yellow plastic Wiffle ball bat he was carrying, then squatted next to the puddle to get a closer look. "Hmm. You sure it's even water?"

"What else would it be?"

Shah sniffed the air then wrinkled his nose. "Not sure. Smells like—"

"Your asshole," Marco interjected.

"You would know," Shah shot back.

Shah wasn't wrong about the stench. I couldn't vouch for whether it smelled like his asshole or not, but it didn't smell like water. It had a noxious odor that reminded me of Mr. Birnbaum's chemistry lab: a mix of sulfur, ammonia, and . . . something else. Something sour.

Shah tapped his finger on his lips thoughtfully. "Maybe it's mercury."

"Like from a thermometer?" Eddie asked. "Where the hell would that come from?"

"A meteor."

"I'm pretty sure we would've heard a meteor hitting the ground next to my house, Shah."

"Hey," Marco said, pointing at the Wiffle ball I held in my hand. "Lemme borrow that for a sec."

"No. Why?"

"Just give it."

Marco tried to snatch the ball away from me, but I dodged out of the way. Instead of reaching for the ball again, he feigned a blow to my groin—the kid was a notorious nut-flicker. I immediately reacted, dropping the Wiffle ball and lowering my hands to protect my crotch. Luckily for my testicles, it was just a ruse, but it had achieved the intended result.

Marco snatched the ball off the ground and tossed it into the water. It landed right in the middle of the puddle. There was no splash. No ripple. It didn't bob or bounce. It hit the surface of the puddle and just . . . stopped. It was like someone had pressed pause on the VCR at the exact second the ball had touched the water. Then, ever so slowly, the ball sunk. That was strange too—it was made of hollow plastic. It should have floated. But it didn't.

"Whoa. That was weird, right?" Shah looked at us to gauge our reactions. "It's like some kind of non-Newtonian fluid."

Marco nodded thoughtfully. "Mm-hmm. Yep. That's what I was thinking too." He clearly had no idea what the hell Shah was talking about.

"Now what do we do?" I said to Marco.

"About what?" he replied innocently.

"About the ball!"

"Just go get it."

"And reach it how?"

"With the bat."

I looked at the yellow plastic bat in my hand. It was about three feet long, nowhere near long enough to reach the ball from where we stood. "It's not long enough, dumbass."

"That's what she said."

"Why don't you just walk in?" Eddie asked.

"Why don't *you* just walk in?" I snapped.

"Use the bat," Shah suggested. "See how far down it goes."

"You do it." I held out the bat to Shah.

"Oh my *God*," Marco groaned. "You're such a pussy." He grabbed the bat away from me. "Gimme that."

My face flushed with a mixture of embarrassment and anger. Kids our age called each other pussies all the time, but I always took it personally. I couldn't help it. None of the other kids had a Dad who was an actual goddamned war hero like mine was. He had saved like fifteen guys in his unit in Vietnam, taking out an entire enemy encampment while getting riddled with bullets and shrapnel, then carrying the wounded one at a time back to the LZ to be airlifted to safety. He had two Purple Hearts, a Bronze Star, a Congressional Medal of Honor . . . he even met President Nixon. My dad would never call me a pussy—he was way too old-fashioned to ever use a word like that—

but I always felt like, deep down, he must be thinking I was. I listened to music by guys who dressed like girls. I was more into books than sports. I didn't like to hunt, fish, or do any of the things that he did with his dad when he was my age. Hell, I was almost a teenager and I was still afraid of the dark. I would never be half the man that he was, and I knew it. I think he did too.

Marco plunged the bat into the puddle to test the depth, sinking it as far as he could without getting wet. "Damn, that's actually really deep," he said as he swirled it around. "I can't even feel the bottom."

"Just like your Mom," I grumbled under my breath.

He pulled the bat from the water and shook it dry. "Ha ha. So funny I forgot to laugh."

"Maybe it's, like, an old well or something," Shah said. "Or a sink-hole."

"That would suck," Eddie replied. "So much for ever playing Wiffle ball again. Or anything else."

Marco handed the bat back to me. A wicked grin formed on his lips. "Dare you to jump in."

"Yeah, right."

"What's the matter? You scared?"

"No. Are *you*?"

Eddie began untying the laces of his Reeboks. "I'll do it."

"See?" Marco said. He clapped Eddie on the back like a proud father. "Eddie's not a pussy."

"Stop it," I growled through clenched teeth.

"Stop what?"

"I'm not a pussy."

"Okay. So, prove it."

I didn't move. I didn't say anything. My face felt like it was on fire.

After a few moments of waiting, Marco nodded. "That's what I thought. Pussy. Pussypussypussy—"

"Fuck you." I started to lunge at him, but Shah stepped between us and put a hand on my chest.

"Chill out, Jack. He's just kidding." He gave Marco a disapproving glare. "Right?"

"Right," Marco said. His tone was unconvincing.

While Marco and I were busy arguing, Eddie kicked away his sneakers and peeled off his socks, shorts, and t-shirt. He stood there in his tighty-whities, swinging his skinny arms as if loosening his shoulders for a swim. "Who else is with me?" he asked. Nobody else volunteered. "All right, then," he said with a smug grin. "See ya later, pussies!" He took off in a sprint toward the puddle and launched himself into the air, drawing his knees up to his chest for a full cannonball. "Kowabunga!"

I spun away and shielded my face in anticipation of a soaking splash of water. Marco and Shah did the same. But no splash came. Instead, there was a sharp slapping noise, the sound of an epic belly flop from a diving board. I turned back to the puddle to see Eddie sprawled on top of the water, staring at the sky with a shocked, pained expression on his face. It was like the water had turned to solid Jell-O when he hit it. Then, just like the Wiffle ball, he began to sink. His arms flailed as the seemingly-solid surface suddenly liquified underneath him. An abbreviated scream escaped his lips before it was cut off by water flooding his mouth. And then he was gone.

Marco squealed with laughter. "Holy shit, that was epic!"

Shah bent closer to the puddle, trying to see past the reflective surface. He looked up at us, his brow furrowed with concern. "Think he's okay?"

"Relax," Marco said, his laughter tapering off. "He'll come back up."

We waited for what was probably ten seconds, but it seemed like forever. Finally, I broke the silence. "He's not—" My voice caught in my throat. I swallowed hard, then continued. "He's not coming up."

"He will," Marco answered. "Eddie!" he yelled. "Come on, man! Quit screwing around!" He laughed again, but I could hear panic fraying his voice.

Shah snatched the bat away from me and thrust it into the puddle. "Eddie!" he called. "Grab on!" He moved it around, trying to find Eddie's grip. "Come on, dude! Grab the bat!"

"Do you feel anything?" I asked. My heart was pounding in my chest. I had a very bad feeling about what was happening.

Shah plunged the bat even deeper, submerging his arm up to the shoulder. "Nothing," he grunted, his voice straining. "He's not—"

Suddenly, Shah was jerked violently forward, plunging face-first into the puddle. His legs kicked wildly at the dirt as he was dragged into the water. Despite his struggling, there was no splashing, no splattering—it happened as silently and smoothly as if he had slipped into a pool of shadow. The puddle barely even rippled.

Marco stared at the spot where Shah just had been. "Guys?" His previous bravado had evaporated. He sounded scared. "Guys, come on."

"We need to get help," I said quietly. But I didn't move. I felt rooted in place, as if my feet had bonded to the Earth's crust. I was frozen solid, utterly paralyzed with fear. Shah hadn't just fallen into the puddle. He had been *pulled*. By what, though? The only thing I could think of was an alligator. But were there alligators in our part of New Jersey? And even if there were, how had they gotten into the puddle? And where had the puddle come from in the first place? And why was the water so deep, and so weird? None of it made any sense.

"Shit!" Marco cried. "What do we *do*?" I didn't respond. "What do we do?" he asked again, his voice rising with panic. When I still didn't answer, he looked back at Eddie's house, searching for some sort of solution. His eyes lit up. "The hose! Let's go, gimme some help!" He pulled me by the arm, finally breaking me from my trance. I ran after him as he sprinted across Eddie's yard to where a long green garden hose was coiled up beside the front porch. "Pick it up!" he ordered.

I began gathering heavy loops in my arms as Marco unscrewed the hose from the pipe. Once it was free, we carried the messy tangle of rubber over to the puddle. Marco sat on the ground and began wrapping one end of the hose around his ankle.

"What're you gonna do?" I asked.

"I'm going in." He twisted the hose into a knot and pulled it tight.

"No!" I felt tears welling in my eyes. "You can't."

"You want them to drown?"

"No, but—"

"Then help me!" He limped to the edge of the puddle, dragging the heavy rubber hose behind him. "Count to twenty. If I don't come up by then, pull me out." Before I could protest any further, he took a deep breath and stepped into the water. He dropped like a lead weight, instantly vanishing under the mirrored surface.

"Oh my God," I mumbled. "Oh, fuck." I let the hose play through my hands as it uncoiled, ready to pull Marco out as soon as twenty seconds had elapsed. I counted as fast as I could: "One-Mississippi-two-Mississippi-three-Mississippi—"

The hose began to slip through my fingers faster . . . and faster . . . and faster. My skin burned from the friction of the rubber zipping across my palms. It seemed impossible that the puddle could be deep enough to consume dozens of feet of hose, but it was.

"Marco!" I tried to close my hands around the hose, but I was almost jerked off my feet by the force of whatever was pulling it. I had to let it go or risk getting yanked into the puddle myself. Just as the final coils of the hose unfolded, whatever had grabbed it—*had grabbed Marco*—stopped. I tentatively gripped the hose and hauled it hand-over-hand out of the water. It came out easily. Too easily. After about a dozen feet, the end emerged. It was cleanly severed.

"Marco?" My voice was barely a whisper. The tears in my eyes spilled over. The hose slipped from my fingers and fell to the ground. The severed end flopped into the puddle. There was no splash.

A quick flash of movement in the water made my heart trip in my chest. I felt a swell of hope at the possibility that my friends were surfacing from the depths . . . followed by a surge of unspeakable horror at what I saw instead. It was something so alien, so incomprehensible, so *other* that I struggle to describe it in terms anyone can understand. It reminded me of the hind leg of a grasshopper—long, skinny, barbed, jointed—but twice as long as my arm and made of something that looked like black glass. At the end was a churning cluster of smaller appendages that moved like the mouthparts of a crab. They had the ghostly translucency of white quartz crystals, but they were as dexterous and multi-jointed as my own fingers.

The nightmare limb breached the surface of the puddle and extended in my direction. I stumbled backward, tripping over my own feet and falling on my back. Two more identical limbs emerged beside the first. They pressed into the ground by my feet as the creature began to lift itself out of the puddle. With a desperate cry, I drove my heels into the dirt, propelling myself away from the water as fast as I could. Then I rolled over, scrambled to my feet, and ran.

I ran past Eddie's house, down Grape Street, and all the way to my house on Peachtree Lane. Throwing the front door open, I sprinted across the kitchen to the phone on the wall and dialed 911. The operator thought I was making a crank call, but after a few minutes of pleading, I was able to convince her to send the Rescue Squad to Eddie's house. Then I hung up the phone and ran back the way I came. By the time I got to the lot, sweat-soaked and gasping for breath, the police were already there.

But the puddle was gone.

All that was left in the lot were Eddie's sneakers, socks, and t-shirt, exactly where he had tossed them. There was no sign of Eddie, Shah, or Marco. Just like the puddle, they had vanished.

I explained to the police exactly what happened, but they didn't believe me. How could they? A disappearing puddle? Water that doesn't splash? A trio of giant grasshopper legs with alien finger-mouths? I sounded like an insane person who had rented too many horror movies from West Coast Video.

Instead, the police had a much more realistic theory: the boys had run away from home. They assumed I was covering for them—albeit badly—by concocting a crazy story to account for their disappearance. The cops could never explain *why* the boys might have run away or where they might have run away to, but it didn't matter. For the next twenty years, that was the official explanation. It's what Shah's parents believed when they moved back to India, what Marco's mom believed when she hung herself in the garage the next summer, and what Eddie's parents believed when they died in their sleep from carbon monoxide poisoning a few months ago.

After Eddie's folks were gone, a wealthy investor bought their land and knocked down their house so he could build a new mini-mansion on the property. With the addition of the empty lot next door, the new owner had enough room to add a tennis court, a putting green, and even an in-ground pool. It was during the excavation of the pool that a new clue to my friends' whereabouts was found. The construction workers hadn't dug up any bodies or bones, or anything gruesome like that. But a dozen feet underground, in the exact spot where the puddle had been, they made an unexpected find: a large cave with a puddle of strange, silvery liquid inside. And, beside the puddle?

An old Wiffle ball.

A yellow plastic bat.

And a tangle of rotten garden hose.

Some of the cops who had investigated my friends' disappearance were still on the force, so they immediately recognized the significance of the discovery. They contacted me and implored me to drive the four hours from my apartment in Pennsylvania so they could question me once again about what had transpired that day.

I decided to crash at my parents' house on Peachtree Lane while the police conducted their investigation. My dad had passed away a few years earlier, but his commendations were still proudly displayed in a case on the mantel, along with the famous photo of him shaking hands with Nixon after receiving his Medal of Honor. There was also a plaque with his favorite quote engraved on it, from Shakespeare's *Julius Caesar*: "Cowards die many times before their deaths; The valiant never taste of death but once."

There was no question that my dad had died once and only once. But me, on the other hand? I had tried following in my dad's footsteps by joining the Army after high school, but I couldn't even make it through basic training. The closest I ever got to a Medal of Honor was winning the Saturday night darts championship at my local bar. And I was still afraid of the dark. I was the coward Caesar warned about, dying again and again every time I let my fear stop me from doing the right thing.

The police forensics teams spent the better part of a week poking through the dirt and clay for any other evidence that might provide a clue to my friends' whereabouts, but in the end, they found nothing. They closed the case again and told me I was free to go. But I didn't. Instead, I drove my rental car to the empty lot where my friends had disappeared.

With the investigation complete and with construction yet to resume, it was easy for me to access the lot without anyone noticing. I ducked under the police tape, then slid down the steep side of the muddy hole to the entrance of the cave where the bat, ball, and hose had been found. It was a low, flat space, maybe twenty feet across, with a domed ceiling striped with sedimentary rock. The excavation had collapsed one side of the cave, turning it into rubble and exposing it to the open air. Even in the dark, the puddle inside was just as shiny and strange as I remembered.

As I stared at the water, I thought about what happened that day, about how the lot which had been such a source of joy for us had turned into such a nightmare. I thought about Joe Montana and Jerry Rice, about Mark McGwire and Jose Canseco, about Terminator and RoboCop. I thought about Marco, and Eddie, and Shah. I thought about my father. If I had been more like my dad, maybe my friends would have still been alive. Not a day went by where I didn't wish

I had gone into the water after them. Maybe I couldn't have saved them, but at least I wouldn't have had to live with the fact that I didn't even try.

After a few minutes of standing in silence, I sat down on the rubble at the edge of the puddle and took off my sneakers. I removed my shirt and pants, folded them neatly on the ground, then placed my shoes on top, along with my wallet, car keys, and flip phone. Then I closed my eyes, held my breath, and stepped into the water. It was warm, so warm that it barely registered as being wet. It felt comforting, almost womb-like. It surrounded me, cradled me, embraced me. As I allowed myself to sink into the Stygian abyss, I felt calm. Peaceful. Content.

Then, something grabbed my leg.

I should have been scared. I should have been terrified. But I wasn't.

For the first time in my life, I didn't feel any fear at all.

So That Happened

~ Gerri Leen

You make your way through the gray mists to the speakeasy. Sanocles is on the door and he opens it with a bow. "My queen," he murmurs.

No one bowed to you in the above world. Danced and sang and generally made merry with you, yes. Respected . . . not so much. "You've been here long enough to call me Persephone, San."

"Yes, my queen."

"Is she here?"

"She is."

You go through and see her sitting at the bar so you slide in next to her. "E."

She doesn't look over, but a small smile plays at her mouth. "P."

No one else calls you that. And you call no one else by their initials. This is a game only you two play.

The bartenders switch out and you see it's Delphys taking the shift. Sentimental as the gray day here in Hades is long, she rushes over, takes E's hand and says, "Eurydice, I can't believe he looked back. Dumb ass."

"Yep," you say, indicating with a look she should refill E's drink and bring you your regular, and she rushes off.

You handpick your staff and your patrons from your favorites in Hades. Not from Tartarus of course. But those who amuse you from the other neighborhoods. Who seem to be a bit . . . bored with the afterlife. Those who come here to your special place are by invitation only, free to drink and dance and maybe do other things—you'd never tell what else they might get up to in the more shadowed back rooms. Staff and patrons both.

You were going to miss E terribly. It thrilled you to see her turn back, even if that idiot Orpheus had moved you to tears with his song.

A song that comes up on the playlist, and E puts her hands over her ears and says, "Make it stop."

"It's a crowd favorite. Perennial top ten. But I can understand why you'd find it irksome. Considering you left him."

E turns to glare at you. "*He* turned around. *He* blew it, not me."

"You could have said something. The entire walk, you were silent."

"And you were spying?"

"I don't have to spy since this is my realm. I see all." Your realm and your husband's. A man who everyone thinks kidnapped you. When instead you and he made a very advantageous deal. He wanted children but wasn't overly interested in love, and you wanted out of your mother's control and wasn't opposed to bearing a few children to get free. Win win. Other than his reputation of course. But then the god of the dead wasn't generally considered to be one of the good guys. A fact you used to your benefit.

He never cared. He enjoys you both for your body and your company, and he holds so loosely you have freedom to indulge yourself. Your mother, on the other hand . . .

E's voice is just above a whisper as she says, "Everyone here would tear me limb from limb if they knew I'd screwed things up on purpose."

"You're not wrong about that. They're in love with your love story." You touch her chin gently and turn her to face you. "Why aren't you?"

"Who says I'm not? It's a beautiful love story. Well, until the snake." She laughs but her expression holds uncertainty and you suspect you know why.

"It's ironic. No one would probably ever have cared about either of us without our men." You study her and see you're on the right track. "What's it like having everyone lauding you as part of a couple but never as yourself?"

She doesn't answer at first. Takes a sip of her drink and stares into the mirror behind the bar. You look into it too and see two beautiful women sitting close, both with expressions impossible to read.

Finally she whispers, "It's horrible. No one cares about who I am. I was the moon in the wake of his sun."

"Some would say it was the other way around. Given his obsession with—I mean devotion to you. That song moves people."

"And I get that. His music moved me too. It's why I fell for him. It's maybe the only reason I fell for him." She trails off as the song starts again. "Oh, come on."

You laugh and with a thought take the song off the playlist. It stops mid chorus and a new song takes its place. There are groans throughout the bar. "Better?"

"Did you take it off forever?"

"No, but I took it off for now. Who can blame me? You're just back. Why torture you?"

"You're way more clever than most think."

"Don't spread it around. The sweet and innocent act gets us both a lot of mileage."

She laughs so quietly only you can hear her, and you relish the sound, one you thought you'd have to get used to not hearing.

Delphys brings your drinks and sets them down extra gently, as if she's afraid the least thing will jar E into despair. "Something's wrong with the sound system, boss. That song . . ." She glances at E.

You give her the look that means to shut up.

"Ohhhh," she mouths and her expression warms as she touches your hand then goes to wait on other people.

Delphys was one of your maidens. One of your favorites. Your mother didn't let you have favorites. Favorites would have meant she wasn't your best friend, your confidante, your everything. So Delphys was gone one morning and a new nymph was in her place.

That happened again and again. Until you gave up trying to carve out a life for yourself in the above world and turned to Hades for a way out.

"I understand what it is to be smothered with love, E." You reach for her hand and squeeze gently. "I understand what it is to be so intertwined that people don't even think of you separately, just as a duet, everlasting. The perfect daughter." You whisper the last part. "If they knew . . ."

She's squeezing your hand back much harder than you did to her. "If they knew what?"

You want to trust her, to tell her how you broke away, but this isn't just your secret. And if the truth ever reached your mother, it would break her heart—and you do love her.

But it would also probably mean you'd have to spend more time with her. And you love your freedom more.

"It's not important," you finally say and wait for her to let go of your hand but she doesn't. "What I can tell you is how much I would have missed you."

Her smile is luminous. "Yeah?"

"Yeah." You stroke her face, this lovely woman you'd thought you'd lost—but only for a time. She would have eventually found her way back.

Unless of course Orpheus sang his way—and hers—into Olympus. You wouldn't put it past him, and Hera was a sucker for faithful husbands, never having known one herself.

"You want to dance?" E is smiling in a way she never did before, open and . . . available. "Eurydice the woman is asking you. Not Eurydice the wife."

"I'd love to dance." You let her lead you onto the dance floor.

There are a lot of confused looks on the faces of the other patrons. You enjoy that immensely. They have no idea who this woman is, this lovely, intelligent, witty young thing who said not one single word to her husband as they ascended, no matter how desperately he asked if she was there. Who muffled her footsteps by hovering behind him rather than walking. Who looked less and less happy the closer they got to the above world.

"I'm glad he failed," you whisper into her ear, your breath moving her hair.

"I'm glad I made him." For a moment she feels like defiance personified in your arms but then she seems to shrink. "But eventually he'll be back here."

'Sooner rather than later if he continues to piss off the wrong women."

"Will you let him in the bar?"

"Probably not. Although I'll lose business to him. He'll no doubt set up shop in some corner of Hades and sing about you whenever you're not with him." You can feel her tense at your words. "E, down here he'll get to know the real you. Eventually, he'll have to shut up long enough to learn who you are—but you have to let him see that. It takes two to make a marriage work. And you'll learn whether you love him or just his music."

You stroke her hair as gently as you can. "It's all right to still love him."

There are times you wish your mother could be with you, could stroke your hair this way on a day when everything had gone wrong and tell you it would be all right. Hades is kind, but he isn't terribly comforting. "It's always all right to still love. So long as you don't lose yourself. And you'll always have this place to escape to. I don't intend to let him in no matter how many songs he sings." Not now that you've lost her once. Not now that you know how she feels when she's close like this, holding on just right.

"No?"

"No. I'm selfish, I guess. Interfering with true love."

She pulls back just enough so you're eye to eye. "There are all kinds of true love, P."

"Yes. Yes, there are."

Cans of Laugher, Jars of Tears

~ J. P. Oakes

Detective Ansible presses two fingers to the bridge of her nose and tries to will her headache away. "And we're absolutely sure that this guy was dead when he showed up for work this morning?"

The ME pokes in the chest cavity with a ballpoint pen. "Time of death is probably two days ago."

Ansible releases a sigh that is almost a moan. "Goddamn East Theoran bullshit."

Two bodies lie on a hotel-room floor. CSU techs bustle around them. Out in the hall, West Theoran security forces swarm like wasps.

"You know what I would give," Ansible asks the ME, "for this to just be another dumb zombie case?"

The corpse by the ME's feet—until recently a bellhop—is a body become a cavity. The chest has been opened, ribs splayed, reaching imploringly for the heavens. Inside: no lungs, no heart, no liver, arteries, or veins. A space as dry and empty as a butcher's carcass.

The ME straightens, points her ballpoint at the second corpse. It's painted with a filthy palette of bruises, but it has all its organs at least.

"You know who that is, right?"

Ansible wishes she didn't. Wishes it wasn't Konstantin Böhm, part of the delegation come to this hotel to negotiate with the East Theorans; wasn't the main voice of dissension to the trade deal being organized. Wishes that if he was going to get murdered, he could have at least waited until her shift was over to do it.

"A moment detective?" one of the CSU techs calls to her. He's by the door with a brush and jar of black powder. His look doesn't telegraph good news.

"No useable prints?" she asks.

He sucks his teeth and steps aside to reveal the door.

It is like a monochromatic finger painting by a class of deranged toddlers. Fingerprints overlay each other on the door, the wall, the mirror. A veritable trail of them.

Ansible's headache intensifies.

After the Hierophantic Wars, the surviving factions fought over Theora like it was the last pie on the dinner table. As Ansible understands it, the only solution they could agree on was the worst one: slicing the city down the middle; splitting it into East and West. East Theora would belong to the Selazzi Regime, while West Theora would remain under Empirical control.

Border disputes had been constant since then. East Theoran agents—and other more outré things—are forever slipping into the West, and conversely, the West sends its own spies East, although from what Ansible has heard, even with modern technology the number returning sane enough to have useful information is still below ten percent.

And yet, despite all the bad blood, and the history, and the vigorous, violent differences of opinion, the diplomatic process has picked up momentum. And now a trade delegation is visiting from East Theora.

Except now, despite the eyes of the world on this microcosm, and despite all the security, the man who led those railing against the deal is dead, and Ansible is left holding the bag.

Ansible follows a trail of radial loops, tented arches, and plain whorls plastered on walls, stair railings, and doors. She drags two security guards after her, and chides at the CSU tech as he paints his dust on the prints, trying to follow them across patches of carpet and rug for empty, tantalizing yards, before they reappear on an oak door, an elevator panel.

Two floors down from the murder scene, they enter a service corridor, and find a hallway become an abbatoir. Organs are spread across the floor—greasy intestines; a glistening liver; two lungs spread like sagging wings. A maid stands at the corridor's far end, facing the corner, shrieking.

The two guards turn ashen-faced. One bends over breathing deeply. Ansible pushes through the gore, past the heaving guards. As she reaches the corridor's far door, she flashes a glance at the screaming nurse. She's halfway through the door before she registers what she saw: fingers protruding from the maid's screaming mouth, tucking away behind her teeth.

Ansible scrambles to bring her gun to bear, screams, "Freeze!"

The maid backhands her, sends her sliding through gore. Ansible tries to pick herself up, limbs responding distantly, and then the world above her detonates. Behind her, a guard's rifle blares a wild, fully-automatic burst of fire. The maid reels through the far doorway as the rounds strike her.

The gun runs dry. Anisible leaps up, scrambling gorily after the fallen body.

She's not fast enough.

When she punches through the door, the maid is bucking on the floor. Then she erupts like a piñata, ribs flying like candy.

Something bursts out of her. A ball of hands—some white, some black, some spattered with freckles, others knotted with arthritis. Some nails are blunt, others chewed, others manicured to sharp points. The creation—roughly the size of the beach ball she once tossed back and forth with her father on a childhood vacation—is too densely packed with digits for her to see how the palms join together.

It scrambles wildly down the hall, fingers dragging it along at madcap speed. Ansible fires, can't tell if she hits it or not, gives chase.

There's a stairwell ahead. It plunges down, sliding from railing to railing, barely controlled. She crashes after it, hearing the guards clattering after her. But by the time she reaches the bottom of the stairs, it's long gone.

She doubles over, panting, horrified.

Goddamn East Theoran bullshit.

The East Theorans aren't keen on her questioning their ambassador. She doesn't give them a choice.

They meet in a conference room attempting grandeur and failing. He's smaller than she expects, narrow and red-headed, wearing a sharply tailored pin-stripe suit. His face is a blizzard of scars, lines of white puckered flesh intersecting like webbing. Both his ears have been removed. He sits in a chair opposite her. Behind him hulks his bodyguard, looking somehow pieced together, as if not all of his body is organic to him. Next to him sits his translator, a young man dressed as if for a funeral, a slight plastic sheen to his skin.

"We've had an incident," Ansible says as she sits, then lays it out for him—the bodies, the chase, the creature. He doesn't blink. "Anything you want to say?"

For a long moment, she thinks he's just going to sit there staring through her. Then he lets out a long, shuddering hiss, slowly building in pitch until she thinks he's about to scream. Then it cuts off. "It reaches," he says in a voice painfully dry. "It grasps." The he reaches out toward her with a closed fist and pulls a heart out of nowhere. He tucks the bloody organ into a pocket inside his suit.

The translator leans forward. "The creature you encountered," he says, "is known as a Manus Dei. It is a summoning, brought here by a practitioner. It is used to take possession of a host and enslave it to the practitioner's will."

Ansible waits for more. It doesn't come. "The practitioner's name ?"

The heart in the ambassador's pocket is staining his shirt red. He spits something thick and black onto the floor, scratches at it with his shoe.

"The ambassador is committed to the peace process," the translator says. "He believes trade agreements are the first step to a more open and trusting relationship. He is as horrified by this murder as you are and swears he has no idea who would act against him."

"Against him?" Ansible loses the struggle to suppress her incredulity. "The main opponent to his deal was just killed."

The ambassador leans forward, smiles. All his teeth, she sees, have been filed to points. "Through night I wander while around me birds flaps with wings like dark silk borne of worms grubbing through leaves infested with a mushroom that claws like a tower toward the heavens."

The translator runs a hand through his hair. "This deal is delicate," he says. "How does someone painting the East Theorans as murderers help us?"

Later, Ansible sits in a makeshift incident room with a member of Empiricist foreign office, an emaciated-looking woman called Jennings.

"You think the East Theorans put some of it on?" she asks. "I mean, how would we know if they're just hamming it up for us?"

Jennings shakes her head. "I was part of a delegation sent there once. It gets-" She shudders. "-so much worse."

Unsettled, Ansible changes tack. "Is the murder of the ambassador's main opponent really bad for him?"

Jennings huffs mirthless laughter. "You hear that?" she says.

Ansible does. Böhm's supporterss flood the streets outside, their screams and protests breaking against the hotel's thick walls like surf.

"Does that," Jennings says, "sound like good news for this deal?"

"But the talks are still going on, right?"

Jennings chews her lip. "For now."

"So, what's riding on this deal?"

Jennings's attempt at a smile is horrific. "The specifics of the legislation aren't as important as the two sides just working together, coming up with some consistent rules, working on common problems, moving away from being opponents and toward being partners."

"But the specifics?" Murders, Ansible knows, rarely happen because people look at the big picture.

Jennings shrugs. "Updating tariffs means there are some winners, sure. Losers too."

"I'll want a list of those losers."

Jennings calls people. Ansible writes names on a chalk board. Goes back to one that Jennings paused over.

"Pierre Mercier? As in the industrialist?"

Jennings's rictus smile reappears. "As in Konstatin Böhm's former business partner, and biggest financial donor."

Ansible noses her car out through the crowd around the hotel. Protesters smack her windshield with placards, utterly disinterested in who she actually is. The surrounding reporters are no better behaved. But finally, she's out into the densely woven streets of downtown, travelling past the financial spires and into the poor, run-down suburbs. Then she's through those, moving out to where the money accumulates again in great sprawling estates.

Pierre Mercier lives in a large limestone building ensconced in carefully manicured grounds. At the door, a young man introduces himself—without a hint of irony—as, "Mr Mercier's most personal and personable assistant."

Mercier himself—as sprawling as his estate—waits on his patio, trademark cigar firmly clamped between his teeth. It all feels very staged, very indicative of a fragile ego.

"I imagine," Ansible says, "that you've heard the news."

He stares at his box hedges and rose bushes for a moment. When he finally responds his voice is bearish. "The markets have responded . . . sympathetically."

Ansible isn't sure what she's supposed to say to that.

He turns red-rimmed eyes on her. "My stock is up, yet I am poorer."

She hesitates, then decides that, yes, she's willing to be the asshole. "You stood to lose a lot if the talks are successful."

"This is more than I calculated."

"But unsuccessful talks would be to your advantage."

He shifts his weight at that one, leans forward. "You think my objections to the talks are financial? Do you know what it is I export to East Theora, detective?"

"Enlighten me."

"Cans of laughter, and jars of tears. Specifically of widowed men aged fifty-five to sixty-seven. They take shifts laughing into empty tin cans, which we seal up with wax. Then they go and weep continuously into glass mason jars."

"And is that profitable, Mr. Mercier?"

He waves a hand, indicates the estate. "I take advantage of their insanity, yes, but the thought of normalizing relations with people so abnormal . . .That neither Konstatin nor I could abide."

He leans back but his eyes are still lively. "It seems to me," he says, "that if I were in charge of a case where an opponent of the trade talks was killed by an East Theoran Manus Dei, I might look at an East Theoran who stood to gain a lot from the talks."

"You're very well informed, Mr. Mercier."

The hand waves at the grounds again—all the explanation she's going to get.

"Did you know," he says, "that the East Theoran ambassador leads the largest exportation program East Theora has? Do you know what is going to happen to his profits, detective?"

She chews on that. "Thank you," she says finally. "You've been very helpful."

She's doesn't like Mercier, but doesn't like him for the murder either. Killing a friend to just to make a little more dough is hardly a solid motive for someone as rich as Mercier. Although, she thinks, you never can tell with the rich. They're as bad as junkies sometimes, it's just they're addicted to the cash.

Back at the hotel she finds Jennings again. "Tell me about the ambassador."

"He's as deranged as anyone in the Selazzi Regime." Jennings's vehemence surprises Ansible.

"But he stands to profit from this deal?"

Jennings hesitates. "In a way." In the light from the window her hair looks thin, patchy.

"What way?"

"To the East Theorans, money is just a way of dealing with us. Otherwise, it's basically meaningless to them. They care about currying favors with their gods, with the Selazzi themselves."

The Selazzi—vast abominations rotting, and pulsing, and eternally failing to die far beneath the earth, their psychic extrusions leaking into the nightmares of the Empiricist Empire.

"The ambassador has high standing with one of the Selazzi," Jennings continues. "A successful deal will increase his standing with it, make the standing of other's less meaningful."

"So . . . he'll profit."

"He won't want to talk to you again."

"Well, then it's bad days all round then, isn't it?"

The ambassador expresses his displeasure by making her wait. She expected something more creative from him. He leaves his bodyguard behind too, just bringing the translator. A bold move given the events of the day, or perhaps just a way to show how little she means to him.

She starts talking before the ambassador has a chance to sit down. "You weren't wholly forthcoming with me about your stake in these talks."

He doesn't sit down. He grabs his chair and swings it at her.

She yells, dives away. The translator shrieks, apparently as caught off guard as her.

The ambassador advances, chair held aloft. She flings herself sideways as he smashes it down with stunning force. It comes apart, spattering splinters in a detonation of wooden shrapnel. The seat cushion flaps wildly.

How could someone so scrawny have so much strength inside him, Ansible wonders?

Inside him. Oh shit.

Outside she can hear people yelling.

The ambassador holds two chair legs reduced to stakes. The translator is screaming, high and shrill. She's pulling her gun. If she's wrong about this, this is about to be one hell of an international incident.

The ambassador looms over her. She fires.

He lurches sideways but she wings him, spinning him around and sending him to the floor. They both scramble up, her into a crouch, him onto all fours.

People are bursting into the room, screaming at her.

The ambassador darts forward. She fires again, puts three rounds into his looming head.

They are the eye of the storm—an utterly still pair, while around them security forces from both sides of Theora whirl. The translator is on his knees, shaking and muttering to himself.

Someone puts a gun to the back of her head. She doesn't know if it's someone from her side or theirs. It only matters if she was wrong though.

She wasn't.

The Manus Dei bursts from the ambassador's back in a spray of blood and bone. People scream, shoot. The gun leaves the back of Ansible's head, and she starts firing, but the thing makes a powerful, hundred-handed leap into the air, sailing over everyone's heads, crashing into the still-swinging doors.

She's after it in a flat sprint, but by the time she's shoved through the crowd of bodies and out of the doors, the corridor outside is empty.

She seethes, turns around. Chaos still churns the conference room, but the ambassador's eviscerated body and the quaking translator still sit in the quiet eye of it all.

She grabs the translator. "Why didn't the bodyguard come?"

He stares at her, wild-eyed. Up close, the sheen on his skin looks like plastic. There's an edge near his hairline looking red and raw.

"The shimmer in the eyes is the glow that bakes—"

She rattles him hard. "Translate!"

He swallows, his burnished Adam's apple bobbing. "I don't know. In the ambassador's room? I waited for them both but only the ambassador came out. He told me he didn't need his bodyguard."

Because, Ansible knows, he was already dead.

The bodyguard is gone by the time they toss the ambassador's room. Jennings is there, looking like she's shedding another pound of hair into the room, her skin almost as shiny as the quivering translator who Ansible has dragged there in case he can find anything out of place. She knows she certainly won't. The logic of the room is opaque to her: furniture set on angles perpendicular to her expectations, books spread out in a grid, all open to the thirty-seventh page.

"Tell me more about a Manus Dei," she tells the translator.

He coughs. "In among the gloaming waves I wander…" He shakes his head. "Sorry. I mean, it's a religious vessel, a vehicle for an operator's intent."

"An operator," Ansible repeats. The bodyguard?"

He shrugs.

"These people are fucking monsters!" Jennings kicks at the books in disgust. She seems on the verge of screaming.

Ansible ignores her. "Is it . . . made? Summoned?"

It looks like the sweat is stuck under the plastic sheen on the translator's skin. "It's a ritual. The investment of a piece of the Selazzi into a clay model."

"So, the ritual requires clay?"

"Yes."

"What else?"

"Erm . . ." A set of rapid blinking. "Cans of laughter. Jars of tears."

"Like this?" Jennings stands in the closet holding up a can and a jar. Emblazoned on each is Pierre Mercier's logo.

☉

It would be neater, Ansible thinks, if she didn't get a call on the radio on the way over to Mercier's saying that he'd just reported a break in. It'd make more sense if when they pulled into the estate the most personable of personal assistants had been standing over the bodyguard's dead body, tying up his boss's loose ends.

Instead, Mercier and his assistant are locked in a panic room. Security guards have the bodyguard trapped in a windowless study.

Ansible has West Theoran security pull the bodyguard out. He tries to fight, but the rifles on him settle him down.

"You're under arrest for murder," she tells him.

He sneers at her. "Diplomatic immunity." It sounds like a phrase he's memorized.

"He's right, I'm afraid."

Ansible has arranged another meeting with Jennings. The foreign office woman is looking calmer, as if the ghosts haunting her have taken a step back.

"So, the bodyguard just gets to walk?" Ansible's headache is back.

"East Theoran justice is far worse than anything we can offer." She curls her lip. "Those people are animals."

"You're not the most diplomatic diplomat I've ever met."

Jennings shrugs. "They're not in the room. I don't have to pretend."

"How long were you over there for?"

Jennings shudders. "Six months."

"Undercover?"

Another shudder. "No, it was official. That was the worst of it. They would parade their insanity in front of me. They showed me things they were actually proud of." Her voice is rising. She takes a breath, steadies herself. "Did you," she asks, "arrest Mercier?"

"At what point," Ansible asks her, "when you were over there, did you learn about the Manus Dei?"

Jennings blinks slowly.

"Or maybe a better question," Ansible continues, "is when did you meet the ambassador's bodyguard? Maybe the Manus Dei was his idea. You'll have to explain it to me."

Jennings takes a breath. "What are you talking about?"

"It was easy to like the Ambassador for this," Ansible says. "Böhm cast himself as the villain, and so the natural role for the Ambassador is the avenging hero. Plus he had a vested interest in the deal going through."

She strokes her chin a bit. It's showboating, but she's feeling smug. "Except if the government really thought Böhm could affect the outcome," she says, "would they really have let him attend? Because his failure to derail everything would be a great way to de-fang the mob out there." Ansible points to the window and where the protesters still chant.

"But if I didn't bite on the ambassdor," she contines, "well you were there to point me at Mercier. And he's an asshole. It's easy to want to pin this on him as well. And when I didn't quite take the hint, you even had the can and jar as props. That was a nice touch. Except your assassin had failed in his job when he got to Mercier's, hadn't quite sealed the deal."

Jennings looks wild now, her thin face working. "Maybe there was evidence pointing his way," she shouts, "because he's guilty! Maybe the solution is just obvious!"

Ansible sighs. "You know they keep records of who they sell that stuff to, right? I had Mercier look it up. There's not many people in West Theora who buy it. And I checked your bank accounts."

It's so fast, it catches Ansible flat-footed. Jennings breaks for the door at a sprint. But the security guard she posted there catches Jennings by both wrists.

"They're monsters!" Jennings screams as they cuff her. "They're rabid! We have to keep them out!"

"The only thing that mattered to you," Ansible says, more for her own satisfaction than anyone else's, "was that the talks were destabilized."

"We have to keep them out!"

Ansible smooths her hair. "The East Theorans have requested that you be sent over there for the trial," she tells Jennings. "From what I hear, your colleagues are thinking of letting them have you."

Inside the hotel where she orchestrated the murder of three men, Jennings starts to scream.

Noblesse Oblige

~ Frances Lu-Pai Ippolito

Your face was ashen when you first peeked over the lid at me. So sweaty too. I didn't mean to scare you. Go ahead, pull up a chair. Take a seat. Catch your breath.

Let me guess: when they said "cheap seats" at the Apricot Pavilion, you thought you'd get the ugly, fat girls. Or the old ones, so ancient they'd be nothing but loose skin draped over spoiling meat. You didn't expect . . . well what did you expect?

I don't get out of this tank much, but I was young once, more alive than now and I remember (there's a lot of time in here to remember) how it works on the other side of the wall. You came into the Lobby and there were red lights and beaded curtains, and the girls lined up in a beautiful parade. And each one stroked your arm as you walked by. Said "hello," told you her name, offered a tour, and asked if you'd like to talk in private and sample the session you could buy.

But you strode past the ladies to the beechwood bar. Was Lao Wen in the Hawaiian shirt still there? It's been a while. I hope so. Lao Wen was perpetual like a rock—his chubby ass always planted on the high vinyl stool behind the bar. By the way, I loved that stool. I used to sit there as a kid when I came to visit my father's business. Did you notice Captain America's face on the stool under Wen's butt? He bought it from Arnie's Arcade in the building next door. That was before the rioters burned that whole building down.

Anyway, where was I? Sorry Hon, the mind wanders from the body a lot these days. What'd you think of Lao Wen? When I knew him, he drank a lot, didn't shave, and blew gray smoke rings toward the ladies. No doubt he has that lazy right eye and the jeans that don't cover the sideways smiling rear split. But don't be mistaken; Lao Wen looks slow, but he's no joke. Did you see what he's stored behind the desk? Did he show you his dictionary? The man doesn't read. It's a safety deposit box where he keeps pieces and bits of the people he doesn't like in last name alphabetical order.

At the bar, you must have leaned over to whisper "Noblesse Oblige" into Lao Wen's ear. (His ears are gross, right? Untrimmed hairs turned spider legs crawling out the holes.) Being Lao Wen, he wouldn't have blinked (he's seen a lot), but his good eye may have widened just a bit. There are, after all, only two types willing to order off the secret menu: the destitute or the depraved.

I think … you're definitely the former. In fact, you remind me a bit of someone I dated in college. Sweet, quiet, and gentle. He wanted to marry me. We never went all the way. But I think you'll treat me real tender and considerate. Not like the others who regularly visit; they're very mean. Just because I'm used to it, doesn't mean there's no pain. I can feel it, especially when someone wants it to hurt.

You, though, have nice brown eyes. Yes, I'm almost looking forward to spending time with you.

I bet Wen-Wen gave the usual warning in that raspy baritone of his. "Contrary to Reddit threads, these visits aren't free. We charge your account and collect the balance later." Then he pulled out the contract—thick and dense with ant-sized text. You signed. He offered you a drink as part of the house package and let you in.

When the room door opened, I watched you from the domed mirror bolted to the ceiling above my tank (some clients like that angle). You were shown the light switches and the tank keys hanging from a hook on the wall. "Two hours is enough," you said to someone who closed the door. The tank keys fell when you first tried to take them off the hook. Your hands shook and I heard you whisper encouragement to yourself. You dropped the keys a second time when you tried to unlock the partially frosted glass lid. The keys jingled like wind chimes when they fell onto the polished concrete floors. You picked them up and tried again (and again) and eventually (about four minutes and twenty-three seconds later) found a way to put the keys in—three keys inserted all at once, all turned to the right to release the seal. Once the lid lifted, the tank lights flooded on and you screamed.

Without skin, people really do look the same. Red muscle strung over sticks of bone, bangles and dangles of flesh, marbled balls of fat, and sinewed ropes and ties that bind it all together into a cramped chassis caged by bones. I've had a lot of time to think and it finally all makes sense. The inside's rainbow of pink, veiny blue, and even dabs of chartreuse are all colors spelled lowercase. But the colors on the outsides are spelled with Capitals that cause people to close ranks. Black, Red, Yellow, Brown, White, or whichever race, it doesn't matter beneath that largest organ covering our hidden bodies. Peel back the husk to reveal the universal truth: we were all grown and birthed from a mother's womb. A true gospel of sorts. The Gospel of the Flayed.

And you've come to pray.

Do you like older women? Benjamin Franklin said you should: "When women cease to be handsome, they study to be good. To maintain their Influence over men, they supply the diminution of beauty by an augmentation of utility."

I was very old when they skinned me. I won't tell you how old because a man should never ask a lady her age. And, sweetie, without any wrinkles I doubt you can figure it out. I will say, however, that we older women are always full of use. Service—small and great, and love—soft and amiable, especially for a young one in need. Just like Benny said, "There is hardly such a thing to be found as an old Woman who is not a good Woman."

You look twenty. Could this be . . . your first time? No wonder you look like a shivering kitten. Shy and skittish like my college love. Gosh, that was so long ago. Maybe even a hundred years? Right before all the women began to die from the disease. Daddy knew early what was coming. And when Mommy died, he pulled me from school and locked me in my room. (Cream walls, a shelf with a single book by Benjamin Franklin, and two twin beds. One bed covered in Barbie dolls. I loved those dolls until I hated them. Gave them names, pretended they were real people—married, pregnant, divorced, and then dead.)

Daddy fully sterilized the room. Never let me out. (Sixty steps wide by one hundred steps long—I know because I doublechecked and counted the steps all day long.)

He had the money to keep me safe. Built on the backs of the women you passed on earlier. And you'd think when the world lost 75% of its women that the brothels would close and everyone would protect the remaining ones that lived. But Daddy only got richer.

Sure, he had to close a few locations from staffing shortages. Though overall, he had plenty to keep the bars on my windows tight and to pay for the security of our home and his business assets. Plus, he let some of the women have kids—only girls, of course, because the world didn't need any more men. The daughters that survived were offered employment, overtime, and extended benefits.

I never agreed with his management or business practices. We were rich and well-off and Daddy should have shared. So few women left to go around. So few to mother the children and take care of the men. It simply wasn't fair. I was never very good at school, but THIS I knew I could do. THIS I could give. Wasn't it my duty? But Daddy never left me alone, never wavered from keeping me *safe*. "'He that lies down with Dogs, shall rise up with fleas.' I promised your Mother before she died," he said over and over on the other side of my reinforced door, like she would have wanted me caged.

Then Daddy *finally* died. I'm ashamed to say I was excited.

Freedom, I believed. I wasn't young anymore, but before I lost my hair and skin, I was pretty. It's hard to see, but examine my skull, the curve of the lower jawline, the perfectly rounded top of my head, and the smooth path of muscle grains on my face. The buccinator, the muscle around my lips, is particularly strong and well-developed; in college, I was a good kisser.

It's hard to remember sometimes that I haven't always laid in state within this heated glass box, on this platform, in this lacy negligee with the name "Sleeping Beauty" etched on a brass plaque nailed to a wall. (By the way, I feel you fingering the hem of my skirt. You're hesitating. Don't worry, they wash it and me after each use.)

Oh, but I digressed. Daddy was dead, but no one would let me out, no matter how I begged, cried, or threatened to kill myself. It's all because of the fine print in another kind of contract, Daddy's Last Will and Testament. The lawyers explained women, like possessions or chattel, required protection, and the Executor couldn't set me free and violate his fiduciary duty per the signed and binding agreement. "Too dangerous. No telling what a mob of wild men would do if they knew about you. A woman is safest in the home surrounded by a wall of protecting men."

So I remained contained in that secured, air-filtered room until one day, it was my turn to die the privileged death of a geriatric age.

The lawyers came back. This time I read the fine print. This time I forced them to amend the clauses. This time there was nothing they could say for I was the last of the family; I had outlived them all.

When I donated my body to science, I failed to, perhaps, take into account where I might end up. I imagined a training hospital for pre-meds, a history museum of female anatomy, or even the skeletal exhibit in an elementary classroom (I always liked children). But when I was carted away to the mortuary, I realized that the outside air smelled and tasted of burnt things, that the roads were bumpier than decades before, and that much advancement had been made in the preservation of women's bodies.

In a mortuary room of steel walls and no windows, there were a pair of gowned men with latex gloves snapped on.

"Good, we got this one before she was completely brain dead," one said to the other.

"Advanced age. Body is in excellent condition."

"It's a pity about the skin and hair. Imagine what she'd be if we were able to preserve them."

"Yes. . . do you think that we could—"

"You mean before we start the process?"

"Yeah, the body is nearly perfect. All the limbs and digits intact. She even has all her teeth."

"But off the record, right? And only if I get to go first."

"Sure, Bob, you're technically my boss anyway. Not like she's going to tell on us."

They laughed and unzipped their pants. That was "technically" my first time. And though I was almost dead, it stung when they broke through the parts of me that had never been employed; the nerves alive enough to feel the service I delivered.

After my first time, the men preserved me. Filled me up with cocktails of I.V. fluids that transformed me from flesh to forever. Unfortunately, the process didn't, as you see, preserve the skin and hair. Those dissolved. The rest though, including my mind, is maintained in all its plasticity.

I know you can't actually hear me. I've tried to move, to communicate—say things, scream, cry, anything to let people know I'm still here; not just a silent, broken doll for you to hold. But no one knows.

Anyway, back to us, enough about me. I like you. I hope you don't mind me sharing and thinking all these things at you. This is *our* first time and we are about to become close friends.

Oh! Be careful! Don't fall! Climb slowly into the tank, my friend. The contract you signed with Lao Wen absolves the Pavilion of all liability. No one will pay if you get hurt. An assumption of risk. Though I want you to know this is more than an arm's length transaction for me.

You're looking away, avoiding my face. I wish I could stroke your hair, pat that bare chest, and see myself in your eyes. Am I a gorgeous nightmare? Even so, I know you want me, need me. Sweetie, that's alright. I'm here to give. I hope you don't mind that I pretend you're the one I was forced to leave behind.

Oh, good idea! Turn off the lights!

As the wise Benny Franky once said, "In the dark all Cats are gray."

Seren's Day

~ *David Bradley*

As evening stars ignited, Dewin hunted, dripping and muddied, all the lawn dewy, raindrops falling from leaves as he went. The air was thick, the sky dank cotton wetted, all the world descending from day into night; brown'd light, brown'd mist, brown'd sight; water pooled and puddled; midge clouds and mosquito failed on the thick of his arms and the thick of his legs as he trod his way.

He felt all 'round him the spiorad asleeping as they nested, great taproots writhing about them, warm in their places, hollows and hovels, his spell invasive and slowly waking them. His music worked its way to them, whetted their appetites for such love and mystery as he swung to them. His web he spun about them, drawing them sticky and sweet from their drowse. In them they felt the pull of his spinning and his weaving and the lore of straw meadows and blighted harvests and a vow of granges overflowing with gold. And they wept all of them with hungor and drede, all of them but one.

The moment came, the moment Dewin'd foretold, the moment he'd created, the moment that the loose eyes of the feral fell upon him. Somewhere, there, awakened in the periphery, burrowing from hiding, the vines and the crawlers alive, tendrils reaching even deeper still, countless fingers stretched upward and outward from the win-twiges they'd weaved in their waiting, the fantoma felt of his coming and he, mighty Dewin, sensed of their waking. Onward still fair and infinite hedra moved about them, clawing blind through ancient peat, sweat sheets of silt laid by sruth when it was deep and far and wide, ten thousand lives of inundation and inferno and plague and plenty, one after another, lain atop each other and atop each other more, strangling in their cradle Lady's Mantle and spreading thick Foxglove, always; patient and planning and understanding, until the loam and the turf and the very earth itself had become fantoma and they, in turn, had become the very earth. And all their eyes fell upon Dewin, liquid eyes as salt as sea, ancient sea, eternal grandmother's grandfather's grandmother of Etang Bleu, home to all water, she most clear, she most pure, she most serene and chill'd to her icy heart.

Many were they wounded, broken wing and tongues twisted and torn and flayed, Dewin's curse'd damnation having drawn them in and taken them in and then thrown them aside. They lay in states of repose, nursing wounds both real and imagined, some few plotting their escape, some few daring horrible revenge, but more, and more than that, seeking only the dark and the damp and the warmth of their dug dens.

Fated that sweetest of days was Seren, hard of shell, long of gate and thrice eyed, to be drawn by the song of Man from her leafy bed of Vervain. Others withered, their vines bent and misshapen, and withdrawing for all of time. But Seren, weird queen of honey and heat, hidden in lengths of locks, depthless eyes pitch and fire, knew desire as an ocean rising.

On Dewin strode, confident one would follow, one each day, one whose hunger and ache t'would overcome, draw her out, draw her to him, out of the weeds and the stench and the mawing greenwood, moving beside the trail, not so silent as she dreamed, until the moment it seemed she would fail, and this day Seren was called. And she knew him before she saw him and he saw her before he knew her. The cord that bound them was knotted and noosed on the day of days, before even Seren was conceived in the fertile mud of lochan, before even Dewin was hatched in the first of fire, before even rocks were hurled from Hadean's sea. And it knotted them, him to her and her to he, she and his footsteps and he his ritual path, through pools of liquid clay, across the forest floor, their eyes rolling with their fear and their lust and their hunger.

The moon looked down as Seren followed, helpless and wanton to his magick, her trail slick and grease, through a maze of hedgerow battlements and hand hewn bawn. On Dewin's lawn the hives were settled for their slumber, beobread sweet wafted, and the lowing faded from the grange. Meat was hung and netted from slaughterhouse eaves, and baying wolves retreated as he came. Through his garden awash in Beelzebub's Wort and Poppy, Witch Hazel and Nightshade, his home overgrown by Orchid and Henbane, all staggered at Seren's fatal honey'd breath.

Flame gasped in Dewin's grate, dying eyes glowed their last in coal spent, twigs and kindling ash white, wisps of smoke dwindling to the rafters and on into the blackish night. On the hob heated blade and bowl, Dewin's repast, hare and root, thick and fatty, set aside to break his fast come morning light. Dewin's ritual unchanged.

Seren traced the earthen walls, blood pulse and sweated brow, her sapphire eye following Dewin as he led her, and her sapphire eye following Dewin as he turned to her, and her sapphire eye following Dewin as he approached, hard and determined and knowing; Dewin's ritual unchanged.

Seren took her breath and spread herself and braced herself, her sapphire eye following Dewin's steps fast toward her, her sapphire eye following Dewin's lust for her, her sapphire eye following Dewin's eyes upon her; Dewin's ritual unchanged.

Seren hissed and raised her hood, drawing Dewin to her, wrapping herself around him, holding herself to him, closer and closer still, stretching her arm to her arm and her leg to her leg, gripping herself to herself, pulling herself to herself. And Dewin was lost within her, knowing not what was become, until lungful breath escaped him, and bones brittle became. Sweet Serin's teeth, as sharpened blade, were bared and sank, poisoned and painless and deep, into Dewin's bared flesh.

There was a being, the soul of the Man, perched on a particle deep in darkest Dewin, that recognized the moment, the moment of moments, and watched as if from afar, yet within and without it, the crushing of the meat and the splintering of the bone and the piercing of the heart. The light turned blacker still, and cried and called out to eternity as it was extinguished. And then mighty Dewin was no more.

All through the night Serin slumbered and fed, and wept and bled, her lust and love ingested and dead, until the dawn, nursed life unto the fire and built of Dewin a vast and glowing pyre.

And then it was the day, and the keep knew of green shoots and scarlet fruit. And Seren saw it, and named it, and knew it well. For that was the morn of Seren's day.

The Raconteur

~ Phillip E. Dixon

The crowd's thrilled buzzing filled the stuffy, dimly lit tent. An elongated bulb hovered over a canvas-covered mass on the slat-board stage. The dull, orange filament reminded Jacques of a campfire. He elbowed his skinny thirteen-year-old frame to the front, eager to see the Raconteur. The traveling carnival was incredible, with diving horses, a fight club tent, the punch-a-bag game, and the chicken-eating geeks at the freakshow. He'd seen a real automobile too—a Ford. Best of all, Jacques's lone nickel stayed in his pocket—the carnival was free. And those sweet summer strawberries were too if no one was looking.

"Gather 'round! Gather 'round!"

The Raconteur's voice—the squeaky sound of a ten-year-old boy—carried effortlessly from the stage. Spindly arms gesticulated, setting purple sleeves asway. Eight feet tall, the Raconteur's rainbow-colored cloak enveloped a barrel-shaped body. "Who would like to hear a story—"

The audience hollered.

"Who wants jaded heroes and mysterious villains? Absurd comedy and epic tragedy? Blood and redemption? Love and suspense?"

Jacques's fingers found his ears. The crowd grew more intense with each question—as loud as the Magician's tent when he cut the upside-down woman from the audience vertically in half. It was messy—pig slop, surely—but the blue glow throughout was a fascinating trick.

The Raconteur continued from the stage in his child's pitch. "Who would like to sail the Seas of Devilry and shipwreck on the Shore of Dreams? Who will fight the one-eyed beasts in the Forest of Pillars? Who will seek Eternity's Clock and unchain Mother Time?"

"I will!" Jacques shouted, his voice lost in the audience's roar.

The Raconteur still heard him. "You look like a storyteller, my young friend," the Raconteur said, gliding downstage, wooden face drawing close, boyish voice a near-whisper. A hint of pale gray iris pocked two black eyes, one slightly larger than the other. A tiny mouth dashed across a wood-grained face complete with knotted nose, a sharply hooked corner melting into a pocket of black chin-rot. Atop the scalp perched a smear of sienna-colored hair—a dead, fallen maple leaf.

Jacques shivered, wondering why the man had made such a strange mask.

The Raconteur placed a frigid, twiggy finger under Jacques's chin. "It's in your veins, isn't it?" he asked as if sharing a secret. "A boy far from home, hopping trains, eating bull toads, telling tall tales to whomever will listen. Daydreams of jungles and gunfights—a quicksilver escape from the family dust farm."

Yes.

"A boy in need of an audience."

Yes!

The crowd grew restless.

"Get on with it!"

"Tell us a story!"

The Raconteur's head snapped up. "But a story needs inspiration!" he called. "And where shall we find it?"

"Where?" a man shouted, laughing.

The Raconteur floated back to the stage beside the hidden object. "Why, here among you! You, the people, shall become—" The tarpaulin fell. "The Great Orator!"

Audience members gasped. A metal pig's face of rusted wrought iron overlooked the audience. A blotchy canvas ear drooped on either side, worn leather straps dangling from a missing mouth, eyes empty. It was as tall as the Raconteur. Jacques thought the snout made it look like the gas mask his father had brought home from the war in Somme. Acrid metallic tang filled the air.

The audience began to laugh—some with mirth or drink, some with nerves.

The Raconteur ran his hand over the pig's flat nose, looping around the nostrils. "Every story needs turmoil and passion, wisdom and loss. And, most importantly, we need characters! Who shall play the prankster?"

A hand shot up from the crowd.

"The prankster has been found! And who shall be the gargoyle?"

"My wife!" a man shouted to laughter.

The Raconteur pulled people as they volunteered, sliding through the crowd who instinctively gave him wide berth, his long shadow an eclipse.

"We need a bastard! Are there any bastards among you?"

Cheers erupted, jeers and jostling accompanying a slew of raised arms including Jacques's. Mama had called him one enough times. But the Raconteur passed him without a glance, choosing a barefoot man instead. Jacques let his arm flop, disappointed.

"And the widow?"

"Me!" a little girl in a patched wool skirt shouted. The crowd laughed again. The girl's mother, in a similarly worn skirt, shushed her.

"*Tsk, tsk, tsk.* A mother should encourage her little Alice to tell stories." The Raconteur stroked the girl's hair. "Indeed, a mother should lead by example."

The woman tried to step back, but the people behind stood firm. The Raconteur gripped her arm and dragged her to the stage where she stood, eyes wide and anxious. "We have our widow!"

The little girl started to cry. Jacques sidled over and put his arm around her like one of his little sisters. "Your mama will be fine," he said. "She's gonna tell us a story."

The Raconteur pointed to the volunteers who looked jaundiced beneath the lightbulb. "Four characters shape tonight's tale. They make our treatise." The Raconteur positioned them around and inside the pig's head. He slipped the leather straps around the elderly woman playing the prankster, hoisting her inside the pig, her head becoming its right eye, her grey braid trailing down the pig's cheek like a tear. "Every character has a deep desire—a *need.*" The widow took the other eye. The Raconteur helped lay the burly bastard and balding gargoyle down back-to-back, strapping the men's feet to the semi-narrow corners of the pig's upper jaw, then tied their arms and necks together to form the lower jaw. Jacques heard their protests, but the crowd's fever drowned them out.

"A character without motivation is flat, uninteresting, lacking dimension." The Raconteur pointed at Jacques. "Can you suggest a motivation for our characters here?"

"A problem to solve?" Jacques offered, the excitement of recognition tamping his growing unease.

The Raconteur punctuated the air. "That's right, my boy! An obstacle! Our story is almost ready. But *how—*" he hawked the word, "can there be a story if the Great Orator is missing its voice?"

Jacques leapt, eager to be on stage, to act, to be *seen*. The Raconteur pointed at him again but lower, aiming at the widow's little girl. Instinctively, Jacques wanted to shield her, sensing something was awry, but a hairy-armed man beside him hoisted the girl onto the stage. She ran past the Raconteur and wrapped her arms around her mother's strapped-down legs inside the pig's head. The audience laughed.

The Raconteur raised his arms. "The Great Orator, he comes!"

The lightbulb snapped off. Gasps and nervous tittering filled the black tent. Screams from the stage rose alongside crackles and pops like logs in a fire. The crowd froze, a herd of startled rabbits. The screeches rose in pitch and volume. Jacques plugged his ears again, the sound verging on unbearable. Then silence. Blue light filled the pig's eyes and mouth, the lower jaw stretching in a yawn.

The tension broke, and the audience applauded, raucous. The hairy-armed man clapped Jacques on the back and said, "A magic show too!"

In the blue silhouette, Jacques could make out something dripping on stage.

The Grand Orator's mouth moved, and the little girl's voice washed over the rapt crowd. "*Once upon a time . . .*"

The smell of iron grew stronger. Jacques realized the pig's head wasn't covered in rust. He wanted to hear the story, but the voice inside him that warned of Mama's quick hands spoke. *Run.* Jacques hesitated, thinking about the little girl. *Run!* He pushed his way back toward the tent's entrance to slip out.

"Why are you leaving, Jacques? The story has only just begun."

The Raconteur's rainbow cloak blocked the way.

Jacques's voice quavered. "No."

"Ah, but storytelling is a timeless tradition—one which separates man from beast. Story is *life*."

A quiet, hiccupping wail snuck out of Jacques, making him feel like a baby, but he couldn't help it.

"You wanted a story, Jacques. There's a price."

"But—"

"The carnival is free? No. But, you can tell *me* a story. Nourish me with stories—" The Raconteur opened his cloak "—from the inside."

A naked, withered boy of about ten hung from the Raconteur's fleshless chest, arms threaded through bare ribs piercing his abdomen, legs looping at unnatural angles through the pelvis. The boy's eyes glowed blue.

"*Please,*" the boy said. It was the Raconteur's voice. "No more stories."

(Im)Permanence,
A Short and Long Story

~ *Fayaway & Hermester Barrington*

a mockingbird's "Chaw!"
treefrog's prrrrreeeet Robin's panpipes
windowpane cracking

lightwaves and soundwaves
bounce from rippled lake's surface
rocking marriage bed

waterbed island
luna moth fay and satyr
we balance barefoot

carp or catfish leaps
great blue heron squawks and flies
we exchange our rings

"We do!" we both shout
jacaranda petals fall
"we do!" shouts the shore

kiss freezing spacetime
bat flies through cracked window
slips behind the frame

A sound of glass cracking—not dreaming anymore, she guesses, slipping from the now mostly still bed and running downstairs, Zoë chases something that flies into the library and slips behind their watercolor wedding portrait. In the alcove behind, she finds a marbled paper envelope. Inside, a letter in her own flowing script, addressed to her:

> *We had a dream last night, Zoë, and this year I think we should gather everything we've created this past year and hide it, or destroy it. I'm pretty sure that will work. I've talked about this with Robin, and he's already set everything up.*
>
> *And a very merry un-birthday to us both!*

Under her signature is a date—a year ago, tomorrow.

Wheels creaking behind her, she turns as Robin pulled her childhood wagon into the library. Embracing her before slipping her silk kimono over her shoulders—"I don't think you need it, but we should think of the neighbors," he said, then asked: "Are you ready?"

Nodding, she points about the room—"That one, that, and oh, god yes, that"—as he carefully piled into the wagon a Klein bottle containing a dancing Rebis, a Zen garden of hammered gold with a brass cricket chirping in the tree, and a shroud bearing Andy Warhol's likeness, along with a few other items.

"You should be the one to put these in, Zoë," Robin said, handing her a stack of notebooks and sketchpads.

"These are my workbooks, and my journals!" she cries, flipping past sketches of proposed projects—a lava lamp in a vintage Mountain Dew bottle, a chicken claw and human hand drawing each other, notes for a book on vespertiliomancy . . .

"A private archive has agreed to preserve them," Robin replied, "only carefully selected researchers may read them, and to protect us, no one may make copies or photographs until nine hundred and ninety-nine years have passed. I expect that they will be very popular!"

"Well, there's a lot of personal stuff here," she sighs. "But maybe whoever sees them will tell our story, someday." And she places them gently in the wagon, then begins pulling it to the garage to load up the Travelall, the wagon's shocks creaking.

Coming back into the library, Zoë finds Robin pulling a wicker burial basket into the center of the room. "I think I need to be alone for a while," she says, quickening her pace, striding out into the garden and toward the lake. Beyond the lawn, the wild grasses, still covered with dew, tickle her thighs.

She stops to gaze at the fountain in the center of the wild space—composed of shattered clay sundials, water sparkles cheerfully over its surface, and into the basin buried deep in earth, mallow and mustard, and moss. Mounds of earth covered in grass and wildflowers surround it, laid out like numbers on a clock face.

Humming, Robin pulled the creaking wagon behind him to a spot without wildflowers, and picked up a shovel. The blade cutting into the soil released the scent of moist earth into the late winter air. Inhaling those scents, Zoë picks up a spade to join him, and they soon have a good sized pit between them.

"Um, how long have we had this fountain, Robin? Didn't Jorge and Gabriela give it to us when they sold us this place?" Zoë asks as they dig.

Looking away, Robin replied, "Yes, it was their wedding gift to us, so we've had it about two and a half years."

"Only that long? It looks like it's been here longer than that."

"Plants benefit from love, Zoë, and so they grow faster here than anywhere else, I think," he said, laughter in his voice.

"Well, that explains it," she says, grabbing his ass and pulling him close for a kiss.

"I think later would be better, Zoë," Robin said, pulling away. "We should get this done, and we don't want these plants to get fat!"

"I'll hold you to that," she says, and so, smiling, they begin to dig again.

Zoë digs out a few more spadefuls as Robin pulled the wagon closer and slid the basket in. She lights the kindling underneath, uncertain whether the damp earth would extinguish the flame, which finally caught. Through the willow withes comes the sound of clay cracking, metals melting, paper burning. She laughs as a single page with the word "Mitrúvishar" flies out on an updraft and sails into the lake, extinguishing itself with a hiss Zoë could not hear, and she wonders what that word might have meant to her. She tosses damp tissues into the flames as Robin filled in in the hole and scattered seeds on the ground, composing all the while:

the smell of turned earth
and last years' artworks' ashes
wildflowers planting

"How many times have we done this, Robin?" she asks, looking at the other mounds, and Robin smiled, but said nothing.

"Mother Nature is watering the seeds," laughs Zoë, as they finish tamping down the soil, and she counts the rain drops until there were too many. After a supper of fruit, cheese, and wine inside, Robin and Zoë kiss goodbye on the front porch. "I'll be back before dawn," he said, and Zoë listens as the Travelall rattles down the road and onto the highway, going inside when the lake's silence returns with the dusk. Stretching out on the floor of the library with a copy of *The Bloody Chamber*, she smiles as she reads, for the nth time, of the Frog Prince rising up from Devil Reef to marry the Princess, whose children live happily ever after; a moment later, the book drops from her hand and her eyes close.

"Kakā-kakā-kakā!" rising from the lake awoke her, and she laughed—"Yes, I'll be rinsing and cleaning indeed, Ms. Duck!"—just before midnight; slipping out of her kimono, she gathers a few things and heads out to the deck. Settling in, she lights her opium pipe, the first of this year and the last of the next, and watches the ripples, wavelets, the slow movement of the waters toward the dam.

A truck gears down on the highway, and a duck quacks again. Out on the other shore, a frog croaks, several times, and then is silent. Bats fly in and out of the light's glow. Her pipe goes out as she rises, disrobes, and walks down to the lake.

"Cold!" she squeals, as mud squelches between her toes, lily pads brushing past her body, until she is up to her shoulders in the lake. Holding her birth certificate and her driver's license, the flames singe her fingers, until she plunges beneath the surface. Staying under until her head grows light, she floats free of the water weeds and kicks her way towards the shore.

Three glugs of amaretto pouring into a glass to warm her, she settles on the deck to fill out a request for a copy of her birth certificate and a new driver's license, adding one year to last year's birthdate. The asphalt, still warm on her bare feet as she walks to the post office, smells of the recent rain, and mixes with the aroma of algae from the lake. "Hah!" she shouts, as she slams the mailbox lid. "Twenty-five years old again this year!" A dog barks, and she laughs.

A screech owl calls out as she settles down at the lake's edge again; writing a letter to herself, she seals it and lays it aside, then listens as last year's pen and ink splash in the lake below. Taking a new dip pen and journal in hand, she begins to write.

thick white drifting smoke
clinging to journal pages
poppy petals bloom

my birthdate burning
my smiling picture melting
pair of loons wailing

wind guttering flames
water swirling around me
I duck under—shhh!

dip pen scratching self
into paperwork boxes
cold wind drying us

slamming mailbox shut
"hah!" I shout, "another year—
gone!" bare feet warm street

empty picture frame
still warm documents behind
mockingbird singing
dip pen scratching out
poems of the year just now born
wavelets on the shore

past years' leaves' shadows
pinned to the sycamore's bark
torchlight flickering

Venus to the east
melting into the sun's light
his feet on the stairs

This last haiku she hears as Robin read it to her, waking her gently from her sleep. Putting down her journal, he bent to kiss her. "Welcome home, Robin," she says, pulling him close, "I missed you last night," and Robin responded in kind. Moments later, in the garden, they feed the newly planted seeds on the mound, laughing as a car door slamming startles them. Rising together, she brushes the moist earth from his back as he returned the favor.

Zoë settles on the deck to watch the sun continue to rise; Robin, holding a canvas bag, sat beside her and picked up her new license—"Nice photo!" he said—then took out an empty picture frame, a pad of paper and Zoë's colored pencils. "I spilled water on our wedding portrait this morning," he said. "Could you please draw us another?"

"Yes—tell me what you remember about it, Robin—I'm so sleepy . . ."

"Well, it was just lovely. We married almost two and a half years ago, on . . ."—and Zoë writes the date across the bottom in her flowing hand, as he points out toward the center of the lake—"on the island, there. The wisteria and jasmine from the bower got us a little high, or maybe we were just in love—in any case, we couldn't stop grinning, and you giggled the entire time. You wore a bright green peasant blouse and olive skirt, a garland of hibiscus with your hair long. Luna moth wings sprouted from your back, and I . . ."

Zoë's hands move quickly as she sketches an outline for the watercolor. *I probably won't finish it today,* she thinks, *guests are coming at dusk for the party, and there is a lot to do before then, but we have time—we have always had time now.* Robin's voice guiding her hand, she smiles as he recalled for her, as if it were yesterday, a fish leaping at the moment they shout "We do!" a raven watching them from the sycamore, their words echoing from the lake shore, some crepe myrtle blossoms, blown by the breeze, showering onto them as they kiss as if for the first time, again . . .

A Plain, Ordinary Woman

~ Jennifer Worrell

Never use a dull razor to get the job done.

Desima smoothed hot oil over her naked, brown self, ensuring every hair had been waxed, shaved, or zapped from existence. Besides eyebrows and lashes, only her crimson-tipped faux-hawk remained as the barest obligatory effort toward meeting beauty standards. Other girls could keep the waves that undulated to the floor, the boldly colored tresses fanned into exotic flowers, the braids engineered into architectural marvels.

Sweeping the pad of her thumb under her chin, she huffed at a bristly patch that she missed. Desima angled her face to catch the light and stretched her skin over her jaw. The whisker emerged hazy black just beneath the surface. She relit her body oil candle and poked the tip of a cuticle scissor in until it glowed. Snagging the blade under the hair, she met a gentle resistance but scraped it free. She flicked her finger over the tip, a delicious quiver vibrating along her neck. She grabbed the tweezers and yanked hard enough to savor the rip. A fat root glistened like a ripe plum. A rush of calm filled her head, like the roar of the sea inside a conch. One less imperfection, one less beacon drawing attention. The hours spent on this ritual, the constant tenderness that followed, was worth it for a week of invisibility, wolven blood be damned.

She clicked off the high-beam fluorescent bulb and stored her beauty kit in a drawer, slamming it harder than she intended. Idiot boys and outdated traditions—encouraging randos to stroke the tresses of their objects of desire like some creepy valentine—tended to cause that reaction. Too bad her school didn't spend a week before the annual Wolf Moon Festival teaching unpaired students how to mind one's own business instead of new coiffing techniques. But all this pageantry, the styling competitions, the inexplicit yet shamefully direct theme of mating, deepened the connection to their lupine ancestors, who were more inclined to re-inhabit their human progeny during this time of year more than any other, or so the logic went. Another event that managed to both dismiss and spotlight women like her.

A sour taste flooded Desima's mouth. She wished she were outside childbearing age, the only group sheltered against such nonsense. Until those years were over, she'd be surrounded by boys blowing on the nape of her neck and sighing at the baby hairs waving back at them, licking their lips whenever she kicked off her shoes, hoping to glimpse a dark line leading from toe to ankle. Every summer she contemplated never going barefoot again, wearing long sleeves and pants to cover her limbs, maybe even shaving her scalp as bare as the rest of her. But covering up made it worse; their imaginations ran wild, speculating what treasures lay underneath, hardly able to keep their hands to themselves.

Centuries after their lineage was diluted to merely distant kin, too many boys still acted like animals, their memories failing to remember all the yesterdays when she recoiled at the slightest touch from anyone outside her small platonic circle, wanting simply to inhabit her own space and air.

Counting to ten, massaging her jaw in tiny circles, Desima reminded herself to breathe. Stress mercifully made some people bald, but cursed her in the opposite direction. She steeled herself for another day at Lupine High, followed by a two-hour-long Festival Committee meeting, mandatory for seniors.

At least she could console herself with the fact that everyone else wanted to sit in the glare of floodlights, both literally and figuratively—on stage at the history re-enactment, hawking wares at the vendor booths, guiding children's story circles—leaving her alone with the job of prop master. Except for Peter, who she volunteered as her assistant. If she had to suffer through this, she was roping her best friend in too. And since this was his first year in the village, the grandeur of her heritage was yet unspoiled by exploitation, the mystique surrounding the old tales still ripe with wonder. Despite the bastardization of history into a commercial spectacle, some magic remained in it all.

☉

Staring blankly into the turd-brown void in the back of her locker, mind swimming with pre-meeting contingency plans and inventories and all things werewolf, Desima momentarily let her guard down. Before registering the swell of derisive laughter, she sensed a rank change in the air. From the corner of her eye, she saw Uri and his band of Neanderthals slither into a half-circle behind her, preventing easy escape.

"Imagine how pretty she'd be if she grew that hair out."

Desima groped along a row of hooks in the side wall of the locker for her set of knuckle spikes. Shaped like two innocent puppies curled up together, her fingers fit snugly through the eyeholes, ears stabbing between. With her free hand, she pulled a notebook with a silvery cover off the top shelf. The shiny object would distract the boys long enough to conceal the weapon in her pocket.

She turned to see fat fingers, lined with dirt and stinking of piss, hovering inches from her face.

"What the fuck?" Desima knocked John's hand away with the notebook but the dull slap echoing down the hall only made them laugh.

"Almost got a handful, guys." John's sniveling voice was enough to make her fantasize about raking those cute little ears across his jugular.

"What do you want, I'm late for Festival Committee."

They crept closer, their eyes glazed, transfixed on Desima's fauxhawk. "We just want to touch it," John said. "What is it with you?"

Her skin pricked as if she had a legit allergy to them. She itched to roll down her sleeves but they'd pounce on any vulnerability. Shouting for help would probably bring the wrong teacher running, one who'd find this all very charming.

Desima flashed to sixth grade, at a memory she thought had disappeared. Uri and some friend of his had shoved her against the schoolyard fence at recess, balled the top of her t-shirt in his fist, and stared inside, inspecting her sternum for the first fine curls. They tossed her aside, bored, when they saw she was still bare. She'd looked up to see the recess monitors watching like this assault was no big deal, her worth linked exclusively to her physique.

That night she bought her guard dogs and painted the tips with ox blood, then chopped off her knee-length mane and buried the scraps.

Once the novelty of her new cut wore off, no one gave her a second glance, and she'd never needed to use the blades. But the Wolf Moon Festival tended to bring out the beast in people.

The boys' arms dangled as they swayed on the balls of their feet. The hall vanished behind their hulking bodies.

Stifling a yawn, she blinked slowly and set her face to stone.

"Give us a little something." This one had a pretentious name like Zacc. He wore a shirt with a v-neck so exaggerated it exposed his bushy chest and abs, coming to a point at the waist of his pants.

Desima averted her eyes and gnashed her teeth to keep her last meal down.

Zacc raked his fingers over his bushy pecs, a mist of sweat glistening in the fluorescent light. "Maybe I can feel yours against mine." He snatched at her blouse with a hooked finger.

She let her notebook clatter to the floor.

"Relax, honey." Uri licked his wet, gaping mouth.

"I'm not your fucking honey." The air whistled as she drew her claws in an arc.

The boys sprang back, shock replacing lust and intrigue on their faces. Except Uri, who broadened his chest, calling her bluff. A tough-girl façade made from paper and paint.

So predictable.

She swung again, so close his thin shirt billowed. He screwed up his mouth and snatched at the weapon, but she struck like a rattlesnake, piercing his palm. As he pressed the heel of his other hand into the wound, she turned her wrist and jabbed his bicep.

Desima grinned at his yelp of pain and John and Zacc retreating down the adjoining hall.

"You bitch," Uri said, pulling the pencil out of his bun to twist his sleeve into a tourniquet. "You won't have those with you all the time, so—"

Desima stared him dead in the eye, unblinking, and licked his blood off the blades. He turned a unique shade of white and took off after his friends.

The muscles in her arms rippled as though trying to shake off a layer of filthy water. She rolled her shoulders and neck but the feeling wouldn't leave. Uri's voice spread inside her mind. She shuddered at the idea of John's scaly fingers finding their mark, tugging the wiry tip of a curl.

Her body tingled like a rash. She thrust her hands under her sleeves to scratch. A thatch of peach fuzz lined her upper arms. She could see it, faintly, through the white cotton. Most likely the boys could too. They could smell the sweat clinging to every strand, the scent of panic and fury a special kind of perfume.

The day of the festival, Desima was up an hour early, trying to decide between her regular, everyday hoodie or her special occasion hoodie, excited to finally get this mess over with. By nightfall, the rust-red moon hung close enough to touch. The naked branches of the trees had turned to crystal. An inch of snow covered the ground, sparkling with a frosty glaze.

As if superstitious, the planners kept everything the same, down to the food and the paper lanterns lining the arcade. Bright lights and cloying vapors poured from the competitors' ring, where tournaments for most impressive styling drew white-knuckled spectators. Sultry music snaked beneath a purple voile curtain, giving visitors a glimpse of ladies in skimpy outfits performing burlesque dances by torchflame.

Outside noise dulled to a mellow drone as Desima stalked through the dim light of the prop tent, checking inventory against her clipboard. A mirrored dressing table filled with scraps of fabric and sewing notions, random make-up jars and first-aid supplies, sat lopsided among wood trunks and boxes. A mat of straw lined soil still damp from snow and ice. The wolf costume hung centered against one wall, isolated by velvet ropes and accented by spotlights.

Every year the re-enactment required a new costume, and every year the head seemed larger, the mouth crowded with dagger-like fangs. The fibers of the eyes were painted by hand with a single hair from a wolf's tail. Desima leaned in, losing herself in the inky pools of crimson at the center. The pelt's reddish tint implied the hunter returning from a kill, perhaps prowling for another, its belly never sated. The scent was as real as the rest of it: canine mixed with rust and meat, sulfur and smoke.

A surprisingly loud growl tore through her stomach. Though she ate before her shift, planning to score her much-earned free plates of barbecue once the masses started heading home, she didn't know if she could wait that long. According to her watch, there was no time for a break. She ignored the scent of roasted meat wafting through the flaps in the tent and busied herself searching for broken stitches, loose teeth and hair, anything that might come undone on stage. Nothing ruins an atmosphere more than the main attraction falling apart.

After double-stitching a couple of trouble spots, she stepped back to admire her handiwork. A strange flutter curled around her heart. Each artist brought distinct interpretations to their work, trying to make their re-creations of the ancestral beast more realistic, more unsettling, than the last. They always fell short of the mark. This year they outdid themselves, though she couldn't quite articulate why. Something about the depth of the eyes brought a chill of familiarity.

"Deeeesima." Uri's voice wormed through the tent. "Desimaaa."

Nothing in the tent was substantial enough to hide behind. John and Zacc might be waiting outside to trap her if she ran.

For once Desima wished Peter was at her elbow. Though his small stature and quiet voice made him an easy target for bullies, they usually threw a few taunts and otherwise left him alone. A guy who posed no threat in terms of brawn tended to be nearly as invisible as a sexually indifferent woman. They'd probably move along before risking rejection in front of a guy outside their pack.

She ducked under the pelt, careful not to dislodge it from the hooks that held it aloft. The fur felt soft, intimate. The front paws dangled low enough to conceal her dusty gray shoes, and the spotlights threw imposing, disorienting shadows.

Rusty iron stakes held the velvet ropes in place. She contemplated pulling one out for protection, cursing herself for leaving her guard dogs at home. Believing she was safe with the entire village milling around now seemed infinitely stupid. She nudged a stake in the rear with her toe and it wiggled.

Through small mesh-covered eyeholes over the snout, she saw three silhouettes lumbering through the front of the tent. She tugged at the stake, ignoring the pain of the jagged edges perforating her skin. Sweat greased her palms, fingernails squealing against metal as her grip slipped upward. Gritting her teeth, she strangled the stake and pulled, holding her breath even as it burned for release. They would not find her here, would not fucking touch one inch of her body, even if it meant dislocating her shoulders. Finally the stake eased from the earth.

As they neared her hiding place, they lowered their voices and stepped as delicately as ballet dancers on glass. Zacc tilted his head and paused. They seemed to be eye to eye.

Desima tensed, hefting the stake. It was heavy. Too heavy to swing with any efficiency.

Zacc lunged forward, but was knocked nearly off his feet.

"The fuck are you doing?" Uri moved into view, squaring his shoulders.

"What—"

"Get away from that." Uri's voice wavered as though he feared the costume would come to life. "What if it falls in the *dirt*?"

"Sorry man, whatever."

"Not *whatever*. Watch it."

"Hey," John called, from the rear of the tent. How did Desima not see him pass by? Who else did she miss? "She's probably backstage. Let's get out of here before we mess something up."

The crunch of straw slowly diminished, but the threat of an unmet challenge emerged in their wake.

Desima extracted herself from the costume, dropping the stake. She scratched her brow, itchy from the hot fur, but her fingers ignited in pain. A wet trail remained, too sticky to be sweat. She stepped in front of the battered dressing table and inspected herself in the cracked mirror. Blood covered the tips of her fingers where her nails had popped off, leaving gory little stumps.

She cleaned herself up with sterile wipes and wrapped her fingertips in bandages, then readjusted her hood and slipped on a pair of fingerless gloves. She'd sent Peter to the stage with a box full of last-minute decorations, so she figured she'd hunt him down to make sure he was okay. Hopefully Uri and his gang got sidetracked and stayed out of Peter's way.

Outside, volunteers weaved among passersby with samples of sweets and spiced nuts. Musicians roamed the crowd, keeping the spirit lively and joyous, encouraging people to pair off into folk dances.

Some of the couples huddled around stalls for snacks and beer or an excuse to catch their breath between songs. Desima snorted at the men in curly-haired chaps and matching vests emulating fauns. Many of the women wore mittens like wolves' paws or fur leg warmers under short skirts.

Things hadn't changed much since grade school parties, where all girls talked about was boys and how to snag one, from sundown until moonrise, when they traded strategies for dreams.

Coals from fire pits turned icicles clinging to the fringed canopies into twinkling fairy lights. Though the arcade was warmly lit, the staging area between it and the woods fell into shadow. Desima dodged the throng and weaved among mazes of power cords and generators and ice chests, the boring stuff no one gave a second thought to. Between her all-gray clothes and scruffy shoes worn silent, she melted into the background like another set piece.

Treading the boundary between civilization and wilderness, a crackling, guttural noise resonated deep within the trees. Something lingered, hungry. The shadows moved with the wind, a swell of forest out of sync with reality.

She stayed rooted to her spot. The air hummed with tension. The sound of claws digging in the hard-packed ground seemed inches away, but she could see nothing past the dark cloud obscuring the parcel of trees directly ahead. A pair of crimson lights burned into her retinas. The sensation felt like fire in the hearth.

"Des."

She blinked and the red lights receded, the impenetrable blackness blown away. An owl swooped from its pine-bough sanctuary.

Desima turned toward the arcade and a pair of distinctively out-of-style pants carrying their owner into view. "Peter?"

"What are you doing hanging out in the dark like some Goth?"

The lanterns gave Peter a halo effect, highlighting a peach balayage pompadour with an undercut resembling tiger stripes. So that's where he'd been all this time. He must have booked a spot well in advance.

"Bored already?"

"This is *incredible*. You sold it way short."

"I see you got your hair designed."

Peter nodded crisply, then froze, softly touching the waves to make sure they didn't bounce out of place. "So is the front row reserved for staff? Do we get to skip the line or—"

"Chill. Show's not for . . ." Desima checked her watch. Five minutes. How long had she been staring into the woods? "Don't worry, we're getting bird's-eye seats. Follow me."

Desima led Peter through the performers' entrance of the pavilion and up the scaffolding. Sidling past the lighting tech, she perched on the edge of the catwalk hovering above the stage. Peter scootched in close. Any other boy even suggesting this would make her body stiffen and angle toward the exit to regain even an inch of space, but Peter's disinterest matched her own.

The conductor rapped his music stand and the audience's excitement hushed. The house lights dimmed and sweeping symphonic music drowned out the last tittering voices. As the music faded, the narrator's rich baritone thundered into the pavilion and pulsed in Desima's chest.

"Many centuries ago, wolf and human were inseparable. They formed alliances, eventually resulting in offspring, and the first true werewolf was born."

Dawn gleamed over the rocky landscape. Spears and slings were symbolically tucked stage right as man and wolf enjoyed the heat of a fire side by side.

Traditionally, the play was done almost entirely in pantomime, allowing actors to add personal touches that made it worth watching time and again, while the audience's imaginations and familial histories filled in what dialogue left out.

The second act was immersed in war and struggle, the waning sun mutating to blood red, mountains and fallow fields falling into grim twilight.

"Centuries of ecological and political strife, plague and famine, took their toll, causing both beast and man to lose touch with their roots and separate."

The land appeared ravaged, the result of scrabbling hands searching for bulbs and roots as well as a place to bury the many dead. The wolf at center stage seemed immense, powerful enough to bound into the rafters.

"Despite the broken bonds of the past, each being kept aspects of the other's essence."

The exit music swelled as the red backlighting morphed to the golden warmth of optimism and endurance.

Desima held her gaze on the scene, captivated by the crystal glint in the wolf's eyes. Her mouth echoed the coda as if summoned.

"People believe during Wolf Moons, they can transform from human to wolf and vice versa."

"Do you believe that too?"

Desima needed a second to readjust to reality. She nearly forgot Peter was there. The house lights came up as the curtain descended, widening the divide for another year.

"First time for everything." *And damn, would it be nice.* Reluctantly she stood, swatting Peter's shoulder. "Come on. Let's go grab the costume before it gets trampled."

After picking up the specially molded crate from the prop tent, nestling the costume and head inside, and returning it to a safe corner, Desima snuck out to nab a few kabobs and ciders to toast their hard work. One of the vendors even slipped her chunks of shortcake. She and Peter perched on trunks and dawdled through their late-night snack, lost in their own thoughts. As he stretched across the domed lid and licked his fingers clean, Desima gave one last look around.

"All right, there goes your first Wolf Moon Festival, friend."

"We're done already?"

"Yep. The historical society comes for the costume, and porters take down the tents and stuff. We're out."

Peter flicked off the lights and they headed toward the woods, navigating around the heavily rutted ground. He flinched at a howling sound.

"Just the wind," Desima assured him. "How 'bout I walk you home?"

"You don't have to." He didn't sound convincing.

"It's on the way."

The fairgrounds were deserted except for the last few vendors packing up their trucks. Some of the arcade lanterns remained lit, but without anyone operating the stalls, they cast a sinister glow. The wind whipped up, making trees shiver and banners crackle and snap.

"Anyway, I need to protect you from ghosts," Desima said, running her fingers up Peter's arm.

"Ghost footsteps are awfully loud," he muttered, looking suspiciously over his shoulder.

Desima chuckled, but perked up her ears. A third patter of steps joined theirs, then a fourth. The fifth couldn't be far behind.

She grabbed Peter's hand and picked up the pace. But even the most normal movements feel awkward when someone's watching. Her knees jutted out like a scarecrow's. Her jeans seemed to fit wrong, shifting around her legs with each step.

Locking his sights on the edge of the tree line, Peter tripped over a root. Or a cable. Or—

"Figured you were still creeping around." Uri grabbed Desima by the shoulder and forced her to face him. Zacc crouched closer, holding something she couldn't make out.

Peter tried to scramble to his feet, but John stepped on his foot to hold him down. His stance was sloppy, unsteady, like he'd never been in a fight and was unprepared for this one. In the tent earlier, his voice betrayed the same weakness. She hoped she read him correctly.

Uri shoved her back, swinging his foot out to topple her balance. The seam of her jeans ripped as she landed. Pressing her palms into the dirt, she kicked at Uri's groin, but he tilted his hips. She sprang up on her heels, turning to help Peter up, but froze at the snick of a switchblade.

A knife glinted against Zacc's thigh.

Uri's bicep jumped with the flick of his lever. "Told you we'd catch you without your blades."

Desima backed up slowly toward Peter. John laughed as he forced his weight down. Peter yelped and punched the kid's knees. John wobbled, and Desima caught a pearly shimmer in his right pocket. He had a blade too, and either didn't know how to use it or didn't want to.

"Peter, you got this?" Desima caught his eye and tapped her hip.

He bit his lip and stared at her so long she wasn't sure he understood. Then he grabbed the toe of John's shoe with one hand and twisted the heel in the opposite direction. John fell on top of Peter, knocking the wind out of them both. As the two boys wrestled in the snow, Desima grabbed the edge of John's pocket and yanked, howling at the pain in her shredded fingers. The bandages wormed away from her skin, and new nails, straight-tipped and sharp as razors, sheared through the latex.

The knife slid from the torn denim, landing in a circle of snow and bloody bandages. She pressed the button with her left hand and poked it awkwardly into John's side. He didn't need much persuasion to move. Rather than trying to help his friends or reclaim his knife, he ran off into the woods, skidding on patches of ice. Desima would have laughed if her fingers didn't feel like they were being split open from the inside.

Peter held up his fists, but his boxing expertise came from movies and old TV shows. Zacc saw his opportunity and slashed Peter's pristine white shirt. He sucked in his belly and readjusted his stance, fist colliding with Zacc's cheek. Desima waved John's switch in Uri's face, but he thrust at her stomach, driving her further into the trees. Wind gusted through the hole in her sweatshirt. She didn't dare look down, but considering the chill, the gash must have been six inches long.

Her right hand felt shredded, but at the same time swollen and numb. Uri lunged again, plunging the knife into her shoulder.

She shouted for Peter but was sure the sound of tearing flesh drowned her out. Her entire body seemed to inflate, engorged and ready to explode.

Desima tipped her head into the snow. When had she fallen? The intense cold was a welcome sensation, blocking the pain and distended sensation of her limbs.

Uri kneeled on her hip and held the knife at her throat. Desima noticed a male figure running at them, but it was Zacc. Where the hell was Peter?

"Took you long enough," Uri snapped.

"I had something to get rid of," Zacc said, shaking droplets from his knife. Blood dotted the snow at his feet.

"Peter!"

Uri and Zacc ignored her as they shredded her jeans and her sleeves and widened the hole in her sweatshirt, careful to pull the cloth away from her skin.

They drew back, gasping in awe. Sweat poured off her stomach in streams, soaking the fabric, hair sticking to her body. She reached up to her chin, now covered in soft fuzz.

They panted, fascinated, twirling individual strands between their fingers, leaning down to sniff and nuzzle, a contented thrum rising between them. They left her underwear alone, her breasts unmolested, like some perverted sign of respect.

Desima clamped her jaw shut, incisors stabbing into her bottom lip. Breathing hard through her nose, another heaving voice answered her own.

She tensed her hands, surprised her fingers no longer hurt. The stumps of her fingers had been replaced by rigid black claws, casting skeletal shadows in the snow.

Uri pulled off her shoes and socks and tossed them aside. He delicately raised her ankles, inspecting her like rare gemstones, when his eyes went wide at the sight of two massive paws where human feet used to be.

"What the *fuck* . . ."

She kicked up, snapping out of his grip. A delicious crunch caused Zacc to whip his head up. Desima raked her forepaws across his face, stripping his nose to ribbons. He screamed and covered his face, but not before a waterfall of blood gushed into his lap.

Uri was too stunned to make a sound. He snuffled through his broken septum and writhed backwards on his hands, but Desima clamped her fangs into his calf, siphoning warm blood and flesh between her teeth. The boys' screams rang thin and high as they squeezed air from their lungs.

She'd heard a similar sound, halfway in and out of sleep, at some long-ago slumber party. Instead of frightened, Desima had been fascinated, partial witness to terrors only her friend could see.

Uri's face distorted with astonishment and rage. Zacc tackled Uri before he could do anything stupid.

Desima rose up on her hind legs, snarling, barely conscious of the figure beside her.

Peter bent, clutching at his middle, to pick up one of the fallen switchblades. Before anyone had time to react, he jerked forward, impaling Zacc's wrist.

Zacc shrieked, lurching into the woods with Uri stumbling behind.

Desima's fingers uncurled, slowly shrinking to their original form. Her limbs, still thick with muscle, ached with the fresh buzz of a morning stretch.

"You okay, Peter?"

Peter sliced off his sleeves and knotted them into a pressure bandage across his skinny waist. A purple ring blossomed around one eye and a corner of his mouth.

"Yeah . . . he didn't cut me so deep after all, I guess. You, though—" Peter tilted his head, his expression a mixture of bemusement and delight.

Desima caught sight of herself in a frozen puddle, her hair disintegrating, muzzle and fangs retracting with a soft crackling static. Her bones snugged into her flesh with an easy tightness, like stepping from a hot bath into the chill of an open window.

"Never better."

Peter sheared off her own tattered sleeve and knotted it over her shoulder, which was already beginning to heal.

Desima could still hear the boys' keening in the distance. She considered whether she'd ever be haunted by that sound, or if it would come back to her on a future moonlit January, carried on the crisp air like a symphony.

Box #143

~ John Klima

NEW CALDWELL UNIVERSITY ARCHIVES
BOX #143
BUREAU OF CRIME PREVENTION AND DISCOVERY
Misc papers relating to the disappearance of Oliver Wolsey

METROPOLITAN GUARD FORM #18
Requisition for OFFICERS FROM VARIOUS GUILDS of THE NEW CALDWELL MET-
ROPOLITAN GUARD and SUNDRY SUPPLIES for use by OFFICER GURNEY during
the month of AUGUST 1874

- *One (1) water mage,*
- *One (1) air mage,*
- *One (1) fire mage,*
- *Two (2) earth mages,*
- *One (1) Metropolitan Guard armored transit carriage*
- *Five hundred (500) pounds of MIXED BREAD, MEAT, AND VEGETABLES*

OFFICER GURNEY assumes responsibility for the safe return of the GUILD MAGES and METROPOLITAN GUARD TRANSIT CARRIAGE within EIGHT days of this form's expiry.

I certify that the above requisition is correct, and that the articles specified are absolutely requisite for the public service, rendered so by the following circumstances: SECURITY OF THE COMMON GOOD.

Approved by *[illegible]* on AUGUST 16, 1874.

Received at FACILITIES PLANNING the 16th of AUGUST 1874 by Officer Janis Stefanik for processing.

꙰

PERSONAL LETTER
From the Private Desk of Governor Morgan Gurney

Dearest Brother:

I am disappointed and more than a little surprised to hear that Oliver Wolsey eluded capture. Eluded you, specifically. Given your voluminous accomplishments and atypical high arrest rate, I would have thought that you could apprehend a mere minor with little difficulty. Alas, the past is immutable and permanent, holding one's failure in pristine condition for future generations to gawp at and wonder how something so ridiculous could happen.

It has come to my attention that you are making a pathetic attempt to drink away the failure. Unfortunately for you, your efforts are to be focused outside the bottle. At half past eight, a carriage from the Metropolitan Guard will arrive at your address to take you to the Metro Garage. From there, you will meet up with officers from the Omega Grand Lodge whose job is to take you to intercept Wolsey and return him to New Caldwell. Our intelligence suggests that he will not disembark the ship until he reaches Broadfell.

It should not have to be said, but you are not allowed to fail in this endeavor.

I believe you will have everything you need at hand, but should you find your supplies or support lacking, I trust in your resourcefulness to discover a solution.

Sincerely,
Governor Morgan Gurney

FORMAL METROPOLITAN GUARD CORRESPONDENCE #1
New Caldwell
August 17, 1874
Chief Inspector Cromwell
Broadfell Metropolitan Guard

Sir, this letter is to inform you that Officer Marcus Gurney will be conducting an investigation into Oliver Wolsey within the City Boundaries of Broadfell. Gurney is to be given any and all assistance requested while he is in your city.

More importantly, we expect that Gurney shall not be hindered in any way by your Metropolitan Guard while on the business of the Crown.

Signed,
Sir Matthew Andy Prescott,
Viceroy of New Caldwell
Countersigned,
Morgan Gurney
Governor of New Caldwell

FORMAL METROPOLITAN GUARD CORRESPONDENCE #2
New Caldwell
July 1, 1854
Chief Inspector Ligarius
Broadfell Metropolitan Guard

Sir, this letter is to inform you that LIEUTENANT GURNEY will be leading an armored Naval flotilla south to Broadfell to provide succor for the attack on your port. If you are hitherto unaware of CPO Gurney and his numerous accolades, a short summary follows. Gurney has twice received the Distinguished Service Cross and once the St. James Cross for his show of unprecedented bravery. He has yet to lose a man under his command despite being in some of the most brutal campaigns of the Half Coup. Gurney is a consummate warrior, receiving highest marks in his company as a sharpshooter and more recently winning the Naval Forces bare-knuckle boxing competition for the fourth consecutive year.

You will be in excellent hands with CPO Gurney.

Signed,
Chief Inspector Jay Collins

⤳

BATHERS & FISHERMEN
ARE ATTACKED
BY A MONSTER FROM THE SEA

An eyewitness to the event claims that numerous bathers and several fishermen were attacked by a many-limbed beast that rose unexpectedly from the sea. Passers-by on the docks were alerted by the screams of the bathing ladies, and by seeing one fishing vessel pulled under the water. All those affected were found to be unharmed although many of the fishing boats in the harbor had damage to their hulls. Most damage was minor, but two ships require considerable repair.

The Broadfell Navy is investigating the incident under the direction of Broadfell's Mayor.

⤳

NAVAL INVESTIGATION INTO SEA MONSTER ATTACK
CALLED OFF

After mere days of investigation, the Broadfell Navy has called off its investigation into the sea monster attack. Hoping to use this excursion as a justification of the expense of the Navy's new steam-powered war ships, Broadfell's Navy is instead left only with HMS Hollyhock in the harbor, and that is only because the old brass-sides ship was still waiting to be decommissioned. The remainder of the once-proud

Broadfell Royal Navy deployment is now an expensive decoration at the bottom of the harbor.

Loss of life was minimal, a true stroke of luck given the utter destruction of the ships.

"The creatures appeared to target the steamships," said Lieutenant Rhys O'Mangan. "We believe it was due to the noise of their engines." When pressed for more information, O'Mangan was reluctant to answer in more detail. Eventually he admitted, "Our investigation is at a standstill until more ships become available to us."

The harbor is also at a standstill as no new ships can approach Broadfell while the creatures patrol the water. Eyewitnesses describe the creatures as being brightly colored with uncountable limbs that rose abruptly from the water and tore the ships apart. Local long-shoremen claim these creatures are called "Trarowr" among those who work on the ocean.

The city now waits for outside help as all work grinds to a halt.

⊱⊰

Clipping from The New Caldwell Inquisitor, Friday, July 14, 1854

*HIS MAJESTY'S NAVY TO ASSIST
SISTER CITY BROADFELL AGAINST
TERRIBLE SEA MONSTER ATTACKS*

Upon hearing of the tragedy that occurred at the harbor to our south, New Caldwell Mayor Konstantyn Karwacki enlisted His Majesty's Navy to send a flotilla of six ships south to Broadfell.

The ships have been fitted with large iron spikes along their hulls and reinforced masts. Instead of using sails and God's air power, the Royal Navy is working with the Metropolitan Guard to use the mage guilds to reduce the two-day journey to mere hours. Mago dell'aria deliver strong gusts of air to the ships' sails while Mágos tou Neroú control the waves. An Erdmagier will be on each ship to protect the ships from the additional force of the magicked air and water. This unprecedented collaboration may lead to a new method for long-distance travel.

The flotilla is commanded by Chief Petty Officer Marcus Gurney, recently decorated with the St. James Cross. CPO Gurney is widely recognized as a rising talent in His Majesty's Navy, having led a successful counterattack in the Half Coup. CPO Gurney also completed his fourth consecutive defense of the Royal Enlisted Pugilist Championship, the first man to win more than three such championships. One wonders how CPO Gurney would fare in the Royal Commissioned Mensur Championships, but luckily for the commissioned officers, he is ineligible.

Join us in wishing CPO Gurney and his men a successful campaign in Broadfell and a swift, safe return.

꒷

Clipping from The Broadfell Times, Tuesday, July 18, 1854

ROYAL NAVY FROM NEW CALDWELL SUCCESSFULLY SEND SEA MONSTERS BACK TO HELL

Be they Trarowr or some new beast sent from Hell to destroy us for our improprieties, it took barely more than one day for Chief Petty Officer Gurney and his flotilla of Royal Navy ships from New Caldwell to drive the creatures away. The cleverly modified ships' spikes kept the creatures far enough away so that the naval artillery could fire at will. Within an hour upon arriving, CPO Gurney and his men killed three of the creatures.

The assault served to goad the creatures into more attacks on the New Caldwell ships, but the deadly iron spikes limited the amount of damage from the creatures. The blood from the creatures seemed to hiss and steam upon the water while the deafening artillery fired again and again into the sea.

Rumors persist that the Royal Navy worked alongside New Caldwell's Metropolitan Guard Mage Guilds and that those same mages were at least as much a part of keeping the ships intact as the extra iron was. The ships clearly maneuvered more quickly and adeptly then ships of that size normally can. Within ten hours of entering the harbor, smaller creatures were either dead or seen swimming away.

Eyewitnesses claim that at one point a shirtless CPO Gurney dove into the water, armed only with his cutlass. The claim continues that CPO Gurney attacked the largest of the creatures and drove his cutlass deep into its eye. The creature was seen sinking into the harbor, whether to swim away or perish is unknown.

Broadfell is mightily indebted to CPO Gurney. Without his bravery and leadership, it is unlikely that the harbor could have resumed normal activities so soon.

⤙∘

Clipping from Pacifist Coalition News, Monday August 17, 1874

LOUPE SEEN WITH WOMAN NOT HIS WIFE, THE SILENCE GROWING IN NUMBERS, REDHANDS LINKED TO PROPERTY DESTRUCTION IN NINE POINTS

Tenor Gilles Loupe was seen exiting The Fresh Rooftop with a gorgeous brunette who is clearly not his blonde wife. Rumors hold that the brunette was none other than Maria Vélez, a violinist with the New Caldwell Opera. Was it just colleagues enjoying a little tipple after an exhilarating performance of Viktor Sandmeier's *Vaqtning Chidamsiz Marshi*? Or perhaps this was just another in a long string of infidelity for Loupe? The singer makes the most of his prestige and beauty and is not shy from flirting with any attractive lady—or man—he runs across.

In direct opposition to the city's largest gangs—Thomas Brutus' ICE RATS and the terrifying NEW CALDWELL DEVILS—the new street gang THE SILENCE has a membership that is growing without check. It seems that more and more youths are seen every day wearing the gang's signature multi-colored cloth gag. To date, THE SILENCE have not broken any laws; they merely stand around in public in increasing numbers. The NCMG are aware of the gang but cannot act at this time.

Speaking of breaking laws, what is to be done with the recent destruction that occurred in the Nine Points? A particular sanguine-colored tarot guild is rumored to be connected to the fire in a popular downtown pub, The Beautiful Lamp. It seems the guild was looking for a young man named Wolsey and didn't let anything get in the way of their pursuit. But to make matters worse, they didn't even get their man! He escaped south to Broadfell! It is high time for the Governor to step down from his gilded seat in Parliament and do something about the rampant destruction that these tarot guilds cause in areas where people can ill afford it. (Not to mention the guilds' willful disregard for the laws of the city!) Is it up to the humble barman to cover the costs of the fire and loss of business or can the wealthy guilds be held accountable?

Clipping from Daily Beacon, Monday August 17, 1874

VICEROY AND GOVERNOR ORDER
METROPOLITAN GUARD TO FIND WOLSEY
AND BRING HIM TO JUSTICE

Mere days after the Metropolitan Guard bungled the capture of Oliver Wolsey and essentially washed their hands of the case, Viceroy Prescott and Governor Gurney ordered the NCMG to close the case at all costs. The Governor is funding this endeavor through his personal accounts so there will be no additional cost to the citizens of New Caldwell.

If it was not enough that Wolsey committed cold-blooded murder, wantonly besmirching our harbor, he then brazenly stole from the respected tarot guilds. Every New Caldwell citizen knows how the existence of the tarot guilds bring near limitless prosperity and prestige to the city. One hopes that the NCMG brings its significant power to bear to ease the minds of citizens everywhere.

Clipping from The Green Street Mirror, Wednesday, August 19, 1874

WHO REALLY IS FUNDING THE NCMG'S EXCURSION
TO BROADFELL?

Our humble Governor is offering his own funds to pay to send city guardsmen south to Broadfell to clean up their bungled case, but where is that money really coming from? And is this really a case for the NCMG?

Governor Gurney wants to claim that he's using personal funds, but is that money in actuality from his tax-funded salary? Or is it coming from a more unlawful source? Could our Governor be receiving money from the tarot guilds, and is that money holding sway to policy decisions? It wouldn't be the first time that the guilds benefitted from Parliamentary decisions.

Let us not forget that Governor Gurney is sending Detective Gurney, his younger brother, to handle the case personally. There are literally dozens of other detectives in the NCMG. Detective Gurney's military chest is weighed down with accolades but when was the last time he received commendation for good work done? Are the brothers working together to protect the Governor's investments?

There are certainly more questions than answers at this point, but it all seems to be pointing towards corruption starting at the highest offices in the state.

Clipping from The Broadfell Times, Thursday, August 20, 1874

EDITORIAL

There has been a strange overturning in the popular sentiment concerning the management of public interests during the progress of the last ten or fifteen years. Previously to that time, nearly all public interests were also the interests of the communities out of whose enterprise they had grown, and foreign interference was not tolerated. If such interference was in any way attempted, it was resisted with a vigor which stopped at no means to accomplish its object of being let alone. Large sums of money are annually spent to secure vested and isolated rights, and the pleasure of local administration was supposed to be full compensation for all the expenditure which was involved in running a medium-sized city at largely the cost of large city, especially was this the case with the railroad interest.

The Crown's cities to the north, New Caldwell in particular, may provide lip service to maintaining the strength of the sea trade, but that is a mere front while they conduct their real business of trying to take over Broadfell's rail interest. New Caldwell is on an island, and as such, the expense of rail service may be too much to bear. Rather than take on their own expenses, they want to horn in on the efforts of Broadfell and reap the benefits of western expansion without putting out the initial expense.

In the midst of Broadfell's planning stages for railroad expansion, New Caldwell conveniently sends agents (officers? Mages?) from its Metropolitan Guard to our fair city. The official reason is for Lieutenant Gurney to find and apprehend a certain Oliver Wolsey who ran afoul of New Caldwell's tarot guilds. There was no reason to send agents to Broadfell; the city has its own Metropolitan Guard who are more than competent enough to arrest Wolsey and put him on trial for his crimes. This excursion to Broadfell is surely a ruse to place spies into the ranks of railroad workers and planners.

CURATOR'S NOTE:

The following are examples of il pensiero *messages. These delicate pieces of paper worked in pairs so that mages in the field could write messages on a sheet of* il pensiero *in their possession, and that same message would appear on a second sheet of* il pensiero *paper up to 200 leagues away. Mages in the field rarely had receiving paper so the messages were essentially one-way communiques.*

Message #1
ATTACKED ON WAY TO MG FLEET STORAGE. OFFICER McDONALD CRUSHED ATTACKER'S CARRIAGE AT A DISTANCE THEN OFFICER GALLAGHER ENGAGED ATTACKERS BEFORE THEY COULD REGROUP. COORDINATED DEFENSE GAVE US TIME TO GET TO MG FLEET STORAGE. WAS TOLD THE WAY WOULD BE CLEAR. WAS OUR MISSION LEAKED? EXPECT FULL REPORT UPON OUR RETURN.

Message #2
ARRIVED SAFELY BROADFELL APPROX MIDNIGHT. JOURNEY MADE WITHOUT INCIDENT. ROADS MOSTLY CLEAR. FEW OBSTRUCTIONS EASILY BYPASSED. CARRIAGE REQUIRES TYPICAL VIAGGIO REPAIRS. WOLSEY SHIP TO ARRIVE IN BROADFELL TOMORROW MIDDAY. CARRIAGE WILL BE REPAIRED BY THAT TIME AND MAGES READY FOR RETURN VOYAGE. TO WAIT ON GURNEY ARREST OF WOLSEY. GURNEY TRAVELED AS IF A MAGE, NO ILL EFFECTS. WHO IS THIS MAN?

Message #3
REPAIRS DONE. MAGES RESTED. GURNEY ARRIVED LATE AND W/O WOLSEY. SAID BROADFELL MG HAVE W IN CUSTODY. GURNEY HAS SEALED LETTER FOR GOVERNOR. OFFICER PRATA TENDED TO GURNEY'S WOUNDS BUT HE WILL HAVE A LIMP AND A NEW SCAR ON HIS FACE. WILL REPORT TO NCMG STATION UPON ARRIVAL.

⌁

Broadfell Metropolitan Guard Officer Report
Office of the Chief of the Broadfell Metropolitan Guard
City of Broadfell
97 Washington Street
Broadfell
Sunday August 30, 1874

To the Honorable Board of Police Commissioners,

Gentlemen
The following is the 17th Fortnight Report of 1874 of Robberies and Arrests of thieves.

• *August 17th*
William Daley arrested by Officer Valentine— charge breaking into his stable in Ferry Street near Jefferson and stealing a horse blanket.

- *August 17th*

C. N. Gerken. Grocer of 156 George St. complains of some person breaking into his store through the back window and stealing 5 boxes of segars 1 box of tobacco and 1 tin of money. Officer P.M. Breen on Post.

- *August 18th*

Redhands Guild reported another break-in at headquarters. Nothing reported stolen. Reminded by Officer Kelly that BMG has recommended better locks for guild offices.

- *August 18th*

Mr. Chas. Schultz, Lumber dealer on the East Canal, complains of a thug harassing people on the street.

- *August 19th*

John Lewis reports that his stable was broken into and a saddle and a pair of stirrups stolen. Officer Breen on Post.

- *August 19th*

Mr. Meyers of the corner of Washington & Third Streets complains of a large man assaulting members of the public and berating them with questions.

- *August 20th*

John Murphy proprietor of The Bronze Eel's Fantasagoria Emporium on Grand Street between 6th & 7th Streets complains of some person breaking in and demolishing his display of tarot cards for sale.

- *August 22nd*

John Hasting arrested by Officer Slattery charge stealing a set of harnesses from Mr. Chas Schultz.

- *August 23rd*

Confirmation from informants that Bronze Eel break-in perpetrated by Oliver Wolsey, subject of a HIS MAJESTY'S WANTED FOR ROYAL JUSTICE DECREE recently delivered from New Caldwell. Officers advised to take care in approaching Wolsey.

• *August 25ᵗʰ*

Officer Valentine detained NCMG Officer Marcus Gurney for acting outside his jurisdiction while searching for Wolsey. Officer Valentine recognized Gurney from boxing posters from his youth. Due to his heroic efforts in 1854, which likely saved the city, BMG has dropped all charges against Gurney.

•*August 26ᵗʰ*

Mr. L. Weinthal complains of some person stealing 3 dozen vests from his store 56 Washington St. by breaking in his back window. Property recovered.

• *August 27ᵗʰ*

Oliver Wolsey arrested by Officer Valentine on complaint of John Murphy. Wolsey also found to be in possession of several items of contraband. Wolsey will be extradited to New Caldwell after he is processed and arraigned in Broadfell.

• *August 28ᵗʰ*

Officer Marcus Gurney remanded to return to New Caldwell. The case of Oliver Wolsey is now above his and our jurisprudence.

Respectfully Submitted
Sean H. Howard
Broadfell Metropolitan Guard Assistant Commissioner

17th Fortnight Report of 1874 by Assistant Commissioner Howard of Robberies and Arrests of thieves.
Presented read and received and filed
Sept. 8th, 1874
Nath. A. Robertson
Clerk

Arrest Report Broadfell Metropolitan Guard
CONDITIONAL ORDER of LICENSE to a MALE CONVICT made under the Statutes
of His Majesty King Albert VII.
28th day of August 1874

HIS MAJESTY is graciously pleased to grant to Oliver Wolsey who was convicted of breaking & entering and destruction of property at the Bronze Eel Fantasagoria Emporium for the City of Broadfell on the 20th day of August 1874 and was then and there sentenced to be kept in Penal Servitude for the term of two weeks and is now confined in the Long Bay Correctional Center.

HIS ROYAL LICENSE to be at large from the day of his Liberation under this Order during the remaining portion of his said term of Penal Servitude, unless the said Oliver Wolsey shall, before the expiration of the said term, be convicted of some indictable Offence within Broadfell, in which case such License will be immediately forfeited by Law, or unless it shall please His Majesty sooner to revoke or alter such License.

This License is given subject to the Conditions endorsed upon the same, upon the breach of any of which will be liable to be revoked whether such breach is followed by a Conviction of not.

HIS MAJESTY hereby orders that the said Oliver Wolsey be set at liberty within Thirty days from the date of this Order.

Given under my Hand and Seal,
Governor Tristram Geddings
Under Authority of His Majesty King Albert VII

Sealed Letter for Governor Morgan Gurney

Dear Governor Gurney:
It gives me no small pleasure to send this letter. By the time you receive it, your brother should be back in the fold and Wolsey headed north via train under armed guard. Do not congratulate your brother, however; he did more to obstruct our inquiries into Wolsey's activi-

ties than not. Once we detained the younger Gurney, we were able to proceed post haste in the capture of Oliver Wolsey.

This was accomplished with no interference from outside Metropolitan Guard and no interference from tarot guilds. From what I hear, this is quite different from how things are handled in New Caldwell. It is my personal opinion that you allow your guilds too much freedom in the governance of your city.

Had I received your letter in a timely manner, perhaps we could have worked with Officer Gurney. As it was, we thought there was a new gang in Broadfell, mucking about town banging people in the head and asking questions. But no, it was just your half-trained bulldog, as is usual, solving problems with his fists rather than his brain.

Your letter, terse and too informal, arrived after your brother. While Broadfell does not measure up to the cosmopolitan nature of New Caldwell, we are in possession or more than a little funding and have access to modern technology such as *il pensiero* messaging and the telegraph. Either would have worked in getting a message to us if expediency was desired. If apprehending Wolsey was as important as you suggest, surely no expense should have been spared?

Nevertheless, we have Wolsey in custody. We will process him for the crimes he committed in Broadfell and then release him to your care.

We respectfully ask that New Caldwell refrain from interfering in Broadfell concerns in the future.

Yours lovingly,
Chief Inspector Cromwell

Clipping from The Broadfell Times, Monday, August 31, 1874

DARING ESCAPE!
WOLSEY ELUDES TRANSFER TO NEW CALDWELL

An enormous explosion shook the Broadfell Central District Metropolitan Guard station in the early hours before dawn. Smoke lifted in willowy wisps from the area where custody cells are located. The outside wall was breached from inside Oliver Wolsey's cell.

The bunk of the cell was turned on its side likely to shield Wolsey. A tight circle of charred marks was etched into the stone floor of the cell near the destroyed wall. Our sources indicate that the marks are the size and shape of tarot cards.

Currently Broadfell Metropolitan Guard have released no information on the whereabouts of Wolsey or of their plan for his abduction. *The Broadfell Times* will have an update in our noon edition.

Lakeside

~ A. P. Howell

He stood in the lake between the boat ramp and the dock. Just the same as last night, and so many nights before. Sharon no longer wondered if her eyes were tricking her, if the human shape was merely an illusion of shadows and memory.

The moon was out, bright and full and shining on the water. The lake was just the tiniest bit choppy, animating the edges of the long strip of reflected moonlight. The wind set Sharon's chimes singing and carried the scent of the lake to her nostrils. It wasn't a good scent. The algae bloomed in the August heat, nothing she'd want to drink or swim in but more hassle than danger. The brightly colored patches were easy enough to avoid if you knew to look for them.

Sharon felt like she owned the lake, or at least a part of it, no matter that the deed said the property ended more or less where the water began. She knew the curve of the shoreline, the place where rocks gave way to silt, which of the little island coves would clog with weeds, which channels allowed access and which would cost her a prop blade. And he, too, had become part of the landscape.

His body was a black cutout against the water, limned in silver. She couldn't make out any details of his expression, but she could feel the weight of his gaze.

It didn't bother her, not any more. If he was determined to stand in the water all night, every night, let him. She was not about to sacrifice her view of the moonlit lake. Not tonight, not any night.

Sharon had considered selling the place, her spoils of war, her legal entitlement that was worth so much less than she deserved for what she'd been put through. Take the money and never look back. That would be a kind of victory. But she had fought to remain here, had been so very patient. She deserved to sit here, and did not quite know who she would be if she went elsewhere.

Seven years was a long time to wait, but at least he had not made the sort of will he'd sometimes threatened when at his most angry, drunk, or petty. The local fish and game club would see no windfall, nor would the cousin he'd loved like a brother when they were young.

Seven years was a long time to wait, but the years before had been even longer. Sharon didn't like to think of herself as weak, but apparently she had been, given everything he'd put her through. She could have left—especially early, before so many doors closed, before she became so dependent—but at least she'd become strong in a different way.

Seven years, and all the years since, waiting for a story on the news. An angler with a gruesome catch. A dog retrieving an unexpected bone. No one was searching for him, but the lake wasn't deep.

She wasn't afraid any more. She'd spent too many years afraid. At some point, her heart and resolve had hardened permanently, and the way she'd felt on that night long ago had become her constant reality. Most days, she liked that; and even when she didn't, it wasn't as though she had much choice. Hearts and minds had minds and hearts of their own.

For the longest time, it seemed like he'd stood chest deep, deep enough to swamp waders. But as the years passed it became clear that he was coming closer. The water no longer reached his waist. At some point, he would climb out of the water, moving ever closer to the cabin.

It would take a while for him to make his way out of the lake. Years, based on how long it had taken him to get this close to shore. Then he'd have to walk up the little boat ramp and the switchbacked driveway, or else crawl up a ten foot ridge. He'd have to cross the remaining flat ground to the cabin.

And after that, he'd have to come inside.

If he could've done anything from a distance, surely he would've by now. He'd never been patient with anyone, least of all her.

When he was close enough, well-lit enough, would he look like he had in life, the way he used to look in her nightmares? Or would she see the blood from that last night, his expression one of accusation and surprise? Sharon's curiosity was dulled, and she had not felt a fight or flight reaction in years.

There was no need to think about events far off in the future. That sort of leisurely attitude was something she'd always liked about the lake. She had plenty of time. And it wasn't like she was going to live forever. Heart disease or cancer might get her before he came anywhere close to the cabin. Sharon was well past the age of resenting genetic predispositions and the frailty of the human body.

She held her mug up in a good-night toast, drained it, and turned off the porch light before retiring to her bed.

San Juan's Sowing

~ *J. V. Gachs*

I've spent the last three days next to Abuela's deathbed. This morning her ragged breath finally stopped. Of all the Hermanas, I was the one she chose as her heir, and so this was my duty, but I would have volunteered for it delightedly anyway. If only to make sure she endured a ghastly death.

Each painful inhale, her fight for precious air, gave me peace, but denying her the poppy tea that could ease her passing . . . That truly delighted me. I sipped it calmly in front of her pleading eyes. Taunting her with my smile. Mocking her weeping. The woman who brought me and the Hermanas to our knees when we were children, the one who never showed a shred of mercy in the face of our blood, of our suffering, who punished our bodies, was terrified of pain, and death in her last hours. We are but tender flesh in the end, I suppose, even the ones who pretend their hearts are hard and cold as marble.

I consumed no food other than the last bread from the last harvest—as *delectable* as it sounds—as I watched her drown in her own fluids, so the numbing the tea provided was more than welcome. No one else was allowed in, a precaution to prevent her spirit clinging to the wrong vessel. All that fucking nonsense worked in my benefit for once. I put my ear close to her still warm chest and hear nothing but the emptiness of death.

I guess I'm the queen of the hive now.

Standing next to her corpse, I draw with my fingers her wrinkle-covered mouth, each a piece of the tale of a hundred years of pursed lips and spite. The mouth I've feared is harmless now. Dead meat. In the golden candlelight, the shadows of her room dance. I, then, caress mine. My skin covered with old scars. The memories of her hands stitching my lips together shower over me like summer shimmering rain. Pain seeps into my bones. I admit, the seams served their purpose that night, and so did the scars afterwards. They inspire equal parts terror, respect and lust depending on which eyes are looking at me. As the needle pierced my flesh, and the coppery taste of blood mingled with that of salty tears on my tongue, her blue eyes never once hesitated. Her wrinkled hands never trembled.

I spit on the floor beside her body before leaving the room.

"Let the girls in," I order the men guarding the door. "Abuela is dead."

"Just in time for San Juan's festival," murmurs with satisfaction one of the Padres who sit waiting in the little parlor of the Casa Grande. "Así se dijo."

"Así se dijo," repeat the others, pressing two fingers against their lips. A farewell kiss to the woman upon whose shoulders the community had once grown strong, who never admitted how weak it was now. She made sure we were protected from the outside world by the snowed picked mountains, the forests where even expert rangers get lost, the deadly river that devoured animals and humans all the same, but she failed to see our biggest threat was already within ourselves.

The Padres stand up and approach me, respectfully. One by one they kiss me on the mouth as is customary to greet the village matriarch. I recognize the taste of them all, and I despise them. These kisses are the first sign of the transition of power that will be completed tomorrow night. San Juan's Eve. The sowing. This will be the first new cycle in seventy years. Some of the Padres were children back then and barely remember Abuela's crowning ceremony. The whole community is more excited about the festival than they are upset about her death. It's going to be a once in a lifetime event. Something they will tell the children about for years to come.

Outside the Casa Grande, June's sun scorches my eyes accustomed to the gloom of the closed death room. The black-clad girls walking past me carrying white cloth, basins of water, honey, wax and a clay urn look at me curiously out of the corner of their eyes. I am the subject of their dreams and nightmares. I'll be the Abuela they will remember in their deathbeds. A mixture of excitement and fear clutches at their chests and colors their cheeks pink like bougainvillea. This is an honor for them; they have been told.

"I'm not going to call you Abuela, just so you know it, Hermana."

I turn, and Amelia is sitting on one of the stone benches in the porch of the Casa Grande. Her hair, once black and curly, is now sprinkled with gray hairs and only soft waves remain of her crazy mane. But she is just as ravishing as ever. I've seen how all the Padres look at her. Today, she hasn't put on the patch covering her empty right eye socket. There is no longer any need. Abuela will no longer be offended by the consequences of her own laws. We can show our scars proudly now. They mean we survived. They mean we grow into the Hermanas who saved the community from collapsing on itself. Amelia stands up, splitting a fig in half and offering me a piece.

"Go to hell, Sis. You look good with a clear face," I smile, accepting the red, juicy flesh of the fruit before the sun and hunger make me faint. It'd never be a good omen, less so in front of the whole town stirring to prepare for funerals and San Juan's bonfire. It's warm and sweet. It tastes different now that she's gone.

"Come on, you need to get some rest, I killed a rooster for you this morning, the fire is on." She hesitated before mustering the courage to ask: "Is she really dead? Dead-dead?"

"Dead-dead."

"Good," she replies, pulling another sweet fig out of her apron and splitting it so we can both clean the bile taste from what's coming next out of our mouths. "Out with the old, in with the new."

"Así se dijo," I reply and we both try to hide our nervous laughter from the rest of the town.

I leave Amaya sleeping in the Hermanas' room for the last time. She must be exhausted after three days of confinement with the old damned dying Abuela. The broth and roasted chicken I cooked for her will be her last meal until the old woman's honey-covered heart is served to her at the bonfire. As of tomorrow, Amaya will move into the Casa Grande and everyone will call her Abuela. Her every word will become law. Go figure. Padres following her around, memorizing, interpreting. *So it was said.* What a load of crap. It would be hilarious, though. Pity I won't get to see that.

I sit outside the house, guarding her sleep, and peeling fabes de mayo for tomorrow's feast. There's a certain stillness and joy to this morning. Abuela's death has lifted a weight from my chest. A crack in the clouds letting the sun in for the first time after years of darkness. There's hope for the future now. And I'm glad I'll be a part of the change.

I inhale deeply, as if I had been holding my breath my whole life. Kids are allowed to play and roam free while the adults prepare the funerals and the ceremony. Flower arrangements, lambs, cakes. All their busy bees' voices reach me muffled and distant.

I wonder which of those kids playing in the fields are mine. At least three must have survived. Four maybe? I'm sure one died inside me. I couldn't feel it move for a couple of weeks before the pains. And at least another I didn't hear crying, but they might have just taken it away too soon for me to hear.

I know the little girl with the pink dress and gap teeth is mine without a doubt. She is my spitting image. Sometimes I think she looks like Padre Tomás, but others I think I recognize Padre Bartolome's gestures in her tiny face. I loathe them all, so I guess it's a good thing we don't get to know who's the father so we can't blame their crimes on the children. It's already been five San Juan's bonfires since they put her inside me, and since her I have never participated in the sowing again; not as a Madre, anyway. They took that one day of being called a mother from me because I almost died pushing her out of me.

"You are a bad omen, one-eyed girl," Abuela had stated.

Yeah, like we are the problem, stupid old cow.

Amaya saved me and tethered me to this world. She brought me back and gave me a purpose. Tomorrow we'll harvest the seeds I've spread ever since. The other Hermanas told me Abuela tried to take her away from me after the birth, to keep her from healing me so she could nurture the newborns. She whipped her and threatened to disinherit her, but Amaya wouldn't budge. I believe that stubbornness was the main reason why Abuela chose her in the first place. The strong rock upon which we would build a new world. She was the only one whose lips had to be sown together, whose body had to be contented when we were teens and newlyweds in the sowing. Amaya was a force of nature and remains so to this joyful day.

My oldest will be twenty years old now. I want it to hurt if he's one of the Padres this year, but the truth is I don't feel a thing. He had it coming just like them if so. If my first born is one of the Hermanas, she will have already lived through at least four San Juan's bonfires. She might have been the one who died last year. Or one of the punished ones because they produced malformed children. Each year the number grows. When that starts to happen with the dogs, we tie the bitches outside when they are in heat so the wolves would take them and new blood would save the pack. But the Padres are greedier than dogs here. I have no way of knowing if my oldest is one of the Hermanas that sleeps in our room, or the ones that cook with us. Is she working in the fields? It's no difference.

They are all mine.

And yet none is.

"It takes a village to raise a child, so it was said."

I have always suspected that what was *said* has changed over the course of the years. There is no way to prove it of course, writing is only permitted when it comes to keeping accounts and knowing how much wheat, how many goats, how many seeds... Actually, I seriously doubt that Abuela's Abuela had any opinion about a Hermana slipping a love letter between the clean laundry of another, so I'm sure she couldn't have clearly *said* the punishment for that should be to lose an eye . . . And yet, *así se dijo* was what the Padres chanted like a mantra as they held me on my knees in front of Abuela's knife.

The Spring girls finally come out of the Casa Grande, the big old white building at the center of our community. Although no red color is distinguishable on their black wool robes, what is visible is how the previously dry clothes shine soaked now. Those poor kids can't really properly clean a chicken yet, how are they supposed to do a good job with an old fat goat? Whatever. *So it was said, so you have just been butchered, Abuela.* I wonder if they managed to take the heart out. Maybe Amaya will be having liver tomorrow instead. The thought makes me chuckle. Some of the girls have tiny blood flowers on their cheeks and others have puffy crying eyes. The smallest one, who carries the urn with the heart, has vomit stained shoes. Her hands tremble so much that the clay urn sings against her rings. *You thought it was going to be a fun ceremony when you walked in, didn't you?*

I carry the basket with fabes de mayo in. Amaya is still asleep. I've seen the years change her body. The pregnancies, the breastfeeding, the passing of time. She's still the same girl whose smile I fell head over heels for. I slither inside the bed next to her, she turns around and embraces me. Her skin is warm and she smells like sweat and poppy tea. Her heart beats peacefully. She kisses my forehead. I untie her gown and caress her breasts that have nurtured so many eager mouths.

"Out with the old," she murmurs.

"In with the new," I reply while my fingers search for her warm sex under the sheets.

I shiver under Amelia's touch. She's always known how to drive me wild, or soothe my nerves. Her body and mine beat in sync.

"Bathing the new Abuela is the privilege of the Spring girls, not Autumn barren ones," Padre Bartolomé said with a disgusted grin when we left our Hermanas' house with everything ready for my purifying bath before tonight's ceremony.

"I pulled this one out of death myself just so she could serve me until the day I die, so I say now," I replied, feeling my new status fitting me like a glob.

He swallowed his words and let us on our way. Amelia pressed her lips together trying to suppress a laugh, but she let it roam free once we got to the springs.

Naked in the cold water, letting the sun warm our shoulders, we make love as Hermanas for the last time. Amelia tastes of figs and pepper. She's sweet and spicy. Tender under my touch, fierce as a wolf when it comes to defending her cubs. All our cubs. Our future. We sit together as she braids my hair with the ceremony flowers.

"Are you afraid?" Amelia asks.

"I'm more excited than afraid, I feel like I've been waiting for tonight ever since she told me I would be her heir…" I lick the scars on my lips. "Tonight will be fun, don't you think? Just be careful out there and be back on time."

"Don't worry, *Abuela*, I have it all under control," she replies before kissing me.

The whole town gathers around the bonfire waiting for me to light the fire, to start San Juan's festival. The children are asleep in their beds—or spying from the windows as we used to do. The Spring girls put the red wool robe over my naked body. They draw two red stripes of lamb blood from my eyes to my chin. Blood tears for the old-world fire will devour tonight. One of them places a white clay bowl full of the same blood in front of me. I dip my feet, then my hands. It's cold. Sticky already. Its rotten stink will cling to my skin for days. I got a glimpse of myself in the mirrors of Casa Grande's Hall. I've truly become a Goddess. Beautiful but terrible, yet fair.

The Spring girls open the doors. The dim light of the dusk fills the hall. I close my eyes, and breathe in the last seconds of my old self. Once I move, there would be no turning back. My blood-stained footprints in the white cloth leading to the bonfire will be the first signs of the new dawn. I would trust Amelia with my life. I've entrusted her with our future. It all begins with this first step.

I walk out, and the Hermanas in black robes start their singing the Danza Prima accompanied by their bodhrans and tambourines. The Padres and the Madres, in white ceremonial dresses, holding each other by their pinky fingers, start dancing in a circle around the unburned bonfire. They'll go round and round and round. Faster and faster, following the Hermanas' rhythm until the song ends and they are dizzy as drunk. Their feet hurting and blood stained from stepping barefoot and carelessly on the floor while dancing.

I walk towards them. When the song ends, I break the circle and cross to the beacon. The Spring girls bring me a torch. My heart races. Not even the nocturnal birds and insects dare break the silence. I look around and there she is. As promised. Amelia is dressed in the weird clothes of the city people leaning towards the Casa Grande's wall. I could laugh at how ridiculous she looks with trousers and a black t-shirt. Red lips and eyelids as black as if she had rubbed coal on them. But the truth is she looks tantalizing and dreadful, just as I do now. She's been our siren's song. There are some men with her, I can't count how many but I'm sure they will do. We only need a handful. Hiding themselves poorly behind their outside world recording devices, still no one notices them. The festival has them bewitched already. Amelia nods and I throw the torch in. Heat strikes me immediately. The field turns golden. I walk towards the Abuela throne, a high wooden squared chair, from where I'm supposed to contemplate the sowing.

The Madres look at me. The fire reflects on their eyes as they wait for my signal. I clap and they all cover their faces with the ceremony clothes, as usual before letting their robes fall to the floor. They would stay put, waiting for the night to fall over their bodies, waiting for the touch of many hands. They would. If this was any other San Juan. Not this one.

The Padres strip off their robes too. Some already proudly show their erections and a couple of the younger ones can't resist their urges and start masturbating in the heat of the fire. There are still a few minutes to go before the sun has completely set, but they are already lost in their lust. Focused on the Madres. Distracted. Vulnerable.

The Hermanas take their places behind the Padres. They are supposed to be mere witnesses. Silent caryatides holding together the remains of the old-world, strong cold stones to build the new one upon. But tonight, I have turned them into something else. Something entirely different far more useful. Today, I have put sickles in their hands, hope in their hearts.

I have turned them into reapers.

"Tonight we do not sow children, tonight we sow blood, and we shall reap freedom. And future."

I yell the call of our people to the blackened summer sky until there's no air left in my lungs. The Hermanas slit the throats of the Padres. Not a single one of them fails or shows any doubts. It had to be done. Taken by surprise, the Padres never stood a chance. Their moans and labored breaths don't last long. Blood covers the circle around the bonfire. The Madres take their blindfolds off and dip them in the blood. They show the different stains proudly. These clothes will adorn their houses now, and be honored symbols of their new lineage.

So I have said.

Amelia was right. The filming crew hasn't batted an eye at the reaping of our Padres. They haven't even uttered a word. *Yes, Sis, good job, they will do.* The Spring girls bring me the urn with Abuela's heart covered with honey. They have done a truly lousy job taking it out. It's all cut wrong and torn. But it's ok, I don't intend to eat the damned thing. I never did.

"Tonight, a new world is struggling to be born," I scream, holding the heart in my hands over my head for all to see. "Only because the old one refuses to die. Tonight, we burnt the old to let in the new." I walk down the chair towards the fire. I make sure I step on the corpses of the Padres. They are still warm and some are twitchy. Without a word, I throw the late Abuela's heart into the flames. The Madres and the Hermanas cheer on me as I do so. It's done.

Half of it.

We all turn now to the strangers foolish enough to follow Amelia to us. The ones frozen both by fear and excitement. *We have put on a good show for them, haven't we, Sis?* Amelia was the perfect bait. Vulnerable, scarred. She's always been the best faking tears. The survivor of a cult willing to expose our practices to the outside world. Willing to give those strangers the opportunity of a lifetime. But it's them who are going to be our opportunity. Our new blood. Our future. At least, until we make sure our Madres' are with child.

Then, we'll enrich our crops with their flesh too.

So I have said.

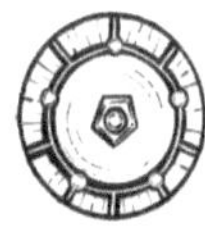

After Image

~ H. L. Fullerton

I'm staring at a photo of B— when I first notice the floater. I mistake it for a smudge on the photograph and let out a cry of dismay. Then I realize there is something wrong with my right eye.

Thank god it's not B—'s picture. I have so few. Only the two I nicked from the impromptu shrine at Cavali's and the blurry one on my camera phone. I blink rapidly—flutter, flutter, flutter—and my vision clears. But of course, I don't realize this is a haunting until later.

I met B— while we were both working at Cavali's—me at my laptop, him as a barista. Working from home sounds grand, but spending all your time within the same four walls gets claustrophobic. You hunger for contact with the outside world so I lugged my laptop from coffee shop to sandwich bar, any eatery equipped with Wi-Fi that didn't mind me hogging a table for hours on end. Instead of calling myself a telecommuter, I dubbed myself a laptop nomad. I stopped roaming once my eyes landed on B—. Cavali's became my oasis and I spent less time staring at my screen and more time glancing at my desert prince.

There's something so electric about the young, as if all their pent up life radiates their tight, smooth pores. I never noticed it when I was that age, but now I am drawn to twenty-somethings in a way I can't explain. The older I get, the more attractive, the more alive, they become. And B—, well, in his black apron over white shirt and dark jeans, he captivated me. His deep set Valentino eyes, green, crinkled when he smiled, which was often, and he had dark mussed hair that cascaded across his forehead. To hide his widow's peak, he once told me, because his mother believed it to be bad fortune. I've heard she blames it for his early death.

I never stalked B—, never once followed him home from Cavali's. But from ten till three I surreptitiously feasted on him whenever he was in sight. My greedy eyes traced the fall of his hair, the almost delicate curve of his ear, the angle of his jaw, the nonchalant way he'd relax against the counter. I thought my staring harmless and even when he fell ill, I didn't stop. Just noted the sallowness of his skin, the bleary eyes and the change in his step; switched to fantasies where I nursed him back to health.

One morning when he brought me a refill without me signaling for it—one of the many reasons I adored him—I ventured, "You don't look so hot. Late night?"

He smiled. "I wish. No, I think I'm coming down with something. I just feel off, you know? Like something's missing." His hand tapped his chest, then fell to his side. I suggested a B-12 shot, wished him well and sipped my coffee. Closing my eyes, I replayed the scene on my eyelids, rewrote some of the dialogue, and let myself be carried away by the aroma of Cavali's dark roast and the memory of his slurry-sounding voice.

No one is sure how he died. Rumors say his doctors are still puzzled over the whole thing. But I have a theory. I think . . . I think it was me and that is why the floaters happened. In my defense, I didn't know what I was doing. My mother always said it wasn't polite to stare, but she never told me it was dangerous.

I'd never even heard of floaters until my vision started periodically blurring. Fuzzy dots blotted out letters on my computer screen, hid numbers and caused me to rub, rub, rub my eyes until the dots disappeared. Then the headaches began. I blamed computer fatigue, grief, the dim lighting of Cavali's and relocated to a brightly lit, chain coffee place. The baristas' green aprons in this new locale were sharp reminders of eyes I once avidly watched and their constant teenage chatter—*he was like* and *I was like* and *that is soooo*—grated my nerves. I found their brew bitter and swore they roasted their beans with napalm. And the floaters still danced in my eyes.

My eyes started playing new tricks on me. Movement in the corner of my eye would signal B—! to my brain and I'd whip my head in that direction only to find no one there. Coming out of the 'customers only' bathroom one day, I caught sight of B— at the end of the short hallway, leaning against the café au lait colored wall. Wearing his black Cavali apron. He was smiling at me.

I stopped, blinked in shock and glanced again. My vision dissolved into floaters. When I reached the end of the hall, I passed a bald, paunchy man whom I couldn't have mistaken for B—. He eyed me with suspicion, I must have stared too hard, and hurried past. I checked my urge to take another gander, forcing my eyes to the table where my coat was slung over a chair back. I never returned to that particular establishment and renewed my round robin of Wi-Fi hot spots.

My troubles persisted. I made an appointment with an eye doctor. I told him about the floaters, the blurred vision, my headaches. I did not mention seeing a dead barista. They ran tests. I have a slight astigmatism, he told me. I might need glasses. No, doctor, I need more than that. Focus is not my problem. There is a dead person flitting in and out of my peripheral vision. Can you do something about that?

I went back to Cavali's last week and saw B— lounging against the counter, one elbow cocked on its top, a smile simmering on his rosy lips. I smiled back before I remembered he was dead and couldn't possibly be standing there. I gave my head a small shake as if to reset my brain. When I looked again he still stood there, same position, same welcoming grin frozen on his face. I blinked and kept blinking, but he didn't disappear. He didn't move either and the smile I so adored turned sinister in its rictus.

Grief, I told myself, *it's just grief.* Spotting a dead loved one is not uncommon. Our minds see what they want to see and here in Cavali's I expect to see B—, therefore I see him. I shouldn't have come back, no matter how horrible the coffee is elsewhere.

I averted my eyes from B—, kept them at half-mast and shuffled in line until I was next. "Can I help you?" the barista said. I made eye-contact and inhaled sharply. The lounging, smiling B— stood before me in vivid color. Unnerved, I dropped my gaze to my hands.

They quaked. "Are you all right?" the voice said and it wasn't B—'s; it had the flat cadence of some mid-west city.

"Yes, yes," I spluttered. "Caramel macchiato, heavy on the cream." I glanced at my server. B—'s insouciant image overlapped him, as if my mind had combined past and present into a double exposure for my eyes to puzzle over. I slammed my eyes shut and, in case B— didn't disappear, averted them while I paid and received my drink. Then I sat at my favorite table, careful not to gaze towards the counter. But B—'s presence crowded me and I left without even checking my email.

I almost wish the floaters would come back. Instead of my vision blurring and clearing, I see the faint outline of B— in that same lounging pose—one elbow akimbo, hair falling into his eyes—superimposed on the sides of buses, etched onto trees, twisting the features of everyone I pass into grotesques. No matter how much I blink, I can't banish him from my sight. In fact, his outline is filling in, becoming more substantial. There is color in his cheeks, I can make out his sweet smile, yet he is still a cardboard cutout of himself. But real, so real that sometimes I think I could reach out and touch him.

This strange double vision causes migraines. I draw curtains, pull shades till my apartment is black and still he colors everything I see—and it's getting worse. Sometimes when I close my eyes, his haloed silhouette is tattooed on my lids.

People tend to think of eyes as cameras, capturing every detail, photographing every moment, snap, snap, snap. Like the optic nerve is a USB cable plugged into your brain, filing away these images for playback or printing at a later date. But that's wrong.

Eyes act more like a television set streaming images. Some are too fast to catch, some linger when you power off, etch-a-sketching the last image until it fades to black.

The wife of a colleague of mine ruined his plasma screen when she paused mid-way through a movie to take a phone call, then forgot she forgot about the movie and went out grocery shopping. By the time he found the paused television, Colin Farrell's face was burned into the screen. He joked, "Some fucker gets the Virgin Mary on a dollar fifty tortilla and I've got the goddamn shroud of Colin Farrell on a eight thousand dollar piece of equipment. Why couldn't she have left it on *The Last Temptation of Christ* instead of *Alexander*."

That after image on electronics? It's called a ghosting.

It's difficult to get anything done when someone constantly interferes with your sight. I squint a lot and people keep telling me to get glasses. I don't think glasses can solve my problem. I do, however, buy a pair of sunglasses and wear them all the time. Now people aren't privy to my eyeball gymnastics as I strain to see where I am going or who I am talking to or what I am looking at.

I keep hoping he'll go away. Go haunt someone else.

But what if he doesn't? What if this isn't my subconscious screwing with me, but something else? I don't think too closely about what that something else might be. But . . .

There are cultures that believe you steal a person's soul when you photograph them. What if my greedy eyes and all their secret staring stole something from B—? He'd said he felt like something was missing and still I ate him up. Staring at a person, day after day, maybe that captures them bit by bit by bit. Maybe that is why we say things like: *the eyes are the windows to the soul* and *out of sight, out of mind* and *seeing is believing* and *what're you lookin' at?* and *Mom! Johnny's staring at me.* Maybe in our collective consciousness we realize that there is a danger in all this eyeballing, that it can go too far and baristas can end up dead and imprinted on our retinas.

Or maybe that's just me.

I watch TV and pretend that B— is burned into its screen inside of my lenses. I know I'm only fooling myself, but I'm okay with that. Unexpected movement makes me sit up on my couch. I didn't turn my head yet B— moved. He appears to be standing straighter, mimicking the actor in the show. I switch off the TV and stare at the white wall across from me so I can be sure of what I'm seeing.

B—'s arms fold across his chest. He turns to face me, full on. "Like what you see?" he asks and I can feel his breath on my ear even though he appears to be six feet away. He throws his head back and laughs.

My heart seizes. My hands clutch at the bottle near my feet. I pour liquor down my throat. *It's the alcohol,* I tell myself. *That's all. You're hallucinating.*

"You're not wasted," B— whispers and his voice slinks down my ear and coils around my cochlea setting off tiny shudders. He takes off his black Cavali apron, leaving him in a white button-down shirt, rolled up to his elbows, and a well-fitting pair of jeans. He undoes a few shirt buttons.

Uh-oh, I think.

"Isn't this what you wanted?" There is menace in his tone.

I shake my head and squeeze my eyes tight, trying to shut him out. He says, "Oh, no. It's too late for that." My eyelids are filled with his green, green eyes, so close, hideously close. Weight presses down on me, as if someone has sat in my lap. I feel myself pushed back into the cushions and struggle to stand, but he's right, it's too late.

Something soft brushes my cheek and I start to sob. "Shhhh," he says. "We'll have plenty of time for crying later. Open your eyes and look at me. The way you used to."

I claw at my eyes.

I am in the supermarket throwing items into my cart. I can't read the labels and B— is refusing to help. I can smell the coffee three aisles over and it nauseates me. B— flicks his finger at me and a stinging sensation burns my mostly good eye. I twitch and curse. Rub the burning eye until the pressure builds as if the whole thing might pop free of my skull. Then my hand is pulled away from my face. B—, who is crystal clear against rows of streaky colors I take for shelves of canned goods, says, "Permanently blinding yourself won't help."

An old woman toddles over to me. I can smell the Jean Nate powder and the urine soaked into her Depends. She is a floating blob behind a smirking B—. "Is there something wrong with your eyes?" She reaches into her voluminous handbag and rummages. "I have drops."

I wave her off, thrust my cart forward. I bump into a display. Packages hit the floor. I'm fine. Everything's fine. There's just a ghost in my eye.

Hand of Glory

~ Roni Stinger

I draw Fred's hand along my body, following the curve of my hipbone, the contour of my belly, tracing the lines of long faded stretch marks with his fingers. My breath hitches, a mix of desire and guilt. I dig my heels into the satin sheets. Lavender essence fills the bedroom with a slight undertone of salt and vinegar. Our love is now forbidden.

He always made me cum first . . . and last. I'd had a few boys before him. They never cared much what I liked. Never taking the time to satisfy me. They took what they wanted and left me to pleasure myself without them. Not that I minded getting myself off, but it wasn't quite the same as sharing it with another.

Fred was different. He enjoyed making me cum. His cock growing so hard as waves of orgasms rushed through my body while he expertly moved his fingers on my clit, slow circles the way I liked, dipping his free fingers into my pussy. God. Just thinking about him made me hot.

His hand is large with thick fingers, calloused from years of labor, but it moves across my body gently. Smooth, thick skin with a touch of dampness lights my nerve endings, leading the way into my pink silk panties. I roll my head back and close my eyes.

He always had a strong work ethic, joining his dad at the lumber mill as soon as he turned eighteen, supporting me and our baby when she arrived right after we both graduated high school. Baby Missy had my dark hair and his blue eyes. His curls and my dimples.

No one thought our marriage would last. We were both so young. Doomed to fail, as parents, as partners. Yet ten years on, our little girl played basketball in the driveway with her dad. He taught her to shoot and dribble. I taught her to bake, garden, and fish.

He and I had our fights. Marriage and parenting weren't easy, but make up sex was the best. We'd find a sitter and steal away, have sex in our car like teenagers.

His hand moves further into my panties, fingers cool, caressing the folds of my labia. My lips moisten in anticipation. I relax into the pillow. His musky tang envelops me.

The other women shocked me, but I tried to understand. I'd had my own temptations but managed to resist. If I were truly honest, I had my own regrets. Times I would have given in had the opportunity arose. Things I wished I'd tried with one or more of my close friends.

It was long ago, and we'd both been so very young. Beneath the surface of any relationship, nothing's as easy as it appears. The many years I tried to understand his secrets and lies were eclipsed by the image of his hands caressing another, working their magic on someone else. That image haunted me through my forgiveness. My stomach grew sick each time I imagined his hands on another. I struggled to push those thoughts away.

I tried not to be selfish. Maybe. there was enough pleasure and love to go around. That's what my polyamorous friends had said. I almost believed, but his hands were mine, meant for only me.

His hand, warmed by the heat of my body, now belongs to only me, working the magic it knows so well. His fingers tease their entrance. Dripping and wanting, I beg and plead. Enter me.

On our twentieth anniversary, Missy went off to college. We were a couple again, instead of just a family. The house echoed with a silence that only my weeping filled. Fred's caresses brought comfort.

We went to restaurants we'd never been. Planned weekend get-aways we'd dreamed of in our youth. We found each other and ourselves again.

I took up painting. Missy's old bedroom became my studio. Fred discovered woodworking. Our garage became his shop. In our bed, I found my voice again. No longer a reason to keep quiet with nobody else in the house. Our moans and my screams filled the rooms as we christened each one with our lovemaking. We were more turned on by each other than we'd ever been, playing new games and buying new toys. Falling deeper in love each day.

I thrust my hips upwards, panting as his fingers enter. They dive deep inside, first one . . . then two . . .then three. Every touch a stroke of erogenous tissue. Almost more than I can take. Almost.

Thirty years after our wedding, we'd beat the odds, made it through the disagreements, the fights, and the transgressions. Fred's hands caressed my arm to ease my nerves, held my waist when I needed comfort.

Missy made us grandparents of a sweet cherubic boy named Danny. He had her dark curly hair and his daddy's smile. Fred played peekaboo and pat-a-cake. Games he'd been too busy for when Missy was a baby.

I baked cookies like any good grandma. I worried so about that little one. What would his future be in this world I barely recognized? Fred's strong hands on my shoulders told me everything would be okay.

When we sent little Danny home, Fred and I made up for lost time together. Our love life had slowed, but his hands hadn't forgotten how to please. He took his time with my pleasure, and I took mine with his.

His hand, inside me. His thumb on my clit. The joints grown stiff but still workable. I guide them to my climax. My moans and screams fill the emptiness of our bedroom.

☉

Fred was working on a new bathroom cabinet for Missy. She took pride in showing her friends the things her dad made.

I painted in my studio, a portrait of Fred and me inspired by a picture taken shortly after we'd met. I'd lost track of time. Fred always came in for a kiss before taking his evening shower. Then I'd clean up my project, and we'd spend the rest of the evening reading or watching old sitcoms we both enjoyed.

When the sun set behind the mountains and my studio dimmed beyond my ability to see, I went to the shop. He should have been in an hour ago.

The roar of the saw greeted me as I opened the door to the garage. At first, I couldn't figure out what I was seeing. Red fabric strewn across the floor. Fred hunched over the saw . . . no. The saw cut through him, still spinning as it protruded from his back. The red wasn't fabric. Blood and flesh flung from Fred's torso and splattered across the floor as he'd collapsed atop the blade. Piles of sawdust and blood indistinguishable from flesh and guts. I'd warned him against using the saw without its guard, but he said he'd be careful.

I stood gaping for what seemed a lifetime, but must have been seconds, before crossing the room and unplugging the saw. But it was much too late. It had been much too late, long before I entered the garage.

Nothing anyone could do, and I knew it. His flesh had gone ivory and scarlet. The blood drying to a crusty brown. I sunk to the concrete floor, cold traveling through my body. I wept for hours before forcing myself to get up and make that call. It was just Fred and me in the garage, adorned with his body parts.

I closed my eyes. It was almost as if nothing had happened, as if we were still happily together. When I opened them, on the floor only a few feet from where I sat, his right hand had fallen free of the mess that had once been my love.

His hand lay palm up, fingers curled like a dead spider's legs, waiting for someone to sweep the critter up. Inching forward, I picked up his hand and cradled it, hugging my love to my chest. The flesh was cool, but still his. The blood congealed at the ragged stump. Not a mar on the rest of the hand.

☉

Holding his hand against my cheek, his fingers open and caress my skin, warm from my hot pussy. I close my eyes and drift.

I washed his hand in the sink and took it to my bedroom, placing it under the covers. Then I made the phone call. The paramedics arrived and called the morgue. The body bag resembled laundry more than something that was once human. No one asked questions, only offered condolences.

Fred came to me that night and whispered in my ear, his hand resting with me beneath the covers, laid on my waist, fingers reaching for the spots that he knew best.

When I close my eyes, he's still here, whispering in my ear. I guide his hand down, his fingers caress my clit, ready for our second round. When we finish, I'll set him back in the jar on the nightstand, preserving our love for another night.

Our years together aren't over yet.

The Mundane Flute

~ Mark Mills

You're probably going to guess that the twist at the end of this story is that Melvin was abducted by the Old Ones because he was a terrible flutist.

That would be wrong.

Well, now that you're forewarned, you might guess that he was abducted because, although he was a serviceable flutist, he was a terrible person.

That's not quite right either. True, Melvin was a terrible person but that had nothing to do with anything. He was abducted by chance, entirely random. None of that "Chosen One" baloney. No destiny, fate, karma, justice, or any of the other meaningless words that we've created to try to wash away the random interactions of meaningless particles which is our existence. Okay, you're right that he was abducted because he played the flute, but it could have been any flutist, in any time or place. Ian Anderson, James Galway, or any other world-renown flutist that you've probably never heard of.

Oh, I may be mistaken—perhaps you do play the flute and know those artists well. In that case, I do hope you keep up with your practice. Otherwise your life has no meaning.

If you would have asked Melvin, he would have told you that, despite his years as a flutist, his life had no meaning, but, like virtually every other opinion he voiced, Melvin didn't have a clue of what he was talking about. He numbered among the few that exist as a balm to the idiot god Azathoth. Among pitiful crawling things that have formed throughout the cosmos, such as mankind and fungi, playing the flute is the only thing that has, does, or will ever matter.

Thus, when the thralls of Nyarlathotep burst into the motel lobby, ripped asunder the registration desk, and dragged Melvin across dimensions, they cared nothing for witnesses. What concern are human eyes or tongues to those that act on behalf of the living nuclear inferno?

Of course, for Melvin, the abduction was more disturbing.

Two or three—no, that's not a vague description: two of the beings repeatedly split and merged back together throughout the ordeal—dropped out of the air while he was upgrading a family of four to a room with two beds. The entities fell from the air, not the ceiling, but from a hole in reality. Slapping on the lobby tile like globs of rancid pudding, one (or two) sent tendrils through Melvin's desk, yanking it to the side. The other creature, a living clot of blood and lidless eyes, shot out a telescopic mouth and sank its teeth into Melvin's torso.

Working with the public had been no joy, but this was somewhat worse.

Melvin, soft and pudgy, put up a token thrashing in resistance before another hole in space opened about a foot above the floor. The unworldly beings leapt through it, dragging Melvin into a direction that was somehow both up and down at once.

Time had no meaning in the dimension that the creatures carried him, but it lasted forever nonetheless. Dumping Melvin in a patch of tangible smoke, they vanished, leaving only a few needle-like teeth in his shoulder.

Slack-jawed and dazed, Melvin looked around. It was space but not the space portrayed in any movie. He was sprawled in a cloud—well, that was how the movies depicted Heaven, but Melvin's clouds were black and full of razor-sharp whirling shards. This was a Heaven in serious need of an OSHA investigation.

Above or below—he couldn't tell if he was looking up or down—the sky or abyss was full of a dark star, a writhing mass of nuclear reactions, mostly the purple of a dank bruise but lined with bright, crimson scars. The comatose star had no eyes, and yet was a huge eye. It was dreaming, but sensed Melvin in its sleep. It began to babble, murmuring guttural obscenities in a language Melvin never knew he knew.

The movies lied. They said: in space, no one can hear you scream.

They were so very wrong.

"Hey, knock it off! Believe me, you don't want to wake the dead." A pale man with hollow eyes slapped Melvin across the face.

Melvin went silent mid-scream.

"You play the flute, right?" The pale man twitched as if he were allergic to the smoke around him. "You must or you wouldn't be here. Don't make any noise except music. Not unless you want that"—he jerked his chin towards the fleshy star—"to wake up."

This was far too much to take in at once—Melvin's mind was unhinged and on the brink of shattering. Fortunately, that was a common state for him.

"What is it?" he managed to croak.

"Azathoth. The creator." The pale man pointed a finger that was far too long to be human. "He made universe through his dreams. Without caring, or even being aware of us, his mind maintains all that is. We've got to keep him dreaming or it all fades away."

"What?"

"What do you mean by 'what'?"

"I mean 'What fades away?'"

"Everything. You. Me. The entire universe." The pale man's voice began to wheeze, as if unused to extended speech. "Now, shut up and start playing."

Melvin was about to protest that he didn't have his flute, but the floating shards in the smoke congealed around his hand into a perfect replica of his own instrument.

"Hurry!" The pale man stared at the dreaming god. "He's starting to stir. Play!"

Melvin didn't want to play, but he didn't want to argue either. He didn't want this Azathoth monstrosity to wake up most of all. So he lifted the faux-flute to his lips and gave it a try. It wasn't like his own flute at all—it was much better. Once he was playing, he could hear weird tunes piping all around him, melodies from alien worlds in frequencies immeasurable to man. He ignored them and played his own song, one that he'd been working on for years, about the girls in high school who had jeered at him.

It wasn't a lullaby, but Azathoth stopped his squirming, letting out a contented purr.

Melvin played his song over and over. He craved neither nourishment nor sleep. He did not, as he so often hoped, slip into a stupor, playing without thought. No, he was aware of every second, and he realized why Azathoth's guardians needed to recruit new players. After months of constant music, he heard one of the alien melodies begin to waver and then end, followed by a burst of alien bleating.

The nuclear monstrosity began to pulse and shudder; Melvin played on, ready to blink out of existence. The abhuman chittering intensified, and Melvin saw far in the distance—farther than a human eye had any right to see—a many-armed yellow beast still clutching a jade-green flute flung from the cloud, falling into the burning corona surrounding Azathoth. A final shriek, and then it burst into flames and was gone, long before it reached the mad star's surface.

Azathoth moaned. and all music devolved into cacophony. It wasn't the playing—no, Melvin, felt the notes from his flute shudder in unison with Azathoth—the universe was moving in phase with the burning void of madness.

On a cosmic scale, this was the equivalent of a child shaking his head and muttering, "No yet, Ma. Five minutes more."

All was lost. The nuclear idiot was awakening.

Then a new piping, a new musician. Melvin continued his own melody, blending it with the new song. The guardians must have abducted a new flutist, from Earth or elsewhere. It was enough. Azathoth quieted and resumed his dream.

Melvin never remembered his dreams so the loss of sleep was hardly noticed. His waking dreams had never truly gelled either. He had never aspired to become a professional musician, at least not with the flute. He only joined his high school band because his mother forced him. He hadn't practiced or even touched his old flute since May when he'd graduated high school.

He ought to play better with this one, but he wasn't. The new cloud-born flute felt like a professional model; he supposed that after tearing holes in the universe, crafting a high-end instrument wasn't much of a challenge. Yet for all its quality, Melvin bleeped and squealed as he shifted notes. The months since graduation had stripped away whatever talent he ever had.

Yet now he wanted to perfect his song. He wanted to make those girls who had mocked him cry from its sadness. He kept playing in the timeless cloud that ringed the burning idiot god. Other musicians went mad and were cast upon Azathoth's flames, but Melvin never wavered.

Was it months? Years? Centuries? No discernible changes marked the passage of time, but he knew he was getting better. His notes were strong, and his song grew until his own heart ached. He was building the sound of sorrow, but something was missing. He was so close.

So intense was Melvin's concentration that he didn't notice when the first musician collapsed to madness. The guardians rushed to replace him but then went another. And another. And another.

Azathoth's caretakers poked reality into a sieve, but they could not replace flutists quickly enough. The nuclear idiot began to mumble obscenities of quarks and gamma rays. The fabric of the universe was frayed enough that it no longer supported the very concept of music. All sound was a gibbering din—the voice of Azathoth. Soon nothing but the idiot god would remain.

"Knock it off!" Melvin's scream cut through the dying reality and stabbed Azathoth through its billions of eyes. "Knock it off! I'm coming to a break-through."

The guardians gaped as the star-sized mass of madness calmed and went still, back to its dreams of depravity and rot. Melvin's song trilled through the ether, perhaps not perfect, but so very close.

The guardians hurried to find more flutists and pipers, restoring the symphony of the cloud. It was as close to order as a universe built on disorder could be.

Some may find the twist to Melvin's story to be unbelievable. These individuals are clearly not musicians.

From the Notebook of Gregorey,
Keeper of Village Elders Meeting Minutes

~ Michelle Knudsen

Friday

Four more headless calves were born this week. After extensive arguing among the village elders and several attempts to interpret the intertwining slug trails in Jonnis's garden, we have determined that the new arrival to our village is a secret sorceress and must be dealt with immediately. Some of us were excited (perhaps too excited, in certain cases, though I will not name names) to unearth the Old Books from their dusty cabinet for the first time in anyone's memory. We spent the afternoon flipping carefully though their pages, looking for guidance.

Friday (later)

It is worse than we thought. We went as a group (Edmund, Jonnis, Old Knickenbocker, Percival the Younger, Tall Steven, and myself) to confront the young woman, who greeted us at her door wearing a blue dress and a bright smile. "Confess, Magic-User!" we demanded, nearly in unison, as the Old Books suggested, but she refused, insisting she was only a simple seamstress and also that her name was Melanie. She offered us sweet tea but we were too wise to be taken in by her tricks. We demanded her confession several more times, with ever-increasing volume, but she would not be moved. Eventually we didn't know what else to do, so we all went home. In our defense, it should be noted that none of us have actual field experience dealing with sorceresses, and the Old Books' entries on the matter were rather limited.

Tuesday

We debated over the long weekend and finally agreed on the next course of action. Tall Steven was sent to fetch the woman, and the entire village population congregated in the market square. Edmund addressed her as head elder. "Once again, we accuse you of being a sorceress! What say you, stranger to our village?"

The woman once more denied the charges. "My name is Melanie, and I am a seamstress, not a sorceress. If anyone is need of mending or hemming or the like, please come visit me at my home by the river! I offer fair prices and free adjustments if you're not satisfied with the initial work."

There was some interested murmuring from the crowd, until Old Knickenbocker cried out, "Enough! Let her say so while she holds the truth stick!"

Silence fell as Percival the Younger approached the woman with the truth stick. She took it in her hands, looking somewhat bemused, and began to repeat, "Fair prices—"

"No, no," Percy whispered. "The part about being a sorceress!"

"I am not a sorceress," she said.

The silence stretched out. "Behold," Old Knickenbocker said at last, his voice wavering with awe. "She must be a powerful sorceress indeed, to overcome the binding of the truth stick!"

The woman rolled her eyes, handed the truth stick back to Percy, and left the square.

"You cannot fool us!" Old Knickenbocker shouted after her, but she did not turn around.

Tuesday (a different one)

It has been a full month, and we have decided that all we can do is try to avoid antagonizing the sorceress. No more headless calves have been born, so either she has chosen to be merciful or the farm doctor was right about staying away from the sketchy-looking feed-grass by that recently discovered cave in the dark forest. Several villagers have been to see Melanie regarding mending and sewing, purely in hopes of staying on her good side. To be fair, her work has been impressive (no doubt she uses magic needles and similar sorceress tricks).

Friday

No updates on the sorceress (except that someone finally tried her sweet tea, and there were no untoward effects, so now we all drink it when we stop by; it's quite delicious) but that cave in the dark forest seems to be getting bigger? Edmund has sent Percival the Younger and Tall Steven to investigate and report back.

Saturday

Percy and Steve never came back last night. Can't write more; must help search.

Saturday (later)

We found them, but they are in rough shape. Percy still hasn't said a word; he only shakes and trembles and huddles in his infirmary bed. Tall Steven is missing two-thirds of his left arm. He cannot recall how it happened. The wound, in some small gift of grace, is perfectly cauterized, so he did not die from loss of blood. He remembers approaching the cave, which did indeed look bigger than the last time he'd seen it, and stepping into the darkness. Then there are only flashes: a sudden numbing coldness, seven floating shapes that he insists were the heads of all those poor headless calves, a pair of glowing crimson eyes.

Jonnis has gone to fetch the sorceress.

Saturday (later still)

She refuses to help us. Even now, she holds to her seamstress story and claims she has no magic to fight whatever is living in that cave. She did come to visit the infirmary with some sweet tea and two beautifully knitted blue blankets, and her presence had a calming effect on Percy. He has stopped shaking and was even able to sit up a little to drink the tea. The rest of us are furious, however. We have granted her every courtesy and haven't persecuted her or *anything* and now in our hour of need she turns her back. I may never wear those pants she hemmed for me ever again.

Sunday

Old Knickenbocker wants to offer the sorceress as a sacrifice to the cave-creature in hopes of placating it. I am uneasy about this idea, to say the least, and Percy (who is much better today) flat-out refuses to allow it, so there is little chance Old Knick will get the unanimous vote required for such an act. We must do something, though. Several other villagers have now seen glimpses of the floating shapes at the edges of the forest, and it seems pretty clear that this can't mean anything good.

Sunday night or maybe early Monday

I cannot sleep. My mind is full of visions of disembodied calf heads and eyes the color of blood. I walked down to the river, partly to try to clear my head and partly because I had half-formed notions of pounding on Melanie's door until she awoke and then threatening or maybe begging until she agreed to come to our aid. When I neared her home, however, I saw that there would be no need to wake her. I could see her through the window in the soft glow of candle-lamps. She was seated at her kitchen table, her head bowed, her hands covering her face. She may have been praying, or pondering, or crying. I could not bring myself to disturb her.

Monday

Percy burst in to the morning meeting just as we were about to begin without him, shouting that Melanie was gone. We followed him to her house, where we found only a pile of completed sewing projects and several pitchers of sweet tea. We looked at one another, then slowly turned toward the forest. Percy took off at a run, and the rest of us followed him again. Several other villagers saw us and followed in turn.

When we reached the cave, we found the seven calf heads neatly arranged in a half circle on the ground, each impaled with a knitting needle that pinned it to the earth. Visible just inside the cave mouth was the head of a monstrous creature, the like of which I have never seen nor imagined, its gray, barklike skin pierced by what seemed a thousand tiny needles. Its eyes were sewn shut with bright blue thread, and sticky black blood trailed from its misshapen ears and pooled around its head on the cave floor.

Just beside the dead monster, a single sewing needle hovered shakily, point down. As we watched, it dipped its point in the pool of blood and then scratched pen-like across the ground, tracing the word *farewell*. Percy fell to his knees with a moan. I placed a hand on his shoulder, trying to contain my own confused emotions. She had saved us after all, been sacrificed after all, been a sorceress after all, and a seamstress too. I suspect the first and last of those were all she'd ever really wanted.

Tuesday

We renamed the dark forest after her, by unanimous vote. It's full of flowers now. All of them are blue.

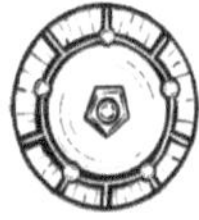

The Clockwise People

~ Christopher Hawkins

He was looking at her hair, the way the little strands of gray caught the noonday sun to shine like ribbons of diamond, when she turned to him, smiling, and said, "Do you think that birds understand each other when they talk?"

"Birds don't talk, dear."

He scratched at his own thinning hair, the high sun hot on his scalp. "Of course they do. It's still talking, even if we don't know the words."

There were little crinkles in the upturned corners of her mouth, and her eyes were dancing. How long had it been since he had seen her eyes like that, lit from within as if every good thought had been born there? As if grief had never had a chance to touch them? "Then I suppose," he said, "they'd have to understand each other. Or else there'd be no point in talking at all."

"Well, yes. But no." She turned away from him, darkening, and just like that the moment was gone. "I mean, a goose can talk to a goose well enough. That makes perfect sense. But what if a goose is honking at a sparrow and trying to tell it something? Does the sparrow know what the goose is saying? Or is it all just a bunch of silly goose noises?"

He thought about this as their feet crunched along the gravel path. Clouds of insects swarmed in the tall grass at the shore of the little pond as starlings darted into their midst. In the distance, out past a stand of dead trees, a hawk was circling in search of a mouse.

"Well, yeah," he said, believing it more with every word. "I suppose they'd just about have to. If a fox was creeping up on their nest, they'd have to be able to warn each other, wouldn't they? It wouldn't matter if they were blackbirds, or starlings, or even seagulls. They may sound different, but they'd get the meaning all the same."

"I don't think they do," she said, shaking her head. "All those bird-calls. All that music everywhere, all those songs overlapping. If the meaning was the same it would all sound the same."

He kicked at a rock, swinging his foot out of its way to do it. "No point in music at all if it all sounds the same," he said.

"I think I'd like it better if it were all the same." Her head was turned away from him, her voice distant, as if she were talking to someone away on the other side of the pond. "I think the world would make a lot more sense that way, don't you?"

He didn't have an answer for that, certainly not one that would satisfy her, so he kept his eyes on the path ahead. They'd be leaving the pond behind soon, winding into a stand of trees and on into the wetlands beyond. The grasshoppers would be thick there, he knew, making their bumbling leaps from cattail to sunflower and back again. It would be peaceful, the white-noise drone of their buzzings loud enough to drown away even his darkest imaginings.

"They say that birds are like guides. That they lead the souls of the dead into the next world." Her eyes were dancing again. Even beneath the shadows of the tall trees they caught the sunlight, and it made his heart lift a little. He wanted to believe what she said was true, even though he couldn't, and he knew that he could never tell her so.

"It's a lovely thought," he said.

She nodded, and said nothing more, as if she knew better than to push the point upon him. She breathed deep and inhaled the scents of the path, wildflowers and lavender, low moss and high leaves. The wind blew them against her cheeks and she turned her face against it to take their full measure.

After they had gone on a bit, he said, "I wonder if we'll see our friends again today."

"Which friends are those?"

"You know," he said. "That couple, with the little dog? Seems like every time we come out for a walk we end up seeing them sooner or later. In fact, I'm a little surprised we haven't run into them already."

"Oh, I remember now," she said, though there was something in her faraway look that made him think that she didn't. "The couple. With the little dog."

"We must be on the same schedule. Sometimes we see them in the woods, sometimes back in the park. Like they have the same route, but just walk the opposite way."

A bird fluttered down from the tall grass. It looked back at them and bounded on up the path, not taking wing but bouncing along on its little feet, putting distance between them. When it paused to look back again and saw them still coming, it hopped further away. He watched the thing, and wondered why it didn't fly.

"Oh, yes!" she said, loud enough to make him jump. "The little dog. I remember it now because it reminded me of our little Skipper. Doesn't it just remind you of Skipper, the way it's always nosing in the grass, pulling so hard on the leash that its little front paws come up off the ground?"

Birds used to be dinosaurs. He'd read that somewhere. They'd been enormous once, so big you had to crane your neck to look up at their bones in museums. Those giants were gone now. What was left pecked along in the gravel and forgot they had wings. Everything passed into something else if you let it go for long enough.

"Why are you looking at me like that?"

He'd been staring again, but in the shade of the trees her hair had lost its luster, and the lines around her eyes seemed full of dark portents.

"I dunno," he said. "Just thinking."

"You look so sad when you think."

It was talking about the leash that had done it. He could still hear the hollow tink the collar had made as it snapped free of Skipper's neck, could still see the dog's joy, the way its tongue lolled out of its mouth as it ran toward the street. He could still see Ethan rising from the grass to give chase, could still hear the naked fear in his wife's voice as she cried out for him to stop. He could hear the squeal of tires, and see the play of sunlight on the car's hood as it rocked to a stop. It had been pure chance that Ethan stumbled in the grass, that little half-step that had kept him from catching up to the little dog. Less than a second, but it had kept the boy from going under the tires. They'd sat at the curb and held him while he called out Skipper's name, but in that moment they'd barely noticed that the dog was gone.

"You blame me, don't you?" she said.

"Blame you for what?" he said.

"For all of it."

They walked together in silence for a while, the little bird hopping out in front of them, looking back at them as if it couldn't understand why they were on the path at all. At last it remembered its wings and flew away, peeping out a warning to the other birds about these two lumbering creatures that had no business in its territory. She watched it go, and kept her eyes on the space in the tall grass that it disappeared through, even after it was long out of sight.

"I couldn't have known," she said. "Not when it started. No one could have."

Little stones and bits of bark scattered at his feet, his footsteps suddenly heavy.

"You remember how it was. Nobody knew anything about it, not for sure, anyway. One week they said it was just like the flu and the next they said it wasn't. Then they said you didn't need masks, until they said you did, and even then it got all political and everyone was shouting over each other until you just wanted to put your hands over your ears, there was so much of it."

He listened to the distant peeping of the birds, their sounds measured and mechanical, like the beeping of hospital machines. He listened to the sounds of their footsteps, shushing softly, like the hiss of a respirator.

"But I did everything right," she said, "or at least I did everything that I knew how to do right. I cleaned all the time. I made him wash his hands. I was careful. I tried to make sure he was careful, too, but it just . . ."

The wind through the trees like the pulling of a hospital curtain. The drone of cicadas like a flatlined EKG.

"None of it mattered. Not one thing." She stopped walking and he turned back to look at her. The sun in his eyes made him squint.

"I did everything I knew how to do and it happened anyway. Sometimes bad things just happen like that. It doesn't make it my fault."

"Maybe," he said.

She folded her arms. With the sun at her back filtering through the trees, the glow was back in her hair. She seemed lit from within, all grief and fire and rage, and seeing her like that broke his heart.

"Maybe? What do you mean, maybe?"

"I mean," he said, "that maybe there was something you could have done, something I could have done, if we had just known what it was."

"No . . ."

"I mean, what if there was some choice we made, some minor little thing that we did without realizing, and if we hadn't made that choice—that thoughtless, insignificant choice—then it never would have happened the way it did."

"Stop."

"Like, what if there was a way that he'd never gotten sick at all? If I'd just taken a little longer eating breakfast one day, or made him go back upstairs to change his shirt when he was wearing long sleeves like he always did, even when it was too hot outside. Or if we'd taken the other way around on our walk one day, or if he'd sat in a different seat on the school bus."

"Stop it," she said. "I don't want to hear this."

"Or if I'd run that yellow light on the way to the hospital and we'd gotten him there two minutes sooner. It's like the day Skipper got hit by that car. If the boy hadn't tripped, the car would have hit him too. But what made him trip? Were his pants too long? Were his shoes tied too tight? Were they not tight enough?"

"I said stop it!"

"Or was it just a low spot in the ground? Like maybe someone was playing football and fell down on that exact spot and made a little divot there, not so much as you'd notice, but just enough to make it so the boy would fall down right there, a week, maybe even a month or a year later. Just one little change like that, just one, and he'd still be here, walking right down this path with us, right now."

"Stop saying it! You can't think things like that. You just can't!" She was doubled over now, her hands pressed against her ears as if she could will his words away. But he'd said them, now, after thinking them a thousand times, and there was no taking them back. He wanted to go to her, to take her in his arms and hold her close, even if it meant that she would only pound her fists against his chest and shove him away. He'd done nothing wrong, and yet he knew that it was no less than he deserved.

"I just miss him, is all," he said at last.

She raised her head to him. Her eyes were dry and there was a hardness in them now that he'd only seen there once before. It was as if a bright light had gone out of the world, and he feared it would never return.

"You can't say things like that," she said. "When you say things like that it's like he's dying all over again."

"I know."

"You can't say things like that."

"I know."

They continued up the path, out of the wetlands and toward the darkening shade of the trees. She kept a half step behind him, as if she was not quite ready to walk by his side. He kept his eyes on the path ahead, on the distant point where it curved, disappearing among the trees.

"I think you're right about the birds," he said.

"About the way they talk?"

He shook his head. "About the souls of the dead. It makes me feel like he's safe. Like there's this whole other world where he's not gone, but just . . . waiting."

She wrapped her arm around his and squeezed reassuringly. He felt his mood lift a little, and resolved to say nothing more about it, to finish their walk in silence if that's what it took not to upset her again. He wished that he could stop thinking about it too, but his mind would not lay still. It coiled like a snake, twisting in on itself until he no longer knew where one thought began and the other ended.

In the end, it was her mouth, not his, that gave them voice.

"I wonder if there really is another world," she said, tightening around his arm, pulling him close. "If there are then maybe he's happy now, wherever he went off to. Maybe it's even the same place that Skipper went to, and the two of them are playing together right now."

He said nothing. He just stared out at the curve in the path, hoping that would be the end of it, that some new thought would come along to distract her. But her grip on him was getting tighter, and he knew then that she would not let it go.

"And what if there's more than one? I mean, isn't that what the scientists say? That every choice makes a whole new universe? A whole new reality branching off from the old one every time someone makes even the smallest choice?"

Above their heads, a blackbird lighted on a branch, bending it beneath its weight. A refugee from the asteroid. One more survivor of extinction.

"Or the smallest mistake."

This last she said softly, almost at a whisper. He craned his neck upward, watching the bird, hoping that she would notice the motion and begin to watch it too, that it would distract her from these thoughts, this folly, that they could finish their walk and say no more of it.

"Because if," she said. "If all those other worlds are out there, then there would have to be one where he never died at all. Maybe more than one."

"You're right," he said. "We shouldn't think about such things."

"How many of those worlds do you think there are? Dozens? Hundreds? Where you ran that red light? Where he took another seat on the bus? Where we went around the path the opposite way?"

No, he thought. *Don't do this.*

"Maybe there are more worlds where he didn't die than there are where he did. Maybe all those worlds are the *right* worlds, and living is exactly what he was supposed to do? What if all the worlds where he died are the wrong worlds, and they were never supposed to have been made in the first place?"

He felt her grip tighten and knew that she had arrived at the same place he had, that those darkest thoughts that he had failed to keep hidden had finally infected her own. He felt the press of her nails against his skin and wished in that moment that he could pull away.

She inhaled sharply, barely daring to speak. "What if this is the only one?"

Around them, insects buzzed as birds hopped and chirped in the treetops. A sharp pop sounded near the ground, some small creature in the underbrush. Still he kept his eyes on the path, on that distant bend that was straightening now, threatening to reveal more of the way ahead.

"We should have seen them by now," he said.

"Who?"

"Those others," he said. "The ones who always end up walking towards us."

"Oh, the ones with the little dog."

He nodded. "I thought we would have seen them by now."

She stopped then, holding onto his arm so tightly that he had no choice but to stop with her. Together they stood, still as statues, listening to the sounds of the forest ahead, of the reedy pond behind.

"We should go back," she said.

The air around them was still, but in the treetops it blew hard and set the branches clacking against each other.

"We're fine," he said, and as it left his mouth it sounded almost like a question.

She shook her head. "Something's not right. Can you feel it? I know you can feel it."

He *could* feel it. He felt it down to his bones, but all it did was make him that much more anxious to move on, to see what lay around the bend in the path. "It'll take longer to get home than if we keep going forward."

"I don't care," she said. "I want to go back."

"Nonsense," he said. "All that talk has got you spooked, is all. You'll feel better once we're out of these trees."

"I'll feel better when we turn around." Her nails in his arms were talons now, about to draw blood. "Why can't we just turn around?"

Her eyes were wide now, shining. He wanted to do as she asked, but could not. He tried to make his legs move to turn around, but they wouldn't budge.

"I see the way you keep looking up the path," she said. "You're looking for them, aren't you?"

"Looking for who?"

"Those people! The ones with the little dog."

Once more he searched ahead into the distance. The path was empty, the air silent, and from somewhere deep within himself he felt a sharp pang of despair.

"You're so anxious to see them again, but do you even remember what they look like?" She let go of his arm, folded her own across her chest. "Go on. Describe them to me. Describe them and I'll keep walking down this path. I won't turn around. I won't even look back. Just describe them to me."

He opened his mouth to speak but no words came out. There was nothing in his thoughts to form them. No memory. Just a blank space. Empty silhouettes against a field of brown and green.

"How old are they? Is her hair long or short? Is he handsome? Ugly? Do you remember anything about them? Anything at all?"

"Well, the dog is small, like Skipper," he said at last, though he was no longer sure of even that. The wind reached down from the treetops and sent a scatter of dead leaves across the path. All of a sudden, turning back felt like a good idea, the right idea, if only he could will his body to do it.

"I don't remember them either," she said softly. "I know they were there. We must have passed them a dozen times, maybe even a hundred, but I can't picture their faces. After all those times I should be able to picture their faces."

"They . . ." The words were slow to come, his mind stuck in molasses. "They had a kid with them." Again the words came out like a question, but as he strained to picture those walking silhouettes he could just about make out a small child walking with them, walking hand in hand. Was it true? Or was it just his own wishful thinking?

"Why can't I picture their faces?"

She stared at him, her mouth trembling, her eyes pleading. Had there been a child with them? Had he remembered that right? And if they were to meet again, would the man be balding like he was? The same height? The same weight? And would the woman be walking quickly with the sun shining in her eyes as the little dog pulled her along by his leash? What then? What would they do if these people passed right by them, close enough to touch?

"You're right," he said. "We have to go back."

He tugged at her arm, but she would not turn around. Her head was turned and she would not look at him. She stared up the path, and inhaled with a gasp.

"There they are!"

He followed her gaze to the distant bend in the path. They were moving there between the trees, too far away to make out their features. Two figures, walking unhurried, taking their time as if time were never a concern. The little dog led them, rebellious and wild at the end of its leash.

"Come on now," he said. His mouth was dry and his voice was barely a whisper. "We have to go."

She pulled free of his grip, tugging away so fiercely that it was as if his touch had burned her. "I have to see," she said. Already she was moving away from him, leaving him behind. On the path ahead, the woman turned to the man and the woman must have been smiling from the way she threw her head back, from the way she slipped her arm around the man's bicep. Their faces were shaded by the trees and they were walking together so closely that he could almost imagine another silhouette trailing behind them, smaller, hurrying to keep up, though he could not tell for sure.

"Please!" He was shouting now, and he could hear the tears building in his voice, threatening to ruin him. "I'm sorry. Let's go back. We can still go back."

He set off at a run to follow her, but knew that she was already too far away.

There Be Dragons

~ Ingrid Garcia

—The Flight Forward—

Marta Lopez moved to her seat preoccupied, her thoughts racing so hard she bumped into the Rastafarian gentleman who was putting his bag in the overhead bin of the adjacent seat.

"Sorry," she said, "my mind's in such a weird place, I forget about my surrounds."

"No worries," the tall, dreadlocked black man said, "and I certainly hope it's a good trip."

As the tall black man nodded in agreement, his dreadlocks softly swinging, he flashed a thoughtful smile and said: "by the way, I'm Kai Menelik."

"Marta Lopez," she said, shaking his hand, "Nice to meet you." Marta put her belongings in the luggage bin, taking out her tablet, and sat down. She had a lot to contemplate, wondering if she'd done the right thing. She grabbed her airpods and was about to pop them in her ears when she saw that Kai Menelik was about to do the same. He noticed, too, and laughed. "We're aping each other." He said.

"Yeah," was all she managed, "If you don't mind me asking: how important is music to you?"

It cut dangerously close to the chase. If he knew what she'd done to the music he was about to listen to, he might not be so amused. Thankfully, he couldn't read her mind.

"Very important," he said, pointing to her tablet, "and if you don't mind my curiosity: how important is technology to you?"

"Very important," she said, wondering where this was leading to.

"Could you live without it?" he asked.

"I suppose I could," she said, thinking it over, "but—"

"—it wouldn't be a life worth living," he said, finishing her thoughts.

Yet, there's more to it that that, she thought, *music can be not just the message, but also the prime mover.*

"Suppose music became so powerful, so compelling," she said, "that—for example—people would actually, well, act out John Lennon and Yoko Ono's 'Imagine'?"

"Imagine all the people," he intoned, "really changing the world for the better? More cynical persons would call that hopelessly naïve."

"It would be," she reluctantly admitted, "but suppose there was something in the music that would compel people to behave like that?"

The moment the words leave her mouth she regrets stating them. For Avitome she helped develop the 'best and most affordable DACs in the world'. In her spare time, though, she went much further by inventing a binaural technique that could stimulate carefully selected parts of the brain with certain frequencies. With a revolutionary algorithm she could aim her aural stimulations with pinpoint precision.

That was all within her field. Much more challenging—for her—was to find out which parts of the brain to stimulate, and to what effect. Until she was put on the right track by ground-breaking research and found a way to impel curiosity in the brain, a way to instill an insatiable thirst for knowledge compelling people to become a vector for change—say a scientist, engineer, entrepreneur or volunteer.

She secretly developed BAD-ASS—her Bin-Aural Deep-Algorithm Stimulation System—that could be embedded in a song, *any* song. The binaural tones were inaudible for anybody and anything but the finest audio analysis equipment. Hacking into popular music streams like Spotify, Google Play, Pandora and Apple Music she converted their most popular songs into the BAD-ASS enhanced ones.

She finished the hacks yesterday, before heading for the Shanghai International Audio Show.

"That might help," Menelik said, "but I suspect people are also motivated by fear, jealousy and greed, probably in that order. What about if we eliminated those?"

"That could be good," Marta said, "but—like love, compassion and joy—I think these are deep-seated emotions, ingrained by evolution."

"I don't want to eliminate these emotions," Menelik said, flashing a broad smile, "I want to eliminate the *need* for them."

They talked in strangely hushed tones, as if afraid other passengers would overhear them, yet secretly wishing everybody would listen. "Technology is basically a tool, albeit a stupendously advanced one," she said, "and it's the people using it that determine if it's used in benevolent ways or not."

"That might be true now," he said, "but what if technology develops so much that it frees us from wanting, that it can provide us with anything we need, for a price too cheap to charge?"

By now, Menelik wondered if he'd said too much. On the one hand, he'd safely cached the encrypted blueprints for the self-repairing nanotechnology he'd developed using the massive resources of MIT's Media Lab, telling his director Joi Ito that his approach was a 'forever-shifting approach to the ideal'—self-repairing nanotechnology that could be adapted for any possible use—while admitting they would never ever reach that veritable point of perfection.

Problem being that one evening, after experimenting all day with one extremely experimental amplitudron-encoded structures, the prototypes started working so well, so eloquently, so effortlessly that Menelik feared he'd actually achieved it. Working through the night, he threw tasks at the novo-prototypes that he'd considered impossible to achieve. Yet his new machines succeeded beyond his wildest dreams.

Then he wrote down the blueprint for his novo-prototypes, encrypted them and put them on several secret caches in the cloud, programming their release—ensuring they'd be both open source and public domain through a carefully crafted legal document preventing that other could retro-actively patent them—in case of his death or disappearance.

Machines that can be programmed to make anything—almost literally anything—needing only the raw materials and energy. The former could be recycled through his novo-prototypes, and the latter was only a matter of manufacturing sufficient renewables—hell, these machines could make their own solar- , geo- or wind power converters.

It could trigger the advent of a post-scarcity society. If everything could be made so cheap it would be pointless to charge for it, then greed, jealousy and even fear—the fear of poverty and destitution— would become obsolete.

Still, Menelik wasn't sure what to do. He could show it to his peers, but was afraid they'd cripple or destroy the technology for a variety of reasons—safety, massive disruption, possibly mis- or malevolent uses. He could go public and face a tsunami of controversy. He just didn't know, so he decided to put it on hold after he returned from his trip to the Nano Tech China Exhibition & Conference in Shanghai.

He could not just spill these beans to the first stranger he met on the plane—no matter how cute, smart and tech-savvy she appeared to be. Yet, by dog, he did need to exchange viewpoints with another intelligent, like-minded human being, and she did seem to fit the bill to a T.

So they kept talking possible scenarios for change in general terms, carefully avoiding telling details. Their animated discussion was interrupted by the meal service. Yet the exchange was so engrossing and invigorating that Marta almost forgot about her environment. Some nagging doubts came up, but she discarded them as fatigue set in, and she decided to take a nap.

She slept well, rarely slept so well in a plane before. And it was so quiet that, as she was awakened by a slight bump—almost like a wrinkle in time—and the sound of a cough from someone in one of the seats behind her, she almost feared that the engines had stopped. But no, they were still flying, albeit in near silence. Wasn't there much more background noise, normally?

She looked out of the window at the left wing. It seemed much sleeker than when they took off, but she must be imagining it. And the windows—they seemed much bigger, too. Strange, but she shook it off as their conversation continued.

"Is it me," she said, "or are these engines really so quiet?"

"Well, isn't this a dreamliner?" Menelik said, mistakenly, "but I also didn't realize it would be so well-insulated. Sometimes technology improves faster than you think."

"Indeed," Marta said, "if only people could improve so quickly, as well."

"Imagine that," Menelik says with a dreamy look in his eyes, "the world living as one."

—Into the Future—

Arrival augurs future shock. From her window seat, Marta sees a flexible trunk like a giant snake curl its way to the plane's exit door.

The crew doesn't open the door, rather it dilates the moment the giant trunk attaches itself to the plane's exterior. Exiting the plane, each passenger enters their own transparent globule, which nictates shut and vacuums each passenger towards their immigration receptacle. Bio-samples are taken so fast and non-intrusively, that both Marta Lopez and Kai Menelik are waived through before they realize they've been tested.

Each immigration receptacle exits into a giant corridor. Next to each exit, a robot arm holds up a plaque with each passenger's name, and several other robot arms proffer a cart holding each passenger's luggage. Baffled, Marta takes her cart and is directed to a moving sidewalk that quickly takes her into the arrivals area. Menelik arrives there at the same time, next to her, looking bewildered, as well.

The arrivals hall is filled to the brim with people who—on closer inspection—each seem to live in a little world of their own. Some gesticulate frenetically, some talk loudly, some move around in state of serenity, yet—as nobody seems to be paying attention to anybody else—nobody bumps into each other, as if some invisible tech bubble protects them. Most of them look strange in a subtle way—their muscular proportions seem off or they carry artificial extensions. Even more disturbingly, there are no signs indicating ground transport, metro links, parking lots or even the exit.

Lopez and Menelik face each other, uncertain what to do. The moment they seem to head somewhere—anywhere—a Chinese person whose androgyny would make David Bowie jealous emerges from the chaotic crowd, heading their way, saying something that sounds like English but is so full of neologisms, jargon and portmanteau words that it might as well have been Mandarin.

"I'm sorry, but I don't understand you," she says, "do you speak English?"

"What's wrong with you two?" The English that seems to appear out of thin air does not synchronize with the speaker's fast-moving lips. "Is your AugRealApp malfunctioning? I pinged you several times."

"My AugRealApp?" Marta says as she takes out her iPhone, checking the App store, "Is that the latest hype?"

The Chinese looks at Marta's iPhone in utter disbelief, then starts laughing uncontrollably. As the laughter subsides, they say: "What's that? A display box? A phone cell or whatever they were called?" They shake their head. "Where are you two from? The Luddite Archipelago? The last remaining Amazon tribe? Anyway, these are useless here. In modern society, you can't get anywhere without ubik-link implants."

"Ubik-links?" Menelik says. "I'm a nerd, utterly up-to-date with the latest shit, and I've never heard of them."

"No problem, dear medieval people," the Chinese says, quickly touching an antenna-like appendage on their head, "I'll set you up."

"Set us up?" Marta says, "I'm not sure if we can pay for that."

"Pay?" The Chinese shrugs. "That's a concept from the Stone Age." They pause and contemplate. "Dear Luddites—I almost forgot people like you still existed—but in our modern, post-scarcity society money has become obsolete. To get around, you need an AugRealApp system, which connects you with the ubik-link."

"But I'm not sure if I want that." Marta protests.

"You can't get out there," the Chinese waves their—weirdly proportioned—arms in all directions, "without an AugRealApp. You'd be run over by an ElectroBus, smashed by a SurfaceZep or chopped up by a HyperDrone, as they can't see you." They sigh in exasperation. "You wouldn't survive ten minutes, out there. Surely you're not *that* stupid, or suicidal?"

"This doesn't make sense," Marta says, "where are we?"

"Über-Shanghai, of course," the Chinese says, their hands operating some invisible interface with blinding speed, "don't tell me you took the wrong flight."

"Über-Shanghai?" Menelik says, frowning, "maybe we should ask what year this is?"

The Chinese rolls their eyes. "Do you have a different calendar, out there in the Luddite Archipelago? It's 2038, of course."

"That's impossible," Marta says, "then we're twenty years into the future."

After they've recovered from their shock, Marta and Menelik check for signals with their smartphones, tablets and laptops. No networks or signs of life anywhere, except for the Homeric laughter of the Chinese as they type on their laptops. With great reluctance, they allow the Chinese person to 'set them up'.

A cloud of insect-like drones—so realistic they're indistinguishable from an actual swarm—descends upon them from somewhere above the huge arrivals hall. The insectoids crawl on their arms, face and under their clothes, weaving in implants everywhere. Especially the eye sensor implantation freaks them out, until they notice the process is completely painless. Either the insectoids work with nano precision—avoiding nerve endings all the time—or they use a highly advanced local anesthetic. In any case, the physical implementation is over in mere minutes.

Just like the semi-autonomous, self-repairing nanobot factories I was foreseeing, back then, Menelik thinks, *this means we're really into the future.*

Then the weirdness begins. . .

Extra sensory perceptions pop up everywhere in their nervous system as the Chinese—Jing Shenteng—moves them around the hall, through the dense, chaotic crowd in order to auto-tune the AugRealApp system. The visual overlays of augmented reality are the most overwhelming and disorienting. But they can't help but notice the subtle controls of their muscles to steer them away from collisions; the calming fragrances of myrrh, lavender and lemongrass; the cacophonous myriad of sounds translated/transformed into an auditory matrix that's almost understandable and the gentle, refreshing taste of tea, chamomile and vanilla on their tongues.

Voices from everywhere/ubiquitous visuals/suffusing smells/palatal effervescence/permeating elation

Look up↑—Look down↓—Look out!—Look around☐

It can happen to you—It will happen to you—It has happened to you

It can happen to me—It will happen to me—It has happened to me

It can happen to everyone—It will happen to everyone—It has happened to everyone

Eventually—Inevitably—Irrevocably

We're coaxed into feeling at ease as we get used to this new technology, Marta thinks, *and it works wonderfully. Scary as hell.*

Because they are guided by the AugRealApp—Marta realizes—they can give their full attention to all the augmented reality overlays, which are overwhelming at first. There are at east six different ones in their forward field of vision, all slightly out of focus until you look at one directly, which then becomes razor-sharp and crystal clear. Instant zoom-in action in a bokeh multiverse.

Fragrance is a profuse and mesmerizing bouquet, shifting all the time. Flavor is a bountiful and exquisite feast for the palate, metamorphosing subtly yet endlessly. Air vibrations are omnipresent—an intricate wall of sound layered by nothing but human voices. An a cappella fractal ring referring a fatal carnal palace, exploding from a center and falling back, all the time, in time, timelessly:

We   We   We

Can   Can   Can

Work

It It It

Out   Out   Out

Then Marta recognizes it: a myriad of voices, overdubbed into an audible eternity, yet placed in precise locations through bin-aural trickery. *The BAD-ASS system I invented,* she realizes, *but then developed to the next stage. Make that stages.*

When zooming in on an overlay, Marta and Menelik are immersed in an augmented reality that feels like equal measures RPG, documentary and advertorial.

- There's Boris the Eco-Warrior who assists in restoring the Amazon rainforest—rewilding the land, re-introducing extinct species or bringing them back from the brink and re-implementing biodiversity, cross-referencing his results with Yuki the Bio-Wizard;

- There's Suzy the Space-Lifter who floats in geo-synchronous orbit, part of the team that designs and manufactures the triple carbon nanotube ribbon that's lowered to the base station while feeding the dreams of Juanito the Master of the Multiverse;

- There's Alex the Zen-Teacher who's immersed in one of the huge neural nets that run the drone, pharmaceutical and self-driving systems, goading them away from catastrophic failures through invisible kōans and the grey box method and feeding their impossible findings to Dewi the Hyper-Transformer;

- There's Yuki the Bio-Wizard, who enchants DNA, RNA and cellular automatons in her fight against all diseases and her search for extreme longevity which then can be used by the interplanetary colonists eventuated by the works of Suzy the Space-Lifter;
- There's Juanito the Master of the Multiverse, who invents, develops and explores an infinity of worlds and possibilities both virtual and augmented, feeding his results to Boris the Eco-Warrior, Suzy the Space-Lifter and Alex the Zen-Master;

- There's Dewi the Hyper-Transformer, who goes to the poisoned places like industrial landfills, nuclear waste dumps and plastic oceans and recycles the pollution into useable materials many of which are shipped to Suzy the Space-Lifter, Boris the Eco-Warrior and Farida the Vertical Farmer;

"What are these interactive . . ."—for lack of a word Marta just points at them—"apps for?"

"Apps?" Shenteng laughs at the parachronism. "They're recruitment virts."

"You mean these RPGs-cum-videos depict actual jobs?" Menelik said. "That's impossible. According to you, we're in 2038, not in 2138."

"Check 'The Shift' on Wikimedia Galactica," Shenteng says, "sometime late 2018/early 2019 things began to shift. Finally, humanity was coming off its lazy ass and started grabbing the future by the horns. Once everybody was truly motivated, things moved really fast."

"Post-scarcity?" Menelik cannot believe it. "In a mere twenty years? And we're building a space elevator? Holy shit!"

"Three space elevators," Shenteng says, "One near Singapore, one at Kobékobe and one west of the Galapagos Archipelago. We've grown up, we demand redundancy. Huge demand for Space Elevator Engineers of all kinds: nanotechnologists, superconducting techs, micro-gravity specialists and many more."

"But it'll take ages and immense efforts just to teach these new skills."

"Education didn't stand still, either," Shenteng says, "We'll have you up-to-date for the required job in six months, a year tops."

"Cyborg enhancements, genetic modifications on demand," Marta notices, "are most of you still human anymore?"

"Unfortunately, quite a few still are," Shenteng says, "as we are becoming more than human. Speaking about that—" he gestures at an overlay, "—our medical nanobots determined quite a few issues with your health. Each of you should get these treated, quick."

"But we can't pay," Marta says, "our money is obsolete."

"It's—" Shenteng pauses as they search for the correct anachronism, "—free. We need healthy people to join our projects. So much to do, so little time."

Something nags at the back of Marta's mind. On top of these highly interactive presentations, Marta gets the ineluctable impression that these people—even if some of the cyborg enhancements and genetic modifications make them look more than human—are in constant touch with each other through their AugRealApps and ubik-links, which also seems to be an entangled social network—always connected, always on, always there.

"This AugRealApp," Marta says, "is it ever really down? Can we switch it off?"

"Switch it off?" Shenteng says, looking flabbergasted, "Why would you do that?"

"Some people might not like it if—search 'George Orwell' on your WikiGalactica—Big Brother is watching them all the time." Menelik says.

"Those can go to the Luddite Archipelago," Shenteng says, "Our hyper-connectivity has made us more aware of each other, more understanding and thus more willing to truly co-operate."

"But what about privacy?"

"Overrated," Shenteng says, "and obsolete."

"And the need to contemplate things alone," Menelik says, "and in silence?"

"There'll be plenty of time for that once we head into space," Shenteng says, "Space is huge and travel speeds are slow. Unfortunately."

"Still, this sounds too good to be true," Marta says, "Surely you do have problems."

"Of course we do," Shenteng says, "and every new solution throws up new challenges. But we know that we can work it out. Will you join us?"

Marta and Menelik don't answer immediately. They're over-whelmed, overloaded, future-shocked even if it's the future they made possible. To succeed beyond your wildest dreams, be careful what you wish for, to boldly go where no man has gone before and other metachronistic clichés.

"It reminds me of the sea charts of yore," Menelik says, "where the unexplored areas were marked with 'There Be Dragons.'"

"I see what you mean," Marta says, "and as our geographical knowledge increases, the areas of 'There Be Dragons' move in time, to the future."

"You old school westerners do really need to know more about other cultures," Shenteng says, "it will tell you that there are two types of mythical dragons. The European kind is an evil, fire-breath-ing chaos-monger. The Asian one is a benevolent symbol of fertility, associated with water and the heavens. Welcome to 2038."

Woodpecker

~ *J. Anthony Hartley*

We woke in the house, our house, to silence. I thought it was unusual, then. Every morning, there was the sound of breakfast and the preparations for the day, but not today. My sister met me in the empty kitchen, and we looked at each other in blankness, wondering where they could have gone. After a brief exploration, we found the house was empty. Just us. We hadn't heard them leave. Though we called, there was no response.

Turning on the television did no good. There was nothing but snow, and as I flipped from channel to channel, we looked at each other, wondering and frowning. I shook my head, killed the static hiss, and dropped the remote. Together, we decided to investigate some more. Outside, the car was still in the garage, and all along the street sat empty vehicles. The sky was blue and clear. Along the street lay silence, like a blanket. As we stood there, outside our front door, I reached for her hand in the stillness.

"What are we going to do?" I asked her.

"I don't know," she said, squeezing back.

We stood there absorbing the quiet and wondering. I think then, disbelief swallowed my fear, at least for a while.

Suddenly, the silence was broken by birdsong from the solitary tree in our front yard, and we looked up, together, wondering even more. A small bird emerged from the leaves and took off into the air, flying swiftly across the roofs of empty houses and away and out of sight while we tracked it.

After a while, we went back inside.

The phone gave us nothing but more silence, undercut by a vague and distant hiss, like the far-off sound of waves.

We were too young to know, I guess, to understand. How could we comprehend the power of collective will? You know, there was talk about it on the television, on the internet, in many places, discussions of cults and new religions and the like, but back then, I didn't even understand what a cult was. Eventually, it turned out to be a movement, nothing else, but even that was enough. They couldn't know either, what power they had given themselves. No one else suspected either.

Have you ever tried to will anything into being? Will something to happen?

It's a dangerous thing.

When all those collective minds grouped and pushed, they had already decided that they would wish certain things out of existence. Bad things. Or so they thought. They were going to make the world a better place.

Some people laughed at them, and well they might. We don't laugh now. Not those of us who remain.

That first morning, we didn't understand quite what it was that they'd done. They never quite called it prayer, because it was never an entreaty to any particular god or divine power. Every one of them, all together, they pushed within themselves.

Desire. You can feel it if you try, stirring deep there within you in the hidden places inside. Stroke it very carefully because just sometimes, it will bite. It's sly. The teeth it owns lie in your own mouth, and it can fill your head with lies.

When my sister—Joanna her name is, though she is somewhere else now, if she is still alive—and I found that there was no change, no one to help us, to tell us what to do, we decided to strike out for the city, to see if we could find anyone there. There wasn't anyone left on our street, nor the next, and if there had been, they had already left somehow, before we started to look.

The scariest thing was the quiet.

We stood at the corner, just staring into each other's faces, helplessly, hearing the absence of noise. It was the first time we'd been so conscious of the sounds that swelled in suburbia, simply by their absence. There was nothing to say. Jointly, we understood, each what the other one was feeling. Without a word, we nodded to each other, and together, headed back towards our empty home.

Our town lay on the banks of a river that curved through gentle hills, muddy and lazy in the summer heat. Clouds of insects rose and glittered in the sunshine on those gentler days, mixing faint hissing with the gentle stir of the languidly flowing water through the long river grasses. We used to play by those banks, getting muddy and laughing together as we splashed around in the mud. We knew that river well. Further downstream, it widened, tracked by a broad highway that ran to the city proper, and then, at its mouth, the clustered cranes, and containers of the city's port. We spoke about it quietly in the silence. The river was our best option. If we followed it down to the city, perhaps we would find out what had happened to the others.

We were lucky; our parents had just shopped the day before last, so the fridge was full of supplies, all of them still fresh. There were other things in the pantry. We grabbed our rucksacks from upstairs and filled them with enough for a couple of days. We reckoned it would take us that long to get to the city and find someone else to help. Joanna didn't think that we'd need anything else. The days were warm and the evenings mild and we had the river and each other. That would be enough.

What if we found no one in the city either, I asked her, but she told me that she thought that was unlikely. As it turned out, she was right.

It took us a couple of days to get to the edges of the city, to the tendrils of suburbia that stretched like roots across the open fields. We had slept beneath clear skies, the sounds of wildlife and the breeze the only things to break the silence apart from our own breathing and the few words that passed between us. Perhaps we were still in a kind of shock, but we didn't really have the urge to talk. Little by little, we were realising that that act of collective will had changed other things as well. Perhaps it was because we were so young, hadn't learned to ask the questions yet, but we accepted a lot of what we stumbled across without thinking about it. Then, and for the time afterward, we knew how things were going to be, no matter how strange they might once have seemed. The world was a very different place; that much was true. Yet, at the same time, we were a part of that new environment, along with everything else.

As we drew closer the city boundary, the road swung back to track the river's edge. Empty vehicles sat motionless in the middle, or beside the road, one or two of them at awkward angles. Buildings, small stores, and low apartment buildings grew more numerous, but still overall silence walked beside us, marking our steps. Eventually, we came upon a tall glass building blocking the road, empty now, like all the rest. A cash machine sat in the wall, and I knew if you punched in the right combination, it would withdraw with the whine of gears back into the space above, revealing a passageway through. It was amusing, I thought, that the cash machine would withdraw rather than someone withdrawing from it. A few attempts and the machine pulled back into the wall and I saw. The space was too small. I turned to her and said, "There's no way through."

"Are you sure?" she asked.

"Don't put your arm in there," I warned. "It will take your hand off."

There was nothing that told me that, but deep within, I knew, just the same way I knew that the thing would pull back into the wall and make us a part of it. Before, if there really was a before, such a thing couldn't happen.

She frowned at my words, looked into my face and she sensed my certainty and nodded. We moved away from the trap space, because that's what it was. It only took a minute more, and we found a door, glass, and steel. It was open. The building was empty, we knew. Empty, that was, except for four security guards in dark blue uniforms, shiny silver letters and numbers on their shoulders, sitting round a low table playing cards. Not one of them looked up from their game.

"Hi," I said. "Can we get through this way?" I asked, looking at the tall double glass doors behind them.

"Sure," one of them said, waving behind him casually, not looking up from his game. "There's no one left," he said.

I rested a hand lightly on his shoulder as I passed, murmuring "Thanks."

"Uh-huh," he said and pulled a card, not even looking at me. It seemed that they were resigned as we were to the new status.

What were they doing there? We did not know. Perhaps they were guarding their corporate memory, trying to still live within what had already gone. I stood and watched them for a few moments from the grassy rise behind the building, but they simply continued their game, stony faces set in deep concentration, not a word between them, as if they were afraid to speak.

I shook my head as we crossed the lawn covered slope and initially, the men, and then the building itself gradually slipped out of sight. I glanced at Joanna, and she looked back at me and shrugged.

The river ran on for an hour or so, gentle hillocks and banks where the sand and earth had broken away, leaving dark miniature cliffs along its side. Eventually, we came to another hill, somewhat taller than the rest, and the river ran around behind it. In that direction, the same way that the river turned, lay the city proper, or what remained of it. We knew that to be true. It was there in our memories, the way it had been before. Whatever they had managed to do, it hadn't touched our memory as such. Along the way, we compared things that we recalled, and reminded each other of things that we had forgotten, though Joanna remembered even more than me. It allowed us better to compare it with what was now. It had given us hope that we had seen real people. At least, we thought that they were real.

For some strange reason, our parents didn't give us pause. They were gone; we knew that much, but that was part of the natural order of things right then. Everyone was gone. Or, at least, just about everyone. I struggled with that, with the concept of what caused us, anyone, to be left behind. Was it because we were not part of that concentrated effort?

Over the rise, we came upon an old pizza parlour set low, low to the ground with sandstone walls, deserted now. Inside, everything was set close to the ground as well, nothing tall, to accommodate the closeness of the ceiling—a cosy atmosphere. We slipped inside, searching for anything that might be useful, but the place had been cleaned out. Whoever was left was fast to recognise their circumstance. They hadn't had long. Or perhaps time was all awry as well. It wouldn't take long for there to be more evidence that that was the case. Suddenly, Joanna motioned for me to be still and quiet.

"Someone's coming," she said.

At first, I thought it was the birds and nothing else. There had been a lot of birds, and I was beginning to discount them. They filled in the lack of other sounds with a sense of comfort. Though there hadn't been so much birdsong near our house. I glanced up and over the edge of one of the window ledges and I saw it there, parked on a low bank by the river, a dark red four-wheel drive, shiny but streaked with dust and I knew that she was right. It looked like it had been travelling for a long time and over a great distance. Lying still, still and we could see, there were men with a family of boys. There weren't many of them, but they stood there, surveying the surrounding area. Before long, their attention swung to the place where we hid, though there was little place for us to hide. A flock of birds came down, calling and screeching over the voices of the kids. One of the boys saw Joanna and pointed. She looked down at me and shook her head, motioning me to be still. It was then that it happened; my sister walked out towards them; her hands held out by her sides.

"I call first dibs," said the kid with the blonde matted dreadlocks. "I'll give up my morning's wages for her."

"Take her; she's yours," said the swarthy man with the black stubble. "Go get her."

She pressed her hand down gently in the air as she walked, signalling me to lie still. I lay there as the birds descended, swooping all around the cold stone interior of the pizza place. One hand was up beside my face as I lay there, barely daring to breathe, motionless, except for my eyes. I watched one of the birds, touched with red, a woodpecker. Suddenly it seemed to notice my hand, my fingers, the fingernail at the top of my index finger. The bird looked as if it wanted to peck at my nail and it made me even more scared. I couldn't cry out. I could not move. I could not do anything except lie there, for fear of alerting the men and their family of boys. My sister had walked out to meet them to keep me free. I knew that. She had known what would happen to me, what would happen to us if she let them find me. Me, I was too young and unwise in the ways of the world then to understand the full implications. Looking back, the thing that I remember most was that act of my own will that kept me from crying out, the strength that I could summon inside, because right then it mattered. And then I would remember her act of will; that must have been so much stronger. She had long gone by the time the woodpecker flew away.

Because of what she did, I eventually made it to the city, in the end, alone, but I found others there. There were only a few, but they were there.

It really mattered. I only understand now, after all this time what she did for me that day. If I could, I would take it back, will that things had happened differently. I can't do that though. There's not enough of me. I am but one. Knowing what happened back then, to all of us, because of that act of collective focus that changed our world, I cannot will it. I do not dare to will it even if I could. I can only think it.

Looking out through dusty windows, here from the place on the fifteenth floor, the sun marking gold and green outside the thick plate glass, I can sometimes see images across the water of the way the port had been, the big ships coming and going and the clusters of activity on the docks. The slick, smooth water, gilded with the touches of sunset lies still now, empty of all but those memories, and they are mere phantoms.

As I drag my gaze away from those images and stare at my fingers, where that bird had thought to do its work, I wonder what really happened to Joanna in the end. She always seemed to know so much more than I did.

Nine Times

~ K. Wallace King

I

The moon is a horned crescent pressed against the sky. Duncan snores softly on the pillow beside her and she turns her head to his profile. He is outlined in moonlight, still as a marble effigy. He could be dead lying there beside her. The cat twitches, its purr vibrates her palm when she strokes it. It's so hot. Suffocating. The air conditioner must have shut itself off. The air stinks from the herbs in the candle; cinnamon, myrrh, aloe. Molly fell asleep with it burning. She bought the candle at a quirky shop—clever greeting cards, tee-shirts with silkscreened pentacles—hipster sorcery. She had picked up a book, *Witch Bitch/Reclaiming Our Fire.* A gift for Cattie's birthday? Cattie played at being a witch. Cattie was her best friend. Most of the time. Some of the time. Not much anymore. Actually, Molly couldn't remember the last time she'd seen Cattie. She'd put the book back, but purchased the candle. It was black and had a label she couldn't read because she didn't have her glasses.

"They used these herbs for wrapping mummies," said the girl in The Sisters of Mercy tee shirt as she put the candle in a bag.

In Molly's bedroom the melted wax and burnt herbs make her feel ill.

II

A half full glass of red wine glows in the lunar light. Molly sits up and the sheet slips to the floor in a puddle. Her heart slips too. Duncan isn't here and he's never coming back. "I can't get close to you." That's what he'd said as he packed his things. "You've got your weapon drawn to cut anyone near your heart."

Molly takes a gulp of the wine, grimacing at the sour vinegar of it after sitting in the heat. As she swallows the rest of the wine, a mouse, its tail twitching, quivers on the floor beside her bed. *Just a trick of the light*, thinks Molly, as she kicks the old catnip toy out of sight.

The cat died. The vet told her that the jerky spasms were only muscles responding to the drug, that it was painless, but Molly didn't believe him. She was to blame for this bad death. The cat had cancer, but she'd refused to let it go. When it cried Molly had shushed it, stroking the dull fur, "It's alright. One more day." Without the cat she would be all alone. With herself.

As it was dying, the vet placed the cat in her arms. Molly had shoved it back to the veterinarian. "I can't. I can't." She had rushed away, leaving the cat she'd had for fourteen years to die with a stranger.

Molly picks up her phone from the bedside table. It's only midnight. She puts a hand to her crashing heart. She looks out the window and sees the moon is not a crescent. It is fat and full, hanging heavy over the hills. The cratered face is so visible Molly's eyes might be telescopes.

Moonlight spotlights the driveway as a coyote, thin and ragged, trots across, carrying something in its mouth. The coyote pauses and, as if it knows Molly is watching, lifts its head to the window. The thing in its mouth wriggles helplessly. From somewhere across the canyon Molly thinks she hears a woman screaming.

III

There's a witch moon through the window and the hills are humps of shadow. A sound grates in her mind, a picture forms. A woman, dark haired, in a diaphanous gown drags a steel sword behind her as she walks down a sidewalk. It grates like a rasping scream. She thinks it will drive her crazy, like the houses that tower over her, leering with windowed eyes, with open-doored mouths. Duncan is dim, distant, on a rocky shore while Molly is aboard a pitching rowboat in wild water, a serpentine river—she watches the coils of it unwind before her.

Angry water slaps the boat, oars dangle like lifeless limbs in the river, and Molly is trying to cry out for help but her throat, how it burns. Where did Duncan go? There he is. Standing against a purpling sky with a hook for the moon. He is but a shadow, a wavering shade on the shore.

Black smoke rises, obscuring Duncan. Like a tornado touching down, the cloud of smoke extends what looks like a leg, then another, until there are four. Molly watches the billowing smoke churn and swirl until the smear of black looks remarkably like a great soot-footed dog.

"Row," says someone behind her. "Row, row." Molly turns, clutching the sides of the bucking rowboat, but she is alone. Red lights flash on the shoreline. The boat rocks dangerously, almost throwing her into the river. Approaching sirens shrill like a woman screaming.

IV

The moon is a lopsided egg hanging above the hills. Duncan snores softly on the pillow beside her, she can just make out his profile. The cat mews piteously, she feels the purr vibrate when she strokes it. A dove laments in the loquat tree outside the window. Or is it an owl? Owls eat smaller birds, gentler birds, they tear their insides out. *Horrible.* She doesn't want this thought in her head as she closes her eyes. *Sunflowers.* She grows a garden of big bright flowers, their shining faces—

Duncan says, "Row."

"Honey." Molly gently pokes Duncan's shoulder. "You're talking in your sleep."

"Row."

Even though he is on the pillow beside her, he sounds far way. *What did you say?* Molly tries to turn her face to Duncan beside her on the bed because this is a dream, this boat, the blurred black dog, but she cannot move. She is paralyzed. Yet Molly feels her heart madly fluttering, terrified feathers batting against bone.

OH wake up wake up wake up.

Molly opens her eyes and witnesses her hands flapping wildly above her body. They shine pale as dove wings in the light of the moon. *Thank god it was only—I was dreaming.* She drops her hands. Beside her the cat still purrs. She snuggles up against Duncan, lays her head on his chest, inhaling the sleepy fragrance of his skin. "Are you awake? Oh Jesus, Duncan. I was having the weirdest dream. Duncan? No answer. Molly once more opens her eyes. Outside the window the moon is laughing.

She pulls down the shade and turns on the bedside lamp. She reads mindless garbage then plays games on her phone until it says it's morning. When she tugs the bottom of the window shade, it curls around the roller at the top with the sound of a slap. The room smells of greasy smoke, burnt herbs.

V

Molly takes her coffee to the balcony and sits there in her tee shirt and underwear. She watches the full moon fade as the sun rises, turning the sky a wounded pink before spreading into a vast dome of metallic blue. She can already feel the heat trapped in the wood of the boards beneath her feet. It is another day of temperatures over ninety-five, even though it is late October. Molly watches two crows surfing the updraft over the houses clumped on the the hillsides above the canyon. She thinks about what she might do today, but nothing comes to mind. Another day of in-between. Between jobs, between relationships, pets. *Hell, my life.*

Molly leans on the railing of the balcony. She had once been able to see the entire Hollywood sign. It was the reason she'd agreed to pay more than she could comfortably afford for the apartment. That had been eleven, no, twelve years ago. *How could I have let it all slip by?* Now trees on the hillside have grown much taller and new houses have been built. The famous sign is obscured except for the *H*, one *O*, a solitary *L*, and the *W*. Molly rearranges the letters in her mind. If she could howl maybe she wouldn't feel so empty. But the neighbors would hear. She feels she is turning into that woman that neighbors whisper about behind her back. She'd once known many of the people on her street, but the familiar faces have disappeared.

When a breeze stirs, Molly smells smoke from the fire blazing north off the 5 freeway. Fire is a season in California. The hills are the beige of dead vegetation. The crows call to one another as they circle. In the sunlit sky, their black wings outspread, they dive like bats. Their shrieks make Molly think of the grate of metal. What should she do today?

Every day feels the same. Molly looks up. The birds are gone. Not a single cloud. The sky is empty. *Like me.*

VI

On the street below the balcony a woman is pulling something out of her dog's mouth. She recognizes the woman as a neighbor. Molly waves, but the woman doesn't see her and tosses whatever the dog had in its mouth into the bushes as they walk away. Molly decides to take a walk herself. It's something to do and if she waits any longer it will be too hot to move.

A half hour later she's sweating. She has neglected to bring a hat and regrets it. The sun is blistering. She has climbed the winding streets above her apartment building and finds herself farther up in the hills than she'd intended. She can't remember what kept her so preoccupied that she hadn't noticed. She must have been thinking deeply to not have even seen the mob of tourists around Lake Holly-wood, she doesn't even recall hiking past it.

It's easy to get lost in the Hollywood hills. Streets begin at one point and snake upward, sometimes concluding in a surprising dead end. Or, you'll drive into the hills and, before you know it, find yourself descending into the San Fernando valley with no idea how you got there or how to return to where you started.

Molly is panting as she climbs the steep street. She passes houses perched precariously on the hillside, greedy for every available foot, every inch of coveted view. The architecture she passes is a jarring jangle of periods and styles. A seventies-era geodesic dome with mirror-tinted windows is wedged between a Spanish revival and a Disneyesque McMansion with fairy tale turrets. As she passes a mock Tudor an unseen dog begins to bay. The woeful sound trails behind her. Something flashes in the dirt beside the pavement. A coin. She turns it over in her palm. It is copper-colored, like a penny, but much larger. It must be foreign, she doesn't recognize the faded images. *Big enough to cover an eye.* Why did she think that? Shuddering, she flings the coin into a bush and resumes her hike.

She pauses, smelling smoke more strongly and scans the sky. It's still cloudless, the one-note turquoise of a dyed Easter egg. A memory tugs—Molly in a candy-pink dress. A little woven basket. The other kids faces are smeared with chocolate rabbits.

"Don't just stand there," says her father with a little shove, "join the hunt."

But when the grownups retreat inside, Molly is the hunted. The children run her down across the green lawn, through the rotating sprinklers. She slips and falls onto the lawn, smearing her dress bowel brown in the damp dirt. She lies there, frozen as marble, when the howling children surround her. Then the boy, brown-eyed, black haired, the one she liked, dumps the contents of his Easter basket—mini eggs, gold foil-wrapped chocolate coins—onto her tear-smeared face.

Molly shakes her head to empty the memory and walks faster. She barely notices the sunflower nodding in a big red pot or the cat sitting in a doorway as she passes.

As she rounds a curve on the upward climbing street, ahead is the neighbor with her little dog, some sort of terrier. Molly doesn't really know her beyond saying hello. In fact, thinking about it, she hasn't seen the woman in a long time, and wondered if she'd moved away. She calls out, "Hello!"

Molly has decided to invite the woman over for a glass of wine in the evening when it cools down. It gives her a twinge of dim excitement, something to look forward to The thought of yet another day waiting for night then waiting for day again is almost unbearable and she calls out once more, but the woman doesn't turn around.

Molly picks up her pace, puffing as she climbs the steep street to catch up. "Hey, Cora, hi, wait up."

 Still, the woman doesn't respond though Molly is no more than six feet behind her now. The woman's dog turns to Molly. "Hey there," she says, reaching forward to pat it. It bares its teeth and Molly quickly draws back her hand. "Cora?" She still doesn't answer even though Molly is almost at her elbow.

Cora shouts, "Go to Hell."

Shocked, Molly recoils from the ferocity in the woman's voice, then sees the shiny white air pods in Cora's ears.

"Drop dead," yells Cora to her phone, walking faster up the street, dragging her dog by the leash behind her.

Molly stops and lowers her face to her own phone, embarrassed. She stays that way in case Cora turns around. Only when the woman and her dog vanish around another bend in the road does Molly continue her upward climb. It's so hot. She passes a tangle of brittle yellow vines and shriveled tomatoes—someone's attempt at gardening. Dead grass crackles and turns to dust when Molly steps on it.

VII

Where has she gotten to? She doesn't recognize this street. She checks her phone for her location. Without touching it, the screen is already showing her a map with a red marker. Was it always her goal? She doesn't remember inputting it, but shrugs the thought away. She recognizes the location as a place where you can see all the way across the canyon to Griffith Park and beyond to the downtown skyline. An impressive vista. She doesn't recall wanting to get there, but it gives her a goal. Something tugs in the back of her mind. *I'm supposed to get somewhere . . .*

The street grows so vertical it's almost as if she's climbing the side of a mountain. She has to bend down low, almost touch the street with her hands. She can smell the tar melting which reminds her of the stink of the candle in her bedroom. She feel nauseous.

The houses to her left seem to be jiggling like jelly, as if they aren't quite sure if they are really there. It's the heat, hot air distorting her field of vision. "Heat devils," she whispers to herself.

A man with a backpack and an alpine hat suddenly appears up ahead, descending toward her. A puffing Molly pauses her climb, "Was the view worth it?"

The man passes Molly without a glance. Irritating, though not surprising. People she passes these days never seem to smile, don't even return a hello, lost in their own worlds.

A few minutes later a car approaches behind her and Molly steps onto the dirt shoulder to let it pass. She glances over at the slowly cruising convertible Mustang. Tourists always rented convertible Mustangs. The driver is looking at his GPS with a furrowed brow, and the girl beside him says something in German. Molly nods to them, waiting for the driver to ask for directions to the Hollywood sign; readying the standard reply that you can't drive to it, but there are spots to get a great shot. But the driver doesn't seem interested in Molly and presses his foot to the accelerator, causing the car to fishtail.

"Hey!" Molly yells, jumping away from the car. It had almost knocked her into the canyon. The car roars up the street.

VIII

When at last Molly reaches the crest she expects to find the Mustang there as well, but she is the only soul at the end of the vertiginous climb. She's so hot she can feel the burn beneath her skin and she wipes her forehead with her forearm as she surveys the panorama across the canyon to Griffith Observatory and the skyscrapers downtown.

"Oh no." Black smoke is rising in the canyon below. When she holds up her hand to shade her eyes, "What the hell?"

There's a river down there. A band of silvery water winds through the canyon streets below. Which is impossible. The only river within miles is the Los Angeles River and it's not only in another direction, but a feeble excuse for a waterway. The scream of a siren wails, and overhead is the pounding pulse of a helicopter.

Molly looks up, expecting to see either a news crew or a fire chopper, but sees only a crow circling above her head. When she surveys the view again, the observatory, the downtown skyline, are still there, but the serpentine shimmer that looked like a river is gone.

A trick of the eye.

But the fire burning in the distance is no trick. Molly looks down at the tumbling jumble of roofs and roads. The smoke is rising from one of the lowermost neighborhoods in the canyon. Red and orange flames explode in great balls of fire as if blasted by a furious dragon.

Molly is typing on her phone, trying to discover any information about the fire, when she has the sensation that someone else is near. She lifts her head. A man is climbing the street toward where she stands at the hilltop, but where light should be is only a block of dark. Is it heat rising from the street that blurs him? Molly feels something twist in her gut, that feeling that something isn't right about this man. She lowers her face and quickly begins to descend. When she glances up, the man, or the smudged figure, is much closer. She goes cold inside and turns her head away. *Wrong.* The man doesn't seem to have feet. He isn't walking, he is drifting toward her as if windblown.

Sun in my eyes.

But she doesn't look at him. She senses rather than sees that the man has passed by. He is behind her now, climbing the hill to where she was a moment ago. Her skin prickles. *Who was that?* Something tells her not to turn around, not to even to look over her shoulder. *What was that?*

She walks downhill as fast as she can, if she runs, she'll tumble down the hill, break a bone. *Jill came tumbling after . . .*

The sky is growing dark as smoke from the fire below obscures the sun. A hot wind gusts. When she licks her lips she tastes ash.

The sky is rouged red. She is astonished at how fast the fire must be advancing to light the sky like this. The road is no longer so steep, it evens out and Molly breaks into a jog, *got to get home, get the cat get the car get out,* remembering horror stories of people trying to flee a tsunami of roiling flames only to be found later, burnt hands still on the steering wheel, the melted metal tags of their pets inside the skeleton of a car.

She stops a moment to check her phone. She types in the call letters of the local TV station. The screen is fire red, but there is no text. Above Molly's head, the sun is a faded disc, pale as the full moon in the early morning sky. A whoosh of wind blows her backward, strong enough to make her totter. She senses, rather than sees, the shadowy blur of a big dog as it rushes past.

By the time she reaches her street, the smoke has cleared and the sky is dotted with stars. Bright hot and white they flare in the smudged black sky. The moon hangs lopsided as a drunk overhead. The smell of smoke and charred wood, of the chemicals used to subdue the fire makes her gag.

A group of people stand in front of the smoldering ruins of a building. A silvery river of water from the firehoses races down the street to a drain.

"What's going on?" Molly asks a man with a baby strapped to his chest. Instead of answering, he turns to the young blonde woman beside him, "Wasn't that building sold a year ago?"

A woman with a terrier on a leash speaks up, "I used to see someone on the balcony sometimes. Was never very friendly."

Molly's heart slips when she spots the man with the alpine hat standing apart from the rest of the crowd, his face in shadow. She feels drawn to him, but as she begins to move toward him, he lifts his head and Molly stops, covering her mouth to keep from screaming. It's Duncan and he is cradling her cat in his arms.

"No, no, he's dead, he died." She is backing away, her ankles splashing in cold water. She backs farther, the water now to her knees. When she turns to run she is in an enormous river tossed with whitecaps. A boat is gliding through the chop almost as if flying. Molly knows the boat is for her.

"Row."

No I can't, no, I can't.

Molly turns, splashing out of the river, onto a muddy bank. Duncan and her neighbors are gone. There is only smoke and heat. She feels hot breath on the back of her legs and she wants to scream when the smoke billows and expands beside her, but her mouth won't open. The cloud of smoke has four legs. Molly can smell the burnt wires in its fur, see the fire in its eyes.

When she is lifted off the ground, she screams so loud it echoes through the canyon. The great dog with Molly between its jaws is running.

Firelight casts shadows, stark and sharp. The smoke dog whips past burning buildings and Molly sees herself, a silhouette with dangling legs, arms flailing.

The river is receding as Molly is carried away, its silvery gleam now far behind.

IX

A grinning moon is pressed against the sky. Duncan snores softly on the pillow beside her and Molly turns her head to his profile. He is outlined in moonlight, still as a marble effigy. She could be dead lying there beside him.

Asylum Cake

~ *Eric Witchey*

I was the last ghost hunter in the haunted asylum. My three-person crew, Garret, Lindon, and Svetlana, had all bolted by one AM.

Garret first.

We had just put several dozen organic eggs, a monster tub of real butter, and a few gallons of whole milk in the abandoned asylum kitchen. Any real ghostly presence would spoil the eggs, curdle the milk, and make the butter go rancid. I didn't like the low-tech ghost detectors, but enough self-appointed expert viewers had left us follower comments that high-tech tools fritzed when real ghosts made an appearance. We added backup to make them happy. Garret checked the eggs and sniffed the dairy. Into his lapel mic, he said, "1:00:00 AM. The eggs and dairy are fine."

As if his words were an incantation, the disconnected industrial dispose-all started up on its own. I got a five second, wide-eyed night-vision selfie from his head-mounted GoPro before my equipment man turned to me and said, "Screw this shit. I didn't sign up for real ghosts."

He bolted. His custom Electromagnetic Voice Phenomenon (EVP) detector and hand-held infrared camera hit the slick tile floor. To my amazement, neither one shattered. Unfortunately, his night-vision headset went with him.

The equipment in my van caught his footage, but I never saw him or the headset again.

Lindon, my roving cameraman, abandoned us second.

He had just arrived to see what was up with Garret when the double doors to the walk-in pantry opened like jaws. Rusted can, rotted label, and spoiled bean stink poured out on a column of cold air just before an ectoplasmic hand grabbed his loose shirt and pulled him toward the pantry maw.

Static from the EVP on the floor died, and a man's clear, midwestern-accented words sounded out. "Turn on the lights! Turn them on!"

Lindon spun faster than an Olympic diver to break the gooey grip then sprinted even faster than Garret, leaving nothing behind except the echo of his girly scream.

Svetlana, my medium, was made of strong Romani stuff. After watching the tail end of Lindon's encounter and hearing the EVP, she cursed the ghost and me in Russian then took a flask from a hip holster she had worn since I first met her. We had all joked about her belt having more pockets and better stuff than Batman's utility belt.

I thought, Good. holy water. She came prepared.

She had come prepared, and I suppose she might have thought she had brought holy water.

"Vodka," she said. She popped the cap and slammed back a deep swallow like the Ruska Roma she was. She then handed it to me. "Is good. Is for nerves."

After what I experienced in my hour in the Willamette Hills Out-Patient Retreat and Asylum, you bet I hit that flask. For nerves, you know?

I was in the reality YouTuber and general streaming game as a way of sharing my quest to find real ghosts and crowd-sourcing research, but I was the only true believer in my crew. The two guys joined me because hey, reality TV, TikTok Followers, Instagram, and YouTube. For them, identity relevance meant being seen doing things other people hoped were real.

Svetlana hadn't joined us to build a community of channel monkeys feeding on content. In her interview, she said, "I come here because Prababushka . . . How you say?"

"Grandmother?"

"Ah. No. Great Grandmother says to me, 'Go there with that boy.'"

I figured she was either adlibbing script to impress her maybe new boss or coming on to me. I'd had influencer groupies before, and she was kind of hot in an "I'll kick your ass if you piss me off tattooed Russian ninja chick sort of way."

I liked her and her story. I liked her because, well… Because I liked her. I liked her story because the Great Grandmother who told her to interview for the job had been dead for five decades. Combining her hot vibe and the story, I didn't care what her real reasons were.

Even so, when the ancient tank of an industrial cake mixer started up on its own, she calmly handed me her vodka and said, "You nice boy. Not so smart American, but nice. I hope you live." Then, she turned and calmly walked out of the building without another word.

Which put me in the middle of a 1 a.m. dark asylum kitchen listening to rustling in the pantry, a spinning industrial cake mixer, a grinding dispose-all, and, unexpectedly, a never before absolutely clear-voiced EVP monitor.

"Turn on the fucking lights!" the EVP screamed. "Turn on the God-damned LIGHTS!"

Precedents that tell you what to do when encountering real ghosts don't exist. I mean, most of the shit you hear about or see on social media is just made up. Ninety percent is scripted to gain followers.

In the olden days before social media, there was that Hans Holzer guy and his friends. In the 1950s and 60s, they did their best to investigate and document. Back in Hans's day, ghost hunters had to be dead serious because they were going to have to live with ridicule and ignominy. Today, all the online and channel-show ghost hunters pretend to use his discovery and documentation methods modified with a few tech updates. A bored population craves the adrenaline boost of a scream in the dark. Visuals and suspense for media feeds are more important than meeting actual ghosts.

Don't get me wrong. No way I was above a boost in "Like, Subscribe, and Click on the Bell." I had my silver YouTube plaque, and my Insta had 100k followers, and I figured my crew bolting one-by-one would send my Night in the Asylum video viral. From the garnering sponsors perspective, the shoot was already done, but there was no way I could leave without learning more. Like I said, I got into it for real ghosts.

By phone flashlight, I found the light switches next to the swinging metal double doors from the kitchen to the asylum's cafeteria. I tossed the switches—all six of them. The place had been abandoned for over a decade, and Garret and Lindon had assured me the whole facility was completely disconnected from the grid. I didn't expect lights, but I did hope for a response from the ghost/poltergeist/whatever the hell was living out its afterlife in the kitchen and giving such a clear EVP signal.

The lights came on.

Like, there's no power in the building, but the lights came on.

Like, all the lights.

The kitchen lights, the pantry lights, the cafeteria lights, the patient room corridor access lights, and probably all the office and dormitory and rec room lights, too, though I couldn't see them from the kitchen.

In an EVP digital voice I swear sounded profoundly relieved, the box said, "Oh, thank fucking god."

Corny, and a little late, I know, but I was scared, so I fell back on my lame scripted patter. "If there is any presence in this place, any spirit with unfinished business, please make yourself known to—"

The mixer stopped. The dispose-all stopped. The noise in the pantry stopped.

My ears strained for anything reassuring in the silence.

The EVP spoke. "Thanks!"

That made me jump and think it would be a really good time to return Svetlana's flask.

Before I followed my crew, the thing went on. "I've been trying to get someone to turn on those lights for twelve years. Twelve years! I thought I'd go insane. Every damned night, living in terror."

Hand on the flask and eye on the doors, I said, "Uh, okay." My script was scrap. Bravely adlibbing, I asked, "Why?"

The EVP, still on the floor, had a QLED touchscreen. It flashed as the apparition spoke. "You know this is an asylum, right?"

"Uh, yes."

"And you came her to find ghosts because you figured there would be disturbed spirits?"

"Yeah . . . ?"

"Maybe some real nut jobs? Serial killers? Sociopaths? Psychopaths?"

"Maybe. I suppose."

"Idiots. They all come here for that, but it isn't that kind of asylum."

The giant mixer snapped on again, spun the massive twisting, off-center mixing blades through one revolution, and stopped.

A little stunned, I mean I was talking to some kind of disembodied spirit, I asked, "What kind of asylum is it?"

"For rich folks. Phobias, mostly. A few low-intensity personality disorders."

Grasping for some sense of who I was talking to, I asked, "Were you a doctor?"

"Cook."

"You were the cook?"

"Didn't I just say that? Look around, ghost hunter. You're standing in a kitchen. Did you come here because the volleyball court was haunted? The tennis court? The patient rooms?"

"You had a volleyball court here?"

"No." Static squawked from the EVP. "Catch up, man. I made that up to make a point."

I felt silly. The ghost was right. We had packed up the van and driven four hours from Vancouver WA to the middle of nowhere coastal foothills Oregon forest to check out the haunted kitchen stories about the Willamette Hills Out-Patient Retreat and Asylum. "Yeah," I said. "We came to check out the stories about the kitchen."

"It's not rocket science. Kitchen ghost. Cook."

"And the thing with the lights?

"Nyctophobia. Perk of the job. Free therapy. I'm afraid of the dark."

God, I hoped the Wi-Fi tethered recorders in the truck were storing all this. My mic was on. So was my head strapped GoPro. The EVP had been online when Garret bolted, but you never knew if what you believed you were hearing was the same as what the equipment picked up. "Did you die here?"

"Well, duh. Are you a ghost hunter?"

Trying to calm the spirit and get past his snark, I asked, "How?"

"Hobart." The mixer clicked and spun up to a pretty good whining, twisting mix pace.

"Was Hobart a patient?"

The mixer stopped. "Hobart is the company that built the mixer."

I checked out the massive machine bolted to the floor. The metal bowl had wheels and was big enough for me and Svetlana to hide in. The metal paddles that mixed whatever went in that bowl looked like two multi-tined forks the size of tennis rackets spinning and twisting in and out of one another's orbits. "How the hell did that thing kill you?"

"It was installed in the 60s. No safety features."

"You would have had to climb in the bowl. Why would you do that?"

"It was the week we were closing. I still needed therapy, and I was pretty bummed about losing my free appointments."

The reason the ghost was stuck on the mortal plane seemed to be coming into focus. "You suicided."

"Hell, no!"

My plan to calm the spirit wasn't going well. "I'm sorry. Really, I'm sorry."

"Yeah. Sure."

"I'm interested. I want to know what happened."

"You'd be the first."

"I turned on the lights."

The EVP went silent for three of my exploding heartbeats before the cook said, "Baking a goodbye cake for all the staff and patients meant using the big mixer, but I wasn't happy about it."

"An afraid of the dark cook who died baking a cake—that's your story?"

"You wanted a ghost. You found one. Now, you want what? Napoleon? Hitler? Maybe Marie Curie glowing in the dark and cackling?" The mixer stopped. "Selfish much?"

"I'm sorry." And I was. I mean, talking to that ghost was everything I'd hoped for, and everything I said seemed to upset it.

The ghost seemed to sense my sincerity. "Technically," it said, "I died mixing the batter. Gordo Tenston, who called himself The Prankster Orderly, stuck a hand in from the cafeteria and flipped the lights off. He thought that kind of thing was funny, and they couldn't exactly fire him in the last week of operations. The asshole had Borderline Personality Disorder and loved triggering phobias because he had decided they were all faked."

"So the sudden dark scared you to death?"

"I told you. Hobart. Mixer. I was startled. I jumped enough that my hand got caught between the mixer blades. By the time anybody showed up, I was pulled into the batter and beaten into red dye number 2."

That was a little more graphic than I wanted. YouTube might demonetize me if I didn't cut that part, but the cook who died making a goodbye cake was brilliant quirky stuff. Nobody had done anything like it, and I had a real ghost talking to me. Finally. In that moment, I wished Svetlana were still with me. She'd have at least pretended to understand my excitement.

"Fear of the dark, then," I said, "and a goodbye cake."

"Look," the ghost said, "Do you mind if I work while we talk?"

"No."

The pantry started to rattle. The doors opened again, and ingredients started to file out of the closet in a silent Sorcerer's Apprentice sort of floating dance.

I was thinking, I'm so totally going to be rolling in sponsors.

The giant Hobart mixer spun up. A spray hose from the sink stretched out and poured water into the giant metal mixing bowl.

"A cake?" I asked.

"Unfinished business," the cook said. "Twelve years of night terror gives a ghost a craving for a calming ritual. Baking is sort of my thing."

"Why didn't you—"

"Bake in the light? Not how it works. I can't haunt in the daytime, and I'm too scared to bake in the dark. Hell, I can't even move."

"But you rattled the cupboards and touched people and stuff."

"I hid in the pantry, shook in my ectoplasmic skin, and tried to get people to help me."

I supposed that made some sense. "And nobody would turn on the lights?"

"You saw what happened when I tried to get your friends' attention."

"Oh."

I watched the ingredients, including all the eggs, milk, and butter we had brought, mixing for a while then kicked myself for not thinking of setting up more coverage. While the ghost mixed and baked, I went to the van and brought in extra cameras to catch all the footage I could.

Several bowls of different colored icing made themselves while the batter in huge cake pans baked. About three AM, the layers of a massive cake came out of the oven, floated across the kitchen to a counter, and stacked themselves. A spreading spatula rose from a drawer, dipped into icing bowls, and spread sweet goo over the layers.

"The asylum is empty," I said. "Who's going to eat all this?"

"You," the cook said, "for one. Others will show up. Bake a cake, people show up to eat it. Of course, I've never gotten this far before, so maybe not."

I checked my cameras and recorders.

"As thanks for the eggs and dairy, here's some advice," the ghost said, "Set up a couple cameras in the cafeteria."

I did. If you're a ghost hunter, you don't argue when a ghost gives you ghost hunting advice.

The finished cake, a gorgeous thing decorated with marbled swirls of brilliant colors and a single sparkling red calligraphy word, "Goodbye," rose from the counter and floated to the cafeteria doors.

Instinctively, I pushed the doors open.

"Thanks," the cook said.

"No problem."

The cake passed through and settled itself on a table. A moment later, a cake knife the size of my arm floated out of the kitchen and poised over the cake.

As soon as the blade touched icing, the entire cafeteria filled with ghostly forms: amorphous spectral wraiths, transparent shambling people in hospital gowns, white-coated doctors and nurses, a couple of janitors, and a handful of casually dressed ghosts who might have just walked in off the street.

"They all died here?"

The cook said, "No, but they all know how important it is to celebrate healing."

Trying to make sense of the confusing gathering of specters, I said, "Your intention in the baking determined who showed up?"

"You're trying too hard," the cook said. "Just enjoy the party. Have some cake."

The cake sliced itself. The assembled ghosts ate and chatted and clapped. As the cake disappeared, they even sang oldie '80s disco and '90s alternative rock songs like bored old people on a European tour bus.

I caught every detail in glorious 4k digital.

When the last ghost finished the last piece of cake, all the apparitions disappeared. A loud, metallic clank shook the walls of the asylum, and the building went dark.

In that first moment of absolute darkness and silence, I discovered my own loneliness in my lost connection to the nyctophobic baker. "Cook?" I asked the silent darkness.

No response.

By the light of my phone, I made my way back to the kitchen. "Cook?"

The EVP monitor cast a low, silent glow on a few floor tiles.

Behind me, a door squeaked.

I jumped and turned.

Svetlana strode in, her hand-held utility belt flashlight burning a white, high-intensity LED beam through the darkness.

Grateful for her stoic company, I said, "They're gone."

"They?"

"The cook, the doctors, the patients."

"For decade," she said.

"They were here. I talked to them. Filmed them."

"Great Grandmother say ghosts only can talk at night."

"It is night. They were just here."

"Is dawn," she said. "Sun up now. No window here."

"Oh."

She swept her light around the kitchen. The beam stopped on a top hat-sized triple-layered cake bearing a calligraphy message. "Thank you. Fill the darkness with light."

Svetlana asked, "You bake?"

I said, "No."

"Ah," she said. "Outside, Svetlana is walking on road. Great Grand-mama appears. She says to me, 'You go share boy's cake.'"

"Really?"

She smiled, nodded, and crossed to the cake.

As morning light filtered through the windows of the asylum and a diffuse glow reflected into the kitchen, Svetlana and I enjoyed the ghost cook's gift. After the last delicious bite, she said, "We are done here?"

"Yeah. They're not coming back."

"Okay." She holstered her flashlight and gave me a sweet, icing-covered peck on the cheek.

A week later, Svetlana and I argued over whether to let Great Grandmother take the night shift driving, agreed to try it, set the destination to our next investigation, and posted the asylum video.

Comments poured in, as they do . . .

RealityGeek49   10 minutes ago
Obviously fake. Production values too high.

more . . .

SpookSpaz12   13 minutes ago

Cook voice a hired actor. Heard them on anime.

SvenTheZombieSlayer   1 hour ago (edited)

More Svetlana. Less moron who thinks cake is cool.
Reply: Prababushka   Sad child. Your grand-mother Sophia taught you read. She weeping.

NEXT VIDEO: Ghosting Hunting at the Heceta Head Lighthouse with Svetlana, Prababushka, and American Boy.

A Fiery Lull

~ Elad Haber

Dear Maria,

I set the field aflame. Again. Third time in three years.

First, it was locusts. They came from the south as a murmuration, huge and curved into the shape of an evil grin. They descended on my crops, ate and ate their bodyweights and more. I had no choice, but to burn them out. We surrounded the fields with flamethrowers, killing everything in our path, plant and bug, native and invader.

Next, it was the *federales.* They got wind of some of my unusual strains and were on their way to investigate. Like the insects before them, they swarmed in black vans, kicking up a dust-storm behind them. I gave the signal to burn the fields and even my precious incubator plants.

And now, it's the latest cartel war budding up against my business. I am not associated with any one family, so I'm in the middle of it, a victim of the violent winds that pass through the country like a traveling tropical storm.

We are packing up to leave to America. Etain is here with me. She misses you. You would be surprised at how big she's gotten! Even picking her up is getting difficult for this old man. She's holding the doll you gave her, with the red hair, like her momma when I first met you.

I turned your old studio into my office. Your artwork still hangs on the walls, the glazing glowing red from the fires. We're watching through the big windows as fieldhands burn my life's work.

I hope they are giving you my letters. Please know that though we are leaving the country, we will be back for you. When things quiet down. When it's safe.

I promise, Maria. I will come back for you.

Te amo, mi vida.

—Jorge.

☉

(Scrawled across a billboard near East Hampton, NY)
TO SLEEP, PERCHANCE TO DREAM.

Yo bro! Check this out.

I was working a quad shift at the farm. You wouldn't even recognize the place. You worked a summer here, like, what, five years ago? We've got three huge greenhouses now. The boss named them after those famous ships, the Nina, the Pinta, and the—uh—I don't remember the last one. Besides, he doesn't let anyone in that one.

So, I'm doing my usual work: Assessing every new flowering plant, making notes about size and color. The rows are endless, green aisles like trees along a highway. Small plants at the front and larger, thicker ones by the back. It takes me half a day to do one row.

Suddenly, there's a whisper beside me. I startle and almost drop my tablet.

"Hey," she says again.

It's the boss's daughter. You remember her, right? She was a little stick of a girl at fifteen. Well, she looks a lot different now. She had on a runner's outfit, a tight crop top and even tighter pants. Her legs seemed to go up to her chest and her hair was tied into a ponytail, it snaked down her back like a tattoo.

You know me, bro, I fall in love easily.

"Hi," I said.

She stepped further out of the shadows. She was wearing inky black so she still blended. She came close to me. "I need your help," she whispered.

"What—what can I do?" I stammered.

"I want to do something bad," she said.

I felt myself stiffen. Maybe love wasn't the right word.

She grasped my hand and started leading me away. "Um, but, I, uh, I have to work!" I protested for some stupid reason.

She just laughed and opened a nearby service door. "It's okay," she said, "I know your boss."

Outside, it was night, but stadium lights created an artificial day. As usual, the farm was abuzz with activity, but the other people were far away or engrossed in their duties.

The girl led me through the shadows of the bright light beyond the dome of the Nina to hug the walls of the Pinta. I could hear the machinery in there, churning along 24/7. The flower was converted to other forms in there: heated oils, crystalline wax, or distilled liquids for tinctures.

"Where are we going?" I whispered.

"Come on!" she replied.

We were exposed for a few minutes while we ran towards the next greenhouse, the one marked S/M. She found another darkened corner and we were hidden again. The building looked bigger and more imposing up close. We were both breathing heavy from the run. She had a wild, expectant, look on her face.

She pressed a button and a door revealed itself from the blank wall. Then she punched in a code and the door hissed opened. She grasped my hand and pulled me forward. The door slid shut behind us.

Inside was a laboratory, of sorts. It was similar to the greenhouse where I worked, but even at a glance, I knew the flowers were different. The strains were - I'm not sure how to describe it - unique. There were alien-like purple flowers, stalks and buds that glowed neon green, a few were an unsettling dark blue, while others looked a natural green, but when I looked closer, they had thorns where they shouldn't or had strange colorful patterns.

"What is this place?" I asked, awed.

She took a moment to let it all sink in. "Experimental strains. My father's life's work."

I crashed landed back to reality. I started to back away. "I shouldn't be in here," I said. "We should go."

I turned away. That's when she kissed me.

"Julien," she said. I didn't know she knew my name. She made it sound exotic, European. "Please stay."

I swallowed and nodded. She smiled and leaned in for another kiss, a peck on my cheek. Then she turned on her heel and started wandering among the strange plants. At various places, random as far as I could tell, she picked off a flowering bud and then went back to searching. At one point, she went back and grabbed a bit more from two bright green plants with orange hairs.

Finally satisfied, she ducked away from the rows of plants to a kind of maintenance area. There was a ladder to a loft. She went up first. I tried not to stare.

The loft was small, but furnished. A couple of couches, a few screens mounted to the walls. A bookshelf.

She sat down on a couch and beckoned me to sit next to her. On the little table in front of the couch, she laid down the buds she had collected. Their multi-colored hues looked rainbow-eqsue. She used the bottom of her palm to start crushing the buds, mixing them together.

She broke the silence. "Have you heard of Lull?"

"No," I said quickly.

"Liar," she grinned.

I sighed. "I have heard of it, but it's dangerous. I think. Doesn't it make you . . ."

"Yes," she said. "Or so I've heard. I've never tried it before."

I had a bad feeling about all of this, but what was I supposed to do at this point?

I asked, "How do you make it?"

As she crushed more of the flower, she said, "It's a cocktail. A blend. Different strains, combined in the right amounts. I've been researching, for awhile. I think this should do it."

She finished crushing all the flower and started rolling a joint from the crumbs.

I gulped. "I don't know if I want to, you know, do that."

She laughed. "It's not for you. It's for me. I wanted someone else here to, I don't know, just to make sure nothing goes wrong."

"Like if you stop breathing or something?"

"Or something."

She used her tongue to seal the joint and took a moment to admire it. It was thick like a baby banana. She rummaged around the table until she found a lighter. She lit the joint, took a long drag, and sat back. Her eyes were closed already and she said in a kind of contemplative tone, "You ever just want it all to stop?"

And then she fell asleep.

☉

ZERO STARS!!

I rarely write reviews, but I feel compelled after your RUDE employees treated my friends and I like garbage last night.

It was my best friend's birthday. We arrived around 2 a.m., already tipsy from the drive over. As soon as the doors swooshed open, we were elated. The place was packed with beautiful people, dancers hovering in the sky, and those interactive projection things—I love those!

The hostess floated in to greet us looking like some kind of goddess. She wore a long flowing green dress, with a wide slit in the front, a little too much skin in my opinion, but she pulled it off. She introduced herself, but it was hard to hear over the pounding music. I think she said her name was Elaine.

Anyway, it started off great. As she took us through the winding pathways of the club to our table, maybe-Elaine smiled and chatted with my best friend. Projection-butterflies came at her command to rest on her manicured fingers. Then she pointed at one of us and the butterfly came to rest on our shoulders or top of our head.

But then things took a turn once we sat down. We ordered a few bottles, a few thousand dollars' worth, just to start! Then your hostess leaned in to me and tried to sell me some "designer cannabis strains."

I said, "Bitch, I don't smoke that street rat stank."

Well, I guess she didn't like that. Even though, what's that phrase, the customer is always right—especially the customer who just dropped a few thousand dollars.

As soon as I refused her under the table deal, she got rude and insulting. I saw her talking to some of the waitresses and looking in our direction. We were practically IGNORED all night and I know it was because of her.

I complained to the manager and I saw him talking to her later that night, there was shouting and some wild gesturing, although I couldn't hear what they were saying. I hope she got fired.

Even if she did, I won't be back to your club and neither will any of my friends until you hire NON-RUDE employees.

☉

(Spotted on a billboard outside Albany, NY)
WE WERE MEANT TO SLEEP.

Dear Maria,

I'm sorry it's been so long since my last letter.

I've never lied to you. So, I need to tell you, it's been tough, lately, with Etain.

She is unable to keep a job and she keeps getting into trouble in the city. As a teenager, she was rebellious and mischievous. I was the same way. Heaven knows I was a terror for my poor madre until I met you and settled down. I have tried to be understanding and forgiving with her, but she tests me. Whenever she is home, we fight. She blames me for her mother not being around. She is starting to hate me, I fear.

I don't know how much longer I can keep the lie from her.

In happier news, Etain has taken a liking to one of the field hands at the farm. He's not a lowlife like her usual boyfriends – he wouldn't be working for me if he was – but he has a big mouth. Always texting some brother who lives in another state. A little too chatty, in my opinion. But she seems happy.

Although she doesn't need the money, I have insisted that Etain hold a job in addition to her studies so she can learn responsibility, just like we did. She's still trying to find the right fit.

I will write again soon.

Te amo,

—Jorge.

☉

hey bro. I think I have a girlfriend. Etain, aka the Bosses' Daughter, likes to hang around the employee's hut waiting for my shifts to end. I get some weird looks from my co-workers, but I don't care.

She usually looks like she is the middle of a workout, all skin and sweat. But not tonight. She is wearing what may have been a chiffon gown years ago, but full of rips and tears, like a Halloween costume. Her hair was half-done up one side and stringy and down on the other. Her makeup was similarly half-done, as if she got bored with the whole thing in the middle.

"Hi," I said when I saw her. She was sipping on a vape. The clouds that surrounded her were a maelstrom of colors. "You look nice. Are you going to a party?"

"We," she said grasping my hand like she does, "are going to a party." She wrinkled her nose in that way that may be considered rude to most

people, but doesn't bother me. "You'll need a shower and a change of clothes."

She smiled wide at the prospect and then took off at a run towards the big house. I followed after her. The house was massive and textured in glass. I'd never been inside the house before, even after working here all these years.

It was, as expected, garish and loud. Artwork on every wall, sculptures in every corner. Massive chairs flown in from Northern Europe, it looked like they still had some snow on them. I tried to stop, to gawk like a gallery-viewer, but Etain yanked my arm and led me up the stairs to her suite.

She had three rooms all to herself, each one larger than the next. Her closet was the size of my apartment with seating and lighted mirrors.

"I grabbed some of my dad's old clothes, back when he was a bit . . ." she made a squeezing gesture with her hands. "Younger."

And then she laughed in such a cute way, I felt my heart pulse.

An hour later, I emerged wearing a button down shirt, slacks, and a belt that squeezed the life out of my stomach. We got high and then went downstairs to the waiting car.

In the backseat, on the drive to the city, Etain was calm, as always, but I was a ball of nerves.

"Are we going to be late?" I asked her.

She smiled and slid open a compartment between us. There was a grey satchel inside. She patted it like a dog.

"Hard to be late when we're bringing the party."

Oh.

She saw my discomfort. "Are you nervous?"

"A little."

"Don't be. It's . . . hard to describe. But wonderful, in its own way."

I remembered the lectures in health class. "Isn't it like death? Like you die for a few hours?"

She laughed. "Not at all! There are these amazing images. Like you are watching a movie of yourself. Or you are experiencing something from a different perspective."

"Different how?" I asked.

"You'll see."

She leaned back and sighed, as if she had already taken some of the Lull. I watched the rise and fall of her chest and lingered on the exposed bits of skin beneath the tattered dress. I was used to seeing her in more relaxed attire. Dressed up as she was, it was like she was a completely different person.

The car pulled up to a high rise and a doorman opened the door for us. I half expected paparazzi, but there was only the busy background chatter of the city.

Her heels clicked against the marble floor of the hallway as she led me towards an elevator. Not surprisingly, she pressed the button for the top floor.

The door opened directly into a penthouse apartment. There were floor to ceiling windows overlooking a bustling night-time metropolis. In the daytime, it's probably flooded with light. But tonight it's all shadows. Even the big chandeliers and floor scones are set to a dim. Sheets hang from the high ceiling, forcing us to push our way through the apartment as if we're under colorful water.

We emerged from the hall to a large living area. Guests, similarly dressed in finery, but somehow damaged or weathered a bit, called out to Etain. She manufactured a wide smile, the brightest I've ever seen on her, before she embraced them. She introduced me, but I didn't catch any of the names.

Etain unveiled the grey satchel from behind her back and the other guests tittered and smiled at her. The hostess, obvious in her pristine gown and impossible heels, separated herself from the gaggle. She fake-smiled at me and then leaned into Etain and whispered, "Wait till you see the Den."

We all followed her down another hall to a bedroom which looked like about the half size of one of the greenhouses. There were blankets and pillows piled up in mazes and cul-de-sacs. Beds lined the walls, more than I've ever seen in one place.

"It's perfect," Etain whispered. She was glowing, excited. I couldn't help it, I was excited too.

In the center of the room were three massive vaporizers. Etain went to study them. The little gaggle of women dispersed expect for the hostess, who hung back next to me. She was a foot taller than me in those heels.

"So you're the new boyfriend?" she said to me with a side-long look. "Must be a special person to keep her interested."

There was malice in her tone. Something else, as well. She gave me a weak smile and walked over to Etain. She put her hands on Etain's *waist and pulled her closer to her, an obviously intimate gesture. They both laughed.*

I wandered the corners of the large room, smiling at the beautiful strangers. I overheard one woman lean into her friends and say, "I read some people used to do it in the middle of the day."

One of the ladies gasped. Another one exclaimed, "How uncouth!"

From the center of the room, the hostess called out, "Everyone find someplace comfortable."

There were more titterings and nervous whispers from the crowd. Etain swung the grey satchel around and started loading the Lull into the vaporizers. They started to emit a mist into the room. It was thick and white like snow.

Etain smiled at me before she was engulfed in the storm.

See you on the other side, bro.

☉

Sleep
From Wikipedia, the free encyclopedia
This article is about sleep in humans. For other uses, see Sleep (disambiguation).

For centuries, mankind has relinquished half of their lives to somnolence. In the mid 21st century, spurred by the Accelerated Evolution Movement, or AEM, which was the scientific movement to reach humanity's evolutionary goals through technology and bio-engineering, sleep became a target. Politicians ran on a campaign of radical change. Without sleep, they argued, how much more could we accomplish? They poured billions in AEM research facilities until a "cure" was found. A combination of drugs delivered to five year old children through a year of micro-doses tweaked their bio-chemistry so that sleep became, after a single generation, eradicated. Some countries banned it completely while most societies frowned upon it, asking instead, What would you do if you had half of your life back?

☉

[static]
"Dispatch, dispatch, reports of active blaze on 66th St. and Amsterdam. Penthouse. Engines en route."
[static]

☉

(Photographed on a billboard near New Platz, NY)
I WISH I KNEW YOU.

Dear Maria,

There has been an incident.

Don't worry, Etain is fine. But some of her friends have died, including her boyfriend, Julien. There was a fire at a party they attended in Manhattan. Apparently, they were *sleeping* at the party. There was an open flame somehow that caught fire, we don't know how yet. The police have been around a few times now, asking questions. They seem to think Etain is responsible.

She didn't come home for days and then she appeared one night in my study.

Once I made sure she was fine, I demanded answers and asked her why the police were asking questions about her and her experience with *sleep.*

We had an argument. Our worst yet. She brought you up, accused me of taking away the only person who ever truly loved her.

I had no choice, I had to tell her the truth. About that day, in the old farmhouse, when she was a baby. About the fire you started.

I will never understand how you left her alone in the house. What would have happened if I came home a little later? I couldn't risk something like that happening again. I had no other choice.

I told Etain everything, finally.

Tears streamed from her eyes, but she was stone-faced, like polished steel.

"I don't believe you," she said.

"You're a liar!" she shouted.

I shouted something back.

Then she ran. Out of the room and out of the house. I don't know where she went or if she'll be back.

—Jorge.

☉

Official transcript of podcast "Mysteries of New York," Episode 16 *[ominous musical intro]*

SC: Hello and welcome to the episode 16 of the "Mysteries of New York" podcast where we discuss mysterious occurrences in New York state. I'm your host, Samantha Cunning, with my co-host, Darius White. How are you doing today, Darius? Staying warm?

DW: Trying to, Sam, but it's not working. We're looking at single digit temps for the rest of the week here in Buffalo.

SC: Brr. Let's get right to today's topic. A topical one, a news story that is getting a lot of play throughout the national outlets.

DW: Although it is very much a New York kind of story, wouldn't you agree?

SC: Definitely, Darius. And what are we even talking about? The billboards, of course.

DW: Yes. The Poet of Poughkeepsie.

SC: So named because of the first spotting of the billboard on a state road outside the city. We only have one picture of that sighting before county officials painted over it. The picture was taken in a foggy winter morning and obscured most of the text. But the style was unmistakable.

DW: Especially when similar fragments in thick black spray paint started showing up on the highways and roads of Long Island and then upstate. This was about six or seven months ago, isn't that right, Sam?

SC: Yeah, that sounds right. It was a news-worthy story almost immediately. There was a whole group of photographers who roamed the roads looking for new fragments.

DW: Before authorities could burn them down.

SC: That's right. A few weeks after the first fragment was painted over by local authorities', other municipalities around the state started doing the same thing. But after every washing over, the fragment would re-appear as if by magic. So, they started taking more violent action. Was it the same person, working tirelessly through the days and nights to re-do his or her work, or was it copycats, fans, or maybe it was some kind of collective?

DW: No one knows for sure, although there have been a lot of speculation about the Poet's identity and motivation.

SC: It was the substance of the words that angered the local governments. The fragments were about sleep. The joy of rest. The lost magic of dreams.

DW: We both can attest to years of demonization of sleep, first in school, then from politicians, business owners, etc.

SC: And that's what scared them.

DW: Yes. They burned the billboards so the fragments could not be redone. It was not uncommon to drive down a highway in New York and see a seemingly endless row of burning billboards.

SC: But who is the poet of Poughkeepsie and what are they after? What is their goal?

DW: We'll dig into that more after a short message from our sponsor.

☉

Maria,

They're allowing me one last letter. Maybe I should have called? We haven't spoken in so many years, I don't know if I even remember the sound of your voice.

I've been arrested on federal charges. It was Etain. She was using a cocktail of my strains to jerry-rig a sleep inducer. The FBI has hundreds of texts from Etain's boyfriend detailing how she manufactured the drug and brought it to the apartment where those kids died. Even if she didn't start the fire, they are blaming her for what happened.

I swear, I didn't know what she was doing. I would have stopped it if I knew.

Of course, the Feds don't believe me. They are sending me away. She'll be on her own now. Maybe she always was.

In the end, I was a liar. I never came back for you.

Good intentions too often turn into broken promises.
Lo siento, mi amor.
Goodbye, Maria.

☉

r/newyorkstate—Posted by u/SheDidn'tDoIt six days ago
[MEGATHREAD] FRAGMENTS

okay, guys, this is it! I've asked the mods to close down all the other sightings threads so we can keep it all in one place.

It won't be long now. State police have closed down all roads and exits out of the state. Federal authorities are going door to door. New York is locked down and it's going to stay that way until the Poet is caught.

It's our last chance to help her get her message out. With the enhanced scrutiny, sightings have been rare, but they're out there. Billboards are being monitored so we're starting to see pieces of her last poem on motel signs, drive thru windows, behind Costco's, in gas station bathroom mirrors, wherever they are, WE HAVE TO FIND THEM.

Remember: Every drawing has a nearby number. Put those numbers in sequence and we have the order. Then it's just a matter of finding all the fragments. Good luck, guys!

EDIT #1: We are over halfway there!

EDIT #2: Have you guys gotten any weird home visits lately? Like, from the FBI? At first I thought it was prank, but then they got all mad at me when I wouldn't let them in. They threatened to arrest me, but then I let them search my house and they were satisfied, I guess? They said they might be back.

EDIT #3: I think we should stop.

☉

(Published on the front page of *The New York Times*)

When I sleep,
I dream of my mother.

My mother I never knew.
My mother who tried to kill me.
Flames
Have followed me my entire life.
When I close my eyes,
I let them take me.

Burn me this time.
I'm ready.

From or Belonging to the Spring People

~ Kiya Nicoll

The girl stood on tiptoe, leaning over the velvet rope to peer into the case, not quite reaching forward to put her hands on the glass. She was albino, perhaps, though her skin lacked the rosy undertones one might expect, and her eyes were an ice blue that matched the bluish shading of her cascade of perfectly straight white hair. Her dress was a green so dark as to seem almost black, and the string of simple red beads she wore as a necklace seemed stark and bloody.

"Don't touch the glass," the guard said.

The girl pirouetted on one foot to look at him, to look him up and down, and then laughed, and spread her arms, dancing into a near-run and wheeling around one case, then another, like a hawk spiraling on a thermal, before she darted out into the hall and was gone. The private communications crackled to keep an eye out for her, and her recklessness, and to scold any parent that seemed attached to her, but she did not reappear.

She was the first, or at least the first that anyone noticed.

The next was a man, at least seven feet tall and broad in the shoulder, brown as an oak and hair dreadlocked into shaggy orange pollen strands. He loomed over the glass cases, looking down at them from above, his chuckle rumbling like thunder as he leaned to read the labels.

When another man slipped in, tiny, fawn-colored and black-eyed, the giant turned to him and greeted him with a booming, "Brother!" that made him jump, eyes going wide and startled. The big man crossed over to him in two strides, setting a hand on his shoulder, and steered him around to the case on the end. "Tell me, brother, do you think it's authentic?"

The skittish little man allowed himself to be rearranged, and peered at the label. "From or belonging to the Spring People," he said aloud, and then said, "Well." He hopped in place once, then twice, and on the third the giant caught him in the air and held him suspended so that he could look down at the necklace. "Hmmmm. Put me down, brother."

"Well, what do you think?"

"It's the eye beads that have me particularly skeptical," he said, in the tone of one who really ought to have spectacles to take off and polish while theorizing. "I'd expect more ambiguity about whether or not they're also roses."

The giant laughed, leaning back, his hands on his hips, as if he had just been told a tremendous joke. "You know, you're right."

"Of course I'm right," he said, peering up high enough to strain his neck. "You wouldn't have asked me to look otherwise." He staggered a little when the other clapped him on the shoulder, but did not stumble into the case or back against the velvet rope. "The greens are quite good for them, though."

"They are. The yellowish sheen there is like that girl I was seeing that time."

The small man rolled his eyes. "I know, you like the Dawn ones."

"Regardless of season!" boomed the giant, laughing, but the smaller man was back to studying the necklace, frowning. "What's wrong now, brother?"

"Oh, just thinking that if the greens are particularly suited to a Spring Person of the Dawn, the reds are more suited to one of the Night and that's an odd combination."

"Is it? Does it have colors that suit the entire daily wheel?"

"Pick me up again, brother," he said, and the giant obliged. "The shimmering golds might do for a child of the Midday, and the olives for Twilight, but that dark green there seems to be a duplication of Night. And of course there are minor times left unmarked, but they often are, that's hardly indicative. The reds could be Autumn, too, though, and that tangles the whole thing up in briars."

The big man did not put him down.

"Brother?"

"I was wondering if it had Sun, Moon, and Stars, in your judgement, actually," he said, thoughtfully.

With a frown, the other said, "Not sure. I could make the argument, but it's a bit muddier than is typical. If the dark green is Night without Stars, the red is still perplexing."

"Night with Moon? On the tulips? Or possibly the Sun at Night in Spring?"

He grunted. "Put me down, brother. I'm stumped."

"Let's go have a beer, then." On that note, they left, in amiable company, and the other visitors to the exhibit clustered, briefly, around the piece in dispute, to verify what they had overheard, and to try to make sense of it.

It was two days before another of the curious museum visitors came to look at the necklace. She leaned on a cane, her stooped shoulders shrouded in a cape made of soft black feathers, her hair curling over it, this lock auburn, that lock silver, like maple leaves edged in frost. Her face had a certain agelessness to it, crow's feet around eyes that seemed full of laughter, yes, but neither terribly wrinkled nor terribly worn, and she said, "Hmmm," to the glass case, and then started to laugh.

"Why is that lady laughing?" asked a child, fist knotted in her mother's coat to tug for attention.

The woman turned, the base of her cane making a sharp noise against the floor as she did, a noise that turned heads. She lowered herself like she could fold downwards and said, "Schöner Streich," and then frowned. "Nein, no . . ." It took her a moment to figure out what language she wanted, and it still came accented with a German that had an odd, mincing lilt to it, as if the entire concept of words was worth mockery. "It is a good joke. A beautiful joke? More ways than one. So I laugh."

The child frowned at that, scuffing one foot against the floor. "What sort of joke?"

"Morgenstern." The old woman stood, unfolding again, hands straining against the head of the cane. "No. Lucifer? A morning-star sort of joke."

"What's a morning-star joke?" asked the child, and her mother tried to hush her, inspiring only recalcitrance.

"Nein, no, I do not mind," said the woman, with a wave of her hand. "Here is the joke: one who brightly burns, who high above the sun flies, but cannot escape, and back he falls, gone, invisible. Poof!

And those who their aim set when the morning star is high, they, too, are lost, into the sun to follow."

"That doesn't seem very funny to me." There was an intense edge of stubbornness in the tone, that bordered on sullenness.

"Should you become as old as I," the woman said, with a curl of a smile at some private joke that made her eyes dance, "perhaps the humor of it you will see. The morning star returns, you know, but humans never learn."

"How old are you?" demanded the child, and her mother gasped. "Never learn what?"

The woman laughed again, and answered, "Old enough to know secrets," with a smile that suggested she had quite a few of them hoarded up, upon which she slept like a smug cat.

The child refused to be cowed. "What sort of secrets?" she demanded, with a little stomp of one foot. Her mother stammered an apology and tried to drag her away, but the woman just chuckled and said, "I do so enjoy young humans."

"Why?"

"You have not yet grown into being conventional and afraid," she said, putting her head to one side and smiling that smug little smile, like she was searching through her vault of treasures, letting them slide over her hands like beads to select one that she might consider handing over. "Come, I will whisper you a secret in your ear, if you can convince your mother to let you."

"Mom," she said, dragging out the word in the pleading note of children possessed of a great desire.

"All right, go ask," her mother said, in the defeated tones of someone who does not care to have this fight right now, particularly not in the middle of a crowded museum exhibit. "I'll be right here keeping an eye on you."

The motley-haired woman said, with grand amiability, "Oh, I haven't stolen any children away for years, I don't have a place to store them these days," and then leaned down again, shifting her cane so she could keep her balance.

"What's the secret?" hissed the girl.

"When someone a favor asks, and does not their name offer? Then is the time to be very cautious. Some people play tricks, like the one who had that necklace brought here."

The girl looked up, eyes narrowing. "What's your name?" she asked immediately.

The woman laughed, head thrown back, and then said, "You may call me Hulda, child."

"Thank you, Hulda." She frowned, with a judiciously skeptical look, and then said, "Hmmmm," and marched back to her mother's side.

Her mother took her hand, firmly, and asked, "Why are you making that face?"

"She didn't say it was her name. Just that that's what I could call her."

The older woman straightened, chortling. "Such a clever girl," she murmured, and then said, more loudly, "When the Queen of Summer hears the gossip, it will be quite a show. But perhaps a show you don't want to see." She gave the necklace another long, studious look, and then made her way out, still chuckling.

Again, the museum staff made note; a Queen of Summer who promised to make trouble probably ought to be prepared for, though nobody was at all certain what to expect of her. It had become something of a game, by this point, to collect the stories of the peculiar visitors who studied that case in particular: the two identical children, dressed in grey with trailing sleeves like the wings of swallows, who trilled comments to each other in a language nobody recognized and then chased each other out of the museum in darting swoops; the girl with the shockingly yellow hair, wearing a ruffled shirt that was streaked with purple and white, who read the label and laughed uproariously; the big man who stood for hours, motionless as an exhibit himself, stone-faced and with crystalline-pale eyes shocking against the darkness of his skin. They debated whether the little crowd of short fat people who resembled nothing so much like a collection of mixed nuts in their shades of brown, wrinkled like almonds or even pecans, was another such apparition, but while those guests were quite interested in the necklace and talked quietly among themselves about it, they spent more time in front of the display of cups and forks.

None of that prepared them for the blue woman.

She was not particularly tall, but despite that she loomed, her clothes billowing turbulently around her in whorls of grey and ultramarine, whipping to white at the edges. Her hair was swept up into plumes and cascades, green and blue and grey, and her skin was genuinely blue, sky blue, summer sky blue.

There were fewer people in the exhibit, at least, so she swept to the obvious case without catching anyone in her undertow. She read the label, lifted her chin in obvious disapproval, and sniffed once, before turning and walking back out again. Her wake filled with eddies of murmurs and exclamations, and appropriate calls were made to management.

The days after the blue woman had visited were tense ones. Not by anyone's deliberate choice; it seemed more that the air in the museum had that electric sense of potential, something waiting to break open, though it lacked clarity as to when or how. There were no further strange guests, or at least not any that distinguished themselves from the milling visitors. The most remarkable thing anyone noticed was a sulky teenaged girl in a grey hoodie who spent the afternoons in the exhibit, hands in her pockets and watching the people more than the displays.

Midway through the next week, a man arrived, thin and straight and upright as a sunbeam, wearing white robes that shimmered with the intensity of a mirage dancing over hot stone. His hair was long and golden under a thin, precise circlet, his eyes a vivid and unquenchable green. He glided rather than walked to the case containing the necklace, and bent his head just the slightest amount so that he might read the label. "This," he said, and somehow everyone hearing him knew it to be true, "is incorrect."

"Who are you?" asked a guard, stepping forward.

The man made of angles and light turned towards him, and did not speak, but everyone present understood, for a fleeting instant, the vast spinning angles of space, the pole bent sunwards for long enough for a breath before sweeping on, the dancing orchestra of planets and moons arrayed in their many chords, tracing ellipses in the breath of stars, angles and arcs all made of light. This, too, was a burst of noonlight shining upon white rocks undappled by shade, and the sharp brine smell of the sea.

"You can't just be at them," said a voice, a swaggering voice belonging to a swaggering man. "You have to use mouth noises to communicate." He was broad and red-brown, tall but not overwhelmingly so, his muscularity softened by his paunch. While he also wore a circlet, it was not precise and elegant, but rather a coiled tangle of oak leaves, golden heads of grain, and some sort of reddish purple berry, from which swept two sharply pointed horns in a manner that suggested that he might have grown them himself, even as every onlooker was certain that that was obvious nonsense.

The pillar of a man turned towards him. "It is imprecise."

"You are hopeless." He heaved a tremendous sigh. "Let me translate a moment, I believe he wanted to say that he can be known as, let's approximate, Stilled Sun in Quartz At Noon, Prince Consort to the Queen."

"And who are you?"

"You can call me Frank."

The shining man turned upon Frank a gaze of burning disapproval and sniffed once.

"What?"

Eyebrows like sundogs arched upwards.

"It's hardly my fault you have no discernible sense of humor," Frank grumbled. "And I do intend to be."

The other sniffed again.

"I suppose it's for the best you're too good to actually talk, that language would probably turn half of them into frogs," he snapped back. "Or something worse."

A twist of the hand, a curl of a smile.

"Ugh," Frank declared. As the other man lifted his chin slightly in apparent triumph, he pivoted on his heel and bowed, spreading his arms wide, and said, "My fair Queen."

The victory fled from the pillar's face as he turned, belatedly, to incline his head with elegant formality, even as Frank stepped forward and accepted the Queen's hand in his own, bowing over it to plant a kiss on the back.

"My dear consort," she said.

A flicker of displeasure crossed the other man's impassive face. "He has told them to call him Frank."

"Has he?" The Queen seemed amused, more than anything. "I suppose he is." She offered her other hand to Stilled Sun in Quartz At Noon, Prince Consort to the Queen. "But it does not please you, my love."

Afterwards, nobody could agree what she had looked like. When one person spoke of her shockingly bonfire red hair, another frowned and said her hair had been black, and others argued about whether it had been a metallic gold or like beach sand. Her eyes were definitely vibrant and stunning, but whether they were clear summer sky blue, or luminous green, or even yellow was a topic of dispute. They did not bother fighting about whether her gown was green or blue or red, not when they could occupy themselves in endless debate about whether her crown was made of wheat wrought in gold, or crystal that refracted rainbows around her, or had the horns of a stag worked with silver. Her skin might have been golden, or pale green, or a velvety black that glittered faintly as if she were made of stars.

Everyone agreed that she was compelling, that she was beautiful, that she was terrifying.

"It does not," said the shaft of light shaped into a man, as if the Queen were not a force that interrupted all thought, as if he might carry on a conversation with her about his grievances as a matter of the perfectly ordinary.

"And how did you introduce yourself?" purred the Queen. "Did you?"

"I told them who I am," he replied, with a little prim huff.

"You gave them your name?" Her humor turned thunderous, and she seemed to grow taller. "Knowing the risks, you gave them your name?"

Frank glanced at the other consort, and then laid a hand gently on her arm and said, "To be fair, my Queen, they could barely comprehend it, let alone pronounce it. You know how he is about the mouth noises." His other hand shaped itself into a squawking bird's beak, thumb tapping the fingertips, mocking the concept of sound.

There was a moment where she turned on him, where it seemed there might be some incomprehensible act of violence, and then she laughed. "The mouth noises, yes," she said, and the hurricane was gone, leaving everything windswept but miraculously undamaged. "You are indeed correct."

He bowed, just slightly. "My Queen." He looked up as he bowed, meeting the gaze of the pale shining man, who gave him a slight, small nod, curt and acknowledging.

"Show me the necklace," she said, then.

"The label is incorrect." Nonetheless, he pointed, one slender finger aimed at the case.

The Queen shook her head, amused, and swept past them both to study it. "I do remember this piece," she said. "It was given to—oh, who was she, do either of you recall? She was of our court, of course."

Stilled Sun in Quartz At Noon tilted his head, and deigned to say, "She was a midday child."

"Like yourself," the Queen agreed. "Though much later in the season, I believe, not a solstice girl."

Frank drummed his fingers on his chin, twirling a lock of his beard around them. "Beech tree, I believe. And the colors did suit her."

"Even as she turned red in the autumn," agreed the Queen, with a little shake of her head. "A pity. As mortal as her tree, she was." She waved a hand. "We must correct the sign, at least."

"Do you wish to reclaim the necklace?"

"The mortals made it, and the one with a claim to it is centuries gone," she said. "But this is—" she left it unfinished, for long enough that the predictable consort grew uncomfortable enough to say, "Incorrect," so that she could turn to bestow a smile upon him.

Most of the patrons had shifted to one side, where they could watch the strange guests without grand risk of interference. The Queen lifted her chin and crooked a finger at a guard, saying, "Please, fetch someone with authority. We must speak with them."

There was nothing possible but obedience, though the guard hesitated a moment before one said, "I will keep order." Thusly, if not reassured, at least affirmed that the man made of straight lines and undeniable facts would stand guard in his place, the guard hurried off. Certainly, none of the museum visitors seemed likely to challenge him, even the little cluster that was pinned between them and the wall with no route to edge around towards the larger group of people. The teenaged girl among them chewed gum ostentatiously and somehow, despite everything, managed to look unimpressed.

The guard returned promptly, curator in tow, and reclaimed his position.

The Queen turned, head cocked slightly to one side, and said, "Your sign is incorrect." She flicked her fingers imperiously. "Fix it."

The curator was a short woman, somewhat round, with grey hair in loose curls, and she met the gaze of the Queen and said, "The sign

The Queen of Summer sniffed, and said, "Fine," before saying, fiercely, to the curator, "I shall return."

Spring smiled as sweetly as her fangs would allow. "Unless you yield, of course, in which case the item will remain in my domain, as it is named to be."

The curator stepped back to let them go, first the Queen of Summer, hand in hand with both consorts, and then the fox, her glorious tail swishing behind her as she went. Once they were safely away, she let out a breath and said, to nobody in particular, "Perhaps if we added 'Origin disputed' they won't come back."

Starfish Sister

~ *Jon Lasser*

Riley's dops lay scattered across her desk. They stretched their tiny legs and arms, sitting or reclining, miniatures of her down to their tiny, exasperated sighs as they studied.

One dop crammed for tomorrow's biology exam—nothing about evolution, Father would be relieved to hear—while others studied quadratic equations or caught up on the Honors English reading, which was—well, she'd find out soon enough. Her social dop chattered away on the cloned phone, gossiping with Sophia and Purvi and Olive about boys or school or maybe both at the same time. Two dops bounced on the blade of a jam-sticky butter knife as though it was a springboard. What were they supposed to be doing?

As hard as Riley tried to keep all the dops on task, the aroma of Mom's roast chicken wafted up the stairs like it was trying to distract her. Her stomach growled, dinner having been one slice of toast with the thinnest smear of strawberry jam spread over it, and how could she focus with the dinner-table conversation echoing through the vents? Every bit of it, from Father intoning grace like the whole congregation was present to Mom's inane questions about school, felt calculated to drive her mad.

Roast chicken was her favorite meal, too, but if she didn't babysit all the dops, she'd be up past midnight with homework. Without her watchful eye, they'd stop working and whisper to each other like they were planning a mutiny. It was probably just high spirits, a mirror of her own reluctance to engage with the work, her own capacity for distraction.

And so Beta, who never appeared distracted, sat downstairs with Riley's family, eating dinner instead of doing PSAT prep or applying for internships or whatever. Mom spoke to the dop in that low, soothing tone that always gave her the heebie-jeebies, even from upstairs. Riley was jealous of how Beta felt nothing when talking with her parents, and how she managed to be so organized. Other than that, Beta was so like her it was eerie; Mom couldn't suspect anything.

"And then Miss Koolhaus took a pin and poked Manish from behind," Beta said, "Where he couldn't see, and the air all went out of him." She must've gotten the story telepathically from the social dop, but Beta was selling it like she'd seen it herself. Riley was jealous: if only she could hear the dops in her head as clear as the voice of God, the way they could hear each other!

"I'm glad *you* don't send a dop to school," Mom chuckled. "Imagine the embarrassment if you got caught!"

"Getting caught isn't the point," Father grumbled. "It's the difference between right and wrong—"

"But I'm not," Beta said, "So there's nothing to worry about." It was true, mostly. Beta wasn't sending anyone anywhere, and Riley usually went herself, Phys Ed excepted. Riley was in charge, if not always in control. But what teenager was? How *could* you be in control when your parents ruled your life, when you didn't know or couldn't admit who you were, and there were so many of you running around, each one spreading you out just a little bit further?

"—like the whole question of dops," Father continued, steamrolling Beta the way he would have steamrolled Riley, or anyone else. "They're a perversion of natural law."

"Yes, Father," her dop mumbled. The poor thing shouldn't have to put up with his Biblical reasoning, even though dops didn't have feelings or thoughts of their own. If Father knew what Riley was doing, he'd disown her, or worse.

Father took dops seriously, even if most of his flock were a bunch of hypocrites. Who among them hadn't set a dop to watch an episode of *Mr. and Mrs. X* so they could chit-chat about it at work on Monday? Whatever Father said about "natural law" while they nodded in their pews, however they parroted his homilies in public, their dops watched a show about dops written and acted in by dops so they'd have something to talk about with their coworkers—or their coworkers' dops. None of them batted an eyelash at the Army's dop platoons, each orchestrated by a single master, thinned by her effort to little more than the desire for victory.

Somehow, like drinking beer or smoking weed, adults thought only other people had a dop problem. Never themselves. Dop dependency might be like sex addiction: only a problem if you believed in it. Say if you went to a church like Father's. Dops weren't a problem for Riley as long as she didn't get caught, and as long as she could keep them in line.

"All done." Her math dop sounded reluctant, like she wasn't ready.

Riley sighed. She wasn't ready either. The dop hopped across the bed, til she got stuck between two large folds of the comforter. Riley picked her up and held her in her palm.

She popped the math dop into her mouth and bit down.

Something went squish. Tiny bones cracked as Riley chewed. She swallowed. She felt a jolt, like touching a nine-volt battery to her tongue, and tasted metal halfway down her throat. Her belly grew warm, like she'd just downed a Jello shot of experience. Quadratic equations weren't that hard. It was just cross-multiplication, if you thought about it. The warmth spread through her, creeping up her hands and her neck, rushing down into her legs and toes and everything else. It was as though she'd written the equations herself, over and over, until it came naturally.

She chewed through her homework: the parts of a cell, *Of Mice and Men*, how Franco's Spain served as an ideal model for America, the effects of vitamin B-6 on the human body. If dops were against the rules, why did school have a college prep curriculum so rigorous that nobody could possibly keep up without them?

Her Phys Ed dop wasn't home yet. That was one class Riley didn't need to attend, even if she had to blow up that dop like a thick-skinned balloon. Since making full-sized dops was a pain in the behind, she always used them twice—once for work, and once for fun. After class, she'd sent it downtown for dinner and clubbing. What Riley would do, if she could get away from babysitting her dops long enough. If she wasn't worried about getting caught.

Her stomach gurgled queasily, glutted on knowledge. No time to think about it. She cleared off her desk and put the mat down, the slice of toast she'd filched from downstairs on top. Four plus Beta would be enough for tomorrow, so she cut it into quarters. With a sewing needle she put a drop of blood from her thumb on each, and applied the compound from the dropper. The toast softened back into bread, folded in on itself, and took her shape. The dops rolled onto their backs and cried out like babies. She blew gently across their tiny faces until they stopped crying and fell asleep.

The window rattled, but it was only the wind. Not her dop come back with the forbidden taste of rum and coke, or even another woman in her mouth. Riley was too wiped out even for mom's chicken, so even though she knew she should wait up for PE, she left the window unlatched and turned off the lights.

Something outside crashed and Riley was out of bed, her head out the window peering into the darkness, before she knew she'd woke.

Father's footsteps boomed as he tromped downstairs. The outside lights came on.

"Who's there?" His church voice, the one he used when he was afraid but ashamed to admit to his fear, reverberated in the darkness. The voice Riley heard in her head even when he wasn't mad, the voice when she imagined talking to him about what she really felt, what she really wanted. Not more college prep, not church.

There her dop was, around the corner from where Father was looking, sprawled face-down in the mulch below the pine. Its arms pinwheeled round like a starfish and cast strange shadows in the light of the full moon. No wonder she hadn't seen it right away. It must have fallen from the tree, climbing up to her window. Riley's stomach turned: she should have stayed awake. If she got caught—

"I'm calling the police," Father bellowed. The church voice probably meant he hadn't seen anything and was bluffing, trying to put a scare into whoever he imagined was outside, threatening their perfect little lives. If only he knew what went on inside the house. Not only Riley's dops. Father still talked about how he wanted a son, that he had never wanted Riley to be an only child, but he didn't seem to understand there was a reason she didn't have any siblings. Mom had never said a thing but Riley knew how to put the pieces of a secret together.

She held still for what felt like ages until Father clomped back up the stairs. His bedroom door slammed and his bed groaned. Mom said something Riley couldn't make out through the wall. Soon he was snoring.

The stairs hardly creaked as Riley tiptoed down. She slipped on her shoes. The alarm chirped once as she opened the back door—darn, she hadn't thought about that. Too late now.

Where was the dop? She turned the corner, toward her room. Her phone's flashlight threw shadows of shrubs and planters that made everything feel faraway and strange.

There it should have been, furrows in the dirt in that sprawled-out shape. Footprints led away, into the grass.

The drainpipe shook. Her dop was climbing back up again. It must have come to while she waited for Father to fall asleep, waited in the grass and come back. She could almost taste it, a marshmallow of sin. It would be soon.

The dop shimmied back down, toward her. No! Had it seen her? Why not wait inside? They couldn't go back in together—someone might see them like that. Besides, she'd set off the alarm. For all she knew, Father was on his way downstairs again with the shotgun. They needed to climb the tree, quick.

"I'm Beta," the dop said as its feet landed in the mulch, as though it sensed her confusion. "P.E. booked it down the block. Let's get her."

Riley had never lost a dop before. Now and again, in their "Scared Straight" assembly, school would show video of people who'd lost too many dops. All those parts of themselves vanished, what remained staring blankly at the camera, emptier than any dop. She didn't want to be like that.

And then she understood: this was it. Beta and PE had it in for Riley. They'd plotted against her. Of course they had. Beta would eat Riley and replace her. It's what Riley would have done, if their positions were reversed. It was all right: Beta deserved better. She was smarter, more ready for college, better under deadlines, more in control of their shared life. Besides, Riley couldn't eat Beta, not any more. She was too big to eat whole, and Reilly hated dop soup.

"You go inside," Riley said. "In case my parents check in." Best to pretend she knew nothing.

Beta shook its head. "You'll need my help to catch her. Let's go."

☉

It strolled across the lawn to the sidewalk and started to jog down the block, towards the main street. Riley reached the pavement and ran, too.

Mrs. Winfield stuck her head out her bedroom window and clucked loud enough for Riley to hear. She'd no doubt mutter about "witchcraft" at church on Sunday after shaking hands with Father, even though Riley had seen Mrs. Winfield making sandwiches at the soup kitchen the same time she was at home glued to the boob tube, even though her daughter Everly's dop sat right next to her in Miss Koolhaus's class. Mrs. Winfield had art on her walls from that dop artist, the one Riley saw the clip about in art class, with the factory where all of him painted the same picture at the same time.

"This way," Beta whisper-shouted, gesturing at the alley. "Hurry!" Riley wiped the sweat from her brow and heaved another breath. Maybe she shouldn't have skipped so much PE.

Riley spun on her right heel to turn. This was as good a place as any. She fell and yelped as though in pain from a twisted ankle, steeling herself for the judgement she was owed.

"Over here," the dop shouted. "She's fallen!" It stood above her as P.E.'s footfalls grew near.

Riley's heart beat faster even though she lay flat on her back, the asphalt smooth and warm below her.

They looked down. Beta—at least, she thought it was Beta—smiled, and pulled a steak knife from her belt.

"This is the part where you tell me how I've hurt you," Riley said. "The part where you stab me with that knife and turn me to soup." She shrugged, though the tar sort of stuck her in place. "Get on with it."

Beta shook her head. "I don't like dop soup any more than you."

"How will you eat me? Piece by piece?"

Riley wanted more than anything to be whole—whether it was in her own body or Beta's didn't matter so much. Some head-shrinker might think she wanted to die, but that wasn't it: she wanted to be herself—her best self, the way Beta was—to herself and her friends and her parents. Even so, she shuddered at the thought of being eaten, no matter how many dops a week she ate. That was different—wasn't it?

"I'm not here to kill you. I'm here to free you." Beta stabbed P.E., then pulled the knife up to slit its neck. The blood fell like warm rain on Riley's face. She licked it and shuddered with the feelings that arose. P.E. collapsed. Beta fell to her knees next to P.E. and sawed off a finger. She ate one, then fed the next to Riley.

Riley recalled running her finger along a woman's leg, her finger tracing the silky line where the other woman's panties stretched over her dop-soft flesh. The woman moaned with pleasure. Riley moaned too, remembering.

"I don't deserve to live." Riley sobbed. "I'm—"

"The Hell you don't." Beta stared into her eyes. "We're the same. Not abominations. Not broken."

"How—"

"We have the same father." Beta nodded. "I never could hide from the knowledge of what he thought of me. Sure, I could keep my mouth shut at the dinner table, just like you, but I couldn't pretend to myself that I wasn't a dop." She bit her lip, just the way Riley did. "I had to sit there, dinner after dinner, seething inside while he called me an abomination. Said I was a sin to my face.

"But I knew better. If you cut the legs off a starfish and toss them back into the ocean, each leg becomes a new starfish. I'm your starfish sister. If you have a soul, so do I. No matter what he said, I knew I was no sin—at least not because of the way I was born.

"You—well, thanks to Father, you never were sure I wasn't Satan's spawn. If—"

"I never said—" Riley shook her head.

"You didn't have to. I know you, Riley. I know your thoughts."

"All of them?" It couldn't be. Beta had to be lying to her. Dop telepathy didn't extend upwards, only outwards. That's what people said. But maybe the dops had lied to them?

"All your thoughts. Including the ones Father believes are violations of God's will. Abominations. Even if he doesn't yet know about you."

Riley wiped tears away from her eyes, but said nothing. Maybe Beta wasn't lying. Maybe they weren't so different.

"It's okay, Riley." Beta knelt over her and wiped the blood from her face with a hankie. She sucked the cotton until only the slightest trace of pink remained. "I'm not an abomination. You aren't either." She kissed Riley on the forehead.

Both girls sighed. Riley choked back a sob.

"You killed her. If you're my starfish sister, then so was P.E."

"She was just started. You grow into your soul over time, the way a starfish leg takes a long while to become whole again. Trust me, it's different."

Riley shook her head, not believing but wanting to. It was just what she would have said in Beta's place.

"Even if I was lying, which I'm not, it's too late anyway. Just one more dop, right?" Beta pulled Riley to her feet.

"Now what?"

"Now what?" Beta repeated, laughing: she hadn't thought so far ahead. Riley was getting a little of that dop telepathy after all.

Without asking each other, Riley and Beta faced downtown.

"Now we run."

And the two sisters, alike as twins, disappeared into the night.

Marnie and Kyle in the Quick 'n' Now

~ *Jason Washer*

Eleven-thirty PM and it's freezing rain outside. I've already swept the store and emptied the trash, and haven't seen a single customer since our shift started. I can't see past the gas pumps and the darkness to the street beyond, but I know it's deserted, too slick to travel. The roads were treacherous on the way in and I should have stayed home.

Kyle's been stocking the beer freezer for what seems like hours. Through the freezer door I watch him sit down onto a case of beer and hunch forward over his phone. He stays like that for a while, his fingers occasionally flicking at the screen, and I don't want to know what he's looking at. I pull a half dozen magazines from the rack and bring them back up to my perch at the register and start flipping through them. Later I'm turning the last page on the last magazine and digging through my purse for nail polish when I hear the squeal of the freezer door opening and see Kyle hugging himself as he walks up to the register. His cheeks are blue.

"You were in there a long time," I say, glancing up at the clock behind the register. Hardly any time has passed at all, but I don't retract or apologize. Instead I lean into it, "I hope it was good for the phone too . . ."

"Don't be a perv, Marnie," Kyle says, not meeting my eye, and then I really don't want to know what he was looking at on his phone. It takes a minute but he eventually blushes and tells me to fuck off, but not with any particular vehemence, only a mild shame. Tonight's my third shift at the Quick 'n' Now, just two nights past my orientation shift with Jamie, and only my first working with Kyle. He's as awkward as he sounds, and always was, even back in school. He sits next to me behind the counter, the two of us up on stools, silently surveying the store, waiting for someone to come in.

No one does.

"Did you sweep?" he asks, like he's my supervisor. He's not. It's my third day but it's only his second month.

"Yup," I say, and then because I can I ask, "Did you stock the cooler while you were in there?"

"Yup," Kyle says, and then glances down at the empty trash bin behind the register. "Did you empty the trash?"

I glance from the empty can to Kyle and try to hold his eye for a moment so he knows just how stupid of a question that was but he quickly looks away. Someone needs to come into the store soon and buy something or I'll lose my mind. I'm certain if this quiet and boredom continues for another seven hours Jamie will find us in the morning at each other's throats like feral dogs, one of us wearing the other's blood as war paint. Or worse yet making out in the cooler.

"How's your mom?" I finally ask, reduced to small talk. He looks at me, an eyebrow raised, confused. I don't know his mom, and hardly know him, other than for the years we passed each other silently in the halls of Ripley's schools. A dozen years of school for a job at the Quick n' Now, and Jamie had me trained in less than an hour: here's the registers, card everyone under forty for beer, and don't forget to sweep and take out the trash. We spent the rest of the shift chatting, and then had beers in his car up by the airport. I'll admit it, Jamie's pretty hot.

"Dead," Kyle says with something like glee. Not glee that his mom is dead, but glee that I asked such a stupid question. Of course she was dead, and had been since sixth grade. Everyone in town knew his mom was dead, even me. She drove into a lake.

"Sorry," I say, and I mean it. I should have remembered. It was a big deal back then, and the only thing anyone in school or town talked about, and then everything went back to the way it was. At least for us. "I forgot."

"It's okay," he says, still not meeting my eyes. When he says it it comes out mumbled, and sounds like 's'kay' and then for some dumb reason I feel even worse, because I remember that I never told him I was sorry when his mom died in sixth grade; and no, I didn't just remember. I knew and I've known that I never did. Even at the start of the shift, I knew. I could feel it between us even if I didn't know at first what it was. I'm not sure if anyone at school ever told him they were sorry about his mom.

"The floor . . ." Kyle says, this time meeting my eye for a moment before looking away again.

"I told you I swept," I say, sharper than I should have. His mom died after all, and for me anyways it's as fresh as if it just happened, though I guess he's been living with it, or without her, so he's probably used to it by now. Could a person get used to their mom driving into a lake?

"No," Kyle says, getting up from his stool and walking around to the other side of the counter. He points to the cooler, "the floor. In the cooler. It's cracked."

I follow him into the cooler so he can show me his discovery and I hope he doesn't think this is the part where we make out, because it isn't. The door seals behind us and it's freezing in the small and brightly lit beer cooler. Neither of us is wearing a jacket. I hug myself for warmth and he points to the floor, and sure enough, there's a crack in the tile.

"It's new," he says, crouching down on his heels. He runs his fingertips lightly up and down the thin foot long crack in the floor. "It wasn't there yesterday . . ."

"Someone must have dropped a case of beer," I say. "Better call the cops."

He squints down at the crack, "Do you see it?"

"What?" All I see is the cracked tile, and Kyle, shivering on his knees in the cooler. It's freezing in here, and I'm freezing too. Fuck this, "I'm going back to the register."

"The reflection in the crack," Kyle leans down, his face inches from the floor. "Or maybe it's a light?"

"I don't see it, and I'm cold," I move toward the freezer door.

"Just look at it," he motions for me to come closer. "Come look. Don't you see it?"

"No, and if you think I'm getting down on the floor with you—"

"Marnie, please."

"Fine," I say, and kneel down beside him to stare at the cracked tile. There's a reflection, he's right. Or maybe it's a light. "So someone left the basement lights on. Big deal."

We're both kneeling on the cold tile, our faces pressed close to the floor staring at the crack and he looks up at me, his face inches from mine.

"Nope," I say, clambering to my feet. "Not tonight. Not going to happen."

He looks up at me, confused for a moment, until his face registers understanding. "Stop being a perv. And don't you get it?"

"What?"

"There's no basement."

Back at the register I glance up at the clock and it's still barely half past eleven. Time is crawling by, and this is officially the longest shift ever. Outside the sleet continued, and the constant pattering of the freezing rain on the roof rang on. I watch Kyle staring down at the slowly rotating hotdogs for what seems like minutes, until I can't stand it anymore.

"Jamie never told me," I say, and Kyle looks up at me, his spell broken. "About the hotdogs? Do they ever get swapped out? Or are those the same ones from the grand opening?"

Kyle shook his head no, and smiled. "I've never seen them changed since I've been here. And I've never sold one. Maybe on the day shift?" He grabbed the tongs. "Want one?"

"God no," I say, "You go ahead."

Kyle sets the tongs down, "Nah, not hungry. Maybe later."

He hops back up onto the stool next to me and we sit silently for what seems like hours. Finally I'm unable to stand it any longer, the awkwardness too thick, and I break the spell and blurt out, "Jamie seems nice."

Kyle snorts, a grin on his face. "Everyone thinks so."

"Don't you?"

"He's a great manager. Really nice," he says, and I see the expression on his face and hear the bitter longing in his voice and realize that I'm not the only one who's been drinking beers up by the airport with Jamie. The manager of the Quick n' Now is an equal opportunity employer.

"So nice," I agree softly, and stare hopefully at the door, willing someone to come in. No one does. This might be the longest night of my life. "Is it always this slow?"

"Maybe it's a crawl space?" Kyle asks, staring over at the beer cooler again. "For the pipes?"

"Maybe," I say, and then add. "It's probably just a reflection."

"An optical illusion," Kyle says. "The way the lights are hitting it."

"A delusion."

"What?" Kyle asks me.

"My dad, he always says 'optical delusion.'"

"Yeah," Kyle says, and then gets up from the stool. He goes into the office and comes out with his jacket in one hand and a screwdriver in the other. "I'm just going to take another look."

I watch the freezer door close behind him, and I sit under the store's buzzing fluorescent lights and wait. After a while I get up and grab another handful of magazines to skim through even though I've read them all before. He's gone for what seems like a really long time, though the clock is still showing barely half past eleven when he comes back out of the freezer with the screwdriver in his hand. He nods at me as he walks past the register and into Jamie's office. I can hear the drawers of the file cabinet banging open and shut, and when he walks back into the cooler he's carrying a hammer in addition to the screwdriver.

I wait at the register for what feels like an hour and then grab my jacket and follow him into the cooler.

Kyle's on the floor wailing away at the tile with the hammer. The walk-in cooler is filled with a haze of dust, and tiny chips of tile are flying through the air and pinging off the cases of beer. The hairline crack is now a hole big enough to reach an arm into. A faint yellow light streams up from the opening.

"Holy shit," I say over the sound of the smashing tile. Kyle's arm is robotically swinging the hammer at the floor, over and over and over again, the hole getting bigger and bigger until it's almost two feet across. "Jamie's going to kill you."

Kyle stops swinging the hammer and looks up at me questioningly, and then says, "It's not so bad, I just wanted to see . . ." He looks down at the ruined floor, realizing what he's done. "Oh shit."

"Yeah," I say. "You're fucked."

"I didn't think I . . . I wasn't thinking. I didn't realize."

"You were in here for a long time," I say. "How could you not realize?"

He pulls out his phone and glances at the clock, and shakes his head, "No, I wasn't."

"Yeah, you were. You're really fucked." I kneel down beside him and peer into the hole. It drops six feet down to another ceramic tiled floor, and a hallway that veers off to the side. The light is coming from off to the side, further in. "What is this?"

Kyle shrugs and wipes sweat from his pocked forehead with the sleeve of his jacket. "An unfinished basement. Utility room, maybe."

"With no stairs?" I say, thoroughly creeped out. I shiver, maybe from the cold. I'm pretty sure that Kyle has stumbled into someone's murder hole, and that there's probably a dozen body's stacked like cordwood just out of sight around the corner.

"And no door," Kyle says, and then, "There has to be a door."

"Where?"

Kyle shrugs again, "There has to be."

I stand up and say "Nope. That's enough. Fuck this. We'll sweep all this shit down into the hole and just tell Jamie we dropped a keg on the floor."

"You think he'll believe it?"

"Sure. And it doesn't matter if he doesn't. I'm going to get the broom out of the office."

I grab the broom out of the office and glance at the clock as I head back into the cooler to see how many more hours of this I have left. 11:30. It has to be broken, or the clock's batteries are dead, so I pull out my own phone to check the time and my battery's dead too. Awesome.

"Kyle," I say as I'm pulling open the cooler door. "What time is it?" He's not in the cooler. "Kyle?"

"Down here," He pokes his head up through the hole in the floor.

"What the hell!" I jump back, startled, and may have peed a little bit. "You scared me. What are you doing?"

"I just wanted to see where the light was coming from," Kyle says, ducking his head back down into the hole.

"And?" I crouch down near the hole just in time to see him duck around the corner and out of sight. "Kyle?"

"Just a corridor going down, and then it turns off to the right again."

"Come back out," I say, and I can hear his feet scuffing away. "Right now. You shouldn't be down there."

His voice echos up to me, "I'm just going to look. I'll be right out."

"Jamie's going to kill you," I say, and then regret it.

"It's fine," he calls. "I just want to look. Be right back."

"Kyle," I say as I listen to his footsteps get further and further away. I stare at the hole in the cooler floor and I wait.

I pull out my phone again to check the time before I remember my battery's dead, and then I walk back out into the store and pull a charger off the shelf next to the Tylenol and tampons. I rip open the charger and then try to plug my phone in behind the register but of course it's the wrong size phone plug. Of course it is.

I look up at the broken clock and try to work backwards to figure out when Jamie will come in and our shift will be over, and I think about the magazines and the sweeping and Kyle breaking open the floor with the screwdriver and the hammer and I don't know. It has to be four a.m. by now, or later. It feels later. It's been such a long shift. When Jamie gets here in the morning I'm going to quit. I go back into the cooler and sit down on a case of beer to wait for Kyle to come back. I try not to imagine Jamie wearing his skin.

I stare at the hole and wait and before long I can't even feel my hands anymore and my ass is numb from sitting for so long. My nose runs from the cold, the sleeve of my jacket damp with snot. Occasionally I give a halfhearted yell down into the hole for Kyle, but he never answers and after a while my voice goes hoarse and my throat grows sore from shouting.

I try counting to measure the passage of time, but invariably my mind wanders and I forget where I am in the count and have to start over. I consider leaving my vigil at the hole more than once, but I don't. Where would I go? And once I stop expecting the shift to end, or anyone to come into the store, the waiting grows less painful.

I think about Kyle's mom a lot. Was there a point in the lake as the water rushed up around the car that she changed her mind and said fuck this? A moment where she fought back? And if she did change her mind how hard and how long did she try to get out of that car? At some point did she just give up and accept the water rushing in and over her?

I yell for Kyle again, loud, and this time when he doesn't respond I drop down into the hole.

I walk for longer than I can remember. The passage slowly descends, each long and tiled hallway eventually turning right into another and then another, and in this way I slowly descend until I almost forget where I'm going or what I'm looking for. Hours or years later, I don't know anymore, I turn right for must be the thousandth time and the hallway terminates in a dimly lit and low ceilinged alcove no bigger than the beer cooler.

Kyle and Jamie are sitting at a card table and Kyle's laughing like he just heard the world's best joke. Jamie can be wickedly funny, especially when he has you alone in a car by the airport, or in a small room deep underground.

"Hey guys," I interrupt, a little worried that I'm ruining Jamie's joke.

"Hi Marnie," Kyle says, holding up a hand in greeting.

"Want a beer, Marnie?" Jamie grins and holds up a sweaty can of Pabst. I love his smile, I can't help myself, and almost take the beer, but instead I shake my head no and offer him a tight smile in return.

"I'm not thirsty," I tell Jamie, and I notice Kyle's not drinking either. I turn to Kyle, "I was waiting for you. You didn't come back."

"Sorry," Kyle says. "We were just hanging out. I lost track of time."

"Let's go back up to the store now, Kyle," I say, and instead of answering me Kyle just looks at Jamie, waiting for him to answer. "Our shift is almost over."

Jamie smiles that smile he has, all charm and promise, and he looks at me like I'm the only person left in the world, like it's just me and him alone at the end of the world, as if Kyle's not even here, and then he shoves out a metal folding chair from the table with a small booted foot and says, "Sit and have a beer, Marnie. Let's hang out for a while."

"I'd love to, but we left the story empty," I say, and then add, "Sorry."

"No worries," Jamie says after he downs the last of his Pabst and crushes the can. He tosses the can onto the floor near my feet, and then he's somehow popping the tab on another can. "It's fine, really. The store can take care of itself. Kyle, tell her to sit down."

"Sit down Marnie," Kyle says, not meeting my eye. "Jamie was telling a story."

I smile politely, but I don't sit. I know I can't sit if I want to leave, and I really, really want to leave, even if the beer is starting to look good now. I didn't think I was thirsty, but maybe I am. I'm also very cold. I tell Kyle, "We should go now."

Kyle looks from me to Jamie, hoping for his permission. It doesn't come. Jamie just smiles that smile of his like this is all perfectly normal. Nothing's wrong, and why would anyone ever want to leave?

"Kyle," I say, and he smiles apologetically, and this time meets my eye, but doesn't move. Maybe he can't move, I don't know. I turn to Jamie, and try not to think about what we did together in the backseat of his car, because he doesn't look quite the same anymore; he seems older now, thinner, his hair greasier than before, his bones prominent. He's wearing a thin pair of blue jeans with the cuffs tucked into the brown boots, and a buttoned up shirt that I swear is straight out of the seventies, and not retro fashion or seventies inspired, but an actual and threadbare shirt pulled from the seventies. I realize that he's very old, older than even the nineteen seventies. "Jamie," I say to him, trying to smile, trying to not let on that I know how old he is, "we've got to get back to the store. Our shift is almost over . . ."

"Nah," Jamie says, and he's not smiling anymore, and maybe he never was. "Stop me if you've heard this one."

"We have to leave," I say again.

"I know you've heard it before," he says to Kyle, and he winks, his eyelid slowly folding shut like a bat's wing before reopening. His hand rests intimately on Kyle's shoulder, his fingernails long and dirty, brown with decades of stain.

"Jamie, please," I say, and I realize that he won't willingly let us go. He can't.

"There was a boy, we'll call him Kyle," Jamie laughs. "And his mom drove into a lake."

"Don't be an ass, Jamie," I say. "I know the story. We're leaving now."

"No. And you don't know the whole story—"

"Kyle," I say. "Get up. We're leaving now."

"Marnie?" Kyle says, half up from his chair, and his eyes are boring into mine, pleading with me, hoping.

Fuck this. Fuck Jamie. Fuck the store. Fuck all of it. I reach over the card table and grab Kyle's arm and try to pull him the rest of the way to his feet. His arm is cold, freezing, and Kyle is shivering, his face pale, his lips blue.

"We're going," I tell Jamie as I pull Kyle up from the chair. Kyle looks at me, his eyes still pleading with me, and I'm remembering back to middle school after his mom died and I really, really wish I had told him how sorry I was. It was a really shitty deal for him, and I should have said something, should have said anything, but I didn't.

We stumble past Jamie and he doesn't look anything like Jamie from the car anymore, not even close, not even human, and then Kyle and I are out of the alcove and we're back in the narrow corridor.

"I'm so sorry," I say to Kyle. I can hear him just behind me, following me, shivering, his breath coming in frozen hitches as we climb the long hallway back up to the beer cooler. "I really am. I should have said something."

"It's okay, really."

"No, it's not. Kids are assholes. I was an asshole."

"Marnie, let it go, okay. It was a long time ago," Kyle tells me, but it really wasn't. Six years, a couple of thousand days. I couldn't imagine how he could let it go so soon. "I've moved past it, and you should too."

"How can you move past it?" I ask incredulously, trudging back up the long halls toward the surface. I listen to Kyle's feet scuffing the tile behind me, but I don't hear anyone behind Kyle. Not yet. I wish I could remember how far away the store was. "I don't believe you."

"She did the best she could," Kyle says.

"Bullshit," I answer, "absolutely fucking bullshit. She was a bitch and should have done a lot better by you," and when he doesn't reply I realize I've gone too far. Awesome. First I ignore him when his mom dies, like he wasn't even there, pretending like nothing ever happened, and then I call his dead mother a bitch. Nice going. "Sorry."

He still doesn't answer, and we keep walking. Time passes, and we must be close to the store by now, but I have no way to know with my phone's dead battery. I spend most of the walk wondering if Jamie's coming after us, and if he is what he'll do when he catches us. I'm tired. After a while I realize that he can't follow us. He's too old, too set in his ways by a thousand years of time and death washing over him. He can't move, and he doesn't want to move. He never moved, even in the car by the airport; he was just a daydream, a passing fancy, a wish sworn and quickly recanted.

He just waits.

Kyle and I are safe, for now.

"Kyle?"

He doesn't answer me, and hasn't for the last hours and miles, though I still hear him behind me.

"I said that I was sorry," still no answer. "I'm sure she did her best."

My mind wanders back to the sixth grade, and Kyle, and his absence. I hadn't told him I was sorry about his mom driving into the lake. Not then and not ever. How could I?

"Kyle, don't be a dick. Answer me. Say something." And then even though I know I shouldn't, I turn to look at him, and then he's gone, vanished from the long tiled hall.

He's been gone for a long time, forever twelve years old.

A woman who drives into a lake, that's tragic, I remember my dad saying. Who knows what demons that poor woman might have been facing? But a woman who drives into that same lake with her twelve year old son in the back seat? Then she's not a woman facing demons anymore, is she? That's too generous of an assessment. She is the demon.

A minute or a lifetime later I finally see the fluorescent lights of the beer cooler. I climb up through the hole and stagger out into the Quick n' Now. The clock is still stuck at eleven-thirty. It's still sleeting out, still dark. No one has come in all this time.

"Kyle?" I call softly to the empty store, and I know he won't answer. I'm alone. I grab the same magazines I've read a dozen times before from the rack and bring them up to the register and start flipping through them. Nothing has changed. The fluorescent lights buzz overhead, the sleet rattles on the roof, and I wait.

A Short History of Decay

~ Matthew Cheney

Who first named the eastern edge of the city *the flats*, nobody seemed to know. The designation likely dated to the days when the region was all farmland, before the building of the papermill that turned the village into a town, the town into a city. A particularly large and level field could not help calling attention to itself in the hilly landscape. And so, *the flats*. After decades of abandonment, the papermill got demolished twenty-something years ago in a last gasp of hope for the new millennium. But the flats remained.

As Walt looked out at the expanse of rubble and sod, he felt no impulse to seek an early etymology. The name remained an accurate description. Luxury condominiums may have risen recently a mile away, but the field, the derelict buildings, the rutted roads, the tufts of weeds bedeviling crumbled sidewalks—all offered testament to the collapse and neglect that had infected the city for half a century. Here and now, everything in sight was fallen, forgotten, flat.

He had given little thought to why there was a solitary park bench at this corner of the flats. He assumed there were other benches somewhere farther down, though he could not see any. Perhaps there had once been a park here that was maintained by the city, perhaps there had been numerous benches and they had been taken away, their iron and wood repurposed, and this one got forgotten or left in homage to the past, or perhaps it was simply a little too big to fit on the final truck hauling the benches to a more favored location elsewhere. No matter. Speculation is pointless when no answer is possible. The bench was there and he sat each day on it and ate his lunch.

One of the reasons Walt liked this spot for his meagre lunches (peanut butter and jelly sandwich, can of seltzer water) was how abandoned and empty it was. The offices of the regional art museum where he worked were cramped and stuffy. It was nice to be able to get away from people, nice not to feel eyes glaring or questions haunting faces, nice not to wonder what people were thinking about him, or if they were thinking about him. The previous tenant of the little apartment he rented had left behind a tv, and at night Walt watched whatever happened to be on. Recently he had seen, for the first time since childhood, *The Invisible Man*. When Claude Rains unwrapped the bandages covering his face and revealed his invisibility, Walt found himself suddenly sobbing.

For a few days, perhaps a week, he did not notice any other people at the flats. Then, as he stared idly across the field of greenery and ruins, clouds dawdling in the sky, a breeze jostling litter on the ground, his sandwich half eaten in his hand, he saw figures. They were far off, out in the tall grass and shattered cement. How odd to see people in the flats! (Perhaps there had been people on other days and Walt had not noticed them; he could not be sure.) They were just far enough away to be difficult to see in any detail. They hardly moved, just stood out there in the field. Maybe vagabonds, drifters, people unencumbered by deadlines or expectations, no reason to go from one place to another.

Every day that Walt took his lunch out to the flats, he saw the people. They seemed like sculptures at first, like a public art display, or maybe a weird yoga group or practitioners of tai chi. Day by day, almost imperceptibly, the figures moved closer to his side of the flats. He could see that their clothes were dirty, ragged, torn; their faces grimy. They did not interact with each other. Now and then, one of them knelt down in the field and rubbed their hands in the soil, sometimes then bringing their hands to their face. A few even seemed to eat whatever it was they had pulled from the ground. Remembering an exhibition of medieval paintings he had curated early in his career, he began to think of the figures in the field as mendicants. All those paintings titled Man of Sorrows; all those images of naked, suffering men, of flagellants and the glory of pain.

Every couple months, Carlos sent Walt a package with a card from the girls and sometimes some of their drawings, as well as whatever random mail still came to the house in Walt's name. Occasionally, Carlos added a brief note of his own. Walt sent a few hundred dollars in child support every month, even though it was not required in the divorce agreement. Carlos, who worked in real estate development and made that much money every hour or two, told him it was ridiculous and refused to cash the checks. "There is no need to punish yourself," Carlos wrote in one of his notes. Walt sent a brief reply on office stationary: "I am not punishing myself. I love the girls. Please deposit my checks."

More and more, Walt wondered if perhaps he should stop sending checks, maybe even stop opening the packages Carlos sent. Move on. Forget that old life, be whoever he was now. Whoever he was now.

He began to rush through his morning work, finding himself more annoyed than ever before at the pointlessness of the emails he wrote and the phone calls he made, the interruptions by staff who needed a signature on a form or an answer to an obvious question, the vapid meetings. He would dash from the building at the moment his lunch hour began, all but running to his place on the lone park bench. He returned to work a few minutes late and made his way through the afternoons distracted and lethargic, his mind always partly back at the flats. Some days, he walked by the flats after work, but there were never people there. On weekends, the streets around the area were busier with pedestrians and families, and one of the nearby churches offered meals to destitute people who gathered nearby. Walt usually found some excuse to walk through on a Saturday or Sunday, but he only saw the mendicants standing in the field on weekdays during his lunch hour when nobody else was around.

Though he disliked churches and priests and the sanctimoniousness of religion, Walt approached a group of church volunteers one Saturday when he saw them handing out packages of food at the flats. "Do you happen to know anything about the people who are out there on the weekdays?" he asked. "The people who stand out there in the field?"

The volunteers gave him shrugs and perplexed looks. A woman with thin grey hair and skin as wrinkled as rotting fruit said, "Lots of people hiding out. Squatters. They never really finished tearing down the mill. Turned out there was a graveyard there or something, a bunch of old bones, had to get permission to continue. Nobody bothered. The houses for the millworkers are still up all around, abandoned. Rotting away. Police clear the place out now and then, but not enough. Folks wander."

"It seems more regular than wandering," Walt said. "It's every day, rain or shine. They just stand out there."

"We don't really know anything about this place," another volunteer said, a younger woman with bright blue eyes.

"But your church is here," Walt said.

"No," the blue-eyed woman said. "All the churches here are abandoned. We're from the other side of the city."

"The good side of the city," the older woman said.

"Yes," the blue-eyed woman said, smiling. "The good side."

"So, how are you adjusting to life here in the boondocks?" Walt's boss, Kelly, asked.

"Fine, I think," Walt said.

"Finding enough to do?"

"Oh yes."

"Are you going to come to the donor event next month?"

"Do I need to?"

"I think it might be good if you were to interact with more of the donors, patrons, folks in the community."

"Okay."

"I'm sure it was different in your city. You probably had dozens of people and didn't need to get everybody out there schmoozing. But we're so small, it's kind of important."

"Right."

"They will love having a new person to share old stories with. You'll be positively exotic. They'll write us checks just for the novelty of chatting with somebody who hasn't been here since Teddy Roosevelt was president."

"Sure."

"You're like our very own new, living-breathing exhibit piece."

Kelly smiled and slapped Walt on the shoulder, then walked off to whatever it was she did all day. Her background was in business and public relations. When Walt was hired, Kelly said she was excited to have somebody in the office who would know what all the art meant.

He suppressed a groan with a forced smile. He had worried about what he had gotten himself into, but it turned out that the three curators were actually quite skilled and simply kept Kelly at as much distance as possible. Walt saw his primary job, in fact, as protecting the curators. These days, that often meant trying to highlight the importance of their work to Kelly, who repeatedly said she did not know why a museum of their size needed more than one curator.

Some nights, he found himself telling an imaginary Carlos about his work day. It was the thing he missed most, that opportunity they had to share the ups and downs of their very different jobs, to get the perspective of somebody who wasn't embroiled in all the personalities and politics. As Walt cooked some spaghetti, he said to the invisible Carlos, "She just doesn't understand that no one person can have expertise in paintings and sculpture and materials and fabric and everything else from the dawn of time till now in every country of the world. Yes, we specialize in some things, but the specialties were not planned, they were just what the museum happened to be able to get collections of a hundred years ago, and she thinks one person ought to be able to know enough to conserve it all and present it all and—"

He stared at the boiling water on the stove.

"I'm talking to myself," he said. He tossed some dry spaghetti into the boiling water.

"You are not here. Just me." He stirred the water around the spaghetti.

"I am talking to myself. I am the only one here." He continued to stir the spaghetti as it softened and swirled through the water.

"This is who I am now."

He turned the stove off and left the spaghetti to disintegrate. He was not hungry. He would watch some TV and hope to fall asleep.

It rained every day for a week. Nonetheless, Walt took his lunch down to the flats each day and sat on the park bench and watched the people in the field. They were now only thirty or forty feet from him. They did not look at him. Mostly, they looked at the ground. Rain soaked the rags they wore and the rags clung to them like irrelevant skin. Dirt dripped down their bodies.

Walt's sandwich got soggy. His seltzer water tasted of dirty clouds.

Before Walt went out on the third day of rain, Kelly said, "You should get an umbrella."

"I don't have enough hands," he said.

She stared at him in the same way she would stare at an abstract painting.

On his first day back to the park bench after the week of rain, Walt thought there were fewer people now than there had been before. Before, their numbers seemed to be ten or maybe twenty. Now, he could count the mendicants with a glance: seven. They stood distant from each other. The closest one was only ten feet or so from Walt. The person looked like a man, though perhaps, Walt thought, it was a woman with short hair and small breasts and thin hips, or perhaps a person for whom gender was not so defined. It did not matter. The person stood there, barely moving, never looking at Walt. They knelt down and ran their hands through the dirty soil. They wiped dirt on their face and in their hair.

"We are beginning to know you." A voice from behind—Walt turned around and saw a tall woman with long hair wearing overalls that were filthy but intact. Heavy work gloves covered her hands.

Walt smiled. He wanted to say something, but all the words in his head sounded false.

"You are seeking something," the woman said.

"Am I?" He had not intended to speak.

"An answer, perhaps."

"I would, yes, like to know," Walt said, "what this"—he gestured to the field—"what it is. What it's for. The why of it."

The woman smiled slyly. "The answer is likely less than you have imagined."

"Answers often are."

"Better not to defile with words. Come tonight. After dark. To the old mill chapel. It's at the other side. You'll see our light."

Before Walt could say anything in response, the woman walked into the field and found a place partway between two other people. She removed her gloves, reached down, and covered her hands with soil. She rubbed the soil over her hair and skin as if she were bathing in it. She stood up then and stared straight ahead at Walt until eventually he broke from her gaze and wandered back to his office in the museum.

Carlos always wanted Walt to go to church with him, and now and then Walt did, but it was invariably uncomfortable. He let the girls go if they wanted, but he and Carlos agreed that they would never be forced to go. There was nothing wrong with Carlos's church—it was one of the very liberal Congregationalist churches with rainbow flags out front—but Walt nonetheless felt overwhelmed with hypocrisy when he was inside during a service. He could not understand how anyone could bring themselves to believe in the stories that were being told, the idea of reality that the congregants shared. He had wanted to ask Carlos about it, to have a real and honest conversation where they could both ask each other the actual questions hiding in the backs of their minds, but he did not dare, because he loved Carlos and he feared that what he might learn would disappoint him or that what Carlos would learn about Walt's own beliefs would horrify him and in some way increase the sense of distance that had been growing between them, the sense of distance that ultimately led to Walt not caring about anything anymore and openly fooling around with Evan (the intern with the magnificent eyes and sensuous lips) and then throwing everything away because nothing, in the end, seemed worth saving.

"What do you actually believe in?" Carlos asked him at the end.

"Entropy," Walt said.

"The heat death of the universe? Everything getting cold? Appropriate."

"It's from Greek," Walt said. "Similar to transformation. Literally: a turning."

"A turning away."

"Everything changes," Walt said. "Everyone."

"Everyone," Carlos said, "goes cold."

After work, Walt drove to the flats and parked near the old chapel, a building only distinguished from the ones around it by a small steeple at the top. The buildings must once have been boarding houses for mill workers. They were boxy wooden structures with decades of dull paint faded or flaking from their clapboards, their stoops and porches sagging. Two balconies with haphazard railings reached across upper windows that were cracked and broken, a few covered with wooden planks. As Walt sat in his car, he watched an old man hobble down the sidewalk. No other cars drove by. No other people appeared.

A dim light flickered in the chapel. Shadows floated across the windows. Walt got out of the car. It was a humid night and a sweet but sickly smell lingered in the air, a scent of rot. As Walt approached the front door of the chapel, he heard soft, murmuring voices.

He opened the door slowly. The air here felt even heavier, more humid. He eased his way into the shadowy room. The only light came from candles at the front, candles of various sizes and shapes, all stuck to what once had been an altar and now was a skeleton of rotting boards pustulent with melted wax. There was no other furniture in the room. People—maybe a dozen—walked slowly around the floor in no particular order or pattern. Each person mumbled or hummed, filling the room with a burbling tone.

The woman from the afternoon appeared at Walt's side. "Thank you for coming," she said quietly.

"What is this?"

"Worship," she said.

"Of what?"

"Come, join us."

She led him in and walked with him.

Soon, he began to feel the rhythm of the group.

And then he noticed that the woman had disappeared, that he was walking with the others in a syncopation he could not have described but nonetheless felt, a movement he had become powerless to stop without, he was certain, the whole group stopping. He discovered, too, that sounds issued from his mouth, low rumbles from his throat. He was intoning with the rest, and the sound was not a type of communication but rather an involuntary action, a byproduct of movement.

Hours and seconds danced together, then lost meaning, disappeared.

He thought of the word *clock* but had no image for it. The word was only sound.

The woman appeared from the shadows at a corner of the room. She carried a large silver platter on which meat, fruit, and vegetables had been heaped indiscriminately. She moved to the center of the room slowly, her arms shaking with the weight of the platter. She knelt down and set the platter of food on the floor.

The rhythm of the walkers changed, a focus shifted, and they all turned and faced the food pile, which Walt vaguely perceived to be not only rancid but shimmering with flies and pulsing with grubs, larva, worms. A foul aroma rose from the platter and spread through the room like smoke. People stepped toward the pile. Despite the noxious scent, Walt felt himself drawn toward it. No-one touched him, and yet he was sure he had no more choice of movement than if he were in a suffocating crowd.

Their murmurs quieted to whispery breaths, a tone now the same as that of the many flies buzzing delightedly over the rot. Each person crouched down, fell to hands and knees, still inching forward, soon pressing against each other uncomfortably, jostling as they made their way toward the putrid mound of meat, vegetables, and viscous fruit. Hunger energized the room.

And yet they did not eat, did not open their mouths. Instead, in ecstasy, they rubbed their faces against the pile of food, their skin and hair smeared with ooze and slop, freckled with flies, maggots crawling across necks, scalps, cheeks, noses, mouths.

One person pulled back from the crowd and cried out in orgasmic joy, then another and another, while other people dove in to take their place. Walt, too, found himself caught in the rapture, pressing his way in, closer—closer—closer—until finally the miasma stung his eyes to tears, his nostrils filled with mucus and with fetid beads of pulp, and then his forehead plunged into the reek and slime, necrotic juice sliding down the sides of his face, insects crawling and biting at his sticky flesh, and he could not stop his hands from grasping at the ever more liquid sludge, bringing it to his face, slathering himself with the glory until he, too, could no longer remain on the floor and his legs shot him upwards and his voice called out with primal ache—and gorged with wonder he exclaimed at the beauty of the all.

☉

Sylvia says her favorite color is blue. Sarah says her favorite color used to be blue but now her favorite color is green. Sylvia says her favorite color is green. Carlos laughs and Walt smiles—

Carlos should really be the one doing the cooking, he's the one who spent a term in culinary school, but he says he loves Walt's cooking. Walt laughs and Carlos looks hurt. "I'm serious," he says—

There was rain in the night but the sun shines in the morning through a water-streaked window in their bedroom. The girls bounce into the room, ready for the day. Carlos groans, wanting more time to sleep. In the window, Walt sees sunlight held by a fading drop of water—

They go on their honeymoon to Hawaii. They learn to snorkel, they try surfing, they sit for long hours on the beach. Their last night, they eat a seven-course dinner at the most expensive restaurant they can find. As they walk into the hotel, Carlos stops. He holds Walt's hands, looks into his eyes. "I love you," Carlos says. "I will always remember this night. Forever." They kiss in the warm darkness—

The woman helped him up. Hours, seconds, days fell like refuse to the floor. He and the woman stood alone in the room.

She shuffled him toward shadows where a door waited. "Where are we going?" he asked quietly.

"You need to speak with the elder acolyte. It is close to transition."

Wooden stairs led to stone steps curling down, arriving in a basement lit with candles, the stone walls and dirt floor heavy with inadvertent sculptures of wax. In the dim light, the ceiling felt both distant and dangerously low. The air hung heavy and still, infused with a stench of sewage, mildew, and smoke.

They came to a bed in a corner. Two people wearing rags, their hair wild and unkempt, sat beside the bed. They stood as the woman and Walt approached.

In the bed, a figure lay unmoving beneath a heavy sheet.

The woman put her hand on Walt's back and pressed him forward. "Go close. Be seen. Hear the whispers."

Walt knelt at the bed and leaned in toward the hairless head of the figure lying there. The body breathed slowly. The head turned and beheld Walt with dark emerald eyes sunken deep in the skull. A voice less than a whisper: "You seek . . ."

"Yes," Walt said.

". . . this . . ."

Walt held the body's hand, a scatter of bones dusted with flesh. Tears washed his cheeks as he waited for more words.

Walt felt something move across his hand. A crawling insect, many-legged, winged. It scuttered toward the elder acolyte's head. Walt saw bubbling movement beneath the sheet. Antennae and mandibles appeared, bodies and wings, countless thread-thin legs.

"The greatest creatures," the desiccated being whispered. "The survivors. The gods. Have arrived."

The people beside the bed stood and helped Walt to his feet. Together, they ascended to the morning while the transmigration continued in glory below.

Walt wondered if Carlos had told his minister about it all, about Walt's straying and his abandonment of the family. He imagined Carlos saying to the minister, "I do not understand how he can just walk away. Did he ever love us? What are we to him?"

Walt ought to call Carlos, or even go back to the city and see him, see the girls, try to clear some things up. But what could he say? *You are and always will be my family. Yes, I love you. All of you. But—*

His instinct was to say, *But not enough*, and yet he wondered if the true words were, in fact: *But too much.*

"Did something die in a garbage can or something?" Kelly asked from the corridor. She stuck her head into Walt's office. "Is it coming from in here? Do you smell that?"

"No," Walt said. "All is good." He smiled beatifically.

Kelly stared at him. "You need a haircut. And, if I may be frank, some new clothes? You look like a hobo. Christ, the donor dinner is tomorrow. Get your shit together."

Walt continued to smile.

Only three people stood in the field. Walt did not feel compelled to join them, but he wondered if he should. Perhaps it would satisfy his craving. He reached down near the park bench and grabbed dirt with his hand. He held the hand to his nose, rubbed some of the dirt on his cheeks and lips, tasted it. It was not enough.

He found his way down into the field. In between the other people, he knelt and plunged his hands into the soil. A dark richness to the soil here. Worms undulated just beneath the surface. Below, he knew, though he did not know how he came to this knowledge, the gods were still transforming the elder acolyte, as they had done for countless others and would do one day for himself, if he maintained his faith. His bones would then be brought to the catacombs directly beneath him, the catacombs which had been a burial ground for the mills, though that was hardly when burials here began.

He washed his face with dirt. He spread soil through his hair. He scoured his arms and legs and feet and hands with damp dust of all that had once been something and was no more itself. He stood in the soft sunlight and let the air mingle with his scent and shape and being. The ants and beetles that crawled on him also crawled on the other people standing here, and crawled over all who had been here before.

For the first time in many months, he wished Carlos and the girls could be with him. He wished they could feel the beauty. This was love, true love, the strong love born of connection and unity, of life itself.

Standing still, he imagined what he would soon do, the long drive back to the city where Carlos and the twins waited, and he imagined the wonder with which they would perceive him, the new acolyte. He envisioned the love they would feel once he brought them to a place of rich soil and served them a feast honoring decay, and he imagined their love as they observed him become ready for the gods to give his body purpose and meaning. He saw now in the bright blue sky the faces of his loved ones shining smiles upon him, while in the catacombs below, the gods scurried and swarmed, rendering flesh, cleaning bone, proceeding with the duty which was their desire, the reunion of life and death.

Clouds darkened the sky. Walt looked around and saw that he had been joined by other figures. They moved closer, slowly, in unison. Low murmurs resonated from his chest, throat, mouth.

The woman arrived first. "Welcome," she said.

She held her hand to his cheek. He felt a tickle, then a bite. She took her hand away.

Mendicants approached and one by one made offerings with hands holding gods. They touched his face and hair, they opened his shirt and touched his chest, they unbuttoned his pants and touched his hips, legs, groin. People continued to arrive, continued to bring welcome to him until twilight faded to darkness while he stood in the center of the field, the sacred expanse, stood there garbed by gods wriggling and scampering, raising their wings, quivering their legs, running feelers to and fro, cutting hair and flesh with mandibles, laying new life in pores and wounds. He began to exclaim his joy, but the sound was muffled, muted by the holiness crawling its way down his throat.

Wolven

~ *Daniel Dagris*

Ellis dismounted his horse and joined the men already scalping the dead. Remnants of a small tribe, most of its men probably already killed in one fight or another. Blood soaked into his clothes and dried on leather meant to keep the western sun and arrows from biting too deep. Wiping gore from his forehead, Ellis was insulted to share a promised land with superstitious folks who blew across it like autumn leaves, but also glad for the sport of it. He pressed one nostril with a bloody thumb and blew out of the other a considerable amount of congestion.

The men built a fire just out of sight of the day's massacre as night took hold. Bedrolls were loosed and bellies filled. A few hats rested on saddles while others held back the tide of firelight from men drifting to sleep, mid conversation. Shadows shrank from the blazing fire, flickering a comedy of demons, teasing and chasing about. As the fire matured, the demons inched out along the sand, towering longer than any man sitting against a rock or curled up sleeping.

Ellis awoke and wandered away from the orange glow. His pistol hung loose on one finger as he gripped his works and relieved himself. Finished, he turned back in the direction of the fire. Surrounding his troop stood the silent forms of painted men assumed dead by those asleep at their feet.

Knives flashed across the throats of the sleeping men, loosing spurts beneath eyes that flickered with only the slightest awareness before life left them.

Firing his Colt from his waist, the gun thumped a bruise into Ellis's thigh. Its lightning burst Ritchie's head as Ellis fumbled to tuck himself away while running. A stranger dressed in Ritchie's brain matter dragged the headless body onto the embers, blotting out their light, and gave chase, his footfalls more a pounding echo of Ellis's heartbeat than Ellis's terrified jangling sprint.

Ellis whistled to his horse, but hands found him first. Fighting their grip, he tossed and kicked and fired off his pistol into a night so thick he could only see men for how they blotted out stars from view. He was dragged back toward the glow of coals on which Ritchie cooked, clothes smoldering with lines of slow crawling flame.

Someone sat among the dead. The form sang out a quavering rasp, words Ellis didn't understand, and then spoke the same, back and forth. The tune first chanted skyward then down at Ellis, who readied himself for the tear of blades. The old man then stood, walked into the dark, others followed. Ellis moved and found that no hands held him in place and no foot on his back.

"What now?" Ellis shouted. "Quit fooling! What now?"

A wolf howled, far off. Otherwise, silence answered. Not a star obscured in any which way.

Ellis whistled again.

"Rhaebus, here!"

The horse sidled up to Ellis, lips pulling at the man's shirt.

"Seems we're standing in the food dish." Ellis said, while fumbling in the dark to strip each body of valuables.

Saddlebags brimming, he mounted.

Rhaebus fled at a gallop just as the wolves fell upon the dead men; fangs ravaging the bodies with the same devouration the men had shown the frontier. The horse veered over and around obstacles Ellis couldn't see. Ellis held tight, suspecting Rhaebus might be guessing at their course. The horse soon slowed. Only then did Ellis's lungs unlock. Deep breaths filling the vast quiet between himself and the snarling feast they narrowly escaped.

Bedded down again, Ellis watched the sky sparkle in the moonless night as he listened to Rhaebus snore. Back home in Pennsylvania, nobody he'd known had ever been murdered, not by strangers nor neighbors or kin. A town of people not worth killing.

The Lord's Prayer was one of the only things Ellis had ever learned by heart, and by the time the sun came, he made plans to memorize something else for variety's sake. "*Our father*," Ellis said to Rhaebus, "that's you and me pal. We've got the same creator. *Who art in heaven* . . . Heaven, that's green grass and fruit slop and lady horses to you.

Hallowed be thy name. That's mostly tricky wording. Means His name is holy. Powerful. At least I think that's right. *By kingdom come . . . is it 'by'?* I think it is . . . *thine will be done,* so by the time of judgement, because only the Lord should be judging yours and my choices, his wishes will be carried out; *on earth as it is in heaven.* That last bit explains itself. He will make this world as it is in heaven."

He'd heard the natives committed their legends to memory. No books at all. They would tell stories to their young until the young knew them well enough to do the same when they grew older. In the firelight, the scalps slung in many strands across the saddlebags looked to Ellis like furry book jackets, disemboweled of their tales.

At sunrise Ellis's eyes felt glassy and long. Enraptured by a single spine of a barrel cactus on the farthest hill, on which a caterpillar's orange hairs swayed. If the creature were to wiggle its head or tail, Ellis might burst into a sprint. He yearned for it to move. Rhaebus snorted and nuzzled Ellis, breaking the spell.

Ellis stood, and his legs quaked like a newborn deer. He chewed some jerky, while stripping dead branches from underneath a spindly tree. Once piled, he kindled them with a dry cactus the size of his fist. He stopped often as his gut fought with its contents. Stomach pains followed and soon he doubled over twice: The first terrible. The second as if his body wanted to know if, with enough force, one could turn oneself inside out.

"That food is like a handful of blister beetles, Rhaebus."

He couldn't figure out how wine or jerky could spoil, but somehow, they had. Feeling all the weaker, Ellis rifled through his rucksack and saddlebag for every scrap of food available, piling a collection of jerky, biscuits, flasks and bottles of alcohol, water skins, apples, and a dead squirrel in a sack that Drexel must have killed and meant to eat for breakfast. It's aroma of early rot hit Ellis's nose and he was surprised to find that he enjoyed the stink.

"Seems a waste to toss this little fella seeing as he's already dead . . ."

Rhaebus turned away.

"You're right. It depends on how we cook 'em."

Ants had now claimed the jerky, biscuits, and apples, and Ellis was surprised that he found the idea of eating the ants more appealing than the food they crawled upon. He returned to the fire, added scraps of dead foliage, then began ripping the pelt from the tiny squirrel carcass, licking his fingers as black blood ran down them. His knife stripped bones of their meat with an easy practiced hand. He was disgusted at the idea of licking the rancid blood, but the tang of it was pleasant and to leave it seemed a waste. He talked with his mouth full about the best ways to prepare squirrel, and as he finished tossing aside the skin and bones, he was only holding a pulpy palm full of entrails. The meat was gone.

"Well, that was redder than most."

He snacked while watching the ants.

He reached for a cloth to wipe his hands but there was no blood left to wipe, just the slickness of his hunger.

"I guess this fire's just for sitting next to."

A hard gust of wind tossed the strands of Rhaebus's mane, the quick motion overwhelmed Ellis's attention with the promise of chase. The impulse passed, fought down like swallowed bile, but the implication remained, cold and stone, that ultimately his body would decide.

As if peeking out from behind a curtain, the crescent of a new moon flirted with the night sky. The sound of animals nearby drew Ellis to his feet, his body taut with energy. The night was young and teased him with a bouquet of sounds and smells.

Cresting a rise, Ellis smelled pollen and dander on the air and spotted a troop of familiar horses in the distance. Captain John's palomino, Lightning, and Steven and Simon's horses, a couple of buckskins named Troy and Buck. Troy after the Trojan horse of ancient lore, and Buck, because Simon had been a man of limited words and imagination from a wet town out west named something equally dull thanks to a coin flip. Maybe Simon did the same with ol' Buck. Had the coin landed otherwise, the horse might have been named something less generic, like Kelpie or Botwulf.

Sliding his way along the scree, Ellis ran lightly, but the jingle of his spurs struck him as out of place, every step disconcerting. He was reminded of his family's barn cat when a piece of nature got stuck in her fur and she had no choice but to give up on her prey and wrestle about, trying to free herself. Ellis removed the spurs from his boots and gripped one in each hand, the post and blade protruding from between his fingers.

At the base of the hill a wolf, muscles taut, was also hunting the troop. The allure of pursuit faded enough for him to realize how strange he was acting. Why would he stalk horses he could probably just holler for? And what kind of damned fool would race away from camp with no knife or gun on his person?

The wolf snuck closer to Buck, but Ellis could smell another nearby and readied himself to fight if attacked. He spotted the route of wolves winding their way toward the horses, his hands gripping the spurs tight, their many sharpened spikes forward and ready to bite.

The horses bolted and the wolves followed. The one keeping watch over Ellis loped past, leaving him feeling dismissed instead of relieved.

A stagecoach clattered into sight, drawn by its own team of horses. Again, Ellis felt naked, realizing just how foolish he was acting, now in the presence of other people. But the feeling passed quickly, and this target was all Ellis could see. The four bustling mares, the elegantly carved wheels as they spun, and surely a prize inside. In a burst, Ellis reached the road's edge and latched on as it passed, enjoying the tug that went through him as it lifted him from his feet. Within seconds he was inside.

Ellis's old dog, Argie, used to wake him at sunrise by licking his face, so he dreamed of his lost pup as he awoke to the same sensation. Opening his eyes to the carnage of at least one pronghorn antelope, a wolf licking blood from Ellis's forehead. The wolf seemed as confused as Ellis. It hurried away, looking back every few yards until it was gone.

How many men had woken to being groomed by wolves? Was this something that happened in the stories of these lands? Ellis searched the horizon, but nothing seemed familiar. His memories were muddled, like a fog that wouldn't lift. He had left Rhaebus alone. But what came after had been a whirl of impulse as hazy as a nightmare come the morning sun.

Ellis spent most of the day walking miles of looping meandering steps before he noticed Rhaebus's scent drawing him east. He eventually found the horse—heading home. He whistled like a whip crack.

Rhaebus paused for an instant, then carried on into the falling darkness, faster than Ellis could walk.

Ellis jogged to catch up.

Rhaebus, ears perked, picked up his own pace.

"Dammit, boy," Ellis muttered, running to gain ground. "Rhaebus! Come on now!"

The horse trotted in a circle back toward Ellis, causing Ellis to stop with a hiss of sand at his boots. He raised his hands and inched forward.

"It's okay Rhae. Sorry to leave you alone last night."

Snorting, the horse backed up as Ellis closed the gap between them. Sweat carved streaks in the dried blood on the man's forehead.

"What's wrong, fella? What's got you spooked?"

Rhaebus was calmed by Ellis's voice, but as he came closer, the horse seemed dazed, the wild of its nature surfacing and making them strangers once more.

"You're acting like you don't recognize me at all, and . . . well, I don't get the sense I know me all that well right now either—"

Rhaebus had turned away, as if lost, and again meandered east one final time.

"Rhaebus, here!"

Ellis whistled, loud and hard. A whistle intended to call the horse from miles away. Rhaebus turned his head to the sound but kept trotting. Ellis hurried, gaining a couple of yards on the horse, sending Rhaebus galloping into the looming night.

As the waxing moon emerged, it watched a man chase a horse at a pace that grew as night fell, as if the sun, setting behind him, had been a force tugging him back, from which he was now free.

A sea of pain crashed upon Ellis the instant he awoke. A glint of light twinkled between stalactites high overhead. As his vision cleared, his body ached, and he felt a screaming in his hands, each secured to the ground, one with a pickaxe driven through the palm, the other by rope, his wrist flayed beneath its sinews. He whimpered, quaking with pain that closed his throat and held his tongue. A mining man with small wire-framed glasses perched on his nose, stared down at him.

"You are a quite the trickster, aren't you?" his captor said.

Ellis stared at his wounds. His impaled hand would never work again. "Please, my hands—" Ellis started.

"My intentions are not to help you," the man said. "You may not look like your previous self, but I assure you, this man will be made to pay for the actions of that beast."

"Please. I need a doctor," Ellis said.

"And I need a number of strong men to take the place of the ones you, the former, took it upon yourself to dismember and devour," the man said. "I need a reasonable story to tell my employer because *man-beast*, *night monster*, or even *wolf attack* won't quite do. We are equipped for wolves. We have munitions for men of all type and mammals of all shape and size, but as you have crossed the two, well, our bullets no longer seem to do the trick."

Ellis's stomach churned looking beneath the surface of his own wrist.

"Now tell me how you got this way," the man said.

"I was attacked."

His captor laughed. "Not how you are now. How you were in the night."

"I think I'm dying."

"As well you should. But you will not if I can help it. Silver runs throughout these hills. Lining them like the pockets of King Louis himself. But last night I found gold. Or it found us. A circus will pay handsomely for a monster like yourself."

"I'm just a farmer's son from Pithole, Pennsylvania."

"Oh, you're no child. Underwhelming as you seem here and now, that creature inside you has my attention."

"What did you see?" Ellis asked, worried to hear a truth as raw as his flesh.

"I saw a wolven man. A cyclone of violence. I would offer you food and water to keep you alive, but no man this side of the Mississippi has ever eaten as well as you did last night. If seeing the remains should help you come to terms with your evils, I can oblige."

Ellis shook his head. He had no recollection of what had come after sunset. Only chasing Rhaebus across a land as empty as he felt now. No hunger or thirst possessed him, but surely pain was enough to drive that from any man. He'd lost everything just to be captured by a loon who had bound him like a tent, both stake and tether.

The rattle of wagon wheels soon echoed into the cave and Ellis was manhandled and tossed into a cage with a wooden floor gouged by the claws of something great, a bear or cougar maybe.

The cart moved east, toward the nearest settlement sizable enough to rally an audience—this from snippets of conversation between the men driving. Nobody addressed Ellis directly, as he was a commodity now, they knew how to treat him as such.

Beyond the bars, the waxing moon punched through the darkening blue like a button, appearing when the world had blinked. Soon the chatter of men, alongside the clatter and toss of wagon wheels, struck Ellis as nothing more than the chirp of birds, ineffectual but charming. He no longer felt the shackles he wore as the sky called to him. The swell of evening rose within him from a tease to a tumult. The implications of the bars or the previous tenants of the cage faded as the wood beneath Ellis felt like twigs and he hungered to observe the men as they discussed their nothings of consequence. To pounce, chase, overpower, and devour.

Ellis opened his eyes to the wreckage of a trading settlement, decorated by its occupants, unmoving, and unlikely to do so. His hand no longer bandaged nor punctured. The skin folded and stretched back to good health. A crescent of scar tissue white and devoid of grain.

A silver sheriff badge had been folded in on itself and gleamed from between a dead man's broken ribs, mashed into the meat of his heart. Ellis wondered if he himself was also dead. Had been dead for days. A ghost remaining on earth more out of confusion than unwillingness to depart. Awaiting the discovery of his ragged corpse to provide some sense of certainty. Hunger had left him more than a week ago, but he had not shrunk, quite the opposite. Still, these daytime nightmares felt like he was watching the past fight the inevitable future; a violent unraveling of westward expansion. A manifest tragedy where that which his people had built on the dead was being just as brutally dismantled.

A banker lay in the street, black hat covering his face, belly emptied like a safe. Spitting image of Ellis's older brother, from what flesh remained. This bad dream, this curse, it couldn't follow him home, could it?

He picked up bits of fruit from a tavern floor, but they seemed as appetizing as pinecones. He would have kept a bottle of spirits had they not all been smashed from toppled shelves. Buzzards picked at the corpses throughout the silent township. Ellis gathered cash from the fallen. Gold nuggets, jewelry. He even packed it onto the one carriage that hadn't been destroyed or toppled. But soon found there wasn't a horse left alive to pull the damn thing.

He filled his pockets with gold and notes, slung water skins over each shoulder and, unable to shake the banker's missing entrails from his mind, he gathered food in the hope his appetite would come roaring back and prove he was normal, alive, and in as much danger as this town had been, instead of being the danger that razed it.

A man stood on a plateau overlooking the settlement with claw marks through his shirt, the fabric glued to his back with dried blood.

"You should clear out of here, sir." Ellis said. "As far as you can manage."

The man turned toward Ellis with flower petals of veiny flesh blistered across his eyes. He spoke with a broken voice. Not one hoarse with screams—but crushed by them.

"I was a fool to try to hold you."

Ellis recognized the man beneath the ravaged voice.

"I meant to profit from you after you destroyed my venture," the blind man continued, "but you are more than this world can hold. I ran while you slaughtered this town. I knew what you were, so that gave me an advantage when you revealed yourself. But I was not fast enough, only faster than the rest."

Flashes of running, the snap of bones, the pelting of bullets—slowing but never stopping him—shuddered through Ellis's mind, feeling like a daydream. Ellis ran his fingers across his chest, knots of scarring, hard just beneath the surface, like seeds of destruction. He said nothing.

"You are the wrath of God come to shuck our broken souls from this realm."

"I'm just a kid from Pithole in a land of monsters," Ellis said. "I want to go home."

"This is your home," the blind man said. "That land will always be beneath your feet."

Ellis walked east. He had come west hoping that dealing in death would build him a legacy and grant him a fortune. Now there were empty houses everywhere, wealth he could not carry, and a shadow he could not shake. No matter his offering, no witchdoctor from this land would free him, and no priest back east would believe him. If he were to chase the sunset for an eternity, could he outrun the beast inside? Or would night always find him, and anything that breathed nearby pay the cost?

Unable to concede that home could not offer some protection, he walked east, imagining Rhaebus trotting beside him, and Argie at his heels.

Within an hour he came across railroad tracks, an engine steaming, passengers boarding in fine clothes with luggage enough for a long-distance journey, and a prison car—empty. He didn't have to look far to see gallows with a substantial man hanging from them.

Ellis climbed behind the bars, pulling them closed, the latch falling into place. Looking at the thick timbers and steel that clenched around him, he hoped his cage would hold.

At noon the train chugged out of the station. Someone on the platform said that it was the Lone Liberty Crescent, next stop Emerald, Texas.

"Lord have mercy," he said to himself. But whose lord, he wondered.

The landscape grew greener as the day gave way to night. Ellis prayed that distance could break the spell. That returning home could make him whole again. He tried to picture every face he had paled, purposefully or otherwise, as he traced his evils far beyond the night of the new moon song. His apologies and promises to any god who would have him became a chant of his own, as if to never quit speaking, would leave the other unable to surface. But as the full moon swam into view over Emerald, Texas, the cart began to feel like a matchbox beneath him. As the beast emerged, his last thought was that he would join the tales written on the forgotten pages of the book covers once slung across the back of his horse. Lost.

CONTRIBUTORS

Fayaway & Hermester Barrington

Hermester is a retired archivist, a rogue protozoologist, and a deliberately genre ignorant artist, whose ficciones have recently appeared in *Fate Magazine*, *Mythaxis*, and *Robot Butt*. Fayaway, who usually works in ephemeral media only, is a gardener, urban archaeologist, and on again, off again member of the postfolkpunk group Medusa's Greatgreatgranddaughters. This is the first of their joint projects to be published; their next project is the book *Munchausen by Proxy—A Child's Guide to Getting There First* (Golden Press Books, forthcoming Autumn 2023).

Warren Benedetto

Warren Benedetto writes dark fiction about horrible people, horrible places, and horrible things. He is an award-winning author and a full member of the SFWA. His stories have appeared in publications such as *Dark Matter Magazine*, *Fantasy Magazine*, and *The Dread Machine*; on podcasts such as *The NoSleep Podcast*, *Tales to Terrify*, and *The Creepy Podcast*; and in anthologies from Apex Magazine, Tenebrous Press, Eerie River Publishing, and more. He also works in the video game industry, where he holds 35+ patents for video game technology.

For more information, visit warrenbenedetto.com and follow @warrenbenedetto on Twitter and Instagram.

David Bradley

David Bradley is a freelance writer with one non-fiction book (*The Historic Murder Trial of George Crawford*) to his credit. His short stories and poetry have appeared in *Broken Pencil*, *The Adirondack Review*, *Down in the Dirt*, *Main Street Rag*, *The South Carolina Review*, and *Pennsylvania English*. He has spent a dozen years as a newspaper reporter and columnist in Northern Virginia.

Matthew Cheney

Matthew Cheney is the author of the collections *The Last Vanishing Man and Other Stories* (Third Man Books, 2023) and *Blood: Stories* (Black Lawrence

Press, 2016) as well as *About That Life: Barry Lopez and the Art of Community* (Punctum Books, 2023) and *Modernist Crisis and the Pedagogy of Form* (Bloomsbury, 2020). His stories have been published by *Conjunctions, Nightmare, The Dark, One Story, Weird Tales,* and elsewhere.

He lives in New Hampshire, where he works at Plymouth State University.

Daniel Dagris

Daniel Dagris is a Pacific Northwest author of rural fantasy and horror, with a literary bent. His work has been nominated for the Pushcart Prize, received honorable mention from *Glimmer Train*, and has appeared in *Orca Literary Journal, Open Ceilings*, and elsewhere.

Phillip E. Dixon

Phillip E. Dixon is an English Professor from Las Vegas whose fiction has appeared in *Cosmic Horror Monthly, The Fabulist, Book of Matches Literary Magazine*, and elsewhere. He holds an MFA in Writing from Lindenwood University, speaks lousy German to his two cats, and spends his rent money on coffee as a good addict should.

Sarina Dorie

Sarina Dorie has sold over 200 short stories to markets like *Analog, Daily Science Fiction, Fantasy Magazine*, and the *Magazine of Fantasy & Science Fiction*. She has published over ninety books, including her bestselling series, *Womby's School for Wayward Witches.*

A few of her favorite things include: gluten-free brownies (not necessarily glutton-free), *Star Trek*, steampunk, fairies, Severus Snape, and Mr. Darcy. She lives with twenty-three hypoallergenic fur babies, by which she means tribbles. By the time you finish reading this bio, there will be twenty-seven.

You can find info about her short stories and novels on her website: www.sarinadorie.com

Daniel David Froid

Daniel David Froid is a writer who lives in Arizona and has published fiction in *Post Road, Black Warrior Review, Lightspeed,* and elsewhere.

H. L. Fullerton

H. L. Fullerton writes fiction—mostly speculative, occasionally about being haunted—which can be found in more than 60 anthologies and magazines including *Mysterion*, *Kaleidotrope*, and several issues of *Underland Arcana*, and is the author of the somewhat haunting novella: *The Boy Who Was Mistaken for a Fairy King*.

You may follow them on Twitter at @ByHLFullerton

J. V. Gachs

J.V. Gachs is a Spanish classicist, and writer, currently working as a Latin teacher. Writing in English and Spanish her work has been featured in anthologies like Scott J. Moses' *What One Wouldn't Do* and Chelsea Pumpkins' *AHH! That's What I Call Horror!* Her debut novel, *Epiphany,* will be released by Off Limits Press in December 2023. Obsessed with sudden death, ghosts, and female villains, she always writes with a cat (or two) in her lap.

Find more of her work: jvgachs.com

Ingrid Garcia

Ingrid Garcia help to sell local wines in a vintage wine shop in Cádiz, and writes speculative fiction in her spare time. For years, she was unpublished. But to her utter surprise—after years of receiving nothing but rejections—she's sold stories to *The Magazine of Fantasy & Science Fiction,* and the *Ride the Star Wind* and *Sword and Sonnet* anthologies, amongst others.

She can be found on Twitter (@ingridgarcia253) and is busy setting up a website.

Elad Haber

Elad Haber has been quietly publishing short fiction for twenty years. He attended Clarion when he was just eighteen years old. You might find his stories in various forgotten corners of the Internet or in the dusty backrooms of basement bookstores. He has forthcoming publications from *Lightspeed, Space & Time Magazine,* and the *Simultaneous Times Podcast.* This is his second appearance in *Underland Arcana.*

Visit eladhaber.wordpress.com for links.

J. Anthony Hartley

J. Anthony Hartley is an Australian/British author and poet. He has had pieces appear in *Short Fiction, Hybrid Fiction, Short Circuit, The Periodical, Abandon Journal,* among others and has had poetry in *The Quarter(ly), New Myths, Space & Time* and in *Twenty Two Twenty Eight.*

He currently resides in Germany and can be found at http://www.iamnotaspider.com. He no longer lives on Twitter or whatever it might be called.

Christopher Hawkins

Christopher Hawkins is an award-winning horror writer, and the author of the short story collection Suburban Monsters. His debut novel, Downpour, arrives in October. He is the former editor of the One Buck Horror anthology series and co-chair of the Chicagoland chapter of the Horror Writers Association. When he's not writing, he spends his time exploring old cemeteries, lurking in museums, and searching for a decent cup of tea.

For more information about his upcoming projects, visit his website, www.christopher-hawkins.com, or follow him on Twitter @chrishawkins and Instagram at @hawkinswrites.

A. P. Howell

A. P. Howell's jobs have spanned the alphabet from archivist to webmaster. She lives with her husband, their two kids, and a pair of rambunctious puppies. Her short fiction has appeared in various venues, including *ParSec, Martian, Dread Space* (Shacklebound Books), *Bicycles & Broomsticks* (Microcosm Publishing), and *Darkness Blooms* (The Dread Machine).

She sometimes hangs out online on Mastodon (wandering.shop/@aphowell) and her homepage is aphowell.com.

Frances Lu-Pai Ippolito

Frances Lu-Pai Ippolito (she/her) is a Chinese American writer in Portland, Oregon. Her writing has appeared or is forthcoming in *Nailed Magazine, Buckman Journal,* Flame Tree Press's *Asian Ghost Stories,* Strangehouse's *Chromophobia, Startling Stories,* Not a Pipe's *Stories Within, Mother: Tales of Love and Terror, Death's Garden Revisited,* and *Unquiet Spirits: Essays by Asian Women in Horror.* Frances also co-chairs the Young Willamette Writers program that provides free writing classes for high school and middle school students.

K. Wallace King

K. Wallace King has been hired as a screenwriter, teacher, bartender, paralegal, and by her late father, who fired her before her first week was out. Her most recent short fiction has appeared or is upcoming, in *Nightscript VIII*, *Chthonic Matter*, and *Aseptic and Faintly Sadistic*, an Anthology of Hysteria Fiction. She lives in Hollywood, California, where the hands of dead dreamers are pressed into the sidewalks.

John Klima

John Klima previously worked in New York's publishing jungle before returning to school to earn his Master's in Library Science. He now works full time as the Technology Manager of a large public library. John edited and published the Hugo Award-winning genre zine *Electric Velocipede* from 2001 to 2013.

When he is not conquering the world of indexing, John writes short stories and novels. He and his family live in the Midwest.

Michelle Knudsen

Michelle Knudsen is a New York Times best-selling author of fifty books for kids and teenagers, including the award-winning picture book *Library Lion*, which has been translated into nineteen languages and was named one of *Time* magazine's 100 Best Children's Books of All Time. Her middle grade fantasy and young adult horror-comedy-musical-theater-romance novels have won honors including VOYA Top Shelf Fiction for Middle School Readers, YALSA Best Fiction for Young Adults, and the Sid Fleischman Humor Award. Her next book involves a giant spider mistaken for a kitten. She also sometimes writes for adults.

Michelle teaches writing in Lesley University's low-residency MFA program, where she is currently the Writing for Young People genre chair. She lives with her family in Brooklyn, New York.

You can find her on Twitter at @michelleknudsen, on Instagram at @michelle.knudsen, or at her website: michelleknudsen.com.

Erik Kollmer

This is Erik Kollmer's fiction debut. He tells stories with data for a living. That's what he tells himself anyways. He feels that his data storytelling work does not allow him full narrative control, so his fiction seeks to reclaim that.

Reggie Kwok

Reggie Kwok dreams of dragons in his sleep when he is not summoning their powers for writing. He holds a B.A. in English and a master's in education. He currently lives in Massachusetts, USA. He had a short story published at *Samjoko Magazine* and another one forthcoming at *Zooscape*.

His Twitter is @KwokReggie.

Jon Lasser

Jon Lasser lives in Seattle, WA with his wife and two children. His stories have appeared in *Lightspeed, Interzone, Galaxy's Edge,* and elsewhere. He's a graduate of the Clarion West writers workshop.

Find him online at twoideas.org.

Gerri Leen

Gerri Leen lives in Northern Virginia and originally hails from Seattle. In addition to being an avid reader, she's passionate about horse racing, tea, and collecting encaustic art and raku pottery. She has work appearing or accepted by *The Magazine of Fantasy and Science Fiction, Nature, Strange Horizons, Daily Science Fiction,* and others. She's edited several anthologies for independent presses, is finishing some longer projects, and is a member of SFWA and HWA.

See more at gerrileen.com.

Mark Mills

A Cincinnati resident, Mark Mills teaches composition, literature, film, philosophy, music appreciation, and basic Noa robotic. He has published work in *Tor.com, Grievous Angel, Necrotic Tissue, Short Story America,* and other publications. He worked on and appeared in several low budget films, including *Satanic Yuppies, Live Nude Shakespeare, Chickboxin' Underground, Zombie Cult Massacre,* and *Uberzombiefrau.* Having recently survived advanced stage cancer, he hopes to have his brain implanted in a robotic body and avoid any further health woes.

Kiya Nicoll

Kiya Nicoll is a writer, poet, and artist living in a New England oak grove. They dabble in a wide variety of assorted obsessions when permitted to do so by the children, the cats, and the limitations of physical embodiment. Their work has previously appeared in magazines including the *Escape Pod* podcast and several anthologies, most recently *Bioluminescent: A Lunarpunk Anthology*.

They can be found at kiyanicoll.com, on Twitter at kiya_nicoll, and in the Fediverse at @gehennan@wandering.shop.

J. P. Oakes

J. P. Oakes is a writer and creative director living on Long Island. His debut novel, *City of Iron and Dust* is available from Titan Books, and according to *Publishers Weekly* "offers lovers of the bloody and fantastical plenty to enjoy."

He can be found online at jpoakeswrites.wordpress.com.

Roni Stinger

Roni Stinger's fiction has recently been published in *Dark Matter Magazine, Unnerving Magazine,* and *Rewired: Divergent Perspectives in Horror,* among others.

Find her online at www.ronistinger.com.

Jason Washer

Jason Washer lives in New Hampshire and divides his time between caring for his family, running a small business, and writing stories late into the night at his kitchen table. His work has appeared in the *No Sleep Podcast, Mystery Tribune, Theme of Absence, Bards and Sages Quarterly,* and in the anthology *In Darkness, Delight: Fear the Future.*

Find him on the web at www.jasonwasher.net.

Eric Witchey

Eric Witchey has sold stories under several names and in 12 genres. His tales have been translated into multiple languages, and his credits include over 160 stories, including 5 novels and two collections. He has penned dozens of writing-related articles and essays, has taught over 200 conference seminars, at 2 universities, and at a community college. His work has received recognition from New Century Writers, *Writers of the Future, Writer's Digest,* Independent Publisher Book Awards, International Book Awards, The Eric Hoffer Prose Award Program, Short Story America, the Irish Aeon Awards, and other organizations. His How-to articles have appeared in *The Writer Magazine, Writer's Digest Magazine,* and other print and online magazines.

Jennifer Worrell

Jennifer Worrell (she) works in a private university library in Chicago. Her debut novel, *Edge of Sundown*, was released November 2020 by Darkstroke Books. Her short prose and essays appear in *Across the Margin, Write City Magazine, Writing Disorder, Raconteur,* and *Little Old Lady Comedy*, among others.

More information is available on her website, http://jenniferworrellwrites.com. You can find her on twitter (@JWorrellWrites).

EDITOR

Mark Teppo

Mark Teppo is the publisher of Underland Press. He has written more than two dozen novels across a wide variety of genres, including historical fiction, eco-thriller, horror, western, mystery, science fiction, and dark fantasy. He lives in the Pacific Northwest, where he is busy making things.

His favorite Tarot card is the Moon.

Underland Arcana

Underland Arcana is an on-going project tarot-themed project of Underland Press. Forthcoming collections will focus on both the Minor Arcana and the Major Arcana. For more information, visit the website:

htts://www.underlandarcana.com